DRAGON GOD
OF THE
HINDU KUSH

WAYNE T. HAALAND

An errant parachute jump in the Hindu Kush Mountains during a search for a lost American biological weapon lands Marine lieutenant Jack Flashhardt in fabled Shangri-La. Is it the Utopia of legend? The intrigues and conflicts of the outside world have infected Paradise. Jack must fight his way to safety, then return to save his long-lived friends and the rest of the world from the deadly biobomb and the al Qaida who have captured it.

Praise for Dragon God

New York Times best selling author of Defcon One, Shadow Flight, and Rules of Engagement, Jack Weber, says Dragon God is an action-packed adventure. "This yarn gets high marks in suspense and readability. I thoroughly enjoyed it."

A rip-roaring page turner. A real time combat tale by someone who has actually experienced it. Gunnery Sergeant Charlie Smithson, USMC (ret)

Others add: Humor, action, sizzling and sensual

508 West 26th Street KEARNEY, NE 68848
402-819-3224
info@medialiteraryexcellence.com

Contents

We make war that we may live in peace.
— Aristotle

The person who has nothing for which he is willing to fight, nothing which is more important than his own personal safety, is a miserable creature.
— John Stuart Mill

The object of war is not to die for your country but to make the other bastard die for his.
— General George Patton

God Odin's instructions to Freyja, the Goddess of War: *You must stir up war. And as soon as each warrior is chopped down, bathed in blood, he must be made to stand up unharmed and fight again. Whether they wish it or not, let men rip one another to pieces.*

Prologue

Location: The Wakhan Corridor, Afghanistan
Altitude: 50,000 feet
Time: 0914 Zulu

Jim Peterson, the USAF B-52H pilot of Flight AG-1 shouted into his helmet mike, "I declare a Broken Arrow, y'all copy?" *Goddam, it's not a Broken Arrow, but what do I call this calamity of a weapon—Long Island Iced Tea? Now… this fire's… it's gonna automatically safeguard dump the damned thing—and I can't stop it.*

The co-pilot, quivering and ready to bolt, clutched his commander's arm and shouted, "Colonel, the fire's spread to the passageway! We gotta get out now!"

Chapter 1

The Marine lieutenant watched the lights of a U.S. Army truck arc around the corner onto Ramna 5 Road. He picked up his rucksack, suppressed a feeling of dread, patted his gear for reassurance: one of his two scarred ice axes strapped to the sides of the pack, the slightly stolen XM-25 OICW rifle, a lumpy bulge of borrowed M-67 grenades in a side pouch of his web gear, a holstered Beretta snugged tight at his waist. Finally, he touched the pocket holding Ashley's *get-lost* letter.

The truck hit bumps lights bounced up and down it looked like a warily blinking leviathan as it approached the U.S. Embassy compound. A post-monsoon rain had fallen in the night, and every time the lights dipped, glare flashed from the drenched pavement. Matching flashes of pre-dawn lightning flickered in the Margalla Hills.

The M998 truck slammed to a halt, its huge tires skidding and squealing. Lieutenant Mick Nakamura leaned out the passenger window of the GMC troop carrier, grinned at his former college classmate. "Hey, climb aboard, buddy. Let's go get 'em." Chopstick Mick had a high-pitched voice belied by his monster physique. He had been tagged with the nickname at OCS when his bunkmate discovered he hated Oriental food.

Jack Flashhardt shivered in the cool air, smiled an uncertain greeting, clambered into the cab.

"Good luck, Sir," from one of the Embassy guards.

He waved, put his pack between his legs. *Right, let's go get 'em. No, I'd rather be going after a good grade back in law school.*

"Your climbing class," Mick enthused. "It'll be cool. After we absorb your training, we'll search in Hindu Kush heights we haven't been able to reach. Your call sign'll be, Teach." Gave him a small ISR a palm-sized, intersquad radio. "We have a PRC 117 for satellite comm to Islamabad but this's just for us.

"Good, Chopstick. I'm happy to give the class." *Yeah, right eager as a cobra entering a den of hungry mongooses. Just let me get through this without getting' my ass shot off.* "But why isn't your unit already trained and up to speed?"

Mick smiled. "We were in Fort Greely, Alaska, doin' cold weather training at CRTC when the lost LIIT bomb emergency came up. One day I'm lookin' at Gunny Sack Mountain and hopin' to head to the 10Th after completing training, all of a sudden, they packed us up and sent us off to
Southwest Asia to search for the missing device."

Same as me, Jack thought. *The curse of being an experienced mountaineer unlike Chopstick's crew. That wonderful capability got me activated, sent to Southwest Asia.* He glanced at his climbing boots. No crampons but they wouldn't be ice climbing.

During the ride to Islamabad airport, Mick, a very short, hugely wide, extremely muscular Army lieutenant, with Asian eyes that disappeared when he smiled, oriented him on a topo map. He spread it over his PASGT Kevlar helmet.

"I figured you'd appreciate our jump zone," Mick said. "It's right where the Himalayas and the Hindu Kush meet. Very significant joining of the two highest mountain ranges in the world."

Jack, longer and leaner than Mick, blond and blue-eyed in contrast to Mick's dark hair and eyes, had grown up in the mountains of Montana, had climbed a half dozen "Fourteeners" in Colorado mountains over fourteen thousand feet above sea level had climbed major summits on four continents, but not in Asia. The impromptu class he had dreaded teaching looked better, considering this unexpected payoff.

"There's a ridge on the west side of the valley where you can give my team the climbing class." Mick grinned, his eyes disappearing, and his canines appearing: he didn't have buckteeth, but when he grinned, his teeth were definitely out there, making him look hungry for flesh. "Best of all, Colonel Farley got a HUMINT report from Camp Rhino in Kabul. The lost Air Force bomb might be hidden in a highlands vil. So, your class is a cover to check out Pakistani territory. If we find it, Farley's off your back."

Oh, great! Can't shake Colonel Farley. Gotta win the War on Terrorism for him after climbing class. Told the colonel no go on joining the search for the bomb, but I'm here anyway. He plans this? Feeling trapped, Jack glanced at the sidewalk, saw a group of early-rising mullahs shake their fists at the Americans. One picked up a rock, then the truck was past.

"Screw off, you pissant ragheads!" one of the troops in back.

"So, Jack," Mick asked, "you a little more excited about action than you were last night? Cause I promise you; we'll get some! The Taliban dudes aren't gonna expect an American force on the Pak side of the border." The two had bumped into each other in the Marriott Hotel bar. Mick had asked Jack to give his men the class.

"Sorry, dude," Jack responded. "I'm 0302 but right now I'm a temporary 0203 Intel poge with a day off. You're Regular Army, I'm a Reserve Marine. I didn't sign up to win a war. I thought I was gonna be a JAG lawyer—4402—not an oh three oh two infantry grunts." *I'm missing out on law school and fighting bullshit wars in goat herder countries that make Death Valley look like the hanging gardens of Babylon.*

Mick smiled—showed his canines but no sympathy. "Luckily, you're a mountaineer. We needed one. Fortunes of war, buddy."

"Yeah, I know you gung ho types. Vivere militare est—To live means to fight." He lowered his voice, "But, Mick. Aren't you a little—" he stopped himself from asking the rest of the question: *scared... no, terrified about combat?*

Sensing Jack's nervousness, Mick sang:

*"My eyes are dim.
I cannot see…"*

Jack laughed, finished the old Stanford drinking verse:

*"For I must find a place to pee,
On the Leland Stanford Junior Farm."*

Fifteen minutes later, outside a military hanger on the west end of Islamabad Airport, one of Mick's grinning troopers handed Jack a mushroom parachute and a reserve, helped him double-check the rigging on the tarmac while the rest of the team headed for the waiting helicopter. The young pilot, who was standing next to the CH-47D helicopter, grinned and greeted him, somehow recognizing him as a fellow officer.

After liftoff, they hightailed north at 120 knots. He sat against a bulkhead at the rear of the chopper, end of the team from Mick. He debated reading the printed-out get lost email.

Mick sat down next to him, glanced at the bagged XM-25 OICW rifle.

"Really shoot around corners? I've never seen one. How'd you get it?"

"I delivered it from Camp Hansen. Supposed to drop it off at the colonel's office yesterday, but everybody had secured by the time I got in from Okinawa. So, after you talked me into giving your soldiers the climbing class, I thought the XM-25'd give me extra security — problem is it's damned heavy—maybe 40 pounds."

"So, you brung it," Mick slapped his knee. "I love it! What's OICW mean—I forget."

"Objective Individual Combat Weapon."

"That's right. I heard about it at Benning. How's it works?"

"In the 20-millimeter mode, each shell has a mini-computer in it," he explained. "The sighting video camera's laser determines the range to—say, a boulder. The computer explodes the shell just above and past the boulder."

Mick giggled. "Bad guys can't hide behind anything—that's great!" He shifted back to his assistant team leader to check last minute details with the aid of a laptop computer. Jack loaded the XM-25 with a magazine of 5.56mm ammo and a six-round clip of 20mm computer-directed shells, put its bag in his pack. He glanced up and saw the dawn's light was blooming orange over the Himalayas, shining through the starboard gun port.

Wandering thoughts were suddenly interrupted minutes before the racing helicopter reached the jump zone north of Gilgit— the helicopter lurched, the big Lycoming engines roared. The aircraft's AN/ALQ-156A missile approach warning system suddenly fired flares.

Glancing out the rear hatch, Jack was astounded when a short missile with a bright-white nose, green body blazed past the 47, shot upward in the dark blue sky. Heart went into overdrive—a Stinger Missile or a Russian SA-18. Would've blown them out of the sky if it had hit. Hopefully, the
MAWS worked.

White-hot anti-missile flares blossomed in every direction as the M130 dispenser kicked in again. The chopper banked. Flight engineer braced himself, then yelled, "Just short of your jump zone. Taking fire."

Chopstick Mick Nakamura leaped up. "Let's go, guys." He unholstered his M-9, chambered a round. "Looks like we got lucky—a hot
LZ! Go, go, go."

Troopers on the ten-man team stiffened—a few eager, some looked terrified—eyes bulging, some anxious—eyes blinking; they passed, hooked up to the jury-rigged overhead line, jumped, one after another.

Mick locked eager eyes with him, holstered his weapon, spun away. *Damn, Mick. Wait, he thought. Muffins, coffee, something?*

The gunners fired the two door-mounted M60D 7.62mm machine guns to port and starboard. The crashing sounds drowned out the engines. "Stop firing!" the engineer screamed.

Standing at the hatch, he looked at the gunners, at the scared flight engineer. Took a deep breath, pushed down goggles, buckled his line, forced the jump into the howling air stream. Once away from the aircraft, pounding sounds faded—but his heart was loud in his ears, thumping in his throat.

Jubilance when his parachute, a low-level static line chute, banged open between the peaks and the valley floor, two thousand feet above ground. Fleeting thought: *Fortes fortuna juvat—Fortune favors the brave— but in this case, it favors the scared shitless.*

A twisting updraft caught him. Big problem with looming peaks ahead. He let the OICW hang by its sling, tugged on the back shrouds, struggled to turn the parachute. No luck. Glanced down— most of the team far below, but above his level, two other jumpers caught in the same swirling winds.

He heard a voice crackle over his ISR. Fumbled in a cargo pocket, pulled out the palm-sized radio.

Mick shouted, "Hostiles in that rock terrace to the north! Form on the white rockpile. Break. Teach, that you up there?"

Pushed the transmit button, controlled fear, answered in a level voice,

"Six—this's, er—Teach. Caught in an updraft."

Mick's voice yelled through the radio, "We're taking fire, my pos. See that rock fence? Get your spacegun out an' blast the hostiles with the defilade ammo—keep their heads down."

Shoved the ISR in his breast pocket, turned on the OICW sighting system, switched the selector from 5.56mm to 20mm grenade launcher.

Tried to ignore wide swings caused by the swirling updraft, peered into the gyrating, bouncing video screen, spotted the terrace dividing two small fields. Waited, put the laser dot above the rocks, chambered and fired a round. It arced through the air, exploded a hundred meters short, closer to the scrambling soldiers than the terrace.

Pissed at his poor shooting, he raised the weapon another inch, waited for a blast of air turbulence to pass, fired the remaining five rounds with a spraying motion, then fired the thirty round M-16 in short bursts until it emptied.

The parachute spun, jerked upward again. Looked over his shoulder, saw a hostile erupt from a cloud of dust on the terrace, do a comical pinwheel sprawl.

He would never reload in time, so he slung the empty weapon, pulled out the radio, yelled, "Six, that's it."

"No sweat, Teach," Mick answered. "I'm on the deck. I think you scared some, hit a couple with your suppressing fire. Sit rep?"

He looked down. A parachute draped over a ridge to his left, far below. "One of your guys hit hard. He's not movin'. The other is still sailing—like me—but he's not gonna clear a serac—" The trooper smashed into the ice ridge, bounced away.

Mick's voice crackled on the squad network as he shouted at his men on the ground, "Form on me."

Across the valley, the departing CH-47 belched another set of flares. A Stinger-type missile sliced through the fiery decoys, another blasted the chopper into a huge ball of expanding orange fire; out of it spiraled the crumpled, burning aircraft.

Shocked, Jack sucked in frigid air. The captain, no more than thirty. The co-pilot, the sergeant engineer, both in their twenties— dead. Gunners, maybe teens—dead. Two jumpers on the cliffs— maybe hurt bad. A blasted disaster.

Far below, the sounds of small arms fire banged again. Caught in a powerful, murky storm cell—he sailed up, over the first Hindu Kush peak, down through the air at a terrifying pace. Swung wildly at the end of his shrouds like a surfer tumbling in wave after wave of mountain peaks.

Hit, bounced off a snowy cornice. Careened over a jagged ridge, finally the chute caught on a rock outcropping. Slammed him to a stop on a steep snowfield. Impact knocked the wind out of him; he lay without moving, tried to regain his senses.

Long minutes later, revived by ice-cold snow jammed down his neck, up his wrists, he looked at the snowfield below—too steep, too dangerous. Above: a hanging cornice, eager to become an avalanche. Right side: a leaning serac. Left side: another icy pillar. Straight down the only way out, but it was near vertical—far below—a green valley checkered with hedge rows. Decided to rest, be at his best before he attempted an escape. What kind of people down there? Friends or foes?

He gave up, cautiously reached into a pocket, took out the copy of the email from Ashley. Still too shook to read, but after a month, he knew her important phrases by heart: miscarriage of the baby… re-assess my life… forget marriage… end our relationship… pursue my career… good luck, Jack. *Yeah, right. Luck.*

He pulled out his activation order by mistake. Glanced at it. To: yeah, me. Subject: Reassignment to Active Duty… report no later… Camp Hansen… assume duty of mountaineering instructor.

The orders had doomed his first year at law school, changed his whole life. All because of a bunch of fanatical Muslims. He was starting to hate the whole Middle East-Asia thing.

Crumpled the wrinkled document, let the wind whip it away. Pulled out the email. Mashed it, tossed it. The wind caught the slip of paper—it skipped across the snow, disappeared.

The baby had also disappeared like a wind-tossed scrap. Dreamed of— now gone. Ashley, brilliant, tall, smoky hazel eyes, pouty lips, tangled blonde hair—gone. Might've been different if he hadn't been activated, jerked out of law school, out of his life in Palo Alto and sent to Asia.

Resting was a mistake—he caught a mental vision of the falling, flame-engulfed helicopter. The pilot's cocky grin and greeting, the young gunner's friendly "Mornin', sir." Gone.

The memories flooded through his mind, wouldn't stop. Pressed his gloved hands to his head. Realized his helmet and goggles were missing, one of his axes, as well.

Crack and rumble of a distant avalanche, loosened by the dawn's light, snapped him back to reality. Still hung up by his snagged parachute on the sixty-degree slope, he carefully dug a last clod of snow from under his collar, grabbed his ice axe, tucked in the M-25, took a deep breath, and released his chute.

Slid down a huge expanse. Self-arrested with his axe, kicked up a rooster tail of snow, but he tumbled: bounces stunned him. Slowed, flipped to his back, continued to skid: kicked-up more snow trying to dig his heels and elbows and ice axe into the snow, spotted a huge bergschrund ahead.

The giant crevasse—the end of a glacial ice flow. Too fast for terror, he slid over the deadly opening on a sudden snow bridge. Plummeted down another long, steep slope, through a long, narrow ice chute, sprawled over a ledge, fell into a stream.

Frigid water rushed over his face. He gasped, staggered to the iceencrusted bank. Reached for a jagged rock, but was unbalanced by his pack; the gushing water knocked him away. Flailed, floated, struggled to twist around so that his feet were downstream, shot over a waterfall.

Screamed "No—o!" Tumbled through the air. Landed in a glacial-melt tarn pool at the base of the falls.

Underwater: then pushed up by the blowback of the falling torrent, he bounced above the surface, was immediately pushed under again. Dazed by the impact of the descent, he fought the drag of his gear-laden rucksack, his web gear. Failed to release it, watched air rush out of his mouth in huge bubbles. Sinuses, lungs burned. Water had a murky blue tint to it, the white bubbles squirmed, wiggled upward, left him behind.

Suddenly, hands appeared, grabbed him. He clutched his rescuer's waist—glimpses, a naked body—a swimmer guy helped him to the pool's surface. Scrambled to safety, shivered uncontrollably—wiped water out of his eyes—looked at his rescuer.

The blonde woman spoke over her shoulder. He didn't understand her —yeah, she was naked! Thick wet hair spread over square shoulders.

Kneedeep in water, he unstrapped his ax, pulled the M-9, quickly checked the surroundings: snowfields above, but here— halfway to the valley floor—stunted pine trees, scattered bushes, jagged boulders. No danger: only a second girl, unarmed and naked, bending over the side of a steaming pool. Two horses—a bay and a palomino—grazing nearby. A pastoral setting at the end of the horrendous adventure.

Unable to control his shivering, he holstered the M-9, unslung the XM25, shrugged out of his rucksack, waded to shore. The first girl looked so much like Ashley, he felt disoriented, as though he were somewhere else— maybe a dream world—with his lost girlfriend instead of in hostile territory.

Her teeth also chattering. She knelt, undid his waterlogged boots, helped him strip off his jump suit. Led him over a smooth rock ledge, into a nearby shallow pond of hot water. Skin burned, tingled. Sulfurous-smelling steam rose from the pool. He shivered uncontrollably, still managed to check out her perfect pale skin, blue eyes, thick eyebrows and eyelashes bleached almost white, her full red lips on a Nordic face. He sank into the hot water, finally relaxed. Her skin looked silky smooth—it shone like white satin across her square and broad shoulders.

"Who are you?" In a loud, slow voice. "Speak any English?"

The girl smiled, replied in accented but perfect English, "I'm Penel Kong and she's my sister, Wantonal. Welcome to Shangri-la of the Hindu Kush."

Chapter 2

Stripped to his skivvies, comfortable in the pool's hot waters, Jack commented to his rescuer, "You're twins." Managed to add, "How come you two looks so... like white babe—er women?"

"Not twins, Wantonal's much older." First girl sold that thought with her voice. "We're here for a sunrise soak."

The second girl, pulled skin-tight, black leather pants over her long legs, added, "We're white because Five Northmen joined and then deserted and hid from the Grand Army while on a quest to find the original land of the Aesir, the gods of Asia that built Troy, then moved on to Asgard—" "And conquered the Vanir—the gods of fertility," Penel finished.

"They deserted when the Grand Army turned back from the Indus
River. We True Hunza live in the valley of Shangri-la, descendants of those Vikings."

"Vikings in—so this is Shangri-la? You mean the real Shangri-la? One in Lost Horizon? It was in Tibet. This's the Hindu Kush."

Penel smiled. "We know where we are. Did your guide know where he was when he gave you directions?"

"Guess not. How come you have a Greek name? And what army did they desert from—those wayward Vikings?" The two girls looked like misplaced Hollywood starlets.
"From Alexander's Grand Army. He traveled through in your 321 B.C.
He was a Greek."

"Wow! That's two thousand years... well, thanks for pulling me off the bottom." Could have bought the farm. And thanks for knowing English, even if you can't read calendars.

Penel floated to him, grinned, massaged his body.

Her medicinal actions were lost on him, just like the history lesson— suddenly he felt horny—not a shock, considering she could've been a high school cheerleader—enough sex appeal to incite riots on the team bus.

"Drink." She cupped her hands, trickled sulphurous-tasting water into his mouth. "Drink and be restored. The waters have healing powers. For now and forever."

He choked, swallowed. *Forever? I might not survive this drink of goat piss.* Glanced around again, checked for stray Taliban or bandits: empty boulders, ten-foot-wide waterfall gushed into the icy tarn beyond the hot spring. No threats. No crazed Ponce De Leon jumping up to steal the now and forever water—whatever that meant.

Leaned back, sank to his neck, felt a change sweep through his body that made him feel rested, fresh. Jack decided he'd feel even better with his clothes on and his weapon handy—so he got out of the pool. The other girl, who didn't look "much older" wore only her leather pants. Murmured a husky hello, dried him with a large wool shawl. She accidentally— playfully?—brushed her full, bare breasts against his chest when she toweled his hair. He inhaled a hint of saffron, fought an urge to embrace her.

Still nervous, he restrained himself until she looked into his eyes with an inviting smile. Her look, her hand, slowly stroking his hip with the shawl.

Girls must be bored stiff. Shortage of guys in Shangri-la? No wonder it's called Paradise. Stick around awhile? Pull her closer, stupid.

Before he could act out his fantasy, he heard a horse's hooves approach on rocky ground. Dropped his hands, glanced at the XM-25. *Bullet in the back from some jealous local. You dumb—*

Guy aimed a huge pistol at him—at least a .44 Magnum. Oldfashioned Dirty Harry revolver. Demanded in an English accent, "What the bloody hell're you doin' to my gels?"

Unnerved, he raised his hands faster than a Frenchman in a war, stared at the glaring stranger. Don't shoot, pal. I don't…

"You should see the expression on your face." English guy—maybe a teenager—bellowed with laughter. "Caught you with your pants down, what? But who the bloody hell're you? And how'd you get into Shangrila?" Guy rode a small roan mare with a white flash on its face. Young, early twenties—dressed in a well-worn khaki shirt, ragged shorts, a bizarre black top hat. Suddenly, the horse reared, he fell off, got up, slugged the horse in the neck. The mount swung its head around, tried to bite him.

Jack gave up on any semblance of dignity. Stepped behind a boulder next to his clothes, pulled them on, answered, "Dude, we were on a recon training jump in Hunza Valley. I got caught in a weird updraft. This really
Shangri-la?"

"Fabulous. Don't suppose you have a radio?" He looked like a teenage Leonardo DiCaprio. Blond, curly hair, thin face, blue eyes, a big nose only a Beverly Hills plastic surgeon could love.

"Nothing long range. I'm lucky I'm alive, pard." Checked—the guy had holstered his piece. "Hey, I didn't know the girls belonged to you. Penel
—whatever—saved me from a deep six."

The first girl, now dressed, grinned at him, white teeth flashed.

"I'd feel a helluva lot more accommodating with my gels if you'd brought a radio. Now you're trapped here, as well."

"Shut up, Dickey," Wantonal said. She approached, wearing a wool sweater. "We're not thy gels."

"Yes, Dickey," Penel added. "We need not thy permission to soak in the waters. Or to rescue handsome strangers."

Abashed, the English kid grinned. "Sorry."

"Where's here, dude? I mean, I just sailed over a mountain ridge. It's not that far back—we can hike up it in a couple days." He looked up at the mountains that surrounded the narrow valley—they did look steep, but he'd climbed sharp peaks all over the world.

"Impassable heights, and I'm afraid of avalanches," the Englishman responded. "I've been stuck here for years. Ever since the Soviets blew the tunnel in '79—it was the secret passage into the valley. I'm Dickey Arses of the SAS." He pronounced his name like R-seas. "From Nottingham,
England. Worcester College, '77."

Jack introduced himself. Pulled his wet boots on, asked, "Don't you mean the Russians? The Soviet Union fell years ago."

Startled, Arses looked at him. "Steady on—you mean the bloody
Afghans threw them out? When did that happen?"

"You forget all the crap you learned in high school? Years ago. And the Soviets bit the dust around 1990-91." *This guy was either crazy or stupid.*

"I'll go to bloody hell," Arses said. "And you're a Yank."

"You said you were in the SAS in '79?" Looked at Dickey's face. "What were you—a regimental mascot?"

"Not likely, I was twenty-four. I'm more'n double that now." Guy was a kid. Stretching it, maybe his twenties.

"Too true," Arses continued. "No mirrors in the valley but it doesn't take long to realize that you'll turn into a wellspring of health the longer you stay. But to more important issues. Let's get back to Asgard, the girls' home. The king—gels' dad—will demand to meet you. Climb on Penel's pony." *Asgard? That was the name of the home of the Viking gods up in Scandinavia—a long way from the Hindu Kush!*

Penel had retrieved his waterlogged pack. He dried, then reloaded the XM-25, filled the 20mm with a fresh six round clip from his pack, hoisted the heavy rucksack and web gear on, mounted her palomino. She and Wantonal doubled up on the third horse, the bigheaded bay with a choppedoff, stubby mane.

The four let the horses pick their way down the rocky trail towards the flatlands. He looked at the steep cliff below the trail, wondered where they were taking him. Thought of the downed helicopter. This had to be better. He hoped Chopstick and his men had survived the gun battle. Mick was so gung ho—trying to prove a Japanese-American kid from a garlic farming family could be a tough guy in the Army.

The sun cleared the vertical Hindu Kush peaks by ten A.M. He looked at the blue skies, saw wisps of clouds swirling above the valley like hovering specters. Feelings of well-being vanished, even after the sun warmed his face. Wondered if the Englishman was a plant—maybe connected to the bomb somehow. Possibly a posted guard. Was the bomb stolen, hidden in this valley? Pulled sunblock out of his pocket, covered his exposed skin with the orange-smelling lotion. Offered some to the two women on the bay horse, they refused.

Snapped back to reality by the Englishman's voice, he heard the kid say, "—every bloody day, vicious winds swirl over the valley. That's why no one comes here by air. That's part of why I've been stuck here for twenty-odd goddam years."

"What's the rest?" Guy had sat on his ass for over twenty years if he wasn't lying. But he had to be spinning a yarn. He wasn't a day over twenty.

"Hard to explain it," Dickey said. "The people're great, of course.
Women all gorgeous—just look at these two. I figger there's something in the atmosphere. Hilton got it right in his book, Lost Horizon. He'd been here—the locals remember him—even though he disguised and fantasized all the features. An' moved the location a hundred miles east when he wrote the book." Dickey looked back at Jack. "I developed a bit of lassitude. You feel so bloody good, it's hard to get motivated. And the issue of living longer—I'm proof."

"You said there was a tunnel that got blown. Why don't you dig it out, pard?"

Arses looked back again, "Miles of tunnel by hand? Haw, haw. Not bleedin' likely. Even so, I tried twice, years ago—but attacks by unknown forces—China Bitch's giant dad most likely—lost five men the first attempt. A suspicious cave-in cost ten more the second go-around. Locals refused after that. And the heights are too dangerous. Avalanches fall all afternoon. I've tried countless times but I've always had to turn back."

The Englishman glanced back at Jack. "I know there's a way, for the blasted Chinamen come to steal the tarn waters. I just can't find it."

Jack had different ideas about climbing out of the valley, but didn't trust the Englishman enough to tell him that avalanches generally didn't launch at night. That was why experienced climbers always started summit attempts around midnight. That was the time for him to take a long hike with no goodbyes.

He didn't think twice about the attraction of living a healthy life in a completely foreign, boring-ass environment. Anyway, if this was Shangrila, a land of peace and tranquility, why'd the Englishman carry a weapon? And who had a weird name like China Bitch? Jack suppressed growing worries while he watched the track ahead.

Ambling down the trail, he guided his horse closer, conversed with the girls. Penel said she and her sister were actually twenty-two and twenty-five years old. She asked questions about the outside world: what were the girls like? What were the men like? What kind of social events did young people participate in? Was he married? Both shut up when he answered he was single, whispered to each other.

He thought of Ashley, wished he hadn't thrown away the Dear Jack email—it was a link—no matter how depressing. Thought of the miscarried baby—maybe a girl, maybe a boy—teaching the child how to ride back home on sunny Montana days. Ranch dogs running ahead, falling back, meadowlarks calling, cutthroat trout hitting the surface of mountain brooks that crisscrossed the ranch.

Snapping out of his reverie, he asked Wantonal how long people lived in Shangri-la. She claimed the denizens lived four score as a youth, four score as an adult, four score as oldsters.

Jack didn't believe her. "How come you're not overpopulated?"

"Our people are too insulated," Penel answered, "Much inbreeding.
Our women lose—well, healthy babies are rare."

Jack thought of Ashley—their lost child—flushed that train of thought again. "After all that time, what… 250 years? When you die, d'you go to heaven?"

"I don't know," Penel answered. "I've never known anybody to die and come back. I've heard Dragon God Baal eats us and we become part of the Universal All." She had a smile on her face.

"Your god? Eats you, huh? What happens when he craps?" Penel, uncertain of his blunt humor, smiled.

Minutes later, he was trying to quit worrying and enjoy the pleasant ride when Arses topped a ridge, cursed.

The two women and Jack joined him, spotted several men sneaking up on a solitary person in the valley below. Jack pulled the glasses out of his pack, saw that the man was leaning over a stream, washing. The men creeping through streamside brush wore turbans.

"Whoever he is, he's in trouble," Arses exclaimed.

"Friend or foe?"

Arses said, "No one I know—but I can see the others are bloody ragheads. They kill us on sight if they can. Let's ride hard, stop the vicious bastards." Urged his horse down a very steep ridge. Suddenly, he slipped half out of his saddle. Jack caught him and pushed him back on his horse.

"Hurry!" Dickey shouted.

Chapter 3

Captain Yassar Ahmoud finished his morning tea, glanced around his tent in remote Panishir Valley of northern Afghanistan. He checked his smooth face on a mirror hanging from a tent pole, stroked his fake mustache. The al Qaida operative left the tent, very conscious of his appearance as he crossed the few steps to the center of the Taliban camp.

Dressed in an immaculate khaki uniform, Ahmoud wore well-shined black boots, avoided a muddy stretch. Whenever he looked up at the forbidding mountains on all sides, he longed to be back on the streets of Islamabad, but he knew he couldn't pass up the opportunity he had long awaited.

When he'd heard about the capture of the young Tajik couple, he had rushed to the Taliban camp—his biggest problem was time. He had to break the boy's will before anybody else could find and grab the American bomb. His other problem was experience: he had no clue as to how to make the prisoner talk, and the Taliban captors had failed in their efforts.

Ahmoud stopped in front of the naked youth. About sixteen years old, the boy was bound hand and foot, with a rope tying him to a wood stake one of the men had fashioned from a wild apricot tree. The youth knelt in the red dirt; next to him, the girl was buried to just below her ample naked breasts.

The boy had found the bomb. He and family members had been caught after they tried to sell it to a Pakistani man posing as an agent of the Second Department, the intelligence section of the Chinese People's Liberation Army. Ahmoud calmed himself and asked in Turkic, "What's your name?" "Sary Tash, sir." The boy looked terrified, desperate.

"You originally found the American bomb? You have one choice, Sary. Tell me where and then die, or don't tell me and live."

He knew that his words had confused Tash, but Ahmoud did not bother to rephrase them.

The youth glanced at his buried companion, stared into Yassar Ahmoud's green eyes and effeminate face. "I choose life, Your Excellency," he responded. He licked dry lips with his swollen tongue.

Ahmoud clapped his hands. "Wonderful. First, let's clean you up, Sary

Tash. You have dust all over your body."

Puzzled by the captain's kind words, the terrified boy stared. He unconsciously urinated in the dust. The odor drifted up.

Ahmoud checked out the boy's tiny penis, the puddle of piss. He selfconsciously stroked his mustache, then gestured to his subordinate, a short, ugly, square-bodied man named Hakim.

Bearing a double handful of two-meter-long elephant grass stems, Hakim approached. At Ahmoud's nod, Hakim gently brushed Sary Tash with the long-stemmed bundle, giggling as he did do. Each razor-sharp blade of stiff grass made a tiny cut in the Tajik's skin. The boy rolled, bucked. The grass sliced into his body, made innumerable slashes, until his skin looked painted from the bright red blood intermingled with splotches of dampened dust.

Ahmoud glanced up at the hot sun. "That's enough. He's clean enough. Sary Tash chose life." Ahmoud walked away, swallowed bile that tried to escape his stomach, turned back and added, "Oh, and dig out the girl. We'll save her for later." He noted tiny Ponerine ants swarming over the bloody prisoner.

The boy writhed, rolled, tried to kill the insects until he was so exhausted he could not move. The ants bit and feasted in the hot autumn sun. The boy forgot about his earlier show of bravery, screamed until he lost his voice.

Ten idle soldiers squatted in a small perimeter around Tash; Yassar Ahmoud, sat at a campaign desk in his temporary headquarters—the dusty tent—listened to the sometimes-audible voices of the Afghans. They were making bets: how long before the boy passed out, or asked for death, or died.

Occasionally, with much laughter, they speculated whether the strange Pakistani dandy would allow them to have their way with the girl, who was now being kept in a tent. One voiced disappointment that they hadn't been able to stone the girl.

Ahmoud composed a report for his superiors:

I will have the location of the bomb by this time tomorrow. Then we can accomplish our goal of defeating the hated American capitalist swine.
With the bomb, we will strike the American dogs. We will make the fascists wail just as we cry for the pain they have imposed on our families and the peoples of Islam.

The captain closed the journal, satisfied that his vitriolic language would cover his actions and please his superiors. He glanced in the mirror, smoothed his fake mustache—it was perfect.

An hour after sunset, Ahmoud checked on Tash. The boy refused to talk. He revived slightly, croaked for water. Marshaled his strength, screamed once an hour until daybreak.

At sunrise, Ahmoud dressed and approached Sary Tash. When the prisoner begged for water, Ahmoud shouted, "Bring water. It will be a long day. Bring water at once."

The Tajik guerrilla moaned, opened his mouth.

When Hakim brought a bucket he had prepared, the prisoner stared up at him. Hakim taunted Tash for a moment.

At Ahmoud's order, Hakim slowly poured the solution of bitter salt water into the prisoner's mouth, all over his body. The prisoner vomited, screamed, sobbed when the brine burned the cuts and bites on his tortured flesh.

The sun rose in the sky, the air became hotter. Sary Tash's screams were reduced to a keening whimper. At noon, with a valley temperature of ninety degrees, Ahmoud approached the boy and asked, "Do you want to change your choice of life or death?" *Get this over with,* he thought. *What's the point of your hold out? Don't you realize I'm running out of time?*

The prisoner whispered unintelligible words.

"Again, please. I did not hear you," Yassar commanded.

The boy's throat was so damaged, he had trouble saying the words. Ahmoud removed a canteen of fresh water from his belt, trickled it into
Tash's mouth. Finally, the youth managed to whisper in Turkic, "Dragon God Baal's lung."

"Thank you," Ahmoud said. "But I need more information."

The boy tried to speak, could not. He whispered, Ahmoud leaned over to listen. The boy's words were unintelligible. Ahmoud shouted, "Take this boy to a tent. Give him water. He's ready to talk."

An hour later, a sergeant rushed to Ahmoud's tent to report the boy had died without speaking.

Enraged, Ahmoud threw his pen. "The girl?"

"She slashed her wrists with a piece of glass. Dead."

When he verified the report, he found that the boy and girl were both deceased. He returned to his tent, wondered what the hell "Baal's lung" meant. Wondered if his personal exposure was worth the scant knowledge he had gained. Worried that he might be censured for his unauthorized interference and botched handling of the interrogation.

Chapter 4

Kicking his pony into a scrambling, clattering hooves on rock gallop, Jack reluctantly followed Arses down the ridge. Heart pounded: he gripped the skidding horse with his legs, sat back, absorbed the jolts with his knees. He kicked his feet out of the stirrups in case the horse fell. What the hell had he gotten into? But he couldn't ignore the victim. Couldn't act like an indifferent coward in front of the women and the kid.

Arses partially fell off his horse two more times, Jack shoved him back into balance both times. They held up at the bottom. Jack reined up behind the Englishman, looked: fifty meters away, four men held down the victim. Another had dropped his pants, was taunting the captive, waving his penis. But the attackers had problems: bodies suddenly flew, tumbled away from the roiling scene. Outraged screams rang out.

Arses pulled out his pistol, flashed a crazed smile, urged his mare ahead, gun hand on his top hat. He fell completely off his horse.

"Dude, you can't ride for shit!" Jack held out a hand, helped Dickey back on his plunging horse, then urged his mount across the boulder-strewn plain, wished he had time to use the OICW. Glanced back, saw Penel and Wantonal had just reached the base of the cliff, were reined up to watch.

Valley floor was flat, undeveloped at the attack scene. Farmlands in the distance, boulders and scrub brush covered the near ground. Beyond the struggling mass, the stream wound its way around house-sized rocks. Attackers and victim just inches from the grayish-blue, glacial melt water.

Jack, several horse-lengths in the lead, ducked when a man fired, then returned fire. Tumbled an attacker head over heels. Shot until he ran out of bullets. Three shocked men still stood, stared at the impromptu posse.

Jack reined in his pony, slammed another magazine into his M-9. Knocked a young turbaned guy over with his mount. Boy screamed, fell to the side.

Second one grabbed his reins, drew a long Khyber knife, stabbed at Jack's leg, hit the saddle—Jack shot him, guy flew backwards like he was jerked on a chain. Shot the first guy when he struggled to his feet: gun bucked in his hand, the aggressor heaved up, arms outspread, eyes popping out of his head.

The last rapist, a big man with a full beard, long hair, was on his hands and knees over the victim, oblivious to the carnage around him.

Arses fell off his horse again, jumped up, flipped a rope noose around the man's neck. Wrapped the rope around his saddlehorn. Guided his horse, dragging the man, who kicked, hollered all the way to a rock outcropping. Arses backed his horse, hoisted the man aloft.

The hanging man grabbed the rope, pulled himself up, hand over struggling hand.

The semi-naked, dust-covered rape victim approached at a run. She wore a rough woolen cape over a ripped shirt, a short skirt torn open in front. Long, flowing black hair, huge breasts, a spectacular Zena look-alike body. She hit the guy like he was a tackling dummy. The rapist clutched the rope. Was pulled higher by Arses' horse. The woman hung on.

When she realized the man was still climbing, she reached to her waist with one hand, pulled a knife, shredded the guy's crotch like it was beef chimichanga. He screamed, tried to protect himself, let go of the rope. Neck snapped like a breaking branch of dead wood.

Dust-covered woman dropped, stood under the hung man, tilted her head; the drenching flow of blood coursed over her face and breasts.

When the deluge of arterial gore slowed to a drizzle, the big woman— she had to be over six feet—turned, glared at Arses and Jack. Upper body, lean, lovely, blood red: a copper collar around her long neck, a broad forehead under wild hair, a sensuous mouth— overall a spectacular, malevolent Chinese beauty. But young— maybe fourteen, fifteen. Shaded her eyes, stared, slowly licked her gory lips.

Hey, babe, Jack thought, *I didn't rape you—I saved you.* Despite her awful appearance, his shock turned into stirrings of desire. *No, I guess I won't ask you to dance.*

She glowered at Dickey Arses, exclaimed, "Hate you!"

The girl ran to the stream, her long legs flashing. Splashed through the water, disappeared through a cave opening on the side of the cliff. What the hell was she pissed about?

Arses pointed toward the cliff. "If I'd known it was China Bitch, I wouldn't have risked our necks riding to the rescue. I'd have stood aside and cheered like a bloody Irishman."

"What'n the world're you talking about?"

"But she never comes into the daylight. Now we've got a chance to exterminate the bitch." Dickey reloaded his pistol. He glanced up. "We're about to do a great service."

Jack was shocked by Arses' proposal to kill the woman. Was immensely curious about her. "Dude, you can't just kill her. Yeah, she didn't waste energy on gratitude. But we can't—-"

"Worse. China Bitch be Evil Incarnate," Penel yelled as she and Wantonal rode up to the two men.

"The Devil's whore," Wantonal added with a spitting voice. He grabbed Arses. "Can't kill a rape victim—a young girl."

"Ordinarily, I'd jolly well agree. But she's no victim." He kicked the roan, galloped across the stream to the cave, almost fell off twice, dismounted, disappeared in the six-foot opening.

"What's the deal? Why's Dickey so pissed?"

"We call her China Bitch," Wantonal explained. "She's one of the filthy Chinese hermits of the mountains."

Mystified, he fell silent, wondering what the hell was up with the Chinese hermit thing. Knew he wouldn't ever ask the strange girl-woman to dinner and a movie.

After long minutes Dickey returned, cursing, pounding his saddle.

"Can't believe this happened. I'm an idiot."

"Nothing wrong with being a hermit." He could go for a little antiviolent aloneness himself.

"Eater of flesh!" Arses spat.

Eater of flesh—something told him the Englishman wasn't kidding.

"Horror of the night," Penel added. "Thou must know, she deprives us of our home, Fortress Haartgard. After dark, she and her kind stalk its halls."

"Out of control religious fanatics, psycho cannibal women. Guys, you need to upgrade your Chamber of Commerce membership rolls. What's all the violence about? I always heard Shangri-la was, like, Paradise."

"It was Paradise until the Soviets blew the tunnel," Arses answered.

"Resources grew short. These inhabitants—" he nodded at the two women —"they're really Baal-worshiping Animists—they and the Muslims in the valley had it out. The strange KEGYA folk at the south end of the valley stood aside."

"And China Bitch is part of a wild element that emerged twenty years ago," Wantonal added, "after a huge earthquake. Now, she and her kind appear and disappear in Fortress Haartgard like magic of old." "They steal precious children, attack the weak," Penel added.

And chow down on 'em. Jack swallowed disgust.

Wantonal concluded, "She seduces the strong, and when they are weaponless she kills and carries them away."

Seduces? He felt the same stirring of the blood he had experienced when China Bitch first stared into his eyes.

Arses asked, "Stuff you don't see on the telly, what?" He rummaged in his saddlebag, pulled out a leather-covered flask, drank. Offered the bottle.
"Local brew, but it'll do."

"Oh, yeah," Jack said. Hid his feelings of horror, confusion, drank what proved to be apricot brandy. Too sweet, but he appreciated the burning sensation. Offered the bottle to the women, who were staring at him, they refused. These girls didn't drink, didn't sunburn, and enjoyed rescuing drowning Marines.

"What a ball!" Top-hatted Arses exclaimed as he slapped his horse's rump. The animal rose, then settled.

Ball? Baseball, pinball, a dancing ball— anything'd be better than Arses' idea of a ball. He asked, "Playin' cops an' robbers has been fun, pard, but what's the chance of getting out of this creepy scene and finding a decent meal and lodging?"

"Haw, haw," Arses laughed. "Bloody Yanks—and you're a wonderful
Berserker example—never lose their sense of humor. Let's ride back to
Fortress Haartgard and feed you, young Jack."

Why a fort? he mused. *What did they need protection from? One gorgeous cannibal? Looked good enough to eat before she took that bloodbath.* Wondered if he'd see her again.

Chapter 5

A tiring three-hour ride north in hot sunlight: the four arrived in a village of whitewashed brick buildings the girls called Asgard.

When Jack asked why the village was named after the Viking Gods' homeland, Penel testily reminded him the valley had been settled by Northmen.

He looked for the beautiful structures so lovingly described in the original story of Shangri-la, Lost Horizon—saw none. The structures were invariably made of whitewashed brick, and were trimmed with wood around the doors, shutters around the windows. The streets were free of the trash common to Pakistani villages. He also noticed that all the inhabitants looked young, healthy. Perched old crones dressed in black, so common throughout the third world, were not evident. People smiled greetings when the group rode through town, stared at him. He sniffed, smelled appetizing odors of roasted chicken. A whiff of fresh bread made his mouth water. Longed for food, a comfortable bed. Flushed an image of the burning helicopter.

Jack reined in, looked up at the large fortress: the gloomy old stone structure loomed over the hamlet in the fading afternoon light and was at least two hundred feet long; its daunting gray walls built in a curve that started, ended against unscalable cliffs. Flock of ravens circled over the thirty-foot-high ramparts, incessantly cawing. Rock crags straight up from the rear of Haartgard Fortress to immense snowfields high overhead, with summits that surrounded the valley.

When the group rode through the gates of a thick outer wall, he looked up at the snowfields, wondered whether avalanches ever had smashed upon the old fort. Noticed long, narrow, ancient archer's shooting slots rimmed the empty ramparts. *Make a great Gunga Din movie set. Doesn't look like anybody left the lights on.*

Young boys appeared in the central yard, took the horses.

Penel led him through empty passageways to a room overlooking the valley.

Basic, with a mullioned window, a bed, a fireplace in one corner, interior bulkheads of rock, colorful rugs covered the floor. So bare, he figured it was a prison cell. But the door had a crossbar on the inside. Dropped his rucksack, gear, and weapons, next to the narrow bed.

Penel opened the window, smiled. "Let me welcome thee to Haartgard of Shangri-la. Jack Flashhardt, you are a tremendous, fearless warrior. I've been thinking about this all the way across the valley. Wantonal and I argued, wagered. I won." *Won what?*

She thrust the security bar across the door, pushed him backwards; they tumbled across the low cot against the bulkhead. Penel kissed him, traced hands over his body. Pulled his clothes off. The two undressed each other, hurried under muslin sheets covered by a heavy, slightly mustysmelling wool blanket.

Shivered: Penel pressed her body against him, rubbed her breasts against his chest, kissed passionately. He became aroused, she climbed on top of him, took him inside, rose, descended. He drowned in her long blonde tresses, her intense eyes.

Rolled her over. With Penel under him, he gained control of his senses, kissed creamy soft breasts, pulled fingers through thick hair. She stroked hands down his back, clutched rump muscles, dug nails into flesh.

"Jack Flashhardt, have my baby," she murmured. Felt like she hit him in the face with a bucket of cold water.

"Have my baby," she repeated. "Have my baby."

His rational mind turned off. The thought of a child—even with this strange woman—was powerful. Sharp jolts of pleasure wracked his body.

She moaned, rocked with him.

Slowed, kissed her neck, her breasts. Skin had turned a wonderful, wild rose color. Moments later, they convulsed again, tumbled out of the bed, onto the cold wood floor.

After regaining his breath, he exclaimed, "Wow! What a greeting.
You're incredible. Beautiful." *Thought about volunteering for Welcome Wagon?* Climbed back into the bed, pulled her under the covers. "You're wonderful." What a cure for a lost love. She could make him forget the real world in a hurry. But the baby thing…

Penel laughed. "Take me away to thy world, Jack Flashhardt. Thou art the best that has happened to Shangri-la in years."

Whoa, this girl is looking for a relationship and a family on the first date. "Dickey claimed the mountains were unclimbable."

Penel rolled on top, stared into his eyes. "I saw the assessing look thou gave the mountains. Thou're not afraid."

"Why d'you want to leave Shangri-la?" He stalled, tried to keep the magical feel of their tumble in bed. "The outside world's full of violent people, tax collectors, traffic jams, crappy reality TV. Here you live a much longer, healthier life."

"The most exciting event in Shangri-la is sunrise. The second, sunset." *Exactly my impression,* he thought.

"And I want children—they are rare in Shangri-la."

"Really? Why?"

Penel stroked his short hair. "Our men are not very fertile. That's why we practice polyandry."

Jack sat up. "You're kidding!"

"It takes much effort to produce children. Our men—"

"Yeah, not fertile." He twisted a lock of her blonde hair. "You said your dad was king. What would he say if you split?"

"He would be upset, but he has Xander, my brother. And Wantonal." "Have you heard of a lost bomb?" Asked on a whim.

"Mayhaps," Penel asked.

Jack sat up. "Somewhere in the mountains. An American bomb."

"Yes," Penel answered. "An ugly thing. A Muslim woman in the market told a house girl of something. A huge, repulsive thing—not in Shangri-la. In a cave in the mountains—a sacrifice to Dragon God Baal. Why do thou ask? All her people are abuzz, says she. Do thou seek it? Be that why thou're here?"

He changed the subject. "I thought the god, Baal, was a dude with horns like a cow. Why do you call him a dragon?"

Penel smiled. "Legend has it that Alexander the Great found the statue of Baal that Moses tried but failed to destroy. In the Valley of the TigrisEuphrates. He took Baal's horns and attached them—as a prank—to the gold-encrusted Dragon God, which other ancients had looted from China. Then, the horned statue was rescued by our ancestors, who stumbled on this valley during their escape. Probably," Penel concluded, "it was a marriage of two cultures, Babylonian Jews—Baalists—and Chinese Animists, many years ago. There are powerful legends attached to the God."

"Let's talk about it later." Rolled back on top of her. Grew hard, slid inside her hot velvety center, stroked her wild rose skin.

Long moments later, he sprawled away with a huge smile.

Penel beamed. "Rest, I will send fare, and Wantonal wants you." She slowly rose, dressed and instructed, "Thou must not leave or let anyone in after dark. Bar the door, thereby sleep in peace, Jack Flashhardt." With that double warning, she ignored his questioning look, removed the heavy security bar, opened the door.

"Dracula roaming the halls of the fort? Why don't I stay with you?" *Get me out of this prison cell.*

"My father, a suspicious man, decrees strangers must stay alone in Haartgard until he meets them. He's engaged until tomorrow, no doubt. Just bar the door, Jack Flashhardt. Save thyself for Wantonal."

Crawled under the covers, dozed, thought about the rosy-skinned girl. Flashes of her beauty, her sensuous lovemaking, her skin, her soft breasts, the crumpled, falling helicopter, the men he had shot, the angry woman's bloody visage. Thoughts of Ashley brought jarring reality, a pang of guilt. Remorse, homesickness. He dozed.

A half hour later, a knock on the closed door. After he hurriedly dressed, two giggling blonde girls, accompanied by two armed but smiling soldiers, entered. They served a meal of flavorful mutton, rice, green raisins, a pot of jasmine tea.

Girls looked like mature fourteen-year-olds. Twins with rosy cheeks, dancing blue eyes; they wore gray wool parkas trimmed with red stitching. While they served him, a young blond guard put down an ancient boltaction rifle, started a fire in the fireplace—warmth spread through the room. Girls lifted his spirits with their bubbly giggles, bouncy enthusiasm.

They offered salacious hints—the guards nudged each other.

He demurred, thought, *After Penel, a covey of beauties couldn't arouse me, let alone young kids.* Disappointed, they left, assuring him that they would return. He took off his clothes again, slept.

Much later, he jerked awake, noticed complete darkness. Suppressed a latent fear of dark places. Listened, heard a scrape, a shuffle outside the door. Realized he'd forgotten to bar it. Heart nearly stopped in fear. Groped for his M-9. Pitch dark in the room. Door opened with a creak. Heard the rustle of clothing removed. Not a lethal visit. Breathed again.

Caught a glimpse of bare skin in a faint shaft of moonlight from the window. A tip of breast—felt a surge of excitement. *But who the hell was it? The twins? Penel? She's insatiable. Guess her dance card is empty. Maybe Wantonal?*

Woman confidently walked to his bed, leaned over, sensuously stroked his naked body under the blankets, grasped his rapidly growing erection.

Decided it was Penel, spread the covers back.

Raised her leg, stepped over him, guided him inside her already wet center. Heard her hurried breathing. He put his hands on her hips, stroked upward. She felt different. Must be Wantonal. But her smell was unbelievably rank.

She crushed her pelvis down on him—searing heat. Pushed against him with powerful hips. She was faceless in the dark.

Leaned closer, stroked his shoulders, his cheeks—terrible breath, panted against his ear, kissed his cheek, wrapped her hands around his neck.

"I hate!" she whispered. "I will have." She hissed, "I will eat."

Horrified, he tried to heave her. China Bitch bent into his upper body, pressed on his neck for long seconds—his vision blurred. *Christ—trying to…*

Dwindling consciousness, he balled his fist. Slugged her in the teeth. She flew back, regained her balance, pushed her forearm down on his neck, her groin continued pounding him. Panting breath blew against his ear. He reached, tried to grab his pistol, hand banged on the ice axe strapped to his pack. Jerked it out of the Velcro straps, grabbed her forearm, pushed it from his neck, she wouldn't stop grinding into him. She twisted away but his strong climber's fingers locked around her wrist.

Hacked her in the shoulder, ripped the pick end of the axe down.

Razor-sharp edge cut a huge slice in her arm.

She bawled from the pain—blood gushed. Reversed heads, struck her in the same shoulder with the axe end. His hand stung, felt like he'd mis-hit a baseball. Sank so deep he couldn't pull it out. She screamed, jumped back. Axe ripped out of her flesh. He heaved his knees, rolled on top. Realized he was still moving against her. Horrified, he jerked away.

China Bitch sprang up—howled, ran spraying blood. He cursed for being stupid, forgetful. How'd she see him in the dark?

Quickly dressed, threw his web gear and pack on, stepped outside with pistol in one hand, small flashlight from his pack. Stood still, looked in all directions. No movement. Flickering candle in a sconce on the bulkhead revealed a massive trail of blood that traced down the hallway. Fort was eerily quiet, empty. Should have been people in the halls after the horrible screams.

He followed the blood track along stone-walled passages until it disappeared in an alcove. Searched for a doorway, found nothing. He turned the opposite direction.

Outside, a half moon still shining above the fort's parapets. No guards atop the walls, no soldiers in the courtyard. Fort was deserted. Penel was right. No one in Haartgard after dark. Just like Herot in the poem. Place is nothing but a damned oversized horse barn.

Crept down the steps, into the stable, selected the first horse he encountered. By the moon's light, he fitted the gray with a rope halter, led it out.

Heaved himself up, slowly walked the horse across the flagstonecovered ground, out the open front gates. Heart pounded, no one appeared in the cold, pre-dawn darkness.

Chapter 6

When the sky began to lighten the rock-terraced fields of Shangri-la to a dull-green, Jack dismounted in an oat field, slapped the small gray gelding. The horse paused to munch on stalks of oats; he chased it into a galloping retreat, then turned into a scree field of loose rock shards piled against the steep valley wall.

He found a nook amongst boulders, crawled in, nervously dozed for two hours. During waking moments, he brooded over the Muslims he had shot, thought of Penel, her rosy-skinned sex. China Bitch's vicious sex—her howling, her bleeding in the fort; Ashley ensconced in the distant dream of Palo Alto. Strange flies buzzed in the rocks, ignored him.

At ten hundred hours, he opened, then ate an MRE—a Meal Ready to Eat—a beef hamburger. Fake grill marks made him smile. Where else but America? He had heated the food by placing it against his ribs, but the butter was hard and the cool beef smelled greasy. Put the M&Ms in his pocket.

He longed to be back in Palo Alto, walking to class, maybe heading to The Oasis on El Camino Real for a sizzling-hot burger, a cold beer.

Finished, he stuffed the trash in his rucksack, looked at the narrow valley below him. Felt an unwillingness to leave beautiful Penel. He recognized the feeling of lassitude Dickey Arses had described, overcame the emotion, forced himself to put one foot in front of the other.

At low altitude just over the valley, ten thousand feet above sea level, steps took as much effort as strides at twice the altitude. Discovered each move became infinitesimally easier, as though he shed gear while he climbed.

Midnight on a high ridge, at about twenty thousand feet, he stared down at the darkened valley of Shangri-la, proud of his accomplishment: ten thousand feet in fourteen hours. Below, dead men and a dead woman. Far down the valley, a few scattered lights of Shangri-la, where a beautiful girl and an eccentric Englishman were trapped—if you believed them—in the most unusual place in the world.

High altitude winds, rare late at night in other heights, tore at his parka and pack. Breath clouded, he panted in the oxygen-thin air, tried to ignore a pounding headache. Valley still tugged at him—he turned from the strange basin.

Shadow of movement below. *A Marco Polo ram? Penel, pissed off for being deserted? China Bitch?*

Too big. Figure, apparently a man, moving rapidly across the moonlit snowfields, disappeared in a ridgeline of black rocks, appeared closer. Following his footprints.

Alarmed, Jack hurried to his right, clambered along a rock outcropping. Spotted a crusty windswept section of snow, traversed over it, left no trace of his passage.

Despite stealthy efforts, saw the big man again, an hour later, much closer. Fellow carried a long, heavy staff. Wore a peaked cap that covered his ears, draped over his neck.

Called over the howling wind, "What d'you want, bud?"

No answer. Cursed Mick for getting him into this mess. More frightened, thought about breaking out the OICW. Glanced up at the summit on his right flank. About a thousand feet higher than his position. Extended his ice axe, started up the sixty-degree slope. *See if this guy can really climb. I'll leave the prick in the dust. Yeah, right: snowdust.*

After two hours, he gained the summit. Paused to catch his breath: heart pounded, throat raw from breathing the sterile, high-altitude air— figured the summit was over twenty-two thousand feet.

The words to John Denver's song rang in his mind: "Rocky Mountain high, in Colorado…" Wished he was on a Rocky Mountain high. Shouted the Marine cry, "Oorah!"

The moment of exhilaration ripped away when he saw the large man climbing, two hundred feet below. Panicked, he crossed over the top. Ran down the snowy slope on the Pakistani side of the crest, into a growing cloud. Prayed the misty whiteout would help him lose the dogged follower. Worried about setting off an avalanche.

Slowed to a creep by the weather conditions, Jack struggled to maintain his balance as he descended. Relaxed slightly when he figured the big guy could never find him in this soup.

An hour later, he saw a white structure, ghostly in the thinning whiteout, barely illuminated by the moon.

Neared the one story, pitched-roof with tipped up eaves. Square building—its stone walls were smooth with no visible cracks or structural seams. Waded through a drift that had accumulated along the side, turned a corner, realized he had stupidly circled back and now stood on a cliff overlooking Shangri-la.

The entry of the temple facing Shangri-la was door-less. Four-foot blank walls created an entry patio. He sized up the structure, wished he had studied Far Eastern ancient architecture. Peered inside: saw a man, naked to the waist, sitting with crossed legs on a low platform.

"Hello," he shouted over the howling wind.

Beardless, the bald-headed monk looked Chinese. Didn't look up or respond. Appeared to be frozen stiff in the sitting position. Touched the man's skin—ice-cold but not frozen.

He pulled his knife, held it under the man's nose. No moisture. Monk was dead. Illuminated his watch—it was two hours before sunrise. Sat at the base of the platform, leaned back, fell asleep.

It was still dark when he awoke. Heard a voice, but too tired to do anything but listen: "You seek approval from Dragon God Baal. That is wise—your fates are entwined."

He listened more closely—evidently, the monk wasn't dead. He glanced around—didn't see a dragon. "You are born, fed, cared for, secured. Your next need is approval." The monk spoke in a sing-song voice, highpitched heavily-accented. "Need grows as you age. First the approval of
parents, then friends, teachers, associates. You try to excel, but you ignore
The Way—the wrong paths loom."

"What paths? I'd settle for a path out of here." He was getting curious but still too tired to turn around. Maybe dreaming one of those nightmares where you can't move.

"Your society lusts for things. The material side." Disapproving tone to the man's voice.

"Yeah, well, a parka an' gloves 'ud be a good start for you, pal. House, four walls—furnace'd be good. Bag ladies, homeless naked guys are sorta
Twentieth Century uncool. Uh, in your case… just cool."

"Can you garner things forever?"

"Til death do us part'd be long enough. Uh, scratch the death part for now."

"You must come to The Way. Only then will you achieve
    inner peace.
Dragon God needs you—ready yourself for service. You have pain. Shed it —it confuses you."

"I killed men and a woman. Human beings with their own feelings, experiences, hopes, dreams. I ended all that. No way out of it."

"You are a kshatriya—a member of the warrior caste. It is your dharma —your duty to fight your opponents. You will make the earth a lake of blood, even an icy grave for many. Remember, a righteous battle leads to heaven for the fallen—they will be washed of their sins by their spilled blood. Ignore your mental pain. We will teach you The Way when you are ready."

"You guys ever hear of 'Turn the other cheek'? Or maybe take a shower instead of washing with blood?"

Woke up with a start. Outside, sun was shining, sky was blue. Turned his head, ice cube monk gone. Looked around the temple—it appeared smaller inside than outside. A bulkhead without a door split the room. Crossed, felt for an opening—found none.

Wondered what was inside the blocked-off space, walked outside, turned towards Pakistan. Saw no tracks in the fresh snow. An hour later he crested the highest ridge, saw Peaked Cap standing on a near ridge.

Plunged down the snowfield, away from the lone figure. Encountered a massive series of bergschrunds—thirty-foot-wide glacial cracks directly across his path. Turned right—punishing minutes later, found a snow bridge, inched across a blue icy abyss.

Paused to clean his sunglasses. Looked around, saw the huge figure stalking down the snowfield, just yards behind! Up close, guy was huge. Over seven feet tall—almost eight feet. A long scarf wrapped his head, covered his face. Jack stopped, drew his M-9, fired into the snow bridge— the shots shattered the overpass.

Big guy reached the uphill side of the bergschrund, stopped twenty feet away. Stared, raised a fist.

"What's your problem, dude?" Jack yelled. Thought about the XM-25, decided he couldn't shoot the guy unless he was in direct danger. The two stared at each other over the crack in the glacier.

"I smell you, Fan Gway. I am Mo Poo. You killed mine daughter, foreign devil." The big man growled in a basso voice so deep it made Jack resonate like a tuning fork. *Jesus, China Bitch's dad.*

He shouted, "Look, I saved her. She was being raped by these Muslim dudes. We killed them. All of them."

Mo Poo peered at him. "It's true, Chin Bit told me she was going to Haartgard. To thank a man. A man who saved her. But when I found her, she was wounded. Your smell was on her. She bled to death." *Chin Bit. So that's why the name, China Bitch. Wow! Dead. But why's this guy named More Shit?*

"I'll seek out the truth. If another killed Chin Bit, I will know. What do you in my mountains?"

He tried to think of an excuse, glad to escape the death incident.

Blurted out the first thing that came to mind. "I'm looking for a lost bomb.

Have you seen it?"

The giant regarded him for a long moment. "Yes, I know of the hidden weapon so many search for, but that is of no matter. Dragon God Baal tends to that egg. Chin Bit's death—it will be resolved." He walked away.

"Wait, Poo. Where's the bomb? I need to know."

The big man strode away, shouting, "When I know the truth…"

Jack turned and clambered down the mountain, as fast as he could move without snowshoes. Gulped snow as he walked, stopped at sunset to gnaw on his last MRE, frozen chicken in iced-up curry sauce. When it became too dark to see, he fell to his knees, dug a hole in a snowbank. Crawled in to escape frigid blasts of air, looked up at the sky to relieve a touch of lygophobia. Zillions of stars stared down, washed away the fear of darkness. Ursa Minor, encircled by Draco the Dragon, high in the sky. *Wish I could plant some dragon's teeth. I could use an army of ancient Greek hoplites or even peltast soldiers to fight off the big guy.*

Lower, near the horizon, he spotted the red star Antares, the Asian dragon, in the constellation Scorpius. *Lotta dragons here,* he thought. *Guess that's why they worship one. Me, I'll stick with my Christian God.* He looked up at the amazing spectacle of stars, felt peace, tranquility course through his body.

"Thanks, God," he murmured. He backed into the snowcave, took two heatpaks out of a side pocket in the rucksack, wrenched them to activate the warming chemicals, slid one inside each boot to prevent frostbite.

Filled in his access, left a breathing hole, curled on top of his groundpad, fell asleep. Last thoughts, fears were of his giant pursuer's final words, "When I know…"

Chapter 7

Mara Bhutto stepped out of the dusty Mercedes Benz taxi, paid the driver two hundred rupees. She wore a full-length, highly prized, dark blue burqa from Herat, Afghanistan, and an intricately embroidered lace veil that covered her face to just below her intense green eyes.

Without glancing up or down Islamabad's Kaghan Road, she practiced her code words: "Bless me, Father, for I have sinned greatly and severely."

Mara climbed the white marble steps of Fatima Church, the only Catholic Church in Islamabad. She entered the nave, paused to dip her fingers in the holy water, crossed herself, unveiled and strode into the peaceful darkness of the church. The temperature felt twenty degrees cooler than outside, where the afternoon sun was blasting the city through a hazy, smog-ridden atmosphere.

Mara Bhutto, the illegitimate daughter of the former prime minister of Pakistan, Zulfiqar Bhutto, sat on a wooden pew and reflected on the last three months of her life, spent in China. With degrees in English and Asian History from Quaid-e-Azam University, an Economic Studies degree from Cairo University, she was the most educated, the most angry, the most dangerous woman in Pakistan.

Angry because, when she was three years old, her mother and her uncle had brought her to the front of Parliament House on Khayaban Avenue, where the Army hanged Prime Minister Zulfiqar Ali Bhutto, a protégé of Mao Tse-tung.

Her father hanging by a rope was Mara's first memory.

The most dangerous woman because when she had returned from Cairo University, her Communist cadre had recommended her for a threemonth course of subversive warfare in The People's Republic of China. The Hainan Island school was attended by revolutionaries from all over the world. Mara learned armed and unarmed combat, tactics, assassination techniques, skydiving, demolitions.

She'd learned to use every muscle and brain cell in her lean, longlegged, five-foot-eight frame.

Mara checked her watch: five PM. She rose, moved through darkness to a confession booth against a far wall of the empty church. Sitting in the tiny structure, she uttered the code phrase. Her heart was pounding, she felt a tingle of sweat on her armpits. The walls closed in on her when no one answered.

Finally, a small wooden shutter slid open on the wall of the booth. A priest's voice. "I will show you the way to purity."

Mara was so relieved she missed the man's first words of instruction. She caught, "a colonel called Shahbaz Bhaddi, also known as Big Sun, will be there. His new appointment as the head of the Pakistani search effort for the lost American biological bomb must be interrupted."

"Where am I meeting him?"

Ignoring her question, the priest droned, "Luckily he has a weakness for beautiful young tarts… but know that he's very cautious and you'll be searched."

The dispassionate priest paused, his hand appeared, the manicured fingers with highly polished nails, held a tube of lipstick. The priest's long effeminate fingers reminded Mara of writhing white slugs that never saw the light of day. She smelled cheap toilet water it almost gagged her. "This is a custom-made single-shot Russian pistol. One twist and click produces lipstick, and a harder twist fires the four millimeter weapon."

"But where, Father?"

"The bar in the American hotel the Marriott. He goes there regularly. You'll meet the colonel tonight, and God willing grant the Muslim heathen an early exit to Paradise."

"Thank you, Father." She regarded the lipstick, saw the priest's face lowered to the cavity in the booth staring up at her. Disgusted by his leer, she fled, stuffing the lipstick in her purse.

Mara caught a taxi, gave an address for her assigned safe house in the Blue Zone, one of the eight districts of Islamabad. The cab stopped in front of a Punjab grocery. After paying the driver, she climbed narrow steps to the apartment, wrinkled her nose at the ugly spiced odor of rancid mutton soaked in curry, that was wafting from the store.

She undressed, threw her clothes about the seedy apartment. Her support team had devoured Chinese food, left the scraps; the smell of soy sauce and noodles filled the tiny furnished apartment.

Donning a tight-fitting, bright violet silk dress cut low over her impressive breasts, and barely covering the tops of her thighs, she inspected her appearance for a second while she pulled sheer nylons over long legs. She thought of the weird Russian gun in a lipstick tube, applied her own vibrant red lipstick, inspected her golden skin for flaws and saw none.

Putting a wig and large sunglasses on to disguise her appearance, Mara threw a floor-length burqa over the Western outfit, slipped a pair of sneakers on—she didn't want to be harassed by stray mullahs upset at the sounds of a woman walking on the streets of the city. An hour later, she strode through the lobby of the Marriott.

In a restroom, she removed the burqa, replaced her shoes with high heels. Carrying the extra clothes in a leather bag, Mara entered the bar; she was seated at a prominent table in the Western-style lounge. The table was near a French expatriate piano player, who played a song made famous by Maurice Chevalier, Thank Heaven for Little Girls.

Little girls. Mara remembered when she had been a three-year-old little girl, held aloft by her uncle to see her father hung—a sight that had taken years to understand. The thought strengthened her. She wondered if the victim would thank heaven for her.

After slowly sipping her first drink—a tart Perrier water—she noticed a half dozen senior officers enter the club, sit at the long bar. The boisterous officers spotted her, soon a lean junior officer approached. Mara acknowledged his presence with a smile; the sour-faced lieutenant informed her, "Colonel Bhaddi would like to meet you."

Too afraid to make a response, Mara forced a shaky smile. The lieutenant asked her to accompany him to the rear of the club. She rose, followed. He led her to a private room, containing a dark leather-covered booth, lit by a fake Tiffany lamp.

The lieutenant eyed Mara's skin-tight dress with the wordless contempt of a devout Muslim, picked up her bag, carefully removed and inspected every item in it. When he pulled out the lipstick gun, Mara held her breath. He twisted the silvery tube until lipstick slowly extruded, looked at Mara with an expression of disapproval. The lipstick gun was aiming at her. Mara forced herself to remain still. *He won't shoot me, he doesn't know it's a gun. Don't twist.*

"The color doesn't match your lips." He twisted the lipstick again, retracting it.

Heart pounding, Mara responded, "Really? I must have grabbed the wrong one. Thank you for noticing."

"How much do you want?"

"Thirty thousand rupees," she murmured in a breathy voice.

Angered by the tone of her voice, the lieutenant pulled out his wallet, tossed down three ten-thousand rupee bills and left.

A few minutes later, Shahbaz Bhaddi walked into the tiny room in a grand manner, like a massive bull strutting across his domain. He carried bottles of Australian champagne, two flutes. He smelled as if he had been riding a horse.

It took almost an hour to get the colonel to finish the first and half the second bottle of cheap champagne. The colonel, looking nervous about being with the spectacularly beautiful young tart, insisted on relating a boring story about flying his antique airplane.

Beyond the curtain shielding the entry, Mara listened to the clink of glasses, the murmur of voices, the piano player singing another old-time song.

Frustrated by his lack of aggression, Mara stroked the colonel's knee, his leg, finally his groin. He sputtered to a stop, wrapped his arms around her, pulled her slim body against his huge frame.

Mara murmured, "My, you're handsome, so big, so strong."

The colonel growled deep in his throat, let her go, poured the last of the champagne. Hoisted her onto his lap, kissed her long neck above her breasts.

Pulling away, Mara, heart beating rapidly, removed the gun from her bag, applied fresh lipstick. The colonel drunkenly pawed the tube aside. Mara suggested that she apply lipstick to his lips.

Intrigued, the colonel puckered. Mara, her heart pounding like thunder in the Himalayas, applied the lipstick to his fat lips.

"Open your mouth so I can get it right," she ordered. Mara lifted the tube, aimed it at the roof of his mouth, gave the tube a twist. The gun made a popping sound. Shahbaz Bhaddi stiffened. His eyes bulged, his mouth opened, closed three times. Gasped as though he couldn't catch his breath.

Clutched Mara like she was a lifesaver. She shuddered, pushed him away— he slid under the table, thumped it once.

Terrified, Mara waited to see whether the colonel's guards had noted the sounds. When no one arrived, she groped under her dress, found a black orchid strapped to her leg by a garter, threw it on the table, grabbed her bag. She slowly walked out of the private room, amazed at how easily the colonel had given up his life in a moment of drunken passion. If she could just get past the friends.

Chapter 8

The morning after he returned to Okinawa from Pakistan, Jack reported the experimental OICW's employment to Gunnery Sergeant Tensht's assistant, left the armorer a report detailing his firing of six rounds of 20mm ammo during the parachute drop, added a note to check with Mick Nakamura to determine the results. Then he went to the gym to work the stiffness out of his over-traveled body.

On the exercise bike, he thought of the chewing-out he had received from Colonel Farley, the senior Army officer in Islamabad. The blackhaired, chubby colonel had shouted, snarling through a downward curving mouth that looked out of place on his cherub face, "What makes you think you're free to gallivant around the countryside on sightseeing tours, Lieutenant? Yesterday, you missed your flight to Tokyo. You're an G-2 courier, not a goddam tourist! Important secret documents had to be there by midnight." Farley had slammed his fist on his desk so hard the 105mm cannon shell penholder bounced. His cherubic face looked strange wearing a grimace, his hooded eyes flashed.

Jack concentrated on a picture of the President hanging on the wall. He looked either embarrassed for Jack or constipated.

Farley had continued to shout, "You refused to volunteer to help out General Harmbruster's search for the missing bomb. And now you couldn't even find time to carry out your orders." The colonel tapped his head, "A sense of mission doesn't come from here." He tapped his chest. "It comes from here."

"Headache? Heartburn, Colonel? Can I get you an aspirin? Or do you just want to sit there and work on a coronary?" *What a pompous ass!*

The colonel had stared, barely understood the sarcastic remarks, decided to ignore them and continued with a loud voice,

"You were absent without leave. AWOL. That calls for non-judicial punishment and loss of pay under the UCMJ. You'll catch a plane this morning to Camp Hansen. Await word on a hearing date." *Uniform Code of Military Justice. That'll give my short-lived career a great send-off.*

Trying to remain calm, Jack responded, "Sir, may I offer an explanation?" *I'm calling this jerk, sir?*

"Offer? You failed to complete your mission. Get out of here. And remember, I'm going to keep my eye on you. The next time you screw up, you're gonna be in a world of shit."

He had pulled out the documents he found in the cave, handed them to Colonel Farley.

"What's this?" The colonel had demanded. He pulled a cigarette out of a pack, lit it as he looked at the much-folded documents.

"I don't know, sir. I found them in a cave on my way out of the Hindu
Kush. I think they're written in Urdu. Might be interesting."

Unimpressed, Farley had thrown the papers aside. "Tell my aide exactly where you found them—just in case they have any value. Now, get out of here, you goddam worthless reserve."

He had about-faced, left the colonel's office, happy to be out of the man's hateful atmosphere.

Angry, he pumped the exercise bike faster while he thought of how hard he had worked to get back to Pakistan: at first light on the mountainside, he had edged out of his tiny snowcave, surveyed the slopes. Immediately had seen a cave-opening in the side of a serac—an ice wall.

Wishing he had slept in the cave, he had cautiously entered it. Six foot high entrance was half-filled with snow but after he waded a few feet, the cave floor was dry. Aimed his flashlight ahead, rounded a corner, found a sheet-metal door. Thought hard about turning around, leaving. Maybe a whole troop of bad guys behind it.

He pictured startled faces, guns rising. It was poorly made, he pushed it open, heart hammering, M-9 at the ready.

An empty room with a desk made of Indian Army ammo boxes.

Papers, in some Arabic-type script, were scattered across the desktop. Much-used numerology book on the desk. Gathered the documents, thrust them in his pack. Saw one scrap of paper crumbled, lying on the cave floor. Picked it up, smoothed it: in English, it was a printout of an email.

Glanced at it, realized someone had asked the San Francisco Giants when their spring home opener was. A baseball fan in the Hindu Kush. Go figure. He looked around, saw nothing else.

After a rapid descent to the valley along rock-covered ridges, through pine tree-filled gullies, he had caught a ride south with a local farmer. Had reported, in the town of Gilgit, to the local Pakistani Army base commander, Major Lialot Soongoon. The major, a Catholic who secretly hated the local mullah extremists, had gladly arranged a ride to Islamabad in an old Soviet-built Hind helicopter.

Jarred back to reality by the triumphant shout of a weightlifter, Jack glanced at his watch, realized he had spent an hour on the workout studio's exercise bike. He looked at the weightlifter a sweaty, popping-muscle enlisted man, sitting on the floor with a triumphant grin on his face. He went back to his room, showered, dressed, pulled the Beretta out of his satchel. He strolled to Gunnery Sergeant Tensht's office. It was cheerfully decorated with multiple pictures of children, Marine buddies.

The big-eared, slight sergeant stood up behind a squared-away metal desk, greeted him. "Lieutenant, thanks for the OICW report. What's up?"

"I got an M-9 in Islamabad, Gunny. I'd like to check it out. See if I can zero it in."

The gunny accepted the Beretta, checked for cleanliness, nodded approval. "Nice weapon, Lieutenant. Little under-powered, but what the hell let's take it to the range and plug Maggie's drawers. You're an officer, ammunition'll cost a fiver."

He handed five dollars to the pale-faced sergeant. They took an open jeep to the practice facility. At the outdoor range, carpeted by a lush growth of green grass, he shot two sets of three rounds at targets downrange; the sets showed a pattern of low right by an inch. The odor of gunpowder tickled his nose as he inspected the targets.

"Excellent groupings, Lieutenant," the gunnery sergeant remarked. He took the pistol, put it on a table, adjusted the sights. The second round of firings shredded the center of the bullseye.

"That'll do it, Gunny."

"Would the lieutenant be interested in doing combat drills?" the armorer asked. "I'd be happy to give specialized training."

He thought about it a great way to pass some downtime. He had shot expert with the pistol and rifle at Basic School. And he wasn't scheduled to instruct would-be climbers the reason he had been activated for two weeks.

The gunny started him with a BB gun, used ping-pong balls as targets, flung them in the air while he gave instructions. Shooting from the hip, Jack missed most of the balls. After an hour, the gunny smiled, ended the session.

"You're tryin' to aim, Lieutenant," the gunny said. "Visualize. Next time, feel the targets. Shut your eyes when you shoot." They made a date for the next morning.

They advanced to two drills a day, two hours each; after a couple of days, he kept his eyes closed and amazingly hit ninety percent of the flying ping-pong balls. Next, he shot at simulated pop-up soldiers hidden behind trees and bushes with an M-16.

The morning after they finished the final class, Sergeant Tensht brought out a new rifle-sized weapon. It was blocky-looking, about as long as an M-16, but it had no barrel. Its gunsight was a miniature video camera.

"I just got this from JNWD that's Joint Non-Lethal Weapons

Directorate in Quantico, Lieutenant. Wanna try it?"

Mystified by the weapon, he asked, "What is it?"

"It's a laser gun. The XM-299. It shoots an energy beam. When it hits the victim, it makes the water molecules in his cells boil. It produces heat far beyond the human tolerance for pain. It's impossible to stand up to it.
Eventually melts the flesh."

After instruction, he looked through a miniature video camera screen at a target. He pressed the button, painted the bull's-eye, one hundred meters away. "Doesn't seem like much," he commented. "In the movies the target goes up in a ball of fire."

The gunny took the weapon back and asked, "Think so, Lieutenant? Lemme show ya. Don' worry, it's safe. You won't be able to stand it long enough to get hurt." Tensht turned the gun on Jack, fired. He felt a warm spot on his arm that immediately became an intolerable point of pain. He jumped away, stared at his arm—there was no flaming hole, just a reddened area.

"See?" The gunny cackled. "It's impossible to take it longer than a couple of seconds." He laughed again. "And it scares the beJesus out of your foe 'cause he doesn't know what happened. He drops everything, pisses his pants, creams his jeans, an' runs like a bat outta hell." "Amazing!"

A corporal approached and informed him that he had a long distance call. Fearing a call from Colonel Farley, he hurried to the First Sergeant's office. Picked up the phone it was his dad. After exchanging greetings, he asked, "What's going on with the ranch, Dad?" The last he had heard, the Crow Nation was offering to sell the 20,000-acre ranch back to Bill Flashhardt.

"A cousin wrote from Texas," Bill responded. "He found a letter in an old steamer trunk, memorializing the original purchase from the Crow Nation. We might be able to re-open the lawsuit, appeal the judgment, if I can round up a hundred grand or so for legal fees." The tribes had sued the Flashhardts, won ownership of their ranch all of it except the house, the barn and stock buildings on 160 acres.

"Anyway, not why I called. Son, I'm proud as hell you joined the Marines. But it burns me that they jerked you outta law school." Jack glanced at the First Sergeant's clerk, turned his back.

"I can get you assigned to the United Nations. You'll be a military attaché. They're sending people to investigate this, that, and any damn fool place they feel like poking their noses."

"Dad, can't believe you'd have anything to do with the UN."

"You're right, I don't approve of the United Nations or any other goddam international movements, but we could keep you out of combat. It doesn't hurt to use every horse in the corral."

"What's involved?"

"Jake that is Senator Jensen, has told me he'll call Headquarters Marine Corps and set it up."

"Are you positive?"

"Absolutely. He's on Foreign Relations. He said he can get it done. The military will jump through hoops for him. You'll probably go somewhere in the Middle East, but you won't be on active duty."

"I'm not sure. The UN would be a whole new deal."

"True, but you wouldn't be a combat Marine."

He again thought of the exploding helicopter, the men he had shot in Shangri-la. Images burned into his brain. China Bitch even more horrible.

He wondered what the change would mean. For a second, he felt he faced two huge choices without enough information. A major crossroad. Maybe one way life, another way death. But the UN he wouldn't kill, get killed. Had to be better.

"Your option," Bill urged. "What d'you want to do?"

"Guess I'll transfer to the UN Alea jacta est."

"You and your Latin what's that mean?"

"The dice have been cast."

After he exchanged goodbyes with his dad, he went to Captain Homer Norton's office. A picture of a young woman and two kids hung on the wall. Another picture of Norton, dressed in shorts, showing off an artificial leg. His desk was covered with stacks of reports, sets of orders, requisition forms. An ashtray, over-flowing like the company clerk's, sat next to the old-fashioned dial phone. He wondered how his new boss had lost his leg.

A shortwave radio was broadcasting the Rush Limbaugh Show. Norton said, "Wait a minute, I want to hear Rush finish what he's sayin." He looked up at Jack. "One of the few that's on the military's side. Ever listen to him?"

"Since I was a kid. My dad loves him. The guy rules in Montana." He waited until Norton turned down the radio, took a deep breath, explained that he had an opportunity to transfer to the United Nations.

The captain stared at him for a moment, responded, "I'm going to try and not be resentful, bigod. I guess I'm just not used to people that have real influence."

He looked at the captain, guessed the guy wasn't going to threaten to throw him in the brig, so he kept his mouth shut.

Chapter 9

After Colonel Farley had the papers Jack found in the Afghan cave translated, he immediately reported to Brigadier General Andrew Jackson Harmbruster's office at the American Embassy in Islamabad. The office was as spare as the colonel's. Both men disdained family and military unit pictures, both men hated greenery in their workplaces. Both were hard men who expected total dedication from their underlings.

Unlike Farley's downward-casting face, Harmbruster had a friendly, smiling demeanor that inspired those under him: sparkling blue eyes, a shaved bullet head, an outthrust jaw. "What'cha got, Fred?" he asked his subordinate.

Farley held up the sheaf of papers. "The Hollywood kid hit pay dirt, General. You were a genius to get him involved especially after he turned down the mission. He went at it in a roundabout way, but he found some important documents. They discuss the bomb, the possessor's intentions. Don't say where it is—only that it's hidden in the Northern Areas. In the mountains."

Harmbruster flashed his famous smile. "I knew that kid was top drawer! Good-looking boy. You're right, shoulda been an actor. Got a jaw and cheekbones coulda been carved by a Mameluke saber. His dad served under me in Beirut, you know. His dad was a brilliant tactician. He had those Lebanese and Palestinian wannabe punks running into themselves. Same blue eyes on the kid. Cold enough to freeze you in your tracks and he doesn't intimidate."

"No shit! Kid is tough as nails I couldn't scare him. And him being a world-class climber helps. His report says he found the cave at fourteen thousand feet on his way down the mountain! I don't know any soldiers or
Marines could operate at that altitude."

"Amazing!" the general commented.

54

"He's a reluctant warrior, General. Personally, I can't stand the wiseass jerk-off. He doesn't belong in your Marine Corps." Farley lit a cigarette.

"I gotta admit, Fred, I was taken aback when the kid flat out refused to volunteer. But it's the new Corps. Gotta adapt. We'll turn him into an asskickin' Marine whether he likes it or not."

"I could hardly believe he turned us down," the colonel added.

"Well, Fred, we're short on assets. And it'd be real kudos for the Marines to save the Air Force's hinder on this one. They're doing what they can with manned and unmanned flights, looking for the lost bio-ordnance. But with its GPS transponder evidently out, they're screwed. And the Army's hiking up and down valleys, hopin' to stumble over it, since they don't have solid Intel."

"His C.O. called, said the kid's got himself in the UN."

General Harmbruster frowned. "His dad's tight with the senator from Montana. Old boy network in the backwoods minor complication. But we'll get around that problem. We'll make sure his UN duty is right where we need him to be. I know the gal heads up Islamabad station." The general
smiled at his subordinate, "I gotta plan, Fred."

Chapter 10

Early on a Sunday morning, Yassar Ahmoud, the young al Qaida operative, sat at his desk in the secret al Qaida headquarters in Peshawar, Pakistan, and gazed out at Khyber Road. The one-story buildings of the Hotel Pearl Continental, white in the blazing sunlight, were across the street.

He tried to imagine Marco Polo riding past. The European visitor had traveled through the city in the Thirteenth Century, on the way to China, and had written of the ancient town, *The people have a peculiar language, they worship idols, and have an evil disposition.*

Ahmoud thought, *I'll show you Christian scum who to call evil.* The first time he had heard of the lost American bomb reportedly nuclear discovered by the Tajik, Sary Tash, he had known it was his destiny to recover the device and destroy an American city. In his mind's eye, he could see the first flare and explosion of the nuclear bomb the dust, the flames, the skeletons of buildings. He could hear the screams of anguish, wailing sirens of ambulances, fire trucks, police cars, the silent moans of staggering living and huddled dead. In his greatest flights of imagination, Yassar could see himself standing over the ruins: a Muslim warrior king, a giant astride the devastation of the broken Infidel city, a hero to all Muslims across the globe. A man.

Even when he discovered the weapon was only biological, he still pictured a black roiling cloud spreading over a city, destroying it, causing panic, looting, death.

He noted his cracked window and wondered why the owner couldn't keep it repaired and clean; returned his attention to more practical matters, opened his journal and wrote his needs:

1-Find the American bomb

Ahmoud looked at the finance issue: al Qaida was a potential source but its leaders would look at a young man like Ahmoud and shove him aside they would want all the glory. They would hinder Ahmoud's vision of himself the Islamic Warrior King.

He remembered his richest friend, a former student of Cairo U: Rama Razi Muhammad nicknamed Razzle Dazzle Rama because he was light on his feet despite being over four hundred pounds. He was a Palestinian. With stolen American foreign aid funds, his family had started an opium cartel that stretched from Thailand and Laos to Afghanistan and Georgia. Ahmoud opened his laptop computer, accessed his Google account. He emailed Rama, left a telephone number.

He regarded the next issue: transport. He thought of his college acquaintance, Ax al Femals. He usually ignored him, because Ax was a homosexual, but his father owned a small shipping company that boated freight down the Nile from Cairo to Alexandria.

Ahmoud was interrupted by the ring of his cell phone he was delighted to discover Rama Razi was already calling.

"Saddam Gandhi," Rama said. "How you doin'?"

After exchanging pleasantries, Ahmoud asked, "I have a proposal I'd like to discuss with you. Can we meet?"

With a dubious tone, Rama retorted, "I've so many operations in my tent, I can't take on new ventures."

"Not business," Ahmoud protested. "I'm serving the Army of Allah. And by the way, I go by Yassar Ahmoud now."

"Praise Allah for your efforts on behalf of Islam, er Yassar," Rama responded. "I have great respect for you who struggle against the foes of
Islam. If only I could contribute more."

"Hey, cut the crap, Razzle," Ahmoud laughed. "This is me, Saddam," he used his old Cairo University name. "I've watched you crawl around too many Marrakech hookah houses to hear you pontificate about anything."

Delighted, Rama laughed heartily. "Okay, okay, Saddam I mean
Yassar. Allah preserve you."

"I think I can strike a tremendous blow for Muslims throughout the world. I want to meet in person."

Rama Razi responded, "I can send my jet for green mangoes in
Karachi and drop them off in Islamabad. My Pakistani-based cousin loves green mangoes. The plane'll pick you up and bring you to Baluchistan. It's a two-hour flight. Let me know when you're ready."

"Excellent!" Ahmoud's excitement grew. "I'll call you as soon as I have the I'll call you."

"Anytime," Rama said. "I'm always in my tent."

Ahmoud hung up, pictured abandoned, rubble-strewn, bloodied American streets.

Chapter 11

A week after Jack Flashhardt's decision to transfer from the Marines to the United Nations, his CO, Captain Homer Norton, sent a young private to fetch him. When he walked into the captain's office, the man smiled, lifted a set of orders and travel vouchers. "I gotta hand it ta you, kid. Headquarters Marine Corps sent your orders. If I'd known you were so goddam well-connected, I'd been friendlier, bigod. No hard feelin's?"

He took the pile of thick papers, sniffed when the man's tobaccosmelling breath reached him, was dismayed when he saw that he was ordered to report to the United Nations in Islamabad.

"You're still a Marine, bigod, and you'll draw pay and a housing allowance at MAACPAC, Islamabad, but now, you're also TAD that's Temporary Attached Duty ta the United Nations. Which means you'll take orders from some goddam UN poge." The captain looked up at him with a grim face. "One thing you're on your own. No Marine Corps to back you up." Norton's expression softened. "Better keep your powder dry,
Lieutenant Flashhardt."

Jack stared at the captain. *Negative, Jerk-face, that's why I'm transferring. So I won't have to keep my powder dry. But why'd the UN send me to Islamabad the worst duty imaginable? Am I still being manipulated by the Army guy, Colonel Farley?*

The next morning, he caught a military transport to Tokyo, traveled on another well-worn, shuddering Air India 767 to Islamabad, took a shuttle to the Marriott, arrived at six P.M. The modern lobby made him feel like he was back in the States instead of halfway around the world; the feeling was reinforced by the Western-dressed men and women around the hotel. Even the odors of the hotel were familiar; he sensed the friendly smells of home, realized how much he missed America. A quick hamburger in the café brought him back to reality—no fake grill marks but it didn't remotely taste American. Back in his room, he fiddled with an uncooperative television, gave up and opened his copy of KIM, by Rudyard Kipling. He read two pages of the Nineteenth Century-paced novel before falling asleep.

The next morning, Jack entered the United Nations at nine A.M., wearing denim jeans, loafers, a tan polo shirt. The building was a twostorey, nondescript, powder blue edifice on Ataturk Street. In the busy lobby, filled with visa applicants, he was directed to a spacious, well-lit office, decorated with multiple plants in the corners, Afghan rugs on the tile floor. There was a hint of curry in the air, but no food in sight. A young man wearing an Australian naval officer's uniform came out from behind his desk, introduced himself as Gil Acton, Lieutenant, RAN.

Gil was his age and size, had short, short red hair, an open and square face with red-toned skin, an infectious grin. His pug nose was sunburned. *Wonder what it's like working for a surfer dude?*

After introductions, Gil said, "Heard you were joining us. Sit down, mate. Make yourself comfortable." Gil took a blue UN baseball cap out of a drawer, tossed it. "Here, you'll need this."

"What'm I goin' to be doing, pard?" Held his breath, sat down on a padded leather chair.

Gil laughed, "Someone has to be a liaison we're two naval officers a long way from the sea, but no worries, mate. You and I are stuck. It's not too bad. I even get into the bush on occasion. Not as fun as chasin' the odd Malay pirate, but there it is."

"Into the bush doing what?"

Gil made a face. "Actually, I hate to do this, but low man gets the backside of jobs, mate." He waved a paper. "This would have been me, but now you're the lucky bloke to go. Our office is sending an observer to check out some atrocity reports in the Hindu Kush Mountains, near the

Chinese border. Some Mormon missionary bird has reported to us by radio.

Any idea where the Hindu Kush is?"

"Are you kidding? Some of the best climbing in the world, that's all. A climber's paradise. The range extends from the northern part of Pakistan down into the southwest, along the Afghan border. I've made a first ascent in the range." Jack stopped, stared at Gil. "How'm I supposed to get there? Area's dangerous, dude." He thought of the CH-47: a ball of flames, pilots, crew dead.

Startled by his knowledge, Gil stared at the American. "Good on you, mate. You know way more than I care to but you won't climb on this trip.
We'll fly you. You'll be above the famed Silk Road to China. The land of KIM."

"I'm reading the book."

"Another good read is THE GREAT GAME," Gil suggested. "By
Hopkins. About the Russian-English rivalry over India in the Nineteenth Century. Anyway, there's a U.S. Special Forces outpost in Hunza and you'll operate out of it."

"What'll I do once I get there? And what's a missionary bird?"

"Oh, you know, a Sheila a woman. Name of Amy Andersen. Antiwar, do-gooder type. Human shield that sort of rot. Once you get there, you'll interview the tribes. Check out her complaints. Talk to her. Give it a go you'll figure it out, mate."

"Sounds easy," he agreed. "Er, you said atrocities?"

A tall, slender woman wearing a simple pants suit and high heels walked into Gil's office, smiled a dazzling greeting. She had huge blue eyes, fair skin, appeared to be a young forty-five.

"Miss Elle, this is our new mate, Jack Flashhardt."

She briskly approached, shook hands. She had a strong grip for a lean woman. "Hello. You're an American? Welcome to Islamabad." Her accent sounded Scandinavian, he detected the faint odor of strawberries.

"Thank you. It's good to be aboard I mean here."

"Another naval officer."

"Yes, Ma'am. I'm a Marine." He felt pride to announce that he was in the Corps.

Gil interjected, "So, I've assigned him to the Amy Anderson problem in the Hindu Kush, Miss Elle."

Miss Elle regarded him for a moment. "I suppose your only knowledge of the local conditions has been fed to you by the press and your military superiors." She brushed her shoulder-length blonde hair back.

"Actually, he's climbed in the area," Gil added.

Miss Elle looked at him. "That's impressive, but remember, the United Nations is here to help, not make war or break things. It's our hope to resolve the issues that have split this country, India, and Afghanistan. I'm personally trying to achieve agreement on the Durand boundaries that expired in 1993." She smiled, shook his hand again. This time, she held it a fraction longer than necessary, pointedly looked him over, gazed directly into his eyes. He felt a flush of heat, totally forgot about questions of any kind. She walked out of the office.

He glanced at Gil who was trying, unsuccessfully, to keep a straight face. "She's quite a broad, eh, mate? I mean fer an old one. Married, but I think she's taken with you. By the way—where you staying?"

"The Marriott Hotel." He thought, *I'd like to see Miss Elle between the sheets at the hotel.*

Gil threw his hands in the air. "Too expensive by half. Go to accounting. Get an allotment for some digs, you can stay in my guest bedroom. Plenty of room. My girl'll be delighted."

"I hate to impose."

Gil smiled, "Tonight we have a guest just popped in from Hong Kong. Name of Mara Bhutto. And well-connected politically, according to my gal."

"She good-looking, pard?"

"I hear the bird's gorgeous. Supposedly got a skin color like a bloody gold statue. Yeah, this's perfect. You'll make it a foursome. I have to work 'til 1800 hours, but you can go over now. I'll call my girl, give her a headsup." Gil wrote directions to his villa. "I'll scare up a ride for you."

After reporting to personnel, he went back to Gil, who told him a driver was waiting at the front gate.

When he turned to leave, Gil asked, "By the way, how do you know you made a first climb of a Hindu Kush peak?"

"I emailed a friend in the States. Looked up all the first ascents in a mountaineering record book. None in that grid." He smiled. But his smile washed away when he thought of his pursuer, Mo Poo, and the giant's threats. *Hope I don't run into that long drink of water.*

Back at the hotel, he went to the bar, saw a soldier and a Marine at a marble-topped table. Was shocked when he recognized Bulldog Mahoney, his oversized drill instructor from OCS, sitting with Chopstick Mick Nakamura, his short buddy from college. Approached the two—they were singing a song to the tune of the Yellow Rose of Texas:

"There's   a   yellow
whore in Karachi, That
I am going to see.
No other GI screws her,
No other, only me."

"Mick," he called. The two shook hands, laughed, delighted to see each other. Mick bared his canines in a big smile, his eyes disappeared.

Jack spoke to the huge sergeant, "Bulldog Mahoney. What a surprise." *Meanest prick in the Marine Corps. Half Irish, half Choctaw Indian, half starving crocodile.*

Mahoney smiled around a huge, unlit cigar he was chewing on, greeted him with a heavy Southern drawl. It was the first time he had ever seen the big, six-foot-five, raw-boned man exhibit a pleasant expression. He remembered describing the beak-nosed, black-haired OCS drill instructor to friends: "He's meaner than a Yellowstone Park mama grizzly bear chasin' tourists."

"Jack, I was glad you got back to Gilgit," Mick said. "That was some day, Pilgrim. I lost one of the two men that crashed in the highlands, but we kicked some ass. You wiped out a whole hedgeline. Took the pressure off us. What shootin'! You and us got nine Ks. Too bad about the chopper crew, though."

Jack visualized the blown-up chopper falling to the valley floor. Was amazed to hear he had killed men without knowing he had done so. Now, he had to put more deceased men in his mental death review file these deaders faceless.

Mick settled his short, muscular body back in his chair. Noting that he was about a foot shorter than the famous actor, Jack wondered why Mick sometimes slipped into a John Wayne accent.

"Jack, I explained in my Sit Rep that you disappeared in a huge updraft headed for Paris or London. I sure was glad when I heard you hiked out. I wanna know all about it." Mick shook his head. "Colonel Farley gave me all kinds of shit, Pilgrim. Almost threw the situation report in my face. Good thing we captured the whole op on video. But he's not too happy with you, and I can't figger why. It was obvious you were caught in a weird storm cell."
"Screw him," Jack scoffed. Threw the blue UN cap on the table. "I'm a
UN military attaché now."

"No shit." Mick laughed. "You tryin' to make peace? Or are you tryin' to get a piece?" He laughed at his pun. "Anyway, the papers you gave the colonel? They were al Qaida documents. Something about attacking a West Coast city with the lost biobomb."

"Really!" he exclaimed. "Did they say what city?"

Mick prodded his drink on the table, looked up, his eyes disappearing as he nervously smiled. "No."

"Dude I found another email in that mountain cave. In English. It asked when the baseball season was opening in San Francisco. I wonder if that's the West Coast city."

"Whoa, that's too close to home," Mick exclaimed. "My family's just down the 101 freeway in Gilroy, remember? Outside of San Jose."

Jack thought about his aunt in Menlo Park, also too close to San Francisco. "On another subject, I'm going on a little jaunt into the bush.
Just south of China."

Mick squinted at the waiter when he put down a fresh drink in front of him, peered at Jack. He'd had more than a couple of beers. "Gil Acton sendin' the pretty boy to the bush?"

"You know him, huh? Just a fact-finding expedition for the UN. But maybe you could sell it to the Army for recon purposes. Could you get attached to my little expedition? I could use some cover. I'm going to the Hunza Valley to check out some atrocity charges the green beanies committed."

Bulldog finished his beer, sounded pleasant but looked mean as he said, "Don't see why not, Lieutenant, I work for Colonel Farley. Not much doin' right now. Let me drop a whisper in the first sergeant's ear and get it passed on to the colonel."

"Hey, that'd be great, Bulldog," Mick smiled at his enlisted friend. "Who knows what could happen? Maybe we'll get a chance to kick some terrorist ass." He laughed, cautioned, "But don't mention Jack's name.
That'd be the kiss of death."

"Bulldog," Jack asked. "What're you doing in rug country?"

"It was like this, Lieutenant. Youngie my assistant Platoon sergeant at OCS and I got transferred to Camp Lejeune after your class graduated. We got drunk the first night there, remodeled the side of the NCO club with a Humvee, tryin' to take a shortcut to the bar. Next thing, I'm in Okinawa for a year, now here."

Jack fell silent, his emotions mixed. He had not hated Mahoney, but had despised the drill instructor during OCS. The man had been humorless and petty during the entire course of training. He'd singled Jack out, tried to run him out of the school. His stated reason was that Flashhardt was too pretty to be a Marine. The guy had been so mean-looking and sounding, he had given Jack nightmares ever since. It was unsettling to be seated next to him.

For a second, Jack wanted to brag about the men he had shot in

Shangri-la. Instead, he asked, "So how's duty? D'you enjoy it?"

Mahoney smiled, "Let's see, Lieutenant. The streets of Islamabad or the swamps of North Carolina. Or maybe we should compare the women. American divorcees in North Carolina: overweight, hostile, chain-smoking, cat-owning, kicked around, peroxide blondes. Or young, happy Pakistani babes," Bulldog laughed. "Hmmm that's a tough one. An' help's so cheap, I can afford a maid an' cook."

Jack asked, "So where're you from, pard?" He guessed a mental hospital for incestuous abandoned orphans in the swamps of Mississippi.

"Kentucky, sir. Boonsboro. But my family moved around a lot. I was a Marine brat. My daddy was a sergeant major in the Corps. And despite my loss of rank back at Lejeune, I'm Marine Corps green all the way. The Crotch has been good to me."

"My dad was in the Corps," Jack observed. "His dad, too."

Mick asked, "That why you're 0302 infantry?"

"Guess so." I remember I would've had to stay in another year to become a pilot. It was bad enough I was a mountaineer. I had to take parachute, dive, survival and escape training. I already knew how to fly— we had a Cessna 172 and an old Bell OH58 helicopter on our ranch.

Anyway, I'm hoping for a legal MOS 4402."

"Montana, right?" Mahoney asked.

"Yeah. I'm bound back to law school soon as possible." *Right, that's starting to sound like a delusional dream.*

Jack, Mick, Bulldog Mahoney drank a round of Heineken beers. Then, Mick and the sergeant left, singing another verse to their version of The Yellow Rose:

> *"She cried so when I stiffed her,*
> *It like to break my heart,*
> *But if I ever pay her,*
> *We never more will part."*

He went to his room, packed, checked out, caught a cab outside the hotel. Wondered if it was wise to invite Mick. However, in any trouble, Mick'd kick ass and then some.

Chapter 12

Stepping out of a taxi in front of Gil's villa, Jack considered the one story building. It had a plain block gray wall with a steel entry door, but no windows fronting on the street. A miniature fortress pounded by a brisk wind blowing bits of trash. Walked through the entry, he found an attractive patio filled with lush apricot trees, colorful hibiscus bushes, mounds of impatiens flowers.

He knocked on the front door, an attractive girl answered. She looked eighteen, had long black hair, very dark skin. Startled at the sight of the American, the tiny girl about five feet tall appeared frightened.

"Hello," he said. "Did Gil reach you?"

"No," the girl responded. "I've been out."

"I'm sorry. This's inconvenient. Gil invited me to stay here tonight.
I'm Jack Flashhardt."

She relaxed and her brilliant smile flashed against dark skin. "Please come in, you're very welcome."

Shook hands with the girl, who introduced herself as Fazila. She invited him into a living room with low profile bamboo furniture, a huge purple Afghan tribal rug on the hardwood floor it looked like a Navajo rug from Arizona.

"I am so pleased to meet you, Mister Flasher. Welcome to Pakistan." She had a slight accent, spoke English in a formal manner. "I glad you could join us for dinner. You are so handsome! Are you married?"

Jack thought of lost Ashley, "Nope."

"Your piercing blue eyes, those long eyelashes you probably scare the girls off," Fazila said. "You must meet my best friend, Mara Bhutto.

She's staying a few days."

Made uncomfortable by her compliments, Jack changed the subject.
"You have a lovely home. What time're we eating?"

She glanced at her watch. "It's five now, so plan on cocktails at six." Smiled up at him. "That'll give you time to freshen up." She took his elbow with a tiny hand, led him down a white-tiled hallway lined with potted queen palms to his bedroom.

An hour later, he found Gil and Fazila sitting in the living room. Jack looked around the villa: place was clean, cut roses in brass vases, plants in ceramic pots. The furniture was bleached white wood. On the walls, charcoal sketches with an Oriental flavor.

"How d'ya like my digs?" Gil asked, his red face beaming.

"It's great, pard." He thought of his barren BOQ room in Okinawa. *This guy has a life. But, hey no more Geisha land for me.*

Another woman, dressed in a blue silk blouse, tight white pants, walked into the room. The three rose. Fazila hugged the taller girl. "Mara, did you have a good nap after your flight? I want you to meet Jack Flasher.
He's an American."

"Flashhardt," Gil corrected.

Jack held up three fingers. "With two h's."

The shorter girl stepped back, he got a good look. The friend was spectacularly beautiful: a tall Eurasian woman with long shiny black hair, large green eyes, golden skin. Self-assured, a firm handshake, broad shoulders. *Whoo-ee,* he thought. *Is this girl for real? Gorgeous!*

An old man, bald-headed with a grizzled beard, entered dressed in a white jacket and black pants, followed the four into the dining room.

Jack held Mara's chair. She smiled, he noted her lush lips.

"It's Aussie wine. A Windy Ridge chardonnay," Gil said after the old man filled their glasses from a decanter.

Jack asked, "Cool. Do the grapes grow upside down in Australia?" *What a lame-ass remark.*

"No," Gil let him down easy. "But since it's the other side of the equator—you stand on your head when you drink."

No knives, forks. He looked at the food in round ceramic platters, wondered how he should eat it.

"Like this," Mara instructed. She held his hand, showed him how to use wedges of the flat pita bread like scoops. Felt a shock when she touched him. Her grip was firm; he noticed that she had perfectly shaped red fingernails. After a few attempts, he was able to feed himself, but kept the skill to himself.

They tried the garbanzo bean paste, mixed with what Mara identified as dundicut peppers, the traditional hot pepper of Pakistan, and mint leaves wrapped in the thin chapatti bread. The appetizers were delicious. Hummus paste was light, flavorful, mint was fragrant and tasty. Tiny red peppers were fiery hot.

"Mara, what kind of work d'you do?"

She sat back, silent. *I blurted something wrong. Gorgeous babe maybe she's a hooker or a stripper.*

Fazila said, "Mara's father was Zulfiqar Bhutto."

"Holy shit," Gil exclaimed. "I didn't know that."

"Who?"

"He was Prime Minister of Pakistan. An avowed Communist and major ally of China," Gil explained. *Scratch the hooker.*

Mara, with a look of annoyance on her face added, "I teach in the university here in Islamabad." With a challenging look, she gazed into his eyes and added, "And I do cultural consultation at the Chinese Embassy."

After dinner, the four decided to take a walk in a park that bordered Rawal Lake, across the Peshawar highway. A taxi took them; when they got out of the cab, the two couples separated, strolled along the tree-lined water.

Mara asked, "Are you used to the heat yet?"

"Are you kidding?" he laughed. "It's ferocious. I'm from Montana, where it gets up to 60 degrees on the only day of summer. I'll never get used to this heat." He enjoyed the moon's illumination of the lake. It made a path across water, rippled from a breeze.

"Yes, you will, it takes Westerners about a month."

"It's funny. I don't think of you as an Easterner." They walked in silence for a while. "So what's the deal on your father?"

Mara frowned, answered, "It gives me notoriety and a small income from my father's estate." She gave him a hostile glance. "The government hung him for treason. They were currying favor with America. He was hated by the American government, even though he went to college at UC Berkeley." *Commie U. No wonder they hated him.*

"I was young when it happened, but my mother and my uncle took me to the hanging. I remember images." Mara gazed at him, added, "My mother was British. She died of Break-bone Fever two years later. Dengue
Fever. You get it from mosquitoes. We have a lot of mosquitoes since
America talked the UN into banning DDT."

"I'm sorry.*" Another dirty look. Can't win for losing with this chick. Don't count on gettin' laid tonight.*

"My little half-sister misses not having a mother."

Looked at the beautiful girl. "How old's your sister?"

"Twenty. She's in the convent. We're Catholics." *Twenty doesn't sound little. She a babe like you? Maybe not as angry as you?*

He said, "My folks were divorced when I was one. I never knew my mom." *Got bored with ranch life, shed my dad like a suit off the rack at Sears. Me, too.*

"Too bad," Mara responded.

Gil and Fazila joined the couple, the four caught a cab to Gil's villa.

He wondered: *Consulting for China mean being a spy?*

Chapter 13

Mara Bhutto tried to absorb a passage in Chairman Mao's Book of

Quotes: *Military action is a method used to obtain a political goal.* Her Communist cadre had criticized her for a lack of fervor. Her reading efforts were not bearing fruit.

"Blah, blah, blah!" Mara yelled. She threw the book against the cracked plaster wall. Chairman Mao had probably never had to conduct a one-on-one assassination.

She glanced at her watch ten A.M. Mara put on a bag-like gray burqa that immediately overheated her but covered her body, left the grubby apartment that had been rented for her next assassination. She was late for her appointment with her control, the English priest.

A half hour later, after enduring the driver's constant horn-toots at other drivers, curses shouted at pedestrians, droned prayers to Allah, she thankfully climbed out of the taxi that had carried her through Islamabad traffic, entered Fatima Church.

In the cramped confession booth, she reluctantly muttered the proper passwords, received the correct response from the priest. He added, "You're late. Don't be so again."

Continued in a monotone voice, "An American officer, a major, is assigned to the new American headquarters. He frequents the bar in the Holiday Inn every afternoon. He has a passion for sky diving, and your cadre has been advised that you are a trained parachutist."

"An American!" Mara exclaimed. "Why an American? Is he searching for your precious bomb?"

"Yes," the priest responded. "He leads the U.S. Air Force search for the lost bomb. I want you to befriend him, kill him."
"Why?" Mara demanded.

"He's a Pakistani-American, name of Sadik Bahli. He is secretly al
Qaida. Hopefully, his death will throw both factions into confusion, giving China's PRC more time to secure the bomb." He handed a photo through the opening. "Meet the man and let nature take its course."

She thrust the photo in her purse without a look at it. What the hell was natural about killing? Especially a fellow al Qaida? One thing was sure this proved the Chinese didn't know she was secretly al Qaida. Or did it? Were they testing her?

At her apartment, she pulled out the photo, looked at the face of a very handsome, very dark man that appeared to be in his mid-thirties. He had a square jaw, lovely brown eyes, a perfect Roman nose. She wondered briefly whether the man was married with children. Would loyalty to his family protect him from her pointless mission? Or would he make a pass at her?

Late that afternoon, after deciding there was no point in subtlety, she selected a bright red sleeveless miniskirt, cut low to her breasts. She put it on, placed a long-haired wig on her head, applied garish lipstick, trashy perfume. Large Vaurnet sunglasses completed her disguise. She checked the time, covered herself with the gray burqa, caught a cab to the Holiday Inn.

In the back of the cab, she idly wondered whether she would ever live in a society where she did not have to conceal herself with a burqa. She glanced at the floor it was filthy, littered with empty cans, gum wrappers, cigarette butts.

Mara removed the burqa in the Holiday Inn's lobby bathroom, impatiently waited in the bar until the targeted officer walked in at six P.M. She took the initiative, stood next to him at the crowded bar, complained to the bartender that she had been given the wrong drink. The American heard a woman's voice behind him, glanced at her, turned back to his discussion with a Pakistani Air Force officer.

Mara decided to press harder. She grasped his arm. "Hello, I'm practicing my English so I can get a job with the Americans."

"I'm Sadik Bahli," he responded. "I'm an American. I work here in Islamabad." He was slightly shorter than Mara.

"I'm Fatima Horez." She pronounced the last name like whores. "How long'll you be in Pakistan?"

The American regarded her, noted her wonderful golden skin, her gorgeous breasts. "Look, I'm married." He pulled out his wallet, showed her pictures of his family.

"I'm also married," Mara improvised. "But I want to meet an American to practice my language skills so I can work for the American government. Do you enjoy Pakistan?"

"It's an opportunity to fight world terrorism." His voice was smooth.

"Are you used to the weather yet? It's so hot here. For you foreigners and for we natives as well."

"I'm from Yuma, Arizona. It's just as hot there."

The American wasn't giving her much. Mara took a deep breath. "The only relief I get is when my husband and I go skydiving. The air's much cooler at higher elevations."

Bahli glanced at her outfit. "You're wearing Western clothes but they're too loud for a job interview. And your English is excellent already.
You an experienced skydiver?"

Mara flushed, quickly misspoke her English, "Yes, very. I guess you right about clothes. My husband would anger if he knew I was dressed like this. But I really need job. Skydiving are so expensive—even when get a free ride with friends."

Major Bahli looked in Mara's face. The girl had a guileless expression and was truly beautiful. "I'm going out on Saturday. My partner cancelled but I want to try a new parasail I just got. You an' your husband are welcome to join me, Fatima."

Mara exclaimed, "We'd love that. Just tell where and when."

"Go to PIA at Islamabad Airport. They have a private Fixed Base

Operator. Ask for directions. I'll meet you two at 0700 hours."

Saturday morning, the American officer was waiting at PIA when Mara walked up, carrying a duffle bag of gear. She wore large sports sunglasses that hid her eyes.

"Where's your husband?" Major Bahli demanded. He glanced at her short hair but did not comment.

Mara dropped her bag to the ground. "He injured his ankle last night. But he didn't want me to miss an opportunity like this," she responded. "I hope you don't mind. I wouldn't skip this for the world." She held her breath, hoped the major would accept her story.

The major frowned, noticed the wedding band on her hand, "We both have had bad luck with jump partners." Suspicious, he opened her bag, appeared to relax when he recognized a well-used French parachute wing, the Prima 230ZP. Reassured by her possession of excellent equipment, he flashed a big smile. "Let's go do it." He led her to a white Stationair 206 that was spotless inside.

The American pilot, a big redheaded man with freckles all over, taxied out after greeting Mara with a smile and an up and down look.

Bahli explained, "We'll jump about five miles from Peshawar, dive from 12,000 feet to 2,000 feet above ground. 12,000 feet is the max service ceiling for this single engine airplane at Islamabad's altitude. After we land next to the highway, we can catch a bus."

At altitude, after he climbed through a smelly haze over the city, the Cessna pilot evaded several large white cumulous cloud cells, while the two skydivers checked their gear, prepared to jump. In fifteen minutes, they were over the jump point. To the northwest, more threatening clouds were building up.

Mara opened the cargo door, jumped first, closely followed by the major. The pilot waggled his airplane's wings, turned east towards Islamabad.

The jumpers drifted together, held hands for a moment, parted for several minutes, enjoyed the scenery below: tiny farms spread in every direction until the patches met the mountains on the Afghanistan border, the broad, brown Indus River on the east.

Directly below was the Grand Trunk Road. Named for the ancient eucalyptus trees planted along its way, it sliced east-west across the landscape. Mara wondered what had inspired Sher Shah Suri, the 16th century ruler of India, to build the sixteen hundred mile long highway that stretched from Afghanistan to India.

The wind whistled in her ears, the coolness enveloped her.

Sadik Bahli finally signed that it was time to deploy, Mara nodded. Her heart was pounding in her chest.

The major tucked his arms, descended to a lower altitude for clearance.

Mara reached inside a cargo pocket, pulled out a long-bladed knife. Major Bahli, two hundred feet below, jerked his chute cord, his chute popped open. He looked up, saw Mara swoop towards him with the knife in her outstretched hand. His eyes widened with shock. He yanked on a steer cord, tried to avoid her. Mara adjusted, expertly sailed past, slashed two of the major's chute cords with her razor-sharp blade.

Exultant, Mara yanked her cord the parachute opened with a bang. The major deployed his reserve chute as his speed increased. It tangled with his trailing main chute, his scream of rage and terror faded away as he hurtled to the plain below.

When Mara drifted to the ground, scant feet from the major's crumpled body, she collected her chute, approached. He was sprawled in the middle of a two-meter high ephedra bush. Red brown branches of the medicinal plant lay shattered by the impact; the acrid smell of the plant's crushed leaves mingled with the odors of blood and feces. Mara removed a black orchid from a pouch, placed it in the major's hand.

"Cirrhopetalumm meet Ephedra wallichili," she murmured as she walked away. She heard a motor, saw a vehicle approach. Her heart raced.

She wondered whether it was the police.

Chapter 14

Entering the UN offices, Gil Acton and Jack saw a young man in a dark green uniform sitting in the lobby. Jack recognized the Russian Army uniform, noticed three red stars on the man's shoulder boards. They continued through the noisy lobby, went to Gil's office.

"We need to get you your own office." Gil rubbed his red face. "Let's go see what's available." He glanced at his desk. "Here, what's this?" He picked up two messages, read them as he led the way to the hall. "It appears we have another new member of the team going north. Probably that chap in the lobby."

"The Russian guy?"

"Yes," Gil responded. "You recognize the uniform? Bit rare around here."

"I climbed in Russia, three years ago."

Gil glanced at the second note. "Anyplace you haven't climbed?"

"Australia."

"We don't have much for mountains, great beaches, though. Say, you're getting an assistant, according to this other note. An enlisted Marine."

"Really? I didn't ask for one." Jack wondered whether the Marines had assigned an assistant to keep tabs on him. Felt a hint of worry.

"Don't turn down a batman, he'll smooth the way. Cover your backside—could be handy up north." Gil turned into a small office with one window that opened on hinged cranks. No furniture, the room smelled dusty. "I'll get this tarted up for you. It'll be ready after lunch. Let' go see our Russkie."

The two returned to Gil's office. Gil called the security lobby guard, told him to send the Russian up with an escort.

Minutes later, the blond, blue-eyed Russian a green beret under his arm—strode briskly into Gil's office. He looked at Jack and Gil. "Bruno
Baeder Utecht, starshij lejtenant that is senior lieutenant, Russian Armed Forces. Lately of the 106th Parachute Guards Division."

Gil said hello. Bruno turned to Jack, shook hands. They stood eye to eye, both six feet tall. Bruno was handsome, if severe in his lean face and frame, had a hawk nose, square jaw, long eyelashes. He wore a cheapsmelling aftershave.

The three sat: Gil behind his desk, the other two in chairs opposite him.

"Your name sounds German," Jack commented.

The Russian smiled. "There's a story best told over vodka."

"I'm an Aussie," Gil said. "Royal Australian Navy. Jack, here's a Yank
Marine."

"A mix. Well, that's the nature of the United Nations forces, is it not?"
Bruno asked. "I've already met the boss. What a" Miss Elle walked into Gil's office, looked at the three. "Good, you've all met. Bruno will accompany Jack on the mission to the Northern Areas."

"Yes, ma'am," Gil responded with a smile. "I gather you already know
Mister Utecht."

"Of course," Elle smiled. "I interviewed him in my office, earlier. We're lucky to have two former adversaries working together. It's the true spirit of the UN." She smiled again, checked out Bruno's crotch, compared Jack's, left the office.

Laughing, Gil glanced at his watch, "It's lunchtime. I have a meeting with a Pak officer in the Embassy mess. You two go ahead and get acquainted. Be here at 0900. I'll arrange transport to the airport, and a flight to Hunza. Do you have weapons?" Bruno nodded assent.

Jack said, "Thought we were peacemakers."

"Carry a handgun, wear your blue helmet," Gil cautioned. "You never know."

"What about that assistant you mentioned?"

"He's reporting in at 1500," Gil said over his shoulder. "He'll be good to cover your back."

"Wanna do lunch?" Jack asked. "Or should my people meet your people?" *This Russian guy a spy or what?*

The Russian stared, baffled. "My people?"

"Just kidding. Let's go to the Marriott. Your treat." The Russian, taken aback, glared.

"Just kidding again." He patted Bruno's shoulder, led him out of the office. *Better cool it before the guy slugs me.*

Ten minutes later, the two sat at the long Marriott bar and ordered beers and club sandwiches. While they waited, he asked, "What's the skinny on your German name?"

Bruno smiled, accepted a beer from a slender waiter wearing a sharp tuxedo and a white turban. "My grandfather was a designer and test pilot for the German Air Force in World War II. The Soviets captured him after the war. Luckily he escaped."

"So, how does that put you in Russia?"

Bruno looked around. "You Americans convinced him to go to Russia as a spy. He allowed himself to be re-captured and worked on Soviet rocketry after the war."

"And your dad? Was he a racketeer, too?" Confused by the term, Bruno stared.

Jack smiled, "I meant rocketeer."

"Yes, well, I can tell you are a jokeateer." Bruno laughed at his retort. "Anyway, when father learned the truth, he turned his parents in to the authorities. My grandmother was sent to a gulag and grandfather was forced to continue his rocketry work."

"Turned in his own parents? That's cold."

"Not really," Bruno said. "My father was a Lebersborn."

"What's that?"

"Himmler's program to create the Master Race. Blue-eyed, blonde women from all over Europe were forcibly impregnated and their babies, when they were born, were taken and given to Nazi Party loyalists. My father was such a baby. So he wasn't turning in his real parents."

"What a story," Jack took a sandwich from the waiter, tasted it. Toast was cold and soggy, meat smelled good.

"It's an unusual tale. And I'm an expert in the telling of it. I did a research paper on the Lebersborn at University of Moscow."

"So where'd you grow up? Star City?"

Bruno tried his sandwich. "No, I went to boarding School in Min Vody. It's in the south."

"Hey, I've been there!" Jack exclaimed. "Pretty town." "You're a climber," Bruno guessed.

Jack sipped his beer. "Exactly. My dad and I took the train from Moscow. Quite a trip. Two thousand miles. A guide took us to Georgia and we climbed Mount Elbrus. Up the ski lift approach. Unfortunately, we got socked in just meters from the summit. So we didn't actually stand on the west peak. Couldn't find the marker it's flat on the summit."

Bruno waved at the waiter and pointed at their empty beer mugs. "I climbed the North Approach. Up the Marco Polo Trail and the German road. The one the German Army made in 1939."

"Oh, yeah. We considered the Northern approach but we heard terrorists from Chechnya hang out on the north side. I didn't know about Marco Polo."

"His route to search for China."

"China? I can't even find the steps out of the swimming pool when I play Marco Polo."

"What?" Bruno looked puzzled.

"Never mind." Looked at Bruno out of the corner of his eye. Guy seemed alright. Was a climber. But was he an undercover agent? And why were they going north together?

Chapter 15

In the UN offices, after lunch, a secretary directed Jack and Bruno to their new shared office: two gray metal desks, four cheap metal chairs, a single photo of United Nations Secretary-General Ban Ki-moon on the wall. The window was old, mullion-paned, its brass hinges and handle were covered with green tarnish; a fly buzzed in a spider web the maids had missed. The air now smelled of Lysol.

On one desk, he found a note and a letter from his dad. The note said his Marine assistant had been held up by a delayed flight. Stared at the man's name: William Howling Dog, Lance/corporal, USMC. His halfbrother. He was astonished, reflected on the history of Billy.

Six months after Jack's mother had left Bill, Jack, and the ranch, Bill had an affair with Little Willow, a Brule Sioux from the Indian reservation east of the Flying Eagle Ranch. The brief relationship had resulted in the arrival of a baby. Little Willow rejected Bill, never told him about Billy until the boy was twelve. Billy and Jack had gone to school together in Red Lodge, had been friends until, at age twelve Billy learned they were half brothers. Caught up in an anti-white movement, Billy was completely upheaved and confused when he discovered he was half-white. Viewing his older brother as a rich white kid even though Jack's six generations removed grandmother had been part Indian and part black slave, he had never been friendly again. When the Crow Nation won the lawsuit and repossessed the Flashhardt ranch, Billy had acted even more arrogant.

Jack crumbled the note. *Is the Red Lodge soap opera over?*

"Trouble?" Bruno asked. He sat behind the second desk writing on a piece of paper.

"No. Just my new assistant. Guy's delayed." He picked up the letter from his dad, opened it, skimmed it. Chief Talking Dog was continuing a tradition: every time a Flashhardt had gone to war, the tribe had sent a member as a protector. Talking Dog had gone to Vietnam to cover Jack's granddad, Running Badger had followed Jack's dad into the Marines in the '80s. Now it was Billy Howling Dog's turn. Jack had heard about the interfamily custom but had never given it much thought. He yawned. "I'm beat see you in the AM."

Next morning, wearing BDUs, boots and his blue cap, he took a taxi to the United Nations enclave, found Bruno dressed in tan cammies and a UN baseball cap, waiting outside next to a white Toyota SUV. The two climbed in and the Hindi driver, wearing a white turban, a long beard, drove them to the airport.

Looking at a mosque, Jack commented, "I was surprised to see a lot of mosques under construction in Russia."

Bruno snorted, "Yes, well, freedom of religion now that Communism is dead and gone to Lenin Heaven."

They continued to reflect on the street scene on the way to the airport. Bruno was intelligent and had a wry sense of humor.

Outside the terminal, Mick and Bulldog Mahoney sat on a bench, wearing desert tan BDUs, had large packs at their feet.

Jack asked over a departing jet's roar, "What's the deal?"

Flashing a big-toothed smile, Mick said, "First Sergeant decided I needed cover. Bulldog volunteered."

"Good to have you, Gunny." Jack returned big Bulldog's salute, introduced Bruno. His fears of being spied upon by the Marine Corps reawakened.

"I snagged a Marine MV-22 for our flight north," Mick proclaimed as they strolled through the hot airport, walked outside, around a half dozen commercial airliners.

The Osprey, a tiltrotar aircraft, sat by itself at the east end of the terminal area. Its twin Allison T406-AD-400 engines, at the opposite ends of stubby wings, sported huge, thirty-eight foot long, three-bladed propellers.

The team discovered the Osprey had a malfunctioning GPS; they had to wait until after lunchtime while it was repaired. A boring day ensued, the group commandeered the terminal's VIP lounge. Played hearts, crazy eights, poker for pennies. Bruno won at hearts, Jack at poker, Bulldog won the crazy eights round. Fitting, Jack thought. He glanced at the guns
Bulldog wore: an M-9 on a shoulder holster, a huge revolver on his hip.

"What you carryin', Gunny?"

Bulldog pulled his revolver. "A Ruger. Shoots a .454 Casull—a 260 grain bullet with around 1900 foot-pounds of muzzle energy. About twice a Dirty Harry revolver."

"Must have quite a kick."

The Gunny smiled. "Need a big hand," he said. "Five times the recoil of a Colt .45, but it'll blow a man near in half." He flashed an evil grin that Jack remembered from OCS.

The Osprey was ready at 1500 hours, it cleared the runway minutes later. Jack sat with the others on a row bench against the bulkhead. The airplane, with helmeted pilot and copilot but no crew chief, lifted off like a helicopter, rotated the nacelles until it flew like an airplane. He inhaled the odor—the Osprey was new.

Mick leaned forward. "They're only taking us to Gilgit. Range is about five hundred miles and there's no fuel up there today."

"Then what?" Jack asked. He had not seen Gil at the house.

"I called Gil last night. He'll have a vehicle waiting for us."

Jack went to the hatch, looked out at the Margalla Hills, just north of the city. Saw a huge mosque, with four minarets. Each looked about twentyfive stories high. Mick moved to his side. "That's the Faisal Mosque. Named after the old King of Saudi Arabia, since he paid for it. It's the biggest mosque in the world."

"Expensive religion. Whatever happened to—It's harder for a rich man to get to heaven than to pass through the eye of a needle?"

"Hey," Mick responded. "Whatever works."

At two hundred knots, the MV-22 swept past the mosque, still climbing. Below, he spotted a caravan of two-humped camels plodding along a dirt road. Landscape was carved up into tiny farms. Returned to the bench, tried to sleep. Before he dozed off, he spent moments wondering why Bulldog was on the mission, why the Marines had sent a very special aircraft to transport them, what they would find in the Northern Areas. At Gilgit airport, the team watched the screaming Osprey lift off, transform to an airplane, ascend and disappear in the southern skies.

Jack looked at the steep, snow-covered mountains that surrounded the town of Gilgit, zipped up his parka against the late afternoon wind blowing down from China. Tried to spot where he had been pushed over the Hindu Kush, into Shangri-la, but it was hard to distinguish peaks that looked different from a new location. Somewhere in the town, a Muslim muezzin wailed his call to prayers. The sound made the group realize they were in a remote foreign land.

With its horn honking, a comical-looking Toyota truck with an oversized bed and wood rails pulled up. Rails and cab were covered with decorations, medallions, attached by screws. An old man, wearing a brown cap, drab clothes, a gap-toothed grin, called out, "U-ni-ted Na-tions."

Bulldog Mahoney, Mick, Jack, and Bruno Utecht climbed in the back. Jack asked the driver to take them to Hunza Valley. The old man said it would be best to leave in the morning. Jack checked his watch. 1700 hours
—five o'clock. "Let's go find a hotel."

The Pakistani took them on a short drive through the center of town. The huddled collection of houses overlooked a rapidly-flowing river. The streets were filled with running children, shoppers, workers heading home. Bizarre buses, even more decorated than the UN truck, honked with abandon as they trundled through. A camel caravan trudged silently from a side street across their path. Impossible tangles of electric lines crossed the littered streets.

The truck stopped in front of the Serena Lodge, a wooden, Swisslooking hotel, its balconies trimmed with intricate woodwork. It had spectacular views of the Hindu Kush. Using a United Nations credit card Gil had given him for expenditures, he rented four rooms at a discount rate of one thousand rupees per room, or about fifty dollars each. His room had a bed, small antique table, two chairs, a television that didn't work, a rough wood plank floor covered by a worn Afghan rug. He dumped his pack next to the bed.

After washing his face, he went to the bar, sat on one of its five stools, next to Bruno, who signaled for another Red Pilsner beer. A pall of smoke hung over the room, noisy talk and laughter rang through the air—about twenty people were seated at tables. Unlike American taverns, there were no beer signs on the walls.

Bulldog and Mick sat across the room at a table with three U.S. Army Special Forces soldiers, and on the last side of the bar, a tall white woman, dressed in a tailored cammie outfit, sat with two senior Pakistani officers. One of the officers filled her glass from a vodka bottle on the table.

"Babe alert, six o'clock," Jack said.

Bruno turned, exclaimed, "Putin is great! To think I could find such beauty in this remote outpost." He walked to the table, spoke into the woman's ear without acknowledging the senior officers. She looked at Jack, turned back to her friends. Bruno returned, "She'll be here. I go to toilet.
Keep my seat."

"You got it, Bruno." He smiled and drank beer. The woman was a beautiful and exotic sight in the dingy bar.

The Americans on the side of the room broke into a rendition of an old Elvis song, Jailhouse Rock:

"Osama One said to Mullah four,
Get the boys ready for a holy war.
Let's rock,
Everybody let's rock.
Hamas Three said to
al Qaida Two, Let's go
kill a filthy Jew."

Outraged Pakistani turned, stared at the Americans, who burst into laughter, called for more drinks. Jack grinned, sensed Bulldog's hand in the provocative verses.

The redhead stood, walked to the bar, stood next to him, smiled. "What're you boyos doing in the Northern Areas? Looking for the bomb?"

Startled by her question, he stalled by drinking beer while collecting his thoughts. "I'm with the United Nations."

When she shifted her eyes to his hat, he realized the woman was drunk. Her skin was very white, covered with freckles, twin spots of red on her cheeks. "I'm Melinda O'Reilly." She held out her hand. "Time."

He glanced at his watch. "Six o'clock."

"No, I'm with Time. Time Magazine."

Jack wondered if he had totally lost his sense of humor or if it was just the wrong side of the world. "Sorry, ma'am."

"And it's not, ma'am. I'm barely older than you—well, not much older." Melinda had a gleam in her eye.

"Here is Bruno," the Russian said as he stepped up.

"A Russian and an American. Therein lays a story. Where're you two heading?"

"Hunza Valley," Jack responded.

Bruno said, "Your room."

Melinda did not catch Bruno's statement, or ignored it. Jack swallowed a laugh. She said, "Hunza? Can I ride along? I'd love to come. It's too dangerous to go alone on the KKH the Karakoram Highway the old Silk
Road from Islamabad to Kashgar, China. It's overrun with bandits."

Bruno laughed, put his arm around the beautiful woman's broad shoulders, stared at her large breasts. "Of course, my dear. Let's go to your room and discuss your coming." He glanced at the Pakistani officers. "Or would my room be more convenient?"

Melinda shrugged off Bruno's arm, her blue eyes flashed. "No free rides, Mister Russian. And be careful, or I'll send you back to Moscow with your balls in a basket."

Jack signaled the bartender, pointed at Melinda. "Sorry, I don't want to lose a reporter on my first mission for the UN. I've a hard time keeping track of the time, let alone worryin' about Bruno's " Melinda interjected, "But I think I can help you. I know a place to stay. Papa Pier has a plantation there. He's a friend of mine. Serves a mean bottle of wine well, he has his own winery."

"Thanks, but no thanks."

Melinda looked at Bruno, Jack. Shrugged her shoulders, returned to the officer's table.

"Jack, that woman she was a cliché but she was my destiny tonight," Bruno complained.

"Didn't mean to cut into your love life," he said. "What say we order some chow?"

The two shared a dinner of beef over noodles, with a side of overcooked curry cabbage and fried potatoes; he left Bruno, went to his room. After reading a chapter of Rudyard Kipling's KIM—the hero was wandering the Grand Trunk Road with a Tibetan mystic—a knock on the door. He opened it, saw Melinda leaning against the wall, with a bottle of scotch in one hand, two glasses in the other.

"Buy a girl a drink?"

He stepped back, held the door open. Melinda walked in, put down the bottle and glassware, sat at the small table. She poured a small amount of scotch from the near-empty bottle into each glass, handed one to Jack. He hesitated, accepted. Melinda downed her drink. "I'm glad you're receiving."

"It's late," he responded.

"Truer words were never spoken." She rose, turned off the tiny lamp on the table, walked to the bed, pulled a bulky sweater over her head. Under it, she wore a silk camisole. Added that to the sweater on the carpet. Her upper body was slender, beautiful in the moonlight shining on the bed area. Looked at him over a broad shoulder, pulled off her boots, pants, climbed under the muslin sheets and down comforter.

"You could've warmed it up," she said as she snuggled.

"I didn't know I was goin' speed-dating in Gilgit." He gulped the scotch. Foul taste, but what a woman. Crossed to the bed, undressed, joined her in the warmed-up bed.

Long minutes later, Melinda sat on top of him. With a throaty voice, she murmured, "I'm coming. Am I coming?"

He put his head back on the pillow, smiled. "You're in, darlin'. I'd carry you to Hunza through a herd of wild yaks." Melinda groaned in satisfaction, then giggled. "You're in too, my dear. Ohh, are you in."

Chapter 16

"Bless me Father, for I have sinned," Mara Bhutto uttered the words to her unseen control. There was no response. Glanced at her watch, 1000 hours—she was fifteen minutes late. She tapped her foot on the church's stone floor. Five more minutes. Seconds later, she heard a rustle beyond the wall of her booth. She repeated, "Bless me Father, for I have sinned."

Control responded, "I will show you the way to purity." He added,
"About time you showed up."

Mara thought about expressing regret, but decided, *Damn it, no. I hate the bastard!* Remained silent.

"You're to travel to Kabul. Seek out a traitor to our cause, Zhang Poon t'ang. This directive comes from the Central Military Commission of the
CPC Committee."

"Zhang? A Chinese traitor? The CPC? Why has the Communist Party of China involved itself in local affairs in Afghanistan?"

"That's not for you to ask!" The priest's voice rose above a whisper. "Zhang Poon t'ang's a grand niece of the general secretary. Because he's so concerned about staying off the skyline, his minions are gravely worried about Zhang's fate. Even if she's a half-breed."

"What'd she do?" Mara stared at the booth's blank wall. *Does he realize that I was Zhang's bunkmate at the Hainan Island school?*

"She works for the Second Department. She secured the American bomb for the People's Liberation Army Institute for International Strategic
Studies."

"I didn't even know she was in Pakistan. She's a famous waist-drum dancer in Peking. Why's she here?"

"She was ostensibly visiting as a cultural attaché to the Chinese embassy. But her real purpose as a clandestine special agent was to secure the bomb for the Second Department's Analysis Bureau."

"Good, isn't that what we're all working for?"

"Of course, but after Zhang traded a dozen Stinger missiles to the Tajik who found the bomb, she turned around and sold its location to the

American CIA for cash and a passport."

"I don't believe it!" Mara exclaimed.

"Then she cheated the Americans, somehow."

"She's from one of the First Families. Her path's golden. Why is she…" Even if she is half Negro. A rare and normally disdained background in China.

"The point is, you're to find Zhang Poon t'ang. Take no action. Just report back. She's rumored to be hiding in Kabul."

Mara tried to calm herself. "How am I supposed to get there? It's at least two hundred fifty kilometers on the Trunk Road. And the Khyber Pass is said to be controlled by bandits."

"Stop complaining," Control ordered. "I've arranged travel with a relief mission transporting medical supplies to Kabul. You'll leave tomorrow with Pak Army guards to the border, and a U.S. Army escort from the border."

Ignoring the irony of a U.S. escort, she said, "The city has a population of at least a million. How do I find her?"

"Zhang's a dancer," Control suggested. "Search the underground club scene. That should be easy for you. Probably find her lap-dancing for some drugged-out mullah."

Chapter 17

Jack rose early, caught a taxi parked outside the Serena Lodge. Directed the driver to go to the Pakistani Army base on the north side of Gilgit. When the cab stopped at the gate guard's shack, he explained that he wanted to visit the Base Commander. The guard lowered his rifle, got on the landline, and after a few minutes, he gave directions to the taxi driver, waved them through the gate of the two-meter-high chain link fence. After telling the cab driver to wait, Jack followed a Pak Army private.

Major Lialot Soongoon, a short thin man with a perfectly trimmed British Army mustache, longer than normal hair for a military man, had a lean face with a big nose, piercing black eyes that looked angry. The major smiled, came around the desk to shake his hand. His office was in an orchestrated state of chaos: books stacked on chairs, side tables, a paper shredder with a regurgitated tangle of shredded documents; pictures on the walls of past commands; polo sports gear stacked in a corner smelling of old sweat. On the major's desk a brown china teapot, a jug of milk, sugar, two cups.

"Good morning, sir. I wanted to thank you again for getting me back to Islamabad when I came out of the mountains."

"Quite all right, Lieutenant, I'm always glad to help U.S. Marine tourists. But you're back in the Frontier. And you wear new head gear." The major glanced at the hat he carried.

"Yes, sir, I've temporarily transferred to the United Nations. Instead of killing the enemy, now I can bore 'em to death with bad jokes. Anyway, I'm on the way to Hunza Valley to talk to a American missionary. About some irregularities between U.S. forces and local Afghan and Pakistani tribes."

The major smiled, returned to his side of the desk, poured two cups of black tea. "I was so informed. Help yourself to cream and sugar."

After the two had sat down, Jack asked, "Any chance of flogging a lift to Hunza, Major?"

The Pakistani frowned, glanced at an update chart that showed the status of aircraft under his command. "You chose a bad time," he said. "I only have one gunship available today. An Apache. No air or ground transport capability. You'll have to drive the KKH unless you can wait a couple of days." He sipped tea, then added, "I could give you a radio and air escort today. Might come in handy in case of trouble." *Everybody talks about this KKH like it's Bandit Alley.*

"I see you play polo," Jack said. "Ever play the goat game?"

"You mean Buzkashi," the major responded. "It's an Afghan game. A team sport on horseback. The rider who's able to pitch a dead goat or calf across the goal line wins."

Trying not to sound sarcastic, Jack ventured, "Guess they never heard of just using inflated pigskin. Sounds exciting, enriching. 'Cept for the calf.
D'they have cheerleaders?"

Major Soongoon smiled as he rose. "I wouldn't know. It's a lower class sport. Not played by officers." He called aloud for his aide, an overweight sergeant, and ordered, "Arrange comm with the lieutenant and set up a slick for escort duty to Hunza Valley this morning. Charge it up as a training exercise."

The sergeant took him to the communications building, presented him with a small backpack that contained a multiband tactical radio, gave him a moniker and the escort's call sign. Arriving back at the Serena Lodge, he noticed that the transport truck, driven by the same gap-toothed man, Akbar, waited on the curb. He found the team finishing breakfast in the hotel bar. He glanced at Melinda—she avoided his look.

He grabbed a hunk of black bread, a piece of wonderful-smelling curried lamb off a platter. "Let's head out in ten minutes. Gunny, can you handle this radio? We have a gunship for an escort. Our call sign is Arrow. Slick is High Ridge. Freq is 25.9."

Bulldog Mahoney, with a look of newfound respect for him, accepted the radiopack, checked it out.

Ten minutes later, the truck sputtered to life, started down the street, belching a fog of diesel fumes.

Mick complimented him, "Good work getting us an escort."

"It was no sweat. I met the base commander on our last ill-fated trip to this vacation paradise." He glanced at Bulldog and suggested, "Why don't you call and inform the Paks we've left the hotel. My taxi driver told me it was twelve miles to the KKH. Slick'll pick us up about twenty miles north." A half hour later, the truck turned onto the two lane tarmac road that paralleled the tumbling Indus River's brown waters, coursing out of the north. The road narrowed as they moved north towards Hunza. Winding along mountainside cliffs, the road showed the obviously desperate efforts of road builders who had hacked it through the mountains in the 1970's and 1980's. Below, the Indus River raged through house-sized boulders that had crashed down from the heights. In the distance, to the right of the highway, Jack looked for and spotted the famous five-peaked mountain, Rakaposhi, at 25,551 feet high. He pointed the mountain out to the others, noticed that Mick did not look outside, was starting to fidget.

"Dude, what's the problem?" he asked.

Mick complained, "I'm… I'm afraid of heights."

"Whoa! Time out! Muscled-up GI Joe, jumps out of aircraft in a single bound, whacks Taliban with crushing blows—afraid of heights?"

"Just in vehicles. Cliffsides, no control—it's the worst!"

At noon, the truck ground up a long rise, slowed next to a grove of trees tucked into a tiny niche valley. Poplar trees leaned over the narrow road; truck crept around a corner, the driver slammed on the brakes. A log barred the narrow road. "Attack, sirs!" he cried. Gunfire accented his scream.

Jack rolled off the truck bed, crawled through roadside brush. Gunfire punched into the side of the truck, rang it like a cracked bell. Mick, Bulldog returned fire, Melinda yelled, "Get out!"

Heart pounding, Jack crawled through dense weeds, kicked a Coke can. *Damn, they're not only terrorists—they're litterbugs.* He flanked the ambushers. Peeked around a big poplar tree, spotted men behind a log, firing at the truck. Aimed his Beretta, shot the closest man in the back, guy flipped over the log, turned to Jack with horrified eyes. Second man screamed, threw up his arms when a bullet fired from behind the truck hit him. Third man spotted him, fired. Ducked behind the tree. Splinters of wood hit him in the neck. The gun stopped.

Bang of a pistol—probably Bruno's—fired. Peered around the tree, ignored a flare of pain, controlled his shaking hand, fired at the third man. Bullet ricocheted of the man's rifle butt. Guy threw his weapon down, ran. Automatic fire, the man tumbled head over heels. An agonizing scream from the road—a friend hit. The remaining ambushers shot at him, attacked.

Jack charged at the onrushing men, shooting and yelling. He fired a full clip without conscious aim. Men fell, men ran away in fear. He ran out of bullets, grabbed a dropped AK 74 and fired until it was empty. Jumped over a dead body, crashed into a running man wielding a long knife, grabbed his arm, wrested the knife away. Jumped for it, turned, slashed the man across the ribs. Guy screamed, bent over: Jack swung him into two rushing attackers. Leaped after him. The four fell into a tangled mass of bodies, fighting each other, punching wildly—someone bit into Jack's arm —he tore away, slashed in every direction with the knife. Smell of shit, sweat, coppery odor of blood.

Mick and Bulldog arrived, Bulldog's gun boomed, Mick's barked.

He saw the last ambusher wave a hand, signaling defeat. Stood over the ambusher, chest heaving—the man drew a pistol. Mick shot it out of his hand. The man's headscarf flew off: a young girl, maybe sixteen. Bulldog kicked her in the ribs, she squalled.

"Man, you laid waste!" Mick exclaimed.

Melinda called for help from the road.

"Are they Taliban, or just bandits?" Mick asked.

"Bulldog," Jack managed a level voice. "You search them. Mick, let's go help Melinda." His crazy actions, the bodies, smell of vomit, blood, shit, made him queasy—his legs shook. The two hurried out to the road. Melinda had dragged the driver out of the cab. Jack checked his watch. Amazed, noted only ten minutes had passed. Pulled splinters out of his skin, touched a burn under his arm from a hot barrel, checked out the teeth marks on his forearm and ear.

Driver was bleeding in the chest area. "I hurt," he said.

Suddenly, shots glanced off the truck hood. The team ducked behind the truck, saw a pickup truck—a white Toyota—parked in the middle of the road, about two hundred yards away.

"Bulldog," Jack yelled. "Call the chopper. We need help." Pickup remained stationary, someone exchanged fire with Mick. "I'd like to laze that sonofabitch!" Mick shouted. Jammed a magazine into his M-4, grinned, showed his hungry canine teeth.

"Laze?" Melinda asked.

"Paint it with a laser, so chopper can take it out," Jack answered. To Mick, "Don't worry, the dumbass is sittin' in the middle of the road. Slick'll knock him clear across the Indus."

After five long minutes of exchanged shots, they saw an AH-64D Longbow helicopter approach from the south. Pickup driver tried to turn in the narrow road, but the Longbow's millimeter wave fire control radar targeted the truck. A man in the pickup stood and fired a RPG at the chopper. The slick jerked in the air, fired two

AGM-114D Hellfire missiles, peeled away. The fire and forget rockets streaked toward the pickup, both overshot the vehicle.

"Damn! You might know the Paks would screw a fire mission up!" Mick yelled.

Bulldog shouted, his voice rising, "I got a reconning Warthog out of
Camp Rhino on the US TacNet. He'll be here in five minutes. Hang on."

An RPG screamed over the UN truck, impacted on a cliffside fifty meters away.

"Let's go get 'em," Mick shouted.

"Hold on," Jack said. "Let the Air Force get some." Look!" He pointed at a speck above a curve in the canyon. A minute later, its two General Electric TF34-GE-100 turbofan engines roaring, the Air Force A-10 raced along the road, fired its gatling gun. The 30mm shells tracked to the pickup, enveloped it. The snub-nosed Warthog fired a Maverick missile and destroyed the vehicle: blew it up in a fiery explosion. Bodies appeared out of the smoke, flew through the air. After the flames disappeared, smoke and dust hung over the road, the narrow valley. Mangled truck was upside down, halfway downslope to the river. Secondary explosion enveloped it. The desert camouflage-painted jet did a sixty-degree bank, waggled its wings and climbed out of the canyon.

"Go, Air Force!" Jack shouted. He felt a surge of affection for the unknown American aircrew that had saved them.

Bulldog stepped onto the road, spoke into the radio, said in a calm voice, "All clear, Lieutenant. Only vehicle in sight. Air Force dude, Redbird, is on station." He turned, went back to the woods.

"Great job, Bulldog!" Mick yelled.

Melinda said, "Akbar is dead."

"Let's load him in the back of the truck," Mick suggested. They looked at the fallen driver—he was drenched in a huge amount of blood, more had flowed across the hard-packed dirt. Mick, grimaced, threw an old tarp to Bruno, who carefully wrapped the body. The three lifted the bundled dead man, put him on the truck bed.

When they finished, Jack walked into the woods to check on Bulldog. Found one of the dead attackers: his jaw was slashed open, mouth to ear, both sides of his face. Looked up, saw Bulldog standing over the girl, pulling up his pants. Girl's pants were down to her ankles, she was on her back, sobbing. She struggled to sit up. Bulldog pulled his Ruger, shot the girl in the abdomen. She squealed, tumbled four feet, limbs flailing.

"What the hell'd you do that for?" The keening girl curled into a tight ball.

Bulldog grimaced. "What 'ud you do, Lieutenant? We can't PUC her way out here. Let her go?"

"Could've taken her to the authorities."

"Yeah, right," Bulldog scoffed again. "Us—bunch of white guys. She'd claim innocent, they'd let her go, she'd be back here with new pals next week. This's better. Crazy bitch won't take a potshot at you or me, next time we pass this way."

Silenced by the big man's reasoning, he noted Bulldog's huge .454 pistol was still drawn. Looked at the still body. "In the future, this won't happen, Gunny. These are human beings—just like us."

The two stared at each other. Pistol still in Bulldog's hand— he smiled. "You got it, Lieutenant. That's an affirm."

"What happened to that guy's face?"

"Gold teeth," Bulldog said. "Supplementasl combat pay." He grinned.

Shocked, Jack tried to speak with a level voice: "Same deal, Gunny. Leave the dead alone." Turned, walked back to the truck, wondered if Bulldog would shoot him in the back. When he made it to the road, he thought, *What else is waiting between the ambush and Hunza Valley?*

Chapter 18

The UN minion at the front of Mara's bus droned, "Kabul was chosen by Babur, founder of the Mughal empire of India, as the site for his capital. His grandson, Akbar, built the city in 1570 A.D., and the Russians and the Americans destroyed a lot of it in the last two wars. At 6,000 feet above sea level, Kabul's one of the highest cities in the world."

Mara tried to tune out the scrawny Brit's disjointed history and geography lesson as the old Mercedes bus rumbled through the outskirts of the dusty, dilapidated Afghan city. The American escort had turned off at the city limits, waving as they drove away.

The UN man continued to ramble, but Mara managed to doze off until the bus creaked to a stop in front of the Mustafa Hotel in the center of the city. She glanced at her watch. It was four PM. The trip from Islamabad had taken eight hours. She hurried off the bus, dressed in man's clothing she had purchased at a Jalalabad street bazaar during a rest stop: blousy gray cotton pants, her own Cairo U sweatshirt under a camouflage utility jacket, a scarf wrapped around her neck and jaw, an expensive Persian lamb karakul cap. She imagined a hot bath, a cold drink.

After she checked in, she took a shower in a filthy hallway bathroom, dressed and left her sparsely decorated room, went to the hotel café.

Two musicians strummed tamburs, long-necked banjos, a young boy played a tula—an Afghan flute. A haze of smoke hung over the long, lowceiled room.

The café host sat her at a table near the musicians. When he turned to leave, she grasped his wrist and asked, "Speak English?" "Of course," the man responded.

"I'm looking for someone. A foreigner. It would be worth a bit if someone could help me."

The host, a small man with a scraggly black beard and a thick turban, answered, "Foreigners hard to miss. Talk to boss." He nodded to a door in the rear.

Ten minutes later, Mara met the manager of the hotel, an Afghan who spoke fast-talking English with an American accent. Wais Faizi was a short but powerful-looking man with a jutting chin. He was a former selfproclaimed body-building champion and said he knew everyone in town.

"Tell me whaddya want, Wais can geddit."

"I'm looking for a Chinese newswoman." She put one hundred dollars American on the table.

Wais looked at Mara's golden coloring, peered into her green eyes.

"You're a broad. Whaddya up to?"

Mara flushed. "You know I can't travel alone in Afghanistan—even after the fall of the Taliban regime—as a female. That's the reason for the disguise. The woman's a friend. I was told I could find her here."

"Hey, I'm from the States. I'm like Hamid Karzai—the president—I don' give a shit about a broad's business. But how do I know you're a friend? I hear she's on the run from some Chinese government assholes." He scooped up the money.

"Tell her Mara wants to see her. Mara from school in Hainan Island.

I'll be in my room."

An hour later, Mara heard a soft knock on her door. She opened it and looked through the crack. It was Zhang.

The two regarded each other for seconds, then Mara stepped back and Zhang entered the room. A spectacularly beautiful, mixed-Chinese woman, she wore a man's peasant garb, a turban with its greasy ends drooped to her shoulders, rude sandals. Her oval face looked Chinese, her eyes were slanted but looked European, her skin was light brown.

"Why are you here?" Zhang asked. Suspicion thinned her voice, made her sound shrill. She removed her turban, brushed her long black hair back.

"I'm here to warn you. SD is on to you. I've been assigned to find you, then report." Her friend, twenty two—younger than Mara—looked tired, older.

"What'll you do?" Zhang asked, fear and defiance mixed in her tone.

"Second Department will——-"

"I'll attempt to call Islamabad. My cell phone has a dead battery. I won't get through, Kabul telephone service is non-existent. I'll hire a driver

—I'll be able to report your location in about twelve hours. Did the Americans pay you? Do you need money?"

Tears welled in Zhang's eyes and she hugged her friend. "Yes. They gave me an American passport and ten thousand dollars in a bank in

California. But I have little here."

Mara looked into Zhang's green eyes. "Do you know where the bomb is now?" Zhang didn't blink, but her eyes went flat for a second, shifted to the right, then back. "No. The Americans have removed the bomb—I think they took it back to Diego Garcia." The same glance at the dirty window.

"We must hurry. Take this money." Mara reached for a handful of bills on the table. Handed half to the Chinese woman.

"Thank you, my friend," Zhang hugged Mara.

"You have twelve hours. Don't waste any time."

Chapter 19

"It's also known as Shangri-la, like in James Hilton's novel, LOST
HORIZON," Melinda said after she stopped the truck at the entrance to
Hunza Valley. "Though long life is a myth."

Jack looked at Akbar's tarp-wrapped body, shivered. Chattering, singing birds from nearby shrubs provided background sound to her Irishaccented voice. It was 1600 hours—four o'clock in the afternoon. She had driven all the way from the ambush site— her knuckles still held the wheel with a tight grip.

"You can see it's an area of stunning natural beauty," Melinda continued. "Way down in the valley, that's the Hunza River thundering along like a freight train. There're endless terraces of orchards, maize, tomatoes, pumpkins. It's all irrigated by the water from the glaciers that crowd the sides of the mountains. And the KKH continues through to China, a few miles beyond the valley." *The real Shangri-la, just over the western heights from this place. Where the people practically lived forever —at least so they claimed. Penel—what a babe! Dickey Arses, Haartgard. Scary Mo Poo.*

An hour later, the truck pulled onto a one-lane dirt road that led to a
French-style manor house. Melinda announced, "That's Papa Pier's place." High clouds cast shadows that swept across the two-story stone building like crawling ghosts.

"Lieutenant Flashhardt," Bulldog suggested, "I'll drop you folks off, take the body to the village. That way you won't have to mess with the details. Then I'll head for the Special Forces camp and hang there."

"Great, Gunny," Jack responded. "But first, let's make sure this Papa guy is home."

Melinda drove up the quarter mile driveway, stopped in front of the big, south-facing house. An older, half-bald man dressed in a white longsleeved shirt, black pants, walked across an unkempt yard, accompanied by two white Afghan hounds. Burly, dark-skinned, but obviously a European. Had a bushy, grey mustache that hung over his mouth, down to his receding chin.

Behind the house was a one-story barn and vehicle park. Toyota SUVs were parked in a row along one side of the building. Bare poplar trees next to the buildings, dead leaves rattled as they drifted across the yard.

"Papa, I'm Melinda O'Reilly. Do you remember me?" Melinda called through the open truck window.

"Of course, Melinda," Papa answered with a high, squeaky, accented voice. "No Frenchman could forget such a lovely woman as you."

Melinda and the others climbed out, Bulldog drove away. She introduced Jack, Mick, Bruno.

After offering a limp handshake, Papa ordered, "Come to my cellar, share a bottle of wine from my vineyard." One brown eye was noticeably larger than the other.

He led the group around the east side of the house, down concrete steps. The door at the bottom opened into a tavern with a dozen small tables, a bar along a twenty-foot wall. Smoke hung over the dimly lit room; the scent of the tobacco was sweet—completely different from American tobacco. Large wooden wine barrels stood like sentries along the walls, and a mounted Indian elephant head eyed the patrons over long ivory tusks.

Jack noticed several tiger skin rugs thrown on the wood floor. The tables were filled with drinking men, some in uniform, some not; the fireplace, with a fire burning, warmed the room. Papa led the group to the last empty table, gestured for them to sit. Melinda sat on one side of Papa, Bruno settled on the other, Jack and Mick sat across from the Frenchman. A waiter brought a dark bottle of wine, set large stemmed glasses on the scarred table. Papa took a small corkscrew from his pocket, expertly opened the bottle, poured red wine. As he worked, he asked, "Melinda, you've brought me important men: two Americans and a Russian. What's the occasion?"

"We're here to visit the Americans in the valley," Jack said.

Bruno added words in French.

Papa looked each of them in the eye, nodded. "Ah, yes. The Americans. They're in the old English fort. It's actually on the Afghan side of the border—on the west side of the valley. I'm not surprised. C'est la vie."

"What's that?" Mick asked.

"The American Special Forces stir up trouble. They've taken local men—Hunza—trained them to fight. There've been problems. That

American missionary—the Anderson woman—has complained that the

American force is harassing

the populace." "Is the

border guarded?" Jack

asked.

Papa glanced at him. "Not by the Afghans. And the Paks don't patrol north of Gilgit. There's still controversy over the border alignment." "You mean the Durand Line," Jack offered.

Papa regarded him. "Yes, you're well-informed. A British officer surveyed the border in the 1890's and an 1893 treaty set the line between the two countries."

"Lord Durand was quite a guy," Jack said. "Some say he lived a normal life, others say he died in Tajikistan at an age of 124, after being gored while hunting Marco Polo sheep."

Papa added, "Anyway, the treaty expired in 1993 and now the border's in dispute. The Americans take advantage of the ambiguity.

They've trying to root out stray Taliban. Now they frantically search for the bomb." *Seems like everybody knows about the missing bomb. Some top secret event.*

"What bomb?" he asked.

Papa stared with narrowed eyes. "Perhaps, being in the UN, you haven't heard. The Americans lost a biological bomb. The whole region's terrorized. It could kill us all."

"Did you mention stray Taliban?" Mick asked. "You got a lotta towelheads around here?"

Papa frowned. "The Muslims don't like to be called towelheads. Anyway, their turbans are made of sheets."

"Mick, you got that?" Jack smiled. "From now on use a little political correctness. Call 'em sheetheads."

Mick burst out laughing, his eyes disappeared into slits of flesh. Jack tasted his wine—it was bitter—he gulped it, noticed Papa's frown. "Sorry, I guess I'm thirsty."

The waiter returned with a basket of warm chapatti flat bread, a bowl of olive oil and roasted garlic cloves. The bread was aromatic, the oil fragrant.

He looked at Bruno, nodded towards the door. Bruno followed him outside. "I think I'll visit the Americans," Jack said. "May as well get started."

"Good," Bruno smiled. "I'll have a bit of bread and wine, go to the village, poke about, maybe find stray biological bugs."

Jack returned to the table, asked Papa for a ride to the American fort. The Frenchman told the waiter to fetch a driver. A minute later, a guy from the kitchen came to the table, Papa instructed him in Urdu. He and Mick made their goodbyes, left the smoky bar. Jack wondered what he would find at the American fort.

Chapter 20

Yassar Ahmoud watched Zhang, the Chinese traitor, slip out the back door of the Mustafa Hotel, enter a waiting car that wound its way through war-strewn rubble of the street behind the hotel. Chunks of concrete, tangled masses of destroyed walls, glittering glass caught in the car's one headlight littered the street. He touched his mustache, stepped away from the hotel window and hurried outside. His Taliban driver, Hakim, waited in front in a rented Mercedes sedan.

Outside, he waved at his driver and jumped in the dust-covered, black Mercedes. He directed Hakim, who could barely see over the dash, to turn onto Flower Road, where Zhang's car had headed. Must act rapidly, he thought. Not much time.

They turned onto another rubble-strewn street—no Zhang Poon t'ang in sight. "Hurry," he ordered. "The next crossroad." What if he had lost her? All his plans—then he saw the vehicle stopped in the street ahead.

Hakim pulled up behind the Toyota. Ahmoud jumped out of the back seat, pulled his Chinese Tokarev 54 pistol, cocked it as he ran to the backing-up Toyota. Holding the weapon behind his back, he ignored a burqa-clad woman, two children in the street.

Ahmoud shot the startled driver in the head at close range. Blood and bone fragments spewed across the car, splattered against the opposite window. Ahmoud pointed the weapon at Zhang, who groped in her handbag. "Don't," he commanded. "Get out of the car, Chinese whore."

With a terrified expression, Zhang slowly stepped out. Ahmoud jerked his gun towards the Mercedes. She stumbled on a chunk of concrete, he almost shot her. She looked in his eyes, must've seen the closeness of his action, hurried to the Mercedes. They both climbed in the back seat.

"Back to the safe house," he commanded.

Hakim raced through the Kabul streets, skidded around collapsed buildings, got lost, backtracked, avoided shellholes in the pavement. Finally, he drove into a compound surrounded by a block wall, stopped in front of a one-story stucco house with iron grills over the windows.

Ahmoud motioned Zhang out of the car. They entered the gated patio, passed dead potted plants, went into the house Hakim had rented on a temporary basis. Trash littered the bare floors, dust covered a table, the ledges, the floors. A light bulb hung from the ceiling in the front room.

Ahmoud pointed at a chair and held the Tokarev at the ready until Hakim entered with a rope and tied Zhang's hands behind her. The Chinese girl's turban fell off and thick black hair cascaded over her shoulders. She sobbed as Hakim, humming a tune, tied her feet.

"Tell me where the American bomb is," Ahmoud ordered.

Zhang closed her eyes, wailed.

"I will have what I seek. You can live or die, be tortured or not—it's your choice." Ahmad looked at the Chinese woman. Her face was swelling, her eyes had disappeared in puffed-up flesh. "You have one minute to respond. I will not be stymied by you. You do not want Hakim to hurt you." *Make this easy.*

Zhang shook her head, her voice reduced to a low whine.

"I'm in a hurry. You're a beautiful woman—you'll be blinded. You are a famous waist drum dancer—your feet will be cut off. You come from a rich and powerful family but you will not write them after Hakim cuts off your hands. You'll not call your family for help—your tongue will be ripped out. Then you'll be released in the streets of a strange city. Think about it for one minute." *You're so beautiful, please don't make me do this.*

Hakim pulled a knife, giggled as he waited. The thought of Hakim mutilating Zhang made Ahmoud's heart pound. *Talk, you stupid bitch!*

Wild-eyed, Zhang looked around the room, said nothing. Ahmad nodded, Hakim reached for Zhang's jaw. She began talking as rapidly as she could speak in English.

Chapter 21

"The fort looks like an old movie set," Jack observed. "Where's Brendan Fraser when you need him?" The Toyota Landcruiser drew near the old British garrison at the west end of the valley. Rays from the late afternoon sun played across it.

The fort had mudbrick walls, parapets, towers at each corner, looked to be about one hundred by one hundred feet, with ten-foot-high walls. Big double doors stood open, a Humvee and a troop carrier were parked next to the entrance.

A tall, long-legged, very black guy with Arabic features, in battle dress utilities, stood at the entrance; several khaki-clad native soldiers walked or stood about. The handsome black looked familiar: they drew near, Jack was amazed when he recognized his college roommate, Omar Johnson. "Dude, way cool!" he called through the open window. Jumped out when the driver stopped at the gate; the two embraced, laughed. Omar clapped Jack on the shoulder with a huge hand.

"The hell you doing up here, bro? What's that all about?" Omar pointed at the blue UN cap Jack was wearing. "Last time I heard, the
Marines were haulin' your sorry ass off to war."

"I'm temporarily assigned to the UN as a military attaché," he responded. "How you been?" Omar, like Jack a descendent of a long line of military men, was an Army lieutenant. Unlike Jack, Omar was very enthusiastic about his military career, despite a conversion in high school to Islam, an action that had made him very unpopular at Willamette High School in his hometown of Portland, Oregon.

"What'n the world're you doin' in the UN? Thought I was as far from civilization as anyone can get. You come in here like Brad Pitt and George
Clooney strolling into Vegas. I can't effing believe it!"

"Remember Mick Nakamura?" Jack introduced the two Army officers. Mick and Omar shook hands, Jack added, "Omar graduated from San Jose State. Affirmative action at its worst." He said to Omar, "Remember? Mick was the only certified war monger at Stanford."

Mick bared his teeth in a grin, said, "At least I majored in something useful—Personnel Management."

"Hey, never know when Ancient Mesoamerican architecture and a Latin minor could come in handy," Jack responded. "Anyway, reports came down to Islamabad, from some babe named Amy Anderson, that American soldiers are committing atrocities against locals. So, the UN sent me up here to check it out. Mick's along for the ride. I might've guessed the terror of East Palo Alto would be the cause of all the trouble."

"Atrocities? Bro, what bullcrap! I'm second in command of a Special Forces "A" team," Omar exclaimed. "My men and I've been assigned here as a FOB—that is, a forward operations base, for Fifth Special Forces. Recruiting the Hunza, building a local militia that can protect the tribes.
And interdict leftover Taliban infiltration into Pakistan."

Jack asked, "Should these people be dragged into war by us?"

"Drag my ass! Task Force Dagger out of K-2 in Uzbek— that's Uzbekistan for you tourists—sent us here to help 'em fight the Taliban coming out of Afghanistan. Without us, they have no hope, 'cause they're Animists. Muslims kill unbelievers on sight."

"Well, Omar, I feel better, I guess," Jack said. "I wasn't looking forward to investigating this. But I need to talk to the Hunza."

"Okay, I'll haul your flabby Marine ass around. But most of my unit is out checking a lead on the biobomb—they're somewhere in interior
Afghanistan. And my boss is up north. Anyway, I've an inspection of the
Hunza in fifteen minutes. You can see them then."

The three walked through a central yard of raked dirt, into a short dark hall that led to several rooms. Omar turned into a small room, switched on a light hanging from the ceiling. A cot sat along one wall, an ammo crate desk had papers strewn on it, several rifles hung from nails in the brick walls. Jack asked, "What's the real deal on this bomb everybody's panicked about?" He glanced at Mick. "General Harmbruster tried to sign me up, but I passed when he said it was a volunteer mission. Then Mick's colonel chewed my ass for not helping out." He glanced at Omar. "But they said it had a secret sonic capability. They didn't mention biological bullshit."

Mick said, "I thought you knew all about it—a B-52 crashed in the Afghan Corridor. That's a narrow strip of rock and mountains that sticks into Pakistan, China and Tajikistan, just west of here."

Omar glanced at Mick, added, "A sonic, bunker-busting, smart biological warfare bomb. Officially, it's the GBU-200. But it's called the

LIIT Bomb. For Long Island Iced Tea."

Jack sat on the cot. "We've got satellites that can read a label on a candy bar. So crank 'em up and start looking for the tea."

Omar continued, "Someone found an' stole the LIIT Bomb, hid it during a freaky hot sandstorm. The storm cooled, they were gone."

"So what if it's a hot storm?"

"Infrared technology can't pick out body heat when the sandstorm temp is over 98.6 degrees. Humans just disappear. And the sand blocks out visual satellite technology."

"How bad's this bomb?"

"It shoots off a tight sonic wave that blasts hundreds of feet into the earth before the bomb activates."

"Sonic waves? You mean it's a military boom box? Wow, I always thought your ghettobuster would make a great weapon."

Ignoring Jack's sarcasm, Omar tapped the desk with his fist. "The shielding is made of depleted uranium. Extremely hard—it protects the biological warhead. Blows right through armor, dirt, and rock. Once it penetrates deep into the earth, weaponized bio-stuff is released. Bug spray inside a bunker. Kills bugs. Kills 'em all." Omar looked up. "It contains Bacillus anthracis—anthrax. But better. The anthrax has a gene added to it. B-lactamase. The gene destroys antibiotics. Makes the anthrax impossible to treat."

"Great!" Jack exclaimed. "They call it a cocktail? Gotta happy hour special on it?"

Omar smiled. "To top it off, it carries a lab-designed, geneticallyenhanced strain of Spanish Lady Flu. It killed over 25,000,000 people in 1918. It's very hard on old people and there's no vaccine, 'cause the strain is so ancient. Except for the U.S. military vaccine, of course."

"Kill off the old folks'll solve the Social Security shortfall."

Mick laughed. "Jack, you're a wiseass—as usual. Anyway, it also carries a smallpox virus. Three different bugs, so—" "That's why they called it a Long Island Iced—" "Bingo," Omar concluded.

A Hunza soldier came to the door, Omar asked for coffee.

"I got my own problems," Jack said. "Like the atrocity charges."

"Wake up an' smell the gunpowder, bro. We're chasin' Taliban. An' the Taliban don't believe in borders. Their philosophy is—if it works an' achieves their goals, it's okay. They'll lie, cheat, steal. Anyway, the
Anderson broad's a pain
in the ass." "How
so?" Mick asked.

"She's anti-war, anti-American, pro-everybody else. She'd human shield any poor, deprived terrorist she could find, against U.S. of A smart bombs, cruise missiles or gyrenes from Podunk, Maine—and she'd be singin' Midnight at the Oasis, while she did it."

"Well, she bodyslammed your unit," Jack said. "She complained to the UN that your forces are committing atrocities against Pak civilians. I think she mentioned a black dude who was a wild man—just kiddin' on the last part."

"What bullshit!" Omar retorted. "We—"

"Easy, Omar," he interjected. "I'm sure you're good to go. Let me talk to your native force. My associate—a Russian—is talking to some local civilians. We'll clear it up."

The orderly, a young civilian teenager, entered with a battered steel kettle. Omar collected three ceramic mugs from a shelf, the boy poured hot black coffee, the odor filled the room.

"I'm down with that—but we're goin' out on ambush after dark. We got Intel that a Taliban force is comin' from Afghanistan. Wanna go along?"

Jack responded, "Don't think that'd be cool. UN might object."

"Hey, I'd like to go," Mick said. "If you don't mind me tagging along, killing all the bad guys, capturin' all the glory."

Omar grimaced. "Brother. Oh, well, come meet the Hunza. I'll introduce you to the leader, Sergeant Major—that's his name. He fought the
Russians in the 'eighties."

The three walked to the central yard, where a large number of men sat or stood about. A voice yelled a foreign command. Men scrambled into a formation, stood at attention, a clump of heels knocked together. An older man, small, dressed in BDUs, with a heavily creased face stood in front. When the three Americans approached, the leader gave a British style, opened-palm salute. Omar returned the gesture with a crisp salute, introduced him as Sergeant Major.

The tiny man about-faced, escorted the Americans down the ranks. They stopped at the first soldier, dressed in a khaki uniform. Omar inspected the man's rifle for cleanliness; it was an old M-14:

at 44 inches and 11 pounds, it was almost as long as the soldier and weighed at least 10 percent of the Hunza's weight.

Jack asked the man whether Americans had in any way injured or mistreated any members of the tribe.

"Oh, no, sar!" Sergeant Major instantly replied. "Mister El Tee an' his commander have saved these peoples from the vicious Taliban, who are always shooting us on sight. Is our protector."

Jack followed Omar, looked at the next soldier in line. The man's rifle was unfamiliar, he took it out of the man's hands, looked at it. Stamped on the barrel was the name, Mauser 1936. The weapon was well-worn, an obvious survivor of the Russian invasion. As he looked up and down the line, he noticed that almost every man had a different weapon. Next man, large and very dark-skinned, had a pump shotgun.

After the inspection, he questioned two more men with no result, then thanked Sergeant Major.

Omar declared, "We're leaving. You ammoed up, Mick?"

"I'm good to go," Mick said. "I could use night visions."

The Americans returned to the office, Omar dug VS-7 goggles out of a drawer, gave them to Mick. "There'll be a quarter moon tonight. You'll have vision to eight hundred yards with these. But we want to get in place before moonrise." Mick grinned at him while he strapped the goggles over his bush hat. "This's great, Jack. You brought me good luck."

"We'll see," Jack responded. "I hope everything goes okay." *Man, if he gets dusted, I'm gonna feel like shit.* Just then, Bulldog Mahoney arrived in the UN truck and Jack introduced him. Omar's assistant—Sergeant Martinez—introduced himself. The Hunza force filed out of the gate, headed into the dark night while Bulldog, Martinez, Jack, returned to the interior.

The three went to an empty room with four bunks but no chairs or other furniture. Martinez set up a kerosene lamp, lit the coal stove and left.

The walls were plastered but either unpainted or coated with paint so old it was unrecognizable. Jack looked at Bulldog. He wanted to talk to him about the rape and murder, but he was still wary of the big Marine, so he restricted the conversation to anecdotes about Bulldog's service at OCS. The two laughed about a pissed-off Bulldog making Jack do pushups on his elbows in the OCS barracks.

Staying in the room with a man that might kill him was unsettling; he found it hard to eat the chicken and rice stew a Hunza woman brought to the room. Bulldog ate with gusto, chewed on a big cigar afterwards.

Jack disassembled, then cleaned his pistol, stretched out on the bunk, pulled a rough wool blanket over his fully dressed body, fell asleep after thoughts and worries about Bulldog were overpowered by exhaustion.

Woke alone at 0700, went to look for the toilet. Guard pointed at an outhouse on the west side of the fort.

During his visit to the diesel fuel-smelling privy, he heard a helicopter approach. Stepped outside, watched an old Vietnam-era Huey land next to the fort's gates. A lone soldier climbed out, the Huey lifted, flew back down the valley. The big Marine, lean, muscular, was dressed in BDUs. He wore a blue UN helmet, web gear, a backpack, looked around uncertainly. Jack was surprised when he recognized Billy Howling Dog, his younger halfbrother.

The two sized each other up; they had not seen one another since high school, five years past. He remembered their White Man—Red Indian hostile relationship that had lasted throughout high school. Jack recalled what had happened the last time he had seen Billy: buddies from the Crow Nation had indoctrinated Billy. The Flashhardt family, in the 1800's, had supposedly stolen Indian land in the mountains the Crow called Amanchab'e Chije. When the tribes prevailed in the lawsuit, the Crow Indian kids, including Billy and other Sioux, had built and burned a huge bonfire in the middle of Highway 212 in Red Lodge, got drunk, danced around it.

He approached Billy. A product of Marine training, Billy saluted. Jack returned the salute, grinned, held out his hand. Billy stared at the offered hand for a moment, slowly smiled.

Relieved, he shook hands with his brother, who had a bone-crushing grip. "Long way from home, Billy. How an' why're you working with me in the UN?"

"Jack, you've goddam dragged my poor redskin ass half way round the world!"

He asked, "What d'you mean?"

"Chief Talking Fox ordered me to cover your backside." The Chief had always taken the Flashhardt side in the land dispute. Had worked on the ranch for years. "I joined the Marines, served in Iraq, was hangin' with First MEU. He got me sent to Okinawa. Said to protect your six. When I found out you were in the UN, I called him—he got me sent here as a UN liaison." Billy grinned. "I didn't ask for it and I'm getting crazy with the changes, but here I am."

"How'd he convince you? How'd he pull all that off?"

Billy shrugged, looked around. "Hey, he's the Chief. I do what he says.
And he knows people. Like Senator Jensen."

Jack stared in disbelief at Billy's Marine haircut. "Your braids! You look weird without them!"

Billy grabbed for a non-existent braid. "Yeah, you're right… goddam Crotch!" He looked at Jack. "Hey, you think the UN'll give a shit if I grow back my hair?"

"I don't know. So you're squared away with the UN?"

Billy slapped his thigh. "Yep. I'm good to go. Your own personal aide.
Or bodyguard. So where are we, boss?"

"Hey, Billy—we're blood—whether you like it or not. Don't call me boss. We're in this together until we get outta here. Let's go inside and round up a cup of tea. You carryin'?"

Billy patted his waist. "I've got two M-9s, enough ammo to take on the

Blackfoot Nation."

"That's good, 'cause, we're in a world of shit. We're not in Islamabad, so wear your pieces all the time." He glanced at Billy's pack. On the side, the words: "Yakety yak, we whacked Iraq."

"How was it?"

Billy grinned. "Awesome! They kicked ass. Sorry I missed it."

Jack glanced at snow-covered mountains that surrounded them. "Think we did any good?"

Frowning, Billy added, "Naw—dudes are crazy."

"They have been for thousands of years. Probly won't change—same as here."

Billy tossed his head. "Who gives a shit. We slammed them— they won't be a problem for a hundred years. We can slam 'em again, need be."

"Billy Howling Dog, Internationalist, Supreme—Montana style." Jack slapped his brother's arm. The two walked through the fort to the kitchen, where a cook poured two mugs of bitter tea. Jack sipped, savored the hot liquid. "I have to go to a village and scope out some atrocities. Drop your pack in my room. Let's head out."

In the room, Billy checked his holstered pistols while Jack brushed his teeth and shaved with water from a pitcher on the table. Finished, he wrote a message to Bulldog. The two left the fort, Billy drove the Army truck towards Papa's tavern. The valley was bathed in bright sunlight, the mountain snows sparkled in the morning light. A cold breeze blew out of the north, bundled-up farmers worked in the tiny fields. The scene could've been in Montana.

At Papa's, they found Melinda the newsbabe in the warm tavern, eating oatmeal covered with yellow raisins. He didn't introduce Billy. Melinda sized up the striking Indian. His dark face, black hair, looked natural in Pakistan—except for his grey eyes. He flashed a big smile, overtly checked out Melinda's breasts.

She noticed his stare. "Seems like all this boyo's friends have nicknames. What's yours?"

Billy flashed a big smile. "I'm call. Call anytime." Melinda laughed so hard she choked on her oatmeal. Jack watched the two, wondered why Melinda had cast him aside after her seduction in Gilgit. Felt a pang of regret: that she was so beautiful, so intelligent, that she had dumped him.

Thought of his former girlfriend, Ashley Dupont—she had retreated in his mind. Tried to picture her. Remembered white blonde hair, broad shoulders, a square jaw. Wide-set hazel eyes, perfect nose, full lips, an incredibly lean body. But the picture was fuzzy: he couldn't really see her. Felt a pang of homesickness, loss intense as a knife stab. "Where's Bruno?" He asked.

"Meeting the human shield trollop," Melinda said through a mouthful of oatmeal. "Give me a kiss." He sat next to the red-headed Irishwoman, kissed her cheek. Her skin was fragrant, soft, perfect.

"Hey, guys," Mick Nakamura called from the entrance. He walked to the table, sat down. His eyes were bloodshot in his cammo-painted face.

Jack rose and gestured to a chair. "I'm glad you're back, Mick. How'd it go?"

"Who's this?" Mick looked at Billy, flashed a toothy grin.

Jack sat back down. "He's my new aide. Lance-corporal Billy Howling Dog, meet Chopstick—I mean Lieutenant Nakamura. U.S. Army. Now, tell me about last night."

Mick nodded, jumped up. "It was great! Omar's Intel was spot on and we caught the Taliban in our ambush. We so whacked 'em good. Real good." Mick sat down. "And we took no—that is zero—casualties. We set up along this dirt road. A line ambush with claymores to initiate the action, and a M249 SAW—that's a Squad

Automatic Weapon," he explained to Melinda, who had taken out a laptop, set up an antenna.

"Air-cooled," he continued. She typed as he talked. "Belt-fed, gasoperated automatic weapon fires 1,000 rounds per minute. Chopped up the hostiles that survived the claymores. Fifty KIAs. Only a handful escaped." "What's a claymore?" Melinda asked.

"A directional landmine."

"Named after a Sixteenth Century Scottish sword," Jack added.

"Where's Omar?"

Mick yawned,"He's composing a report to K-2. Then he'll come over for a victory breakfast."

"Better not brag," Melinda cautioned. "Papa's pro-Taliban."

"Yeah?" Mick wore a cocky smile, baring his large canine teeth. "If

Papa's a Taliban prick, he'd better watch out for me."

Arriving behind Mick, Papa said, "Such harsh words from a guest.

Sacre bleu! Charge him double, waiter." The group turned, looked at Papa.

Only Billy had seen him approach behind a waiter bearing a platter of food.

"So you had a successful ambush," Papa said. "But you're mistaken. I am French. I don't care what happens to Afghans."

"Hey, Papa," Mick asked, "you ever been to Euro Disney?"

The Frenchman sneered, "American glitter. Horrible hamburgers, disgusting hot dogs."

"I guessed you didn't notice the French closed it down."

"Why?"

Jack grinned, waited for the joke.

"It was too close to a French Army fort," Mick said. "And the government got tired of French soldiers throwin' down their weapons, giving up every night when Disney fireworks went off." Papa stared, the Americans and Melinda laughed.

"Where can I find Amy Anderson? The American doctor." Jack put eggs, fried potatoes, chapatti bread on his plate.

"Go to the hospital in the village," Papa responded. "If she's not there, someone will fetch her."

Melinda touched Mick. "Show me the ambush? I need pictures."

Mick shook his head, then said, "I just followed the Hunza. No idea where we went. You'll have to talk to Omar."

"I need to head out to the vil," Jack declared. "Mick, will you go back to the fort after we eat? Call and see about a lift back to Islamabad. And Mick, try to get a non-stop. I don't wanna fight my way back through banditos, terror mongers, or Taliban tax collectors."

Mick laughed, sang with a calypso accent: "Hey, Mr. Tal-i-ban, tally an al Qaida…"

After the group finished their meal, Jack paid for it with a much crumpled thousand rupee note. Billy Howling Dog drove back to the fort, where Mick and Melinda jumped off. Billy turned, headed the vehicle across the valley to the village north of Papa's. Flocks of pheasants walked through sun-lit, partially harvested barley fields; Jack wondered, as they drove on the dirt road through the terraces, how the valley could be so green late in the year. Guessed some kind of temperature inversions trapped heat in the valleys and allowed year-round farming. Wind had let up, temperature was mild, in the sixty-degree range. The vil, just off the KKH highway, was on a one-lane dirt street in a cluster of poplars.

Billy asked directions to the hospital; after a couple of false turns, they stopped in front of a one-story block building with a red cross on a piece of tattered gray linen next to the door. When they climbed out of the Toyota, the lean Russian emerged from the doorway, greeted the two Americans with a smile that lit up his severe face.

"What've you found out, Bruno?"

"Despicable American monsters have turned peaceful tribesmen into baby killers that are plaguing the kind Mujs."

Billy spit a stream of tobacco juice to the side. Bruno looked at the spittle on the ground, at Billy. "Another American."

"Bruno Utecht," Jack said, "meet Billy Howling Dog. He's my… er, a buddy from Montana, USA." The two men shook hands carefully. Just like two armed mountain men in the Rockies, he thought. Very watchful.. Polite.
Asked Bruno, "Where's the doc?"

"We missed her. She left for Gilgit yesterday. We must've passed her on the KKH."

"I hope she had a safer ride than we did."

"She'll return tomorrow. Where's Melinda?"

"Didn't get enough last night?" he couldn't resist asking.

"Ohh, Jack, I detect a wistful hurtness, a sadness of loss, perhaps a hint of jealousy. But she was go—od!"

"What a babe! Yeah, I'm so busted. Sorry."

"I described her as a Hollywood cliché back in Gilgit," Bruno said.
"She's beyond clichés. She makes her own rules. She's like Russian bear.
Goes where she wants. Takes what she wants."

Jack stared at the blond Russian, laughed. "You know, you're exactly right. Big mama bear eats everything in front of her. What say we head back to the fort?"

By late afternoon, Omar, who had left the fort after filing a report, was deemed missing. Sergeant Martinez, Omar's sub-leader arrived, told Jack a frantic-sounding man from the United Nations offices in Islamabad was on the radio.

Chapter 22

No worries for you, Jack," Gil Acton said. Static broke up his voice as it came over Omar's radio. "No, it's that bloody sheila, Melinda O'Reilly—I wonder if she's related to that news guy on Fox? The black Irishman? He's loud and obnoxious, but smart just like Melinda. Maybe it's a family trait. Anyway, she went to some Taliban ambush site. Taliban mutilated— according to Melinda— by American forces. The Americans cut the eyes out of every poor dead soul."

"Wait a minute, Gil," Jack objected. "I know American forces did nothing of the sort. The American lieutenant—I happen to know him— commands a Hunza paramilitary troop." Omar would never allow mutilations. What the hell had happened?

Gil added, "What a vision! No pun intended. Word's all over Islamabad. So, Miss Elle, our fearless leader, wants you to check it out. And the Pakistani military're in an uproar, as well. They think American forces have been operating on their soil."

"What difference does that make? And Gil—I'm telling you—
no
American committed an atrocity."

"Check it out, mate*." Yeah right. But what if the reports were true? No, it couldn't be.*

Sergeant Martinez returned minutes later, with Papa Pier right behind him. Jack wondered what the pompous Frenchman wanted. "What's up,
Papa?"

"Sacre bleu!" the Frenchman exclaimed. "The Taliban have invaded my house. They stormed in and took your black lieutenant. While he ate a late lunch in the bistro. There was a dreadful fight. Blood all over my floors. Wine from casks—ruined by gunfire—

spilt all over the place, even splashed on the walls. Merde, it was terrible!"

Jack stood, moved to Papa. "Forget the wine. What about Omar? Is he alive? Is he alright?" To Martinez, "Go get Lieutenant Nakamura and the gunny." Omar couldn't be dead. Not over some bogus atrocity charge. If he were, that human shield, Amy Anderson, would have to be ready for the wrath—-

"The Negro is fine." Papa interrupted Jack's racing thoughts, "He killed two men, wounded another before he ran out of ammunition. He surrendered. They battered him a bit, but—-"

Jack grabbed Papa's arm, "Where's Omar now?"

Papa wrung his hands, rubbed his long nose. "The Taliban are holding him in my house. They wait for an al Qaida officer from Islamabad. To interrogate him. They've taken over my home. It's all because the Hunza killed and mutilated Taliban dead. What a mess. Sacre bleu." He jumped up and down on his tiptoes, his feet pounded on the floor.

Mick joined them, exclaimed, "No way'll I leave him in Taliban hands."

"No!" Papa shouted. "My house'll be destroyed. You can't—
"

Jack poked Papa in the chest with a stiff finger. "I don't give a rat's ass about your house. We'll get Omar out of there—even if your house is leveled." Martinez and the others entered. Mick added, "Damned right." "No-o!" Papa wailed.

"Where's Melinda?" Bruno asked.

Papa looked thoughtful for a second, then adopted a look of consternation, "I don't know, maybe the village."

"Help us," Jack said. "Only way your house can be saved." "What do you mean?" Papa pleaded.

"First, draw us a house plan. Then we have to figure out how to get the

Taliban out of there."

"No, the Hunza will destroy my home," Papa protested.

"Shut up, Papa. Draw." He found a sheet of paper, a pencil.

The Frenchman drew a house plan while Jack, Bulldog, and Mick, strategized about how to free Omar. Bulldog suggested getting Marines from Afghanistan but Mick pointed out that the Pak government wouldn't allow a force to cross the border.

"The Hunza troop can free him," Jack decided. He took Papa's floor plan, showing where Omar was held, led the others to an empty part of the clearing outside the fort's walls. With a knife, he drew a floor plan of Papa's manor on the ground. A cold wind propelled dead leaves through his sketch.

Sergeant Major, the tiny Hunza leader, collected a ten-man squad, Jack assigned battle duties for the rescue. Placed a half dozen men in aggressor roles, representing Taliban guards in the manor. After each man was assigned, they walked through the rescue exercise. Practiced an approach and getaway. It looked easy on paper and on the ground—he wondered if it would be that easy in Papa's manor when boots hit the ground. He gathered the men in front of him. "We'll free Lieutenant Omar tonight. I'm gonna persuade Papa to pull the guards. If I'm successful, should only be guards at the front and rear doors."

He looked at the troop. "Remember, the rescue will take place at exactly 0400 hours. The red flare if we need it. Understand? Just like we planned it."

Sergeant Major nodded his head emphatically. "Rescue at 0400 hours. Very excellent! I will explain to our mans." As Sergeant Major translated his words to the men gathered in front of him, Jack, Bulldog and Billy went back to the fort.

"Bulldog," he said, "get Martinez and come with me. I want to show you where we're gonna waste the Taliban." In a Humvee, he detailed the rescue plan. Ordered Martinez to stop at the junction of the highway and Papa's entrance. "I want you to place several claymore mines on each corner of the junction. Right after dark. I want a man hard-wired to the claymores. Ready to blow the

Mujahadeen pricks home to their 72 virgins." Martinez, Bulldog took notes in small notebooks.

"We'll set up some doozies," Martinez said with a sly smile.

"Just don't get caught," he demanded.

Papa Pier was outside the gate, still fretting about his manor. Martinez held up next to the Frenchman. Jack ordered, "I want you to get all of the guards except maybe one at the front door and one at the back door, away from the manor at 0400 hours. Tell the Taliban leader that you've learned of a rescue attempt. I want you to convince him to pull his forces in order to ambush the rescuers. To place an ambush at the junction."

He reassured Papa, "I'll get Omar out of here with no fuss if you hold up your end, get the guards out on time. That's the key. If you follow my directions, your farm will be saved. But if anything goes wrong… if Lieutenant Johnson doesn't make it out of here, your estate is doomed." He glanced at his watch, thought, *Damn, I've always wanted to say doomed. Hope he buys it.*

Papa looked at him for a long moment, rubbed his face with his hands, agreed with a soft voice, "Yes. I'll do as you say. Please don't destroy my home." He gulped, his throat convulsed.

Chapter 23

0230: Bulldog shook Jack awake. The two went to Martinez' office. Chopstick Mick, Martinez, and Billy Howling Dog were cleaning and loading their rifles and pistols. Smell of gun oil filled the room. They grinned at him but did not rise. Outside, the Hunza force waited. The team fell in at the rear of the unit, men quickly moved towards Papa Pier's manor. The moon was about to disappear over the Hindu Kush peaks, stars were ablaze. Air temp mild—about forty degrees.

0315: Total darkness. Martinez, Bulldog stopped at the ambush site. The Hunza, Jack, Billy, Mick, circled through an apple orchard, hurried to the back of the manor and stopped behind a row of pickup trucks.

0345: Minutes crawled in the cool night air. 0400: Ambush time. Had the Taliban fallen for the trick? All quiet. 0410: "Everything's set on this end, Jack," Mick's voice whispered over the radio. He sounded excited.

"Hunza good to go?" Jack applied cammo paint to his face and hands with a stick he had found in Omar's desk while he listened.

"Yes, sir," Martinez confirmed. "I set the M18A1 mines myself and we got two Hunza sitting on a blow wire, ready to dust those Taliban fuckers while they set up their ambush." "Where's Bruno?" Jack asked No one answered.

0420: He jumped when the claymores exploded at the intersection. Shouts, gunfire, shattered the night.

"Let's go," he whispered. Two Hunza, though they wore no goggles, crept to the back door, grabbed the guard, who peeked around the corner of the house, silenced him with a knife.

Jack opened the back door—weapon held ready. Billy next to him. Manor was quiet, deserted. Heart pounded—he crept down the hallway, hoped no one saw him. Didn't want to die in a weird misplaced French chateau. Peering through nightvision goggles, the green cast to everything was eerie, the interior looked ghostly. A guard, with an AK-47 at the ready, stared toward the noise from outside the front of the house. Billy silently approached, set himself, swung a sock filled with sand. Hit the man on the back of the head, caught the rifle when he fell. Jack headed for the front of the big house. Papa's floor plan was correct.

Man outside the front door stepped back, lifted his rifle when he opened the door. Shot the guy in the upper left chest—his rifle fired a burst into the air as he flew backwards. More sharp explosions, rattle of automatic gunfire erupted from the direction of the junction. Screams, shouts could be heard when gunfire lapsed.

The Hunza troops, led by Sergeant Major, pounded into the manor, ran to the room where Omar was locked up. Sergeant Major threw a crossbar,
Jack opened the door, "Hey, it's me."

Omar jumped, ran to embrace him. "My God!"

Jack stepped back, looked at Omar in the green light of his goggles. His friend had dried blood from cuts on his forehead, chin, his thin lips were swollen from injuries. "You'll never pass inspection in this condition." "Thank God!" Omar glanced at his Hunza team.

"Hugs and kisses later. Let's go." Turned, ran to the back door, found Billy, the rest of the rescue party outside, positioned in a semi-circle, weapons faced outward. "Head for the fort," he shouted. "Checking our six."

"No—stick together," Omar protested but Jack was already going into the house. He was worried about the man he had shot. Ran through the house, looked out the front door, did not see pursuers. Wounded guy was sprawled on his side with arms thrown wide. Ripped open the man's shirt— inspected the wound: it was an inch below the collarbone, didn't look serious except for the dark stain of blood.

Turned the man onto his front, tore a scrap of cloth off the man's turban, made it into a compress, put it on the wound. Ripped off the drawstring that served as the man's belt, wrapped it around his body to hold the bandage. Started to tie a knot, heard a shout. Heard men run out of the darkness towards the house. The wounded man opened his eyes, pushed hard against Jack's chest. Men in the lead fired their weapons as they ran. Felt a double blow to his head, saw a splatter of colorful lights, smelled baby powder, everything faded.

Chapter 24

Awake in a jarring, jolting vehicle. He could see nothing, smelled the rank odor of a large animal. Felt around, realized he was in a bamboo cage on top of a creature! Put his hand in front of his eyes, couldn't see it. Head pounded, felt wounds on his right and left temples. Terror filled his mind— he was a prisoner. Would they kill him? Maybe not right away—taking him somewhere. He touched rough skin, decided it was an elephant. Sticky blood on his head wound: that fact told him he had been unconscious for a short while. Wondered where Billy and the team were, looked at his hand again, still nothing. He felt like he was in a dark cave, became more frightened. Why an elephant? Maybe they were worried about satellite surveillance. figured they were headed west. Worried about being spotted by an American surveillance airplane. It would destroy the convoy.

Long, tense hours later, the convoy stopped without incident. Still a pounding head.

A slight rain began to fall, he huddled on the floor but the thought of moisture got him up. Crawled around the cage, licked water off the bars.
Must be socked in—that's good—no surveillance. Could be worse. Answered himself, *Yeah, how?*

Rain stopped, it grew cold. Curled up, shivered until he fell asleep sometime in the night. The morning unseen, signaled by crowing roosters. Sounds of bustling villagers verified that another day had begun. He called for water until he heard Ahmoud's voice again.

"Prisoner, are you willing to confess your crimes against the peoples of Islam, of Afghanistan? If you do, we'll feed you."

"No way! I'm a UN officer. You've no right to detain me."

"American Crusader, you're not United Nations. I'm told you helped a war criminal escape."

"I need medical attention. What if I do confess?" *Who gives a shit about a dumbass confession? Sing like a bird.*

"Why, we'll videotape it and execute you." Shattered that idea.

"You nuts?"

"Nuts? No, I said no food until you confess."

He sat down, disgusted with the conversation. Heard someone climb on the truck, smelled the breath of a tobacco smoker, faint odor of perfume. Air moved against his cheek.

"Allah is great!" Ahmoud's voice. "You're blind!"

"I need medical attention," he protested. Heard the guy jump to the ground. "Your accommodations are lousy—the view sucks." A half hour later, the driver entered the truck, drove in convoy with the other vehicles.

Where the hell were they taking him? Pashador—didn't sound familiar.

Chapter 25

When the truck slowed to a halt, Jack remembered the drill, grabbed the bars. Heard men undo the straps holding the cage in place, push it off the bed. It slammed to the ground, smashing his left hand. Men opened the cage, pulled him to a wall, shoved him against it. Heard, then felt crumbled plaster crunch under his feet.

Ahmoud yelled, "American prisoner, confess your crimes."

"Go to hell, dude, I'm the good guy here." Rifles cocked. Heart went into overdrive, thought of the American flag flying, rippling against a clear blue sky. Home. Ahmoud shouted a word.

The hills of the Flying Eagle Ranch back in Montana. Dad, Ashley.

Green grass, a cold beer, huge snowdrifts. Want to be—

"Fire." Ahmoud's voice rang out. Volley of shots crashed into the wall around him. Knees buckled. *No pain, no...* Regained his balance, realized he was still alive. The execution had been a ruse. Trying to fuck with his mind, break him.

"Take him away," Ahmoud shouted.

Giggling guard led him—he stumbled, fell—another guard immediately started to kick him. Terrified, he pushed to his feet, staggered ahead. Shoved into a room—sprawled on a dirt floor. Door crashed shut.

Nursed his left hand, felt around the room with his right. Discovered a bucket in a far corner, ran his hands through it, searched for dead varmints, found none. Sniffed—smelled rank but it was water. Splashed the foul liquid into his mouth.

"Who're you?" a woman's voice asked.

"I'm Jack Flashhardt." Turned his head, tried to catch the direction of the voice. "I was blinded when I was captured." He heard steps draw close. "Let me see."

"Who're you?"

"I'm Amy Anderson. From Iowa. I'm a doctor." Amy. The root of all the trouble. Wondered if he could punch the dumb bitch that had caused all this without seeing her. *No, not stupid. How could she know? Still, the thought…*

He felt fingers probe the wounds on his temple. She held his right eyelid open, then his left eyelid.

"I got shot. Screwed up my eyesight."

"No, the bullet just grazed you. The real damage is from a blow to the left temple. It appears the concussive force of it caused a swelling that has affected your optic nerves." *What the hell's that all about? Somebody hit me? Who?*

"And if it doesn't go away?"

"You'll be blind—maybe forever." *Maybe forever. Easy to say.*

Impossible to imagine. What the hell use having a doctor in the house? Uh, jailhouse.

"You went to Gilgit," he said. "I was at your hospital in Hunza Valley.
But we missed you by a day. How'd you get here?"

"My vehicle was stopped on the KKH. I was brought here. I've treated wounded men from an American ambush. Being put in this cell was a mistake. They'll let me go soon." *A mistake. Amy is dreaming. Hanging in La-La Land.*

She added, "Don't worry, I'll demand they release you. If they don't, I'll go to the UN in Islamabad. But, you've brought this on yourself, you know. You're an American. You shouldn't be running around Pakistan, killing refugees and stirring up trouble with the tribes. I've been complaining for weeks."

Yeah, right. "Amy, I am the UN."

"There must be a mistake. These people won't hurt you."

"Amy, these people hate us. Want to destroy Americans."

"Only because we're meddling in their lives."

"We're meddling because they banged us on 9/11. You think our troops want to be in this fanatico-religious, raghead-donned paradise? They're here to whack these bastards so they'll leave us and leave our stuff alone." *Whoa, I'm starting to sound like a poster boy recruiter for the U.S.*
of A.

"Should stay out of their lives. We're just creating enemies."

"Amy, you're crazy. They already hate us, want to hurt us."

She shut up; he thought about his head wound. He must've been struck by someone from behind: maybe a Taliban or a Hunza. No, the Taliban were taken out and the Hunza had no reason. An American? Made no sense. Door crashed open, several people entered. Shoved to the side, sprawled on the floor. Someone slapped Amy, she wailed.

"Shut up, whore!" Yassar Ahmoud's high-pitched voice.

"I'm a doctor. I'm here to help your people." The thuds of several blows on Amy's body. She cried out again, sank to the floor, sobbed. Sounds were horrifying.

"You're a spy," Ahmoud yelled. "A spy for the Jews and American Crusaders." The guy was crazy. Didn't he know Amy was a basic America hater?

"No! I'm a medical doctor. I'm here to help."

Jack heard more blows. He rose, rushed forward, tried to stop the beating. A blow to the back of his head, darkness. When he awoke, his head was in Amy's lap.

"How do you feel?" Amy asked. Her voice was tender.

Sat up, fought dizziness, pain, asked, "I'm okay, you okay?" No time for stupid jokes.

"I'm sorry about what happened. If only an officer or leader would come, we could explain and solve this mess."

"Amy," he groaned. "It's not that simple. The guy who was questioning you is a captain in al Qaida. He's running the show, from what I can figger."

"Oh, my God!" She was starting to get it. The cell door crashed open. High-pitched, giggling laughs. Men entered. A kick in Jack's face knocked him aside. Agonizing pain flared in his head, heard Amy back up, scream.

This is nuts, they're gonna kill us. I'm gonna die in a stupid mud palace. Gotta get out of here.

The men taunted her with cries of "American whore!" and "American slut!" He heard clothes rip. He jumped up, dove towards the men. Caught one from behind, spun him around, held his arm and punched him three times in the face. Two other men grabbed his shoulders, but he smashed them together. The two dropped, stunned. Heard a pistol cock, froze. *Shit, don't shoot me…*

"One more move, American prisoner. Just one, and I'll forget myself,"

Ahmoud exclaimed. "Now, back up."

Backed against a wall, waited, ground his teeth, clinched his fists with frustration. Amy shrieked again, was slapped. Powerless, he listened to the grunting rapists. When the men finished, they left the room. Laughed, conversed in a foreign language.

Ahmoud turned back, taunted in English, "American Infidel." American accent this time. Sounded like that of an educated man from an Ivy League university. "When my man gets off watch, perhaps I'll have him visit you. He favors your sort. His name is Hakim. I'll be sure to introduce him. You'll like him. And I know he'll think you pretty. It should be fun to watch." *So much for foreign student exchange programs making these assholes like us.* After the cell door slammed shut, he groped his way to Amy, who sobbed on the floor. He found her, held her in his arms.

"No, no more," she whimpered.

"Amy, it's me, Jack. They're gone. I'm so sorry. I tried to help, I failed. But don't worry—we'll get out of here. I promise. I'll get us out of here. Hang in there, Amy." He felt her shake her head. "No, they violated me. Over and over. I've never—" Wordless, she fiercely clutched him, cried into his shoulder. *She's losing it. How do I keep her together?*

"Listen." He held Amy against his chest, squeezed her. "They didn't hurt you. Put this out of your mind. Please, Amy."

"You can't know. No one will ever want me. They took—"

"That's not true, Amy. I'd want you. Anybody would."

"No, I'm—you just can't know." She clutched him tighter. "Prove it," she said. "Make love to me. Please—prove it." Shocked by her words, Jack held her, said nothing.

"See? You can't know."

It sounded like he would know. Hakim—but he'd kill the monster.

Somehow, he would. He'd kill them all.

Chapter 26

Woke on the cell's cold dirt floor, a line of ants crawled over his outstretched hand. The large body of ants headed elsewhere. "Hey, Amy?" No response. Heart pounded. What's wrong? They take her away? Tracked
the ant trail with a light touch, across the cell. Followed, searched until he smelled Amy. His hand brushed her body. "Amy?"

Her body swung in the air, a scrape on the floor. Felt until he found a makeshift hangman's rope, made of her pants, tied to a bar in the window.

Hugged her still-warm body, his face buried in her chest. "Oh, Amy," he murmured into the body. "I needed you. I needed you to be strong. When I said, 'Hang in there,' I didn't…" Suddenly saw a glimmer of light, lifted his head, saw an illuminated area! Held out his hands, encountered the bars. He shouted several times. Finally, others entered. Men removed Amy's body while Yassar Ahmoud screamed, "American, you killed the doctor."

"I didn't. You filthy bastards raped her—she committed suicide. By
God, if I was free, I'd kill the lot of you."

"The mouse—no, the rat roars," Ahmoud sneered. "If you were such a man, you would never've been taken prisoner."

"It was 'cause I worried about one of your wounded men!"

"Your loss—now, we'll try you for murder—in addition to your other crimes. We'll discuss those despicable acts after we dispose of the woman's body. Do you have the time, American prisoner? Well, it's almost time for lunch. And I want a good meal. I believe we're having leg of lamb and mint jelly today. Hungry? If you confess, I'll see you're fed. And after your confession, I'll make sure you're let go. What do you say?"

"Yessir, ah'm mad, you asshole," he mumbled. Too exhausted, too numb to feel anger.

Chapter 27

Another man entered the cell. "Hakim," Ahmoud's voice called. "Send for Hakim." Voice came from the middle of the cell. A moment later, Jack heard a person enter the cell. A foul odor assaulted his nose. Looked, saw the blurry form of a little man join Ahmoud. He carried bundles. Ahmoud gave an order in Urdu, then stepped back. Hakim struck Jack with a wood switch. He held up his arms for protection, pretended his sight was not partially restored.

Hakim pounded with the switch until it splintered. Picked up another switch, continued. Huffed, puffed from his exertions. Each blow left a cut or welt on Jack's arms, head, shoulders. Pain spread, soon changed to a general agony, spiced by each blow. When Hakim picked up a third switch and struck, he rushed forward, grabbed the dwarf, punched him three times, hurled him across the cell. Hakim crashed into the wall, slumped to the floor.

Jack turned, pretended blindness: held out his hands, groped his way across the room. Ahmoud yelled. Guard rushed into the cell, pointed his rifle at Jack. Terrified at the vague shape of the rifle pointed at him, he swallowed his fear, ignored the guard.

"If you move, he'll shoot," Ahmoud yelled.

"Who?" He sat down on the floor, wiping blood out of his eyes, off his face. "You afraid I'll fart an' blow you away? Hey, Ahmoud, chill. Stop and smell the sand dunes and camel shit." The guard dragged Hakim out of the cell, Yassar Ahmoud followed, slammed the door behind him.

Relieved that he had survived the ordeal, Jack rubbed his eyes, looked around. Details in the cell were clearer. Thought about who had caused his blindness. Only an American could've hit him: Omar—no, he was outside celebrating with his troops; Billy—no reason; Mick—he was a pal going way back; Bulldog—the only logical party. But why? Why not just a bullet in the back of the head? Why leave him for the Taliban?

Jack spread out on the cold dirt floor, tried to ignore the pain, finally fell asleep.

Woke in darkness again. Got up, looked towards the window. Could not discern where it was—vision worse. Walked towards it, suddenly saw stars in the black sky with perfect clarity. *Thank you, God. I hope I can take it from here.* He peered at the village, saw a number of trucks, SUVs parked in the road. Houses were dark except for one window.

Looked around the cell, noticed stars shining through a crumbled hole in the wall, just below the high ceiling. Wondered why the Taliban would use a cell with a possible escape hole, remembered they thought he was blind. *No blind man could see the hole. No ordinary man could climb the cell's block walls, anyway. But I can: makes Yosemite's 3,000 foot Half Dome look like an escalator. I'm outta here, you pricks.*

Climbed the cell wall. Strong climber's fingers easily found, gripped ridges, slight depressions in the mudbricks. Squeezed into the hole, forced his body through. Upper body hanging towards the ground, he was unable to twist his body. Heaved, crashed to the ground.

Oorah! He shouted the Marine cheer in his mind. Chanted an oldie's rock tune under his breath:

Sha, na, na... na,
Sha, na, na... na,
Hey, hey, hey... go-odbye.

Looked around, saw no movement. Crept towards the lit-up house, crawled under the window. Peeked inside, saw a group of hard-looking uniformed Chinese military men, Afghans that looked like dregs of a rummy bistro. After he carefully removed a rag stuffed in a broken pane, heard Yassar Ahmoud's high-pitched voice, "—cannot give you the bomb.

We plan on using it. Against the Great Satan."

"It is too valuable," someone with a harsh Chinese accent.

"That is the end of it," Yassar concluded. The Chinese spoke among themselves, filed out of the room, casting baleful looks at Ahmoud and a half-dozen armed Taliban. Jack ducked around a corner, knelt on the frozen ground.

After trucks started, headlights flashed on, he sprawled prone—waited —his heart hammering. Three trucks drove out of the village. Heard the house's door slam, crawled to the corner, saw Ahmoud and his guards walk away.

Five minutes shivering in the night air. Crept to the door, entered the building. Inside, felt his way to the desk. Touched spots on the desktop, encountered a half loaf of chapatti bread, a big piece of cheese. Gulped a bite of each, thrust the rest in his pocket. Teacups sitting in a row, drank leftover cold tea, slurping from each cup. Found a lighter, ignited it, quickly looked around.

A haversack tossed in a corner of the room. Picked it up, swept papers on the desk into the pack. Opened a drawer, found a pistol, a long-bladed Khyber knife. Added the weapons to the pack. In the last drawer was a laptop computer, a cell phone. Stuffed them into the pack. Heard a sound! Turned and saw Ahmoud, who shouted, "You! You can see!"

Dropped the pack, jumped across the room, grabbed the slender man by the neck and the arm. They danced around in a circle. Ahmoud hit him with well-aimed but weak blows. He noticed faint perfume as the two struggled, their faces inches apart. Ahmoud silent because of the neck hold. Couldn't yell.

Smashed Ahmoud's head with his own, slammed the man's head against the wall. A crashing thump. He repeated the move three times. Panted for breath, released the unconscious man. Checked his pulse, felt nothing. Ahmoud was dead. Turned, grabbed the pack, ran to the door.
Outside, he crept through the village, reached the last house, ran.

Chapter 28

Jack headed south into the mountains, figured the al Qaida and Taliban would expect him to go northeast towards Pakistan. His feet pounded across the frozen ground. Prayed the deception would give him time to get clear of pursuit. As he ran, he triumphantly chanted over and over:

> I am the Champ-ion,
>
> I'll keep fighting to the end.
>
> I am the champ-ion of the world. Oorah!

An hour later, Jack had traveled about seven miles into a tree-filled valley. Held up, slumped to the ground. Excitement, adrenaline-rush gone. Opened the pack, found the bread, moldy cheese, devoured the food. The tastes and smells were so piquant his jaw cramped, his eyes watered. He walked off the trail into a clump of trees, heaped dead leaves over his body for warmth, fell asleep.

Awoke just before dawn, checked the pistol—it was loaded—a 9mm semi-auto Makarov. Thrust it in his pocket, immediately ran through the poplar and pine forest in a southerly direction. The dawn sky was blue, clear of clouds. An hour later, he encountered a stream flowing past fernfilled banks. After drinking sweet cold water, he sat down, removed the laptop computer from the pack. Turned it on, double-clicked an icon on the desktop screen. When it opened, he checked mail. Only one note was in English. It read:

Dear Sad Sakam,

I agree that a series of mock bio-attacks in San Francisco will foster antiwar protests. Your idea of releasing balloons to show where such an attack would be borne by the winds is brilliant!

He started to look for more mail but the computer beeped three times, flashed a low-battery warning, turned itself off.

Looked at the gurgling stream, stripped, scrubbed himself with clumps of fern, handfuls of sand from the bottom of the ten-foot-wide, ankle deep icy water. When he was finished, he put on his clothes, boots, parka. I'm clean. What a great feeling. A new start. Shivered as he sat, waited for the sun to warm him. Pulled the cell phone out, called his dad.

Bill awakened from a deep sleep. "Flashhardt."

"Dad, it's me."

"Jackson? Where are you?"

"Dad, this's complicated. I was captured by Taliban and——-"

"I know, son," Bill interrupted. "Omar called me. I'm so happy you're okay! I love you. He——-"

"Listen, dad, I escaped. I'm in Afghanistan. Somewhere in Hindu Kush. Northern part of the country, heading south. I——-" The cell phone beeped, flashed a low-battery warning, turned itself off. Cursed, threw it to the ground. He noticed a trout in a small pool next to the far bank. Forgot about dead cell phones and laptops, quickly pulled out the long Khyber knife, cut a pole, tied the knife to the six-foot stick with a bootlace. Stabs missed, the trout disappeared downstream. Crept to the next pool, saw a trout—about a three-pounder. An inch at a time, moved the spear closer, slashed. The stunned fish floated away, but he chased it downstream until he caught it. Waded to shore, flopped in long grass, sliced it open, filleted it with the knife. Quickly devoured the pieces of raw flesh. Wiped slime off his chin, looked around while he re-laced his boot. He put the knife, the laptop, the cell phone away, followed the stream until it intersected a hardpacked dirt road.

Backed up, looked around, climbed a large pine tree. Flock of redlegged partridges walked onto the road, pecked at the ground.

Suddenly an awesome-looking gray and black osprey dove out of the sky, knocked a fat partridge over in a cloud of dust and feathers. Ran after it, picked it up, and flapped away. Envious of the big osprey's hunting skills, he watched the survivors scatter into the roadside weeds. Flash of white caught his eye: scrawny white tiger limping along the stream. Cat stopped at the fish, gulped the guts, head, skin, in two bites. Sniffed the air, looked directly into his face.

The cat's huge blues eyes glinted in the sunlight; black stripes over the cat's eyes gave it a surprised, friendly look. Now discovered, he spoke to the big cat, "Hey, how's it going?" I wonder if tigers climb trees? Hoped chitchat would keep the cat from thinking about hunger.

The cat rumbled something like a response—did not sound threatening. The tiger sat, wrapped its tail around its feet just like a barnyard cat back in Montana.

"You look a little scrawny. Cause you're limping?
Can't catch anything? Wish I could help, but I don't have
any Cat Chow." The cat stretched its neck towards him,
grumbled again.

"Hey, don't get ideas. I wouldn't taste that good. Honest." He pulled out the Makarov, a round was in the chamber. The cat appeared to recognize the pistol as a threat. It turned, slunk into tall weeds, quickly disappeared.

Thought about getting down from the tree, decided it was safer than playing smackdown with the big cat, stayed for another hour. Reviewed a mental map of Afghanistan—*better yet, Afgoneistan: Tajikistan to the north —a big unknown; the Salang River Valley to the southwest, probably a lot of people—to be avoided; Pakistan to the east and southeast—that was the way out.*

A herd of red Bactrian deer, looking like Montana elk, wandered into the meadow, grazed on the high grass. Watching the meals on hooves made his stomach cramp and rumble; he saw two calves frolic—decided to risk a gunshot.

Crawled down the tree, crept through the high grass. Drew near, pulled out the Makarov. When one calf chased the other towards him, he shot the lead gamester in the chest at a distance of ten feet. Hundred pound deer squalled, crashed to the ground. Dropped his pack, checked to make sure the herd's buck was not attacking, pulled out the Khyber knife, slit the calf's throat. Animal gazed at him, trembled for a couple of moments, died. He quickly opened the calf's hot midsection, cut slices out of the liver, devoured the hot, juicy meat. When he finished the liver, he sliced strips of fat away from the ribs, gulped the high-energy flab. The buck approached, stamped its feet, snorted. All of a sudden, it turned, scrambled back to the herd. All the deer ran in a pounding, dusty mass.

When he was so full his stomach felt like it would burst, he cut a rear quarter off to carry away. Looked up, stared into the white tiger's eyes, huge pink nose, just five feet away. Jumped up, backwards at the same time, scared the tiger and himself. When he stopped scrambling, he was ten yards away. Caught his breath. "Easy, big guy. It's all yours." He stayed low, walked backwards, looked down as he did so. Tiger rumbled, attacked the dead calf. Sounds of ripping flesh, crunching bones accompanied him as he turned, fled the meadow. Under his breath, he sang a ditty:

In the jungle,
The mighty jungle,
The tiger eats the deer.
In the Jungle
The mighty jungle
The tiger's what I fear.

Singing to myself — I'm losing it, he worried. *But, hey—my belly's full and Tigger's eating the evidence.*

Chapter 29

Jack entered a twenty-mile long valley in mid-morning. There was a giant bas-relief of the Buddha carved into the western cliffs overlooking the valley. Probably similar to the Buddha statues destroyed by the Taliban in the Bamiyan Valley when they ruled Afghanistan. Like the eyes in a picture of George Washington in the one-room schoolhouse he had attended for his first six grades, the Buddha's sandy eyes seemed to follow him as he crossed the miles-long valley. Just after noon a group of riders pushed their horses out from behind a hogback ridge, galloped across the valley floor. He ducked behind a boulder, watched as a long dust plume bisected the valley.

After they disappeared, he continued south on the alluvial fan of sand and rock: the valley he traversed all day had no trees, no bushes, no flowers, no grass or weeds, no signs of habitation.

"So, Buddha," Jack asked, after constant glances at the huge rock carving, "or should I say, God. Can I ask you for help in getting out of this country?" He waited: no answer. "Or would that be an insult since you call this part of the world home and I shouldn't want to leave your heaven?" No answer.

Jack looked up at the giant statue. "A little landscaping could do wonders around here—just a suggestion." No answer. "Do you ever answer questions or prayers?" No answer.

"How come, like, you know, at least Moses got a burning bush and a parting of the sea. What am I, dog meat?"

When he encountered a stream, it reminded him of the twenty-six mile, Rio Horcones approach to Mount Aconcagua—at 23,000 plus feet—the highest mountain in South America. Like the Horcones River, this glacial stream wandered back and forth in the flat, empty valley. Its waters had a heavy mineral taste. He shouted, "One wish. Could I at least get, like, a drink of good water?"

The snow-capped mountains rose above the Buddha, steeper than any other mountains he had seen anywhere in the world. The majestically framed Buddha watched him without comment. But a minute later, he crested a small fold in the valley floor and spotted a white metal cup sitting on a rock, next to a spring. He scooped water with the cup: fresh, sweet water.

"Whoa!" Jack exclaimed after drinking his fill. He put down the cup, looked up at the silent Buddha. "So," he continued, "how about a lift out of here? Or do I only get the one wish?" The Buddha remained silent, the skies stayed empty. "I guess I should've asked for something more meaningful— sorry about that." No answer.

"Fair enough," he concluded. "The only thing better than a drink of good water is a breath of fresh air, and you're giving me that without my asking. Thanks, dude—er, Buddha."

At sunset, the setting sun turned the facing ridges red and the snowcaps purple. The near full moon, rising in the east, turned the reverse cliffs a pearly white. He paused on a ridge, halfway between the sun and the moon, thought: *I've survived a day. I'm hungry but I'm alive. I'm cold, but*
I'm alive. I'm alone, but...

Darkness spread across the barren valley, Jack called to the distant, gigantic figure, barely discernable in the failing light, "Later, God. Sunset is great. But the landscape—never mind."

After the sundown, Jack wished he had the shoulder of meat he had left when the tiger had claimed his due as master of the forest and mountains. Could have shot it—thought never crossed my mind. *But, hey— way too beautiful. Way too grand. Anyway, how do you explain to your future kids that you killed Winnie the Pooh's Tigger?*

He saw no shelter, no firewood, no possible place to get warm— continued to walk under brilliant stars. Above, Draco the dragon continually devoured the Little Dipper. *Thanks for your help, God. Or, if you didn't, thanks anyway, just in case you're thinkin' about it.*

Midnight, he reached a lower elevation, found a dirt road. Followed it until he crept into a forest glen, burrowed under leaf refuse next to a rushing brook.

A flock of squawking magpies woke him an hour after sunrise. Sat up, brushed leaves, invading bugs away, saw a child standing in the road. The Afghan boy, about nine years old, carried a cloth sack, was attired in impossibly ragged clothes, wore a faded Detroit Tiger's baseball cap— stared at Jack.

"Hey, kid," he smiled. "What's your name?" The boy smiled back, sat on his haunches, looked at him as if he was an alien from another planet.

"I'm Jack," he pointed at himself, pointed at the boy.

"Kim," the boy said. Reached in the bag, pulled out a dried apricot. Offered it. *If I were thirty years old, this'd be Ashley an' my kid.*

Jack walked to the road, brushed leaves, dirt off his parka and pants.

He accepted the apricot—it smelled, tasted wonderful. Looked at the kid.

"Totally awesome, dude. Speak any English?"

The boy made no sign of comprehension. "I wish I hadn't met you," he continued. "What the hell'm I to do with you? If I let you go, you'll spread the tale of encountering a white man—I'll be sunk. If I don't let you go…" He sketched the outline of a hut with his hands, pointed to the boy. "D'you live nearby?" Boy grinned, pointed downstream.

"So, Kim. Like, I wanna go to Pakistan. Can you show me the way?" Thought with a surge of confidence, *If I get to a mountain pass, they'll never catch me.*

Kim grinned when he heard the word Pakistan, offered another apricot. Jack ate three more while they walked south for a mile, turned east into the mountains. Trail headed through a denuded poplar grove, into a fragrantsmelling pine forest. By noon, when they reached the snowline, clouds formed, cut the glare—trail disappeared under snowdrifts. He turned, pointed up the slope. "Pakistan?" Boy nodded. "Okay. Pakistan, okay." Hearing the word excited him. He looked up the pass—high but doable. Steep ridges flared up on each side. Turned to the boy. "Alright, pal. You can head back. I'll take it from here. I'm outta dis joint!" He pointed down, gestured for Kim to go back. The boy grinned, took a few steps, Jack headed up the pass.

Five minutes later, he looked back. Kim was following. "Kim, you wanna go to Pakistan? You playin' hooky? Skipping' school?" He gestured and added, "Go home. Beat it, kid." The boy stood still, grinned. "Okay, come on. Let's go to Pakistan. But let's hurry. Don't wanna spend the night in this open-air hotel—well, we can't complain about the prices."

The two walked on wind-packed snow, leaned into a cold breeze. Ten minutes later, a mist of clouds reduced visibility to fifty feet. He turned to the boy. "I think we'd better head back." Watched the boy, noticed the youth's eyes widen as he looked upslope. Jack swung around, saw a giant man standing in the middle of the pass like a huge redwood tree, barely visible in the mist. His heart, already pounding in his ears from the hike into the pass, accelerated even more when he recognized the man with the distinctive peaked cap.

"No sweat, Kim, I know this guy. Anyway, I'm armed." He asked Mo
Poo, "How's it goin'?"

"You killed my dot-ter," Mo Poo rumbled. His voice was deep enough to cause avalanches.

"Look, I—"

"Enough! You are guilty."

Jack pulled the Makorov out of his parka pocket, cocked it, turned to
Kim. "I want you to run." He pointed downhill. "Hurry. Go!"

A second giant stepped out of the mist, a third and fourth moved to Mo Poo's other side. Jack looked closer: they were identical in size and appearance! Giant quadruplets! He realized the Makorov peashooter wouldn't stop all the huge men. He ran. In seconds, he caught Kim.

"Hurry!"

The two pulled away from the giant Chinamen until they moved off the wind-packed snow, hit softer drifts. Kim floundered, Jack swung around. Lumbering giants were upon them. Shot the first one—the giant fell in a cascading flurry of spattering white.

Mo Poo threw his club, knocked the Makorov out of his hand—pistol disappeared in the snow, hand numbed by the blow. He turned, tried to run. A giant launched himself, caught his ankle. Mo Poo grabbed Kim, savagely wrenched his head, threw him aside. Jack kicked his aggressor in the face with his free foot, rolled, staggered to a steeper slope on the north side of the pass. Suddenly, he confronted a huge wild sheep—an all-white ram with a six-foot spread of curved horns. The shocked ram lowered his head, attacked.

Chinamen behind him, menacing animal before him, Jack could only run at the ram. He advanced, dove under the Marco Polo sheep's huge, sixfeet-wide horns, rolled, continued to run.

Glanced over his shoulder, saw the ram smash into Mo Poo. Man and animal collapsed in a tangle of feet, legs, arms. Didn't see a cliff, ran off it. Everything turned silent except for the whistling wind as he tumbled through the air, turned over and over with the sky and ground switching places.

Crashed in a steep snowbank, a hundred feet lower on the mountain. Slid, ended on his back, head downhill. Tried to turn but was stuck, with cold snow packed down his neck. Finally, he levered himself to his front, stood. Legs trembled so much he had to concentrate to take a step. Looked up the mountain, his pursuers were hidden by a fold in the terrain.

Tremendously relieved to be alive, he looked around for danger. For the moment, he had outdistanced the giant Chinamen. Rested for a few seconds, then postholed through deep snow until he reached rocky ground below the snowline. Penetrated the fragrant cedar pine forest he and Kim had crossed earlier, stopped and looked around, collapsed under a deadfall. Thought of Kim's horrible death, hugged himself, shuddered, grateful that he was alive. After a minute, remembered where he was, pulled dead branches over his body. Camouflaged, he curled into a fetal position, thought of the boy who had fed him, befriended him, guided him, climbed with him, died alone. He muttered part of Taps as a prayer:

Day is done, Gone the sun, From the sky, God is nigh.

The prayer made him feel a little bit better, thought it probably didn't do anything for the kid. Groaned, hugged himself again, finally slept.

Chapter 30

Still suffering from his fight with Jack Flashhardt, Yassar Ahmoud popped three aspirins supplied by the polite steward, an old bald-headed black man from the Sudan. He drained his second glass of water as the sleek Citation jet turned onto short final for the airstrip at Rama Razi's home base, Chanbahar, in Baluchistan, a province of southeastern Iran. The Gulf of Oman's blue waters appeared under the wing as the white jet straightened out, dropped to the surface.

Ahmoud checked his watch—it was almost lunchtime—fastened his seatbelt. He felt nothing when the jet hit the runway, the rollout was smooth. When the engines stopped, Ahmoud loosed the seatbelt, ignored the smiling British pilot. He exited the small jet, saw a white Ford Expedition waiting just meters away. A bearded driver, wearing a typical Iranian wool cap, opened the door for Ahmoud. He hurried to escape the heat.

After a rapid drive through alluvial fan wastelands, which sustained no trees, no bushes, no flowers, no grass or weeds, the Expedition topped a rise and Ahmoud saw a large white steel warehouse on a bluff hanging over the Gulf of Oman. It looked like a drinking cup with no handle. For a second, he wondered whether he would ever leave this desolation alive. He climbed out of the Expedition into the blast furnace air, walked the few steps to the warehouse. The driver, who had hustled around and preceded him, opened the door.

Inside, the air-conditioned atmosphere was cold, stale. Ahmoud saw a Bedouin tent, about fifteen meters by twenty meters, placed on a wood platform. The sides were rolled up, and when Ahmoud stepped inside, he saw Rama Razi sprawled on a double king-size bed. Two women sat on a rug in front of the bed. One played an oud—a pear-shaped lute, the other played a mijwiz—a

Lebanese flute. The plaintive music accented Ahmoud's nervous anticipation.

Rama, a very handsome man with grey eyes, black curly hair, wore a black aba—a loose Arabian robe—over a white shirt. On his massive head was a red and white ghutra—an Arabian headscarf—tied up with an agal cord fashioned of traditional goat hair. In his lap, he balanced a half-empty plate of mansaf, consisting of stewed lamb on a bed of rice and bread.

"Saddam, it's so good to see you," Rama's voice boomed over the haunting background music. "You look so handsome." Ahmoud had chosen a pressed khaki uniform with no insignia or rank displayed, black boots, a black beret and a red scarf around his neck. Rama pointed at his mansaf.
"Help yourself, friend."

Ahmoud greeted Rama, scooped a handful of mansaf sprinkled with pine nuts and ate. It smelled stale, was rancid. He forced himself to chew, then looked at Rama's body. Rama had been big when attending Cairo University, but now he looked twice as large.

"Yes, my friend, I have grown," Rama said proudly when he noted Ahmoud's startled gaze. "Three hundred ten kilograms. Almost seven hundred English pounds." He stuffed a handful of the vile food into his mouth, excess spilled on the giant bed. He motioned for the musicians to leave with the wave of a huge hand. They scurried behind the pleated curtains that isolated the men's part of the tent.

"But why?" Ahmoud asked. A woman approached with a platter carrying Bedouin coffee in tiny white cups. She was beautiful, with huge brown eyes visible over her veil.

"Yes, my friend, women are wonderful. But to eat—ahh, that is the greatest pleasure." Rama leaned forward. "But tell me, I am eager to know what you have."

Ahmoud sipped the bitter coffee. "The Americans lost a biological bomb not too long ago. A plane crash. A Tajik soldier found it. I now have possession of it. I want to transport it to America and decimate a city. I——-”

“Slow down, Ahmoud. Why? You’ll only stir up a hornet’s nest. The
Americans will go crazy——-”

“I want to show them that they can suffer as the Muslim world has agonized at the hands of the Colonialist powers.”

Rama tossed the empty mansef plate onto the bed, picked up a coffee. He glanced, but Ahmoud held his upside down, shook it, Arab fashion, showing he wanted no more. Rama belched, wiped crumbs off his chin.
“Are you committed to this course?”

“Look, Razzle. We saw how much anguish the Twin Towers cost
America. Just two buildings——-”

“Damned big buildings!” Rama exclaimed.

“American has buildings—cities to spare. But a biological attack—one that could be duplicated many times over, will shake America to its core.
That’s what I want. Fear in the streets.”

“It’s too big, Saddam,” Rama shook his head. “I can’t risk my life, profitable and easy as it is. I’m not a lost Bedouin looking for an oasis in the sand dunes.”

“Money. That’s all I need. You’ll never be touched by a hint of scandal.” Ahmoud looked at the huge blob of blubber Rama had turned himself into, quickly added, “You’ll be the colossus of Arabia after America is humbled and it’s safe to reveal yourself.”

“I like that, I must admit,” Rama smiled. “Let me talk discretely— mind you—through sufficient intermediaries, to certain Americans. If they will support this endeavor, so will I.”

“The Americans! Are you crazy?”

Rama raised a finger. “We won’t tell them the true target or who we are. But we must have American approval at some level, or

we'll never transport a bomb like yours out of Asia. We'll propose a false target. Misdirection, that's the Arab way. Blame Muhammad, the Pedophile Prophet. He was the master of deception. We'll enlist the Americans to further your cause. Then we'll subvert it." Rama poked at the empty plate.
"And you possess the bomb?"

"I have it hidden in a cave in the Hindu Kush. All I need is time and money to assemble a new force, and a good sandstorm to hide our efforts. But the Americans are searching. I'm running out of time." He cursed to himself, thought about Jack Flashhardt. He prayed the man was re-captured or dead.

Chapter 31

Jack tried to sleep but jumped to wakefulness at every sound in the Afghan forest. Finally relaxed at sunrise, ignored cawing crows circling overhead, slept for several hours. Awoke just before noon, noticed a cluster of mushrooms that looked just like the morel mushrooms his aunt used to collect in Montana forests. Sighed when he thought of the taste of morels sautéed in sherry, fresh cream, sizzling in home-churned creamery butter. Picked one mushroom to test it. Sniffed—it had no unusual smell. His stomach growled—he took one bite, spit—it was bitter, foul tasting. He stood, walked for an hour, looked for anything that appeared edible. Reached a stream, followed it, saw no fish. Ducks were common but he could do nothing without the lost Makarov pistol.

When he encountered a woodcutting area, he spotted a number of men a quarter-mile upstream, heading his way. Logs were lying about, he pulled a long, flexible vine out of a tree, quickly lashed two eight-foot-long, dead logs together to make a raft. Each log was about a foot in diameter. They were very light. He found a solid, six-foot pole.

Heard men approach from the left bank. Dragged the makeshift raft to the water, threw himself in the mountain stream. The cold, onrushing water quickly sped him downstream. Raft spun around, slammed into a rock, skidded off, kept moving. He was able to use the pole to navigate the jumping white water rapids. Heard a shout, flashed by an astonished woodcutter who gaped at the blond white man. The man jumped into the water, but he was safely past.

Glanced ahead, saw two men wade into the ten-foot-wide flow to stop him—raised his staff, yelled, bowled them over as they grabbed for the passing raft. Rounded a bend, floated down a straight stretch of quiet water. Slid off a wooden sluice—a giant trough built to pass timber over a waterfall. End of the sluice was ten feet above a pool. He flew through the air, splashed into the water. An armed man gaped at him in astonishment. The pool stopped his progress, gave the bearded man time to aim, fire his rifle.

Chips of wood flew, rounds zinged past his ear. He threw himself off the raft, sank to the bottom of the frigid water. Expelled air from his lungs.

Swam upstream in the slow-flowing, deep waters. Under the wood plank sluice, stood until his head was out of the water. The man, with his back to the structure, was looking for him to exit the downstream end of the murky pool. Ducked underwater, shed his haversack, grabbed a fist-sized rock off the bottom, held onto bottom grass. Waited for a long minute, eased his head out of the water, gulped air.

The man still watched the downstream end of the pool as Jack drifted closer. He rose out of the water, shouted, hit the man in the back with the stone. Guy thought he was shot. Screamed in terror, dropped his rifle, ran into the forest. Jack picked up the SKS rifle, grabbed the tumbling haversack, ran towards his raft, which was stuck against rocks. Threw himself on the tiny raft. It spun, he used the rifle butt to fend off rocks.

A half hour later, he was safely beyond the woodcutters. Decided to leave the raft.

Rolled off, smashed through the tangled undergrowth, entered the thick forest, numb from the cold waters. Glanced at the sky: totally overcast.

Gathered dry twigs, used the Bic lighter, made a small fire, fed it with dead sticks until he was warm and dry.

Physically comfortable, he realized he was growing nauseated, dizzy, was suffering from severe stomach cramps. Tried to sleep, but the cramps kept him awake, finally he dozed off. Much later, he awoke, tried to ignore the aches, pains in his entire body. Pulled out the cell, called his dad in Menlo Park. "Dad," he greeted when Bill Flashhardt answered. "It's me."

Bill sounded sober, crisp, clear-headed. "Jackson! It's great to hear you. Where are you? How are you?"

"Still in Afgoneistan, Dad. Tried to get out but some Chinamen stopped me. They… I was being guided by Kim. He was a good kid and he died… I got away, Dad. But they killed Kim—you know, the kid in the book. It was up in a high pass to Pakistan. I hadda turn back—didn't have a climbing permit."

"I'm so sorry, Jack. I love you. Sorry about your son not making the team. Everything's going to be alright. Little League baseball season's almost here—we'll make sure he tries out. Hang in there. We'll get you out —you'll see. I called the Defense Department. I demanded they raise your combat pay."

"Thanks, Dad. Gotta go now. Sick—nothing serious, don't worry. Just have the cramps, dizziness. Love you." He disconnected and called Ashley.
When she answered, he said, "Hey, babe, it's me."

"Jack! I'm so glad to hear you. Your dad called and told me you'd been transferred to the Taliban. Are you okay? Are you safe? Where are you?" Her voice was so sweet, so concerned. He felt his throat constrict, he forgot his nausea.

"I'm okay, miss you. Wanna go to the Oasis, drink a Sierra?"

"I miss you, Jack. A lot. I wish we hadn't argued. I… Jack, I've been… I've been wrong. And I'm so sorry about our son."

"How'd you know, Ashley?"

"It was on the six o'clock news. Jack, where are you?"

"I'm in Afgoneistan. I was with Kim when it happened. I got him killed. I deserted him. He died because of me. I feel so—"

"Jack, how could you? Now you've lost our son. I've had it with you.
I'm calling Child Protective Services. You're so damned irresponsible!"

"Look, babe…" The phone was dead. He shut his eyes, pictured the beautiful girl. Gorgeous, unattainable.

He turned the cell phone off, put it back in the pack. Cramps, dizziness washed over his body. He looked around. The trees in the forest seemed to wave and bend, dance and moan. A cold rain began to fall. He curled into a ball, threw up bile. After long moments of dry heaves, he stood, staggered through the woods, looked for the stream. He saw a structure in a thick clump of cedars, headed for it.

Constructed of hewn-granite blocks, with no decorations or door— only a ten foot by four foot opening. Overcome by dizziness, fell to his knees in front of the stone building. Dragged himself across the wet ground, into the temple.

Floors, walls, were constructed of brown sandstone. A black marble altar shaped like an elongated cube sat against the back wall of the oneroomed structure, on it sat a silent monk wearing a crimson robe. The monk was middle-aged in appearance, had a shaved head and face, stared without acknowledging Jack. Exhausted by his illness, he sank prone, slept.

Chapter 32

Awakened during the night with a raging thirst. Jack looked around, saw the monk. The only inhabitant of the temple pointed at a pitcher against the wall. Jack crawled to the pitcher on his hands and knees, drank. He felt too weak to stand, but the water was delicious.

"You feel pain." Guy looked, sounded like the same monk he had encountered in the snowy temple above Shangri-la. "We are born in pain, live with pain, die with pain. Such the world is. Pain makes you stronger.
And Dragon God Baal needs a strong partner."

Jack gagged, threw up water. "Pain'll make me stronger? I'd rather lift weights."

"Death is a cessation of pain. Do you seek it?"

Wiped his face. "No… settle for some aspirin. Death seems… I don't know, a bit much."

"Transcend your pain. You can overcome pain. Watch my finger, listen to my words. If you concentrate, pain will be as nothing forevermore."

"Works in the movies, but I don't think watching you wave a pinkie is gonna do it."

"You are in a vortex, it will help you concentrate."

"What's that?"

"A vortex is a power point on the earth's surface. The planet's energy flows forth at a vortex. It travels through you as we speak. This temple is on a small vortex, unlike Shangri-la, where the entire valley floor is a vortex.
The current will help you. Think and it will be so forevermore."

The monk moved the finger back and forth. Jack watched the gestures for long minutes. Guy hummed a meaningless tune. Never would make the Top Forty charts, but semi-entrancing. He shook his head and looked around. Place was as bare as a prison cell. He thought of Amy's body, twisting at the end of her pants, a trail of ants up her body like they were climbing a tree trunk. Amy of Iowa, dead in an Afghan sewer. He shook his head again. The monk noticed his movements, stopped. "You must fight your way to the Dragon God's egg. Prove yourself." The monk stood, assumed a fighting stance. "Fight me. Then, fight your enemies. It'll bring you clarity, then more will be revealed to you."

"Screw clarity and revelations. Screw fighting you or anybody. I'd rather have a helicopter ride home."

"To end your struggle would be sinful. You must fulfill your dharma as a kshatriya—a member of the warrior caste."

"Heard that before. Some other dude in the mountains. Don't want to kill anybody. I'm sick of it. By the way, can you do something for an upset stomach?"

"Remember, the cycle of life: birth, death, rebirth. When you kill a foe, you only kill the body—that is irrelevant. If you do not kill your opponents, you will incur sin."

"Sin's good. I'll take sin over killing."

The monk looked exasperated. "If that is all you want, go— you shall have it." He gestured like he was shooing a pesky fly.

"Okay, but can I get a couple of tacos to go?" The monk shook his head in dismay. Jack turned and crawled out of the temple.

The sky was overcast, a wind blew out of the north. Still dizzy, he cautiously worked his way back to the mountain stream, dropped his pack, parka, crawled forward and drank water. Immediately threw up. His head pounded, his stomach cramped. He doused his head in the water, held it under for long seconds. Lifted his head, saw the white tiger lying next to his pack.

Felt a flush of hope—knew at once it was his companion from higher in the Hindu Kush mountains. He crouched on a boulder, said, "If I'm not imagining you, Tigger, what now? Hey, I didn't thank you for not eating me back there. You like the deer?" The tiger growled as though he understood, was accepting the thanks. Alternatively, he growled as though he was getting ready to pull him off the rock and eat him.

Jack carefully drew nearer, "I didn't come this far to be a substitute for ham and eggs. So why don't you tell me what the hell's going on? I can't outrun you, I can't outfight you, I can't shoot you—Mo Poo mislaid my gun." The tiger regarded him, licked its front right paw.

"We've gotta communicate a little better. I'm sitting here, scared shitless, you're busy chewing your toenails." The tiger arched its neck, roared. Jack jumped, lost his balance, fell in the icy water. When he came up, the tiger was standing. He pulled himself back onto the boulder, the tiger stretched its front legs out, yawned just like a barn cat.

"Okay, so thanks for guarding my pack. Can I put my parka on now? I hate breakfast without clothes. Especially if I'm gonna be breakfast." The tiger growled, licked its foot again.

He swallowed nausea, fought off dizziness. "What's wrong with your toes?" The tiger growled.

After a minute, he edged closer until he could see the foot clearly. He immediately noticed a bamboo shard protruding about two inches through the top of the paw. "Holy shit! No wonder you're limping!" He looked into the tiger's eyes. "You want me to fix it." He slid closer, inch by inch. Slowly picked up the paw, twisted it over. Shard was flush with the bottom of the foot. Turned the paw back, grasped the shard—could not pull it through. Tiger trembled, growled. Breath was hot, foul.

"Okay, Tigger, here goes. Remember, I don't need a scalp massage." He bent down, bit into the shard. Pulled his head back, eased the bamboo through the foot, bit down farther, pulled again. The tiger emitted a shriek that made his head ring with pain. Sat back, spit the bloody, puss-covered bamboo splinter out of his mouth, vomited blood, puss, stream water. Tried to pick up the paw, but the cat jerked his foot away.

"You're gonna be okay, big guy." He heaved a sigh of relief, backed away. "But I recommend you change your mouthwash. You've got serious halitosis."

"Yeah, I know," Tigger responded. "But did ya ever try to hold a toothbrush with a paw? Anyway, you're a piece of work, yourself. Follow me." Tigger retreated. Jack threw up more water. Shakily, he stood, endured waves of dizziness. Knew he had to keep moving, grabbed his parka, pack, followed. Wondered where the animal was going, wondered how it had learned to talk.

Chapter 33

Jack staggered into the Afghan village: when yelling children surrounded him, he ignored their presence. He would have continued plodding mindlessly through the village if he hadn't been stopped by two hardlooking, battle-scarred men, who stared, jumped up and restrained him. He asked for the closest Rexall drugstore. The men held his elbows, guided him to a mudbrick house. They called out. A young woman answered, stepped outside.

"Hey, how's it goin'?"

"Hello," the girl greeted him. "Who're you?"

"Hugh Conway. I'm on my way to Shangri-la."

The girl spoke to the two men, then commanded, "Come inside. I'm Say Wen." She was short, chubby, but had a wonderful smile, pretty eyes under black bangs.

"Okay, when."

Confused, Say Wen said nothing. He thought of food and asked, "Can I order something to eat? I could go for a couple of tacos. I got venison in my pack but no tortillas or salsa. An' Tigger's hungry, too."

Say Wen looked for a companion, saw nobody, went into the house. The men followed, guided him to a pile of rugs. A metal stove in the corner of the room threw off heat. "I guess you seat yourself around here," he said after he flopped down on the pile. "Bring me a menu, please."

Say Wen took a big metal cup from a shelf, scooped stew from a pot on the old coalburning stove, gave it to him: it was a chicken noodle, vegetable mixture. Bits of fiery hot red peppers contributed to the taste, the odors were great. He sipped, burned his mouth, blew on the soup. He looked around, noticed that a small boy had also received a cup. The boy, dressed in ragged but clean pants, a

sweatshirt that had the word Singapore printed across the front, ate as eagerly as Jack. He smiled back at the
American. "Sea' y'self." He laughed, added, "I'm Kim."

He stared at the boy. "Thank God, you're alright, Kim. I thought I lost you in the Great Game—"

"How do you know Milady's son?" Say Wen asked from a table where she had sat. "You've mistaken him for someone."
Elated, then dismayed, he asked, "Where'd you learn to speak English,
Say Wen?"

The girl smiled. "I was a soldier's… friend in Karachi for one year, then I back home."

"Friend." He thought for a moment, figured it out. "You were a hooker," he paused, blew on the stew, gulped it down. Suddenly, he leaned over, threw up the food all over the floor.

"Who the hell're you?" A tall, lean white man stood in the doorway, staring at him. He held a large black revolver, aimed at Jack. He spoke with a British accent, had long blond hair that hung over the collar of his khaki shirt, had the reddish skin of a pale man exposed to a great deal of sun. A patch on his left eye. Jack swallowed, wiped his chin. "Hello, Dickey. You forgot already? I'm the American. Jack Flashhardt. What happened to your eye?"

"Flashman? What're you doing here?"

"No, it's Flashhardt." He held up three fingers. "With two Hs. Say, you don't seem too friendly today." He glanced at the revolver. It looked like a huge Colt .45 with an eight-inch barrel. "I've escaped from a prison up north. Trying to get back to Shangri-la to rescue you. How could you forget me?"

"You're the bloody Yank jailbird! The Marine. What'd you do—get caught snatching some mullah's drawers? Haw, haw!"

He shook his head and looked closer. Man's voice sounded too harsh to be Dickey. And he was older. Much older. Confused, Jack looked down at his vomited stew, wondered if it would be okay to lick it up. Leaned over towards the mess, little Kim jumped up, restrained him, pushed against his ribs.

The white guy appeared very British, with a trimmed mustache, a clean-shaven jaw. Wore military pants, polished black leather boots.
Smiled, holstered his revolver, stuck out a hand as he crossed the room.

"Sorry, just amazed to have a Yank drop in on me. Thought you were a bloody al Qaida or Russian. I'm Robert Nayes Arses. I'm a Brit. SAS, actually." Arses' accent, confident air revealed an expensive public school background in England.

He stood, handed his empty bowl to Say Wen, grasped the Englishman's hand. "Pleased to meet you. I confused you with your brother.
I met Dickey not long ago. I'm going to get him."

Robert Arses stared at him with his good eye, astonished by his words. "You're out of your head, lad. I don't have a brother. Dickey died ages ago. You're sick. And that stew was way too rich for your tummy. Come over to my hooch for slingers—hard tack, a spot of tea. All your stomach can take right now. And some meddies."

Jack thanked Say Wen, looked regretfully at the stew splattered across the wood floor. Noticing his glance, Kim rose and moved in front of the vomit. Jack and Arses, trailed by Kim and Say Wen, walked to a house next to a rushing stream. They climbed steps to a porch, sat on chairs made from bamboo. Say Wen went inside to prepare tea; the young boy brushed black hair out of his eyes, squatted on the ground, watched the two white men above him.

Robert asked, "How'd you get caught up in a Talib snare? Bit far off the high seas for a Marine, aye?"

Jack looked at the windmill palm grove a few yards away, the everpresent, steep mountains beyond. The palm fronds clicked, clattered together like rattling castanets. "Got an Army friend that was captured by the Taliban in Hunza. They were gonna kill him for eating their buddies' eyes. I helped some of his friends rescue him. But I took a blow to the head and I woke up in a bamboo cage, being transported north by Dumbo the Elephant! Guess he escaped Disneyland. Then I followed my talking tiger pal here." He rubbed the healing scar on his head. It was still tender.

"Good God!" The Englishman accepted a mug of tea from Say Wen.

"The lash-up at Papa Pier's farm."

Say Wen handed Jack a cup. He sipped the green tea. It was hot, fragrant, soothing—tasted wonderful. "Yes," he admitted. "You said the Yank. So you knew about me. Probably heard of my first ascent in Shangrila. Me and this big Chinese guy, Mo Poo, climbed together."

"You're making no sense, lad." Arses glanced at his tea. "Sorry, out of cream—well, no refrigeration, you know. Shot the milkman for delivering sour milk. Haw, haw! No foie gras, either. And yes, the word is out on you."

I talked to a friend in Gilgit on shortwave. Major Lialot Soongoon. He told me the whole tale. Papa Pier an' I go way back. Heard he was grateful, though. Papa considered the whole thing to be a mess. And you solved it by extracting your nigger friend. Now, the Talib are frantically searching for you."

"What are you doing out here in the middle of Kansastan?"

Arses grinned slyly. "Kafirstan, actually. Oh, this, a bit of that. Training these blokes how to kill Talibs. The land and people get under your skin. And I've done a bit of treasure hunting. Looking for a treasure Alexander supposedly stole from the Chinese Emperor, then lost on the way back to Greece. A solid gold dragon with emerald armour." Arses looked up with a piercing gaze, "Heard about the spot of… cannibalism. The wog was involved. Bit rough, what?" The Englishman leaned forward, gestured for more tea. "You need rest. You're sick, lad. You were living off the land. You must've eaten something bad. Eat any plants, rotten meat?"

He smiled. "Yes, just the other day. Aunt Hannah served up morel mushrooms in the forest—no butter, though. Usually, she sautés the mushrooms in butter."

"That explains it, lad. Never eat mushrooms in these mountains. Got a deadly poisonous bacteria. I'm surprised you're alive. Shoulda killed you. Off your rocker, lad, but don't worry, we'll fix you up." He instructed Say Wen to get antibiotics out of a medical bag. She gave him several pills. "Take these. And tomorrow, if you've come to your senses, you'll tell me why you think you know my older brother. You musta stumbled on an old SAS report. Confused your mind. You see, he disappeared in these parts before you were born."

He helped Jack to his feet, led him inside. Say Wen put him on a bed in a small bedroom, undressed him, covered him with a down comforter. He smiled. "Goodnight, Penel. Hey, your hair's not blonde—did you dye it?"

Chapter 34

Jack awoke with a clear head, no nausea, in a room with mudbrick walls, a wood floor covered by worn Afghan rugs. The sun, shining through a window, had been up for a couple hours. A very tall young woman, looked to be just under six feet, stood by his bed. When he looked at her, he realized he was still messed up in the head, because he saw blue, green, white stripes painted across her entire face, side to side. She wore normallooking, but tight-fitting cammies, which showed off a great figure. Her black hair was long, straight, full. But her intense brown eyes were surrounded by the bizarre war paint. Her beauty was marred by a ragged scar on her neck, curling up to her right jaw like a baby snake. Her skin was almost expensive car black.

"Hey, I'm Jack."

"I'm Milady," the girl had a friendly voice with the same cultured English accent as Robert Arses. She wore a pistol on a belt, counterweighted by a big knife on the other hip.

"So you're not a bad make-up dream?"

Milady, about eighteen to twenty years old, with flawless skin, lush lips, frowned, stretched. "Do I look like a bad dream?"

"No, you look gorgeous. It's just the paint job—Earl Scheib have a local special?"

"I'm a warrior princess."

"Hey, works for me. I'm sort of a pacifist, but each to his—er, her own. You wanna lay waste, I say get it on."

"Say Wen said you can have thin gruel. Maybe some fruit." Milady lifted the comforter, cast her eyes over his naked body, giggled. "Say Wen did undress you! You're as skinny as she says." He grabbed the comforter, covered himself. "Yeah, well, I've been on the Taliban diet. I'm gonna develop it and sell it as a weight-loss plan when I get home. I'll make millions."

"We could fatten you up," Milady said with a coy tone in her voice. She wrinkled her nose, frowned. "But you smell worse than a carrion crow's leavings. There's a barrel shower behind the house—use it." She turned, left the room. He stared at her saucy walk—accented by her muscular, jutting rear.

Stood, felt weak. Wrapped the comforter around his body, wandered through the starkly furnished house until he found the back door. Outside, he took a shower under frigid water from a raised, fifty-five gallon Avgas barrel with a spigot. Groaning, he scrubbed with homemade lye soap he discovered on a wood plank next to the shower, wondered whether he would ever take a hot shower again. Finished, he grabbed the comforter, hurried inside.

Milady was gone. Stuck his head out the doorway; a watching little girl ran off. "Hey," he called, but she disappeared around the corner of a house.

A few moments later, young Kim arrived with his BDUs, damp but clean, smelling of a strong lye soap that again reminded him of the odors of kid's clothes back on the Reservation in Montana. Jack smiled, accepted the mended fatigues. Shivering, he went back inside the house, and while he dressed, Kim sat by the door, watched for a moment, ran away—returned balancing a big cup of weak soup.

Jack thought of Kim—the boy that had died on the mountain pass. The first little girl arrived, proudly bearing a tray with a teapot, a cup, three pills. The green tea was hot, refreshing. He sat down in the doorway, watched smiling villagers go about their early morning affairs. Reflected on his change in circumstances in the last few days: he had gone from prison to freedom, from starvation to being waited on like a prince. Poor Amy. Poor Kim.

Two hours later, Robert Arses and Say Wen walked up, entered the dwelling, sat at a knocked-together wood table. The girl put down a bowl of watery chicken soup. Arses asked, "Feel better?"

"Dude, I feel much better. I could eat a horse, though."

Arses grinned. "Maybe later."

"Who're these people?" He sipped the soup, it tasted great.

"Kafirs. They're one of many small ethnic groups scattered around this part of the land, which is called Kafirstan," Arses said. "They were pushed into the mountains along the Pakistan border last century. Claim to be descendants of Alexander the Great. Muslims call 'em Kafirs—which means Infidels—because they're animists. The name is considered a pejorative by some."

"Seems like old Alexander was a pretty horny guy. Half the population claims they're his kinfolk."

Arses laughed. "Too bloody right." His face grew serious. "Tell me why you mentioned my dead brother, Dickey. What kind of sick joke was that?"

Jack picked up the brown ceramic bowl, poured the soup in his mouth. He looked around for a clear place to throw up in case he felt an urge. "No joke. I met your brother—he looks like you, but younger—out west of Gilgit. I was jumping north of Gilgit and a fierce updraft carried me over the peaks to the west."

"Dickey went missing when I was ten," Arses mused. His face had a sad, inward look.

Jack looked up. "He was trapped in a remote valley, inhabitants call it Shangri-la. The Russians—I mean the Soviets—blew up the tunnel access into the valley years ago. He says no one can fly in because of peculiar wind shears in the heights, and he thought no one can climb out because of avalanche danger."

"Impossible! Shangri-la is supposed to be in the Himalayas."

"Said he was from Nottingham. Went to Oxford—I can't remember the college. Something like steak sauce, I think. But he graduated or whatever you English do—in 1977." He looked at Arses. The man's blue eye was intelligent looking. "Anyway, the Hindu Kush and the Himalayas are asshole to belly button."

"My God! Worcestershire sauce. You're talking about Worcester College of Oxford University." Robert leaned forward, excited. "You're telling the truth."

"I imagine you'd like to get him out," Jack observed.

"The mountains west of Gilgit. Bloody rough country," Arses said, stunned by the revelation. "My brother! Doesn't seem possible! How'd you get out? Why didn't he come with you?"

"I'm a mountaineer—left in a hurry. Had some trouble—no time to guide tourists. But I could get in there with a little bit of luck and good weather—there's no pass to speak of. It was over twenty thousand feet where I crossed over the divide to Gilgit. Nothing to sneeze at, but doable, if you know avalanche and crevasse country." He held up the bowl. Say Wen took it, left.

"My brother, Dickey. A shame the guv'nor isn't alive. He missed his eldest something dreadful. Never was the same."

"Well, get ready for a shock. Dickey looks like a teenager. Never gets sick. Claims they live for centuries in Shangri-la. Just like it says in Lost
Horizon."

Agitated, Arses stood, walked around the room. "They live long in these mountains. Good thing, for they kill each other at a bloody frightful clip."

"I was climbing in the Caucus Mountains a couple years ago," Jack observed. "My guide claimed his grandfather died in a hunting accident at age one hundred seventy five. Bragged the old guy fought in The Great
War. I asked, 'You mean WWI?' But he meant the War of 1812!"

Say Wen returned with a platter of chapatti bread, another bowl of soup. He enjoyed it—he had been too hungry to taste the first bowl.

Arses said, "Good show escaping. How'd you manage?"

"Blinded by a hit to the head. During the rescue of my buddy, Omar Johnson. My eyesight came back as the swelling went down.

I kept it a secret and they thought I was still helpless. I practically walked out of there." Pounding Ahmoud against the wall. "There was an American girl.

She… died. Amy Anderson. Pass that on if I don't…"

Robert put his hand on Jack's shoulder, "You made it this far. You're a bloody tough lad. You'll make it out, don't worry. We'll get you back to

Packystan."

"What's the story on the painted lady? I thought I was still outta my head when I saw her in that getup."

Arses grinned. "I noticed Milady come out with her war paint on— wanted to impress you. Say Wen had rattled on about your looks. But

Milady's some fighter, for a kid. Widow, actually. Young Kim is her son. Lost her husband a year ago. Kim took it hard, losing his daddy. Taliban.

She hates 'em."

"I thought we knocked most of the Taliban. Sure seems to be a lot around."

"They're like cockroaches. Scurry away, survive. And the madrasas keep educating new recruits faster than anybody can kill 'em. Bloody quandary, that. Dollars can't outweigh religion when it comes to winning hearts and minds." Arses rose to leave and said, "Rest, lad. We'll leave for headquarters tomorrow. Ride?"

"Born in Montana—no problem. How far we going?"

"We'll camp on the trail. We'll reach headquarters by noon the next day—assuming we avoid trouble. Then we'll get you home. I have a new high frequency PRC 138. I could talk to the Queen in her bedroom about her dirty laundry if I bloody wanted." Arses left, called for Say Wen to wait. He watched the Brit leave. Wondered what was meant by "—-assuming we avoid trouble." Went to his pack, pulled out the cell phone. He remembered calling his dad, then Ashley. She had said she missed him. Tried to turn it on, but noticed condensation, rust inside the screen. Reflected, remembered floating down a stream. Tried to recall whether the float had been before or after the calls.

Before. It was before the calls. That means this phone was dead. I never called Dad. Never spoke with Ashley. All in my head. She never said she missed me. I imagined the whole thing. Damn! Eating and talk had exhausted him. Realized he had traveled on will alone. He napped all afternoon.

Early evening, after another bowl of delivered soup, he saw movement at the door, recognized Milady. No war paint. "You smell better," she said, approaching and sniffing his skin. Looked up at him with a challenging gaze. Caught her lip in her teeth, moved closer.

He inhaled, smelled a sweet, natural odor. It was lovely. Couldn't resist her obvious intention, pulled her against his body, kissed her. She responded with unbelievable passion for a few seconds, pulled away, looked at him. "Jack Flashhardt, where've you been all my life?" She pulled his head, kissed him. She led him to the low bed, sank onto it, drew him down. She was strong. Wrapped her arms, legs around him. Ripped at his clothes, tore her own away.

He had a flash of China Bitch—fear: pushed it out of his mind. Ashley —guilt: concentrated on Milady. God! Quit thinking. Long, thick, black hair. Sweet, panting breath, arms like rocks, rear and back like slabs of time-frozen lava. Lips swallowing him with passionate kisses, wonderful breasts pushed against his chest. Hot interior. Incredible passion. Coming together hard, soft, fast, slow-rocking. Rolling, falling, laughing, giggling, panting. Kissing, sleep.

Jack woke when someone crawled into bed, snuggled between them. Another woman? A man? It was a child.

Arses' words: Widow, actually. Young Kim is her son. Lost her husband a year ago. Kim took it hard, losing his daddy.

Oh Jeez, he thought. I can't take this. She wants a man in her life, the kid wants a dad. Crawls in bed with us. Too much. He fell asleep.

Chapter 35

Mother and son were gone when Jack awoke in the late morning. Breakfast was a rich mutton and vegetable stew, waiting just inside the door. On a napkin were three antibiotic capsules. He ate the cold stew while sitting on the porch. The sun was shining, the sky was cloudless. He still felt upset about what had happened the night before with the young boy. Chalked it up as another experience—hoped the boy wasn't scarred by the event.

Finished, he grabbed the last piece of chapatti bread, walked through the village, looked for Robert Arses in the village center. Realized he felt great, physically and emotionally.

The Englishman was directing two young men who were saddling three horses. He smiled at Jack, pointed at a stocky Turkmen roan. "That's yours, lad. He rides easy. Wasn't sure of your abilities."

Milady strutted up, mounted the long-legged black stallion with an athletic, show-off leap. Arses climbed on a large palomino gelding. Each had a rifle slung over a shoulder. Arses wore a pith helmet, Milady had donned a puggaree—a pith helmet wrapped in pure white linen that was a startling contrast against her dark skin. She wore a semi-auto pistol on each hip. Arses tossed him a worn baseball cap with a Havelock—a
cloth cap cover that hung on the back to protect the neck. He checked the saddle—it looked similar to an American western saddle, except for an elaborate wooden saddle horn. The saddle blanket was highly decorated with an intricate weave of red colors. Bridle was made of a hemp rope.

Arses gave him a small rifle, a canvas bandolier.

He checked the load on the Lee-Enfield jungle carbine—he was unfamiliar with it, but the action seemed simple. It had a MARK

V stamped on the barrel, a leather sling. He accepted a belt with a beat-up, holstered Colt .45 semi-auto pistol from Milady.

"All set, lad? It's noon—time to be off. Just a half day today."

He glanced at Milady—she was exchanging a smile with Say Wen.

Her son ran up, she reached down, pulled him up, hugged him and kissed him. The boy glanced at Jack, smiled and waved as he was released by his mother.

Arses kicked his horse, the other two followed.

An hour before sunset, Jack sat on a rock in their evening camp, watched two pheasants walk through the meadow. Suddenly, the male, a beautiful bird with a reddish brown body, an iridescent dark green head and neck, a red face, a neck ringed with a white band, raised his head and looked to the west. A moment later, Jack heard the distant sound of a diesel engine, clanking treads. Arses, gathering dead wood for a fire, dropped his load and joined him. "It's a tank or APC."

"American?"

"No chance. American tanks don't wander about in the Afghan bush. Not without air support and ground troops. Too bloody vulnerable. Let's have a look."

Milady joined the two—they hiked through a poplar grove, cautiously skirted a grassy meadow. Clanking sounds from treads accompanied the roars of a diesel engine as they drew nearer. Arses headed up a ridgeline; soon the three crawled to a rocky crest, looked down at the road. Jack felt an unfamiliar weakness.

"It's an old Soviet T-55A," Arses whispered. "Talibs, most likely. Can't imagine what it's doin' out here."

"It blocks our path, Robert," Milady whispered with a disgusted tone. "That's what it's doing."

"Can we go around?" Jack asked. He glanced at the cliffs.

"Not bloody likely," Arses replied. "Canyon's too narrow. They're settlin' in for the night. Let's go back to camp." Back at the horse camp, Arses said, "We'll have to take it out. Best time would be sunrise."

"Can't we hide and let it go by?"

"Too risky. If they find us, we'll be on the defensive, this canyon's too narrow." He put out the small fire.

"Can we attack it at night?"

"They've the advantage after dark. The T-55A has an infrared searchlight. They're nervous at night. A guard'd see us comin'."

"We can't take on a tank!" Jack protested, fear rising in his throat. "The Poles tried it in 1939. Horses didn't work."

Arses smiled, sat down on a log. "Ah, but they weren't up against the Soviet T-55A. It has several design limitations that'll work for us. One, you can barely depress its upward-pointing cannon. Two, it has no forward machinegun." He smiled again. "We'll come out of the sunrise, drop a handful of M67 frag grenades down their maw an' it'll be beddies for the
Talib tank."

"I guess I could, like, make breakfast while you two're out remodeling the tank," Jack half-joked. Arses, Milady both stood, stared sharply.

"Just kidding, guys. I can't wait to play in the Taliban sandbox. I've been hoping all my life to take on a heavily-armored Russian tank with only a horse and firecrackers. Hey, I'll be the first American to conduct a cavalry charge since Black Jack Pershing invaded Mexico back in 1916."

Later, wrapped in a musty sleeping bag, he tossed most of the night, visions of the upcoming battle plagued his mind. He saw no way out of the action, dreaded its outcome.

An hour before sunrise, Arses shook him awake. "Let's go, lad. Off your bum. Milady has already saddled the horses. Stow your gear. We won't be comin' back this way." He looked around, hoped

Arses was right. "Audaces fortuna juvat: Fortune favors the bold," he muttered.

Startled, Arses stood, "A scholar warrior—you're a piece of work, young Jack. Now, let's try our luck with the T-55. It's what we're here for, idn't it?"

Chapter 36

Horses panting and their own breathing visible as the skies began to lighten behind the three attackers. Arses had led Jack and Milady through the forest to the edge of the meadow, across from the T-55. Arses studied the mountains behind them, turned his head so he could see side to side with his good eye. "The sun'll rise in a minute or so. When it does, the inside tankers should pop their hatch. Then we'll ride out of the sunrise. Milady, you'll watch for any shooters on the flanks. Jack, put your reins in your teeth, your pistol in one hand, grenade in the other. Pull the pin now. When you near the tank, toss it down the front hatch. I'll do the same down the rear opening. Then ride on to the west." A metallic slam interrupted him. "There they are. Let's ride."

"Wait," Jack said under his breath. "I'm not ready. Another cup of tea, a cigarette. Something."

Arses urged his horse to a gallop, the other horses eagerly jumped to follow. Clods of dirt flew up from the lead horse. Jack armed the grenade, put the reins in his left hand, then the reins in his mouth, bit down—the cracked, dry leather straps tasted foul, salty, dried out his mouth. Pulled the Colt Milady had given him, cocked it, hung on as the mare fell in on Arses' right. Halfway across the football field-sized, poppy and corn flower-filled meadow, a shot rang out. His saddle slammed sideways.

Milady returned fire at a small ridge to the right flank. The tank's rounded turret turned. The gun lowered slightly, fired.

As the Brit had predicted, the 100mm rifle shell roared over the galloper's heads. Arses hoarsely shouted out a song:

Cannon in front of us Volley and thunder; Stormed at with shot and shell, Boldly we rode and well. Into the jaws of Death, Into the mouth of Hell.

Arses shot at a man who stood agape over a smoldering cook fire. The man dove to the side, scrambled into nearby bushes, Jack dropped him from ten feet with a tap on the trigger. He headed around the five-wheeled tank, threw the grenade down the hatch, kicked his horse. Seconds later he heard a muffled bang inside the tank.

Arses dropped his grenade satchel down the rear hatch but it caught on something, he reined up, grabbed for it. A wounded man came out of the hatch, desperately tried to push it. Jack shot wildly, the man groaned like a dying cow, sprawled away with the satchel in his hands. It fell into the vehicle, exploded.

Jack galloped down the road, sweat lather flew from his horse. Felt tremendous elation: the tankers were dead. Seconds later, a secondary explosion destroyed the tank.

Five minutes later, Arses reined up, hugged Milady, pounded Jack on the back. "We did it! Blew the Talib bastards to bloody smithereens." "You're great, Arses—what's with the Tennyson poem?" Arses laughed, shouted to the sky:

They that had fought so well, Back from the mouth of Hell. The Charge of the Light Brigade!

Milady threw her head back, laughed. Jack leaned over, kissed her. Her lips felt wonderful. He was alive.

Chapter 37

The three reached the Kafirstan headquarters at 1100 hours. A light rain had dampened their clothes, made the horses smell rank. The rain quit by the time they approached the six-feet-high wood walls surrounding the settlement. Watch towers rose from the four corners of the fort, which was about 100 feet by 150 feet. The place reminded Jack of an old western fort.

A battered 106mm recoilless rifle cannon sat on a raised berm in the middle of the encampment, covering the approaches to the wooded valley. The fort was surrounded by steep, rugged mountains. Apples, walnuts, apricots, grew in orchards on the other side of a dry riverbed.

"Pretty nice set up," he remarked.

"Thanks," Arses replied. "The Kafirs do good work."

The three dismounted, stripped their saddles, handed the tack and horses over to a group of young boys who competed to help. Walked to a central building, a one-story structure. Entered, dropped their personal gear by the door. A communications bench was along one wall, a map-covered table and four chairs were on the other side. Walls and floor were constructed of wood planking.

Milady led him to a small brick building, kissed him, said she would send a pot of tea, would be back with lunch. He watched the tall trim Kafir princess strut away, greeting persons as she went— she clearly ruled this encampment.

A half hour later, Milady, wearing shorts, a shirt tied at the waist, arrived with a basket. Surprised by her casual but attractive attire, he complimented, "You look lovely." *And not so dangerous.*

She smiled. "We have a hot spring, let's go up there." The two hiked a half mile up the mountain to a narrow waterfall that cascaded down a cliff.

Steam rose from a fern-encircled hot spring at the base of the falls. Reminded him of the tarn pool in Shangri-la, where he had met Penel, Dickey, and Wantonal.

Milady pulled him down on the soft, grassy ground, next to the pool. She kissed him, stroked his body. Everywhere she touched, he felt expanding electric shocks. Immediately aroused, Jack undressed her and himself. Pushed her back, moved on top. Loved her physical beauty, her passionate kisses, her embraces. They eagerly rose to heights of physical delight, hovered, panting with pleasure, fell together, the sun burning their backs.

Twenty minutes later, Milady took packages of food out of the basket, placed the packs on a flat boulder. He ate a huge beef and goat cheese sandwich, then waded into the warm water—it was about ninety degrees. Thought again of Penel's hot springs, wondered what was happening in the hidden valley. Swam to the far edge—about twenty feet—plucked large white flowers that looked like magnolia blossoms, smelled like nightblooming jasmine. Held the flowers above the water with one hand, brought them back to the lunch spread.

After lunch, he studied the cliff above them while he chewed on an apricot. "You know, it looks like there was a road going up to that ledge.
You can see where landslides destroyed it."

Milady looked up at the cliff. "I don't see it."

"There," he insisted. "I wonder where it goes?"

"A lot of Buddhist temples are in the sides of cliffs." Milady smiled. "Maybe the golden dragon god is in there." He looked at Milady. "You've heard the legend, too, huh?" He appraised the cliff—it looked climbable. "I think I'll climb up there and check it out. D'you mind?"

"No, have a look. Probably only the millionth to do so." He pulled on his pants, boots, pushed through dense foliage that overhung the water. Got to the first slide that had swept away the visible road, worked his way across the cliff. Climbed an overhang:

his back was to the ground, hung by one hand for a second until he was able to reach, pull himself up. Just around the second wall, still to the left of the cascading waters, he saw a cave opening about ten feet high. It was set back from the road, was not visible from below.

Took a deep breath, suppressed his fears of the dark, stepped into the cool air of the cave. On each side of the cave, at various levels, astounding sights: intricate ceramic and bronze statues sat in niches cut out of the walls of the cave. At least a hundred Buddha statues of varied sizes, colors, some slim—some fat. Human-looking statues ranged from six inches to eighteen inches high, set so that they all seemed to stare at a strange platform in the middle of the cave floor.

All gazed at the same spot, where a shaven-headed monk sat in a lotus position, wore a crimson robe in front of a two-horned dragon, carved of limestone, two feet high and four feet long.

Jack silently watched the monk, a heavily-muscled young man with a shaven head. The man opened his eyes, regarded him. Shocked, the monk stared. Stood, raised his hands, attacked.

Jack retreated to the ledge outside the cave. The monk jabbed, kicked at his head twice. He raised his hands to defend himself. Realized that he had to fight, punched the monk with a quick right to the jaw. Sent the man reeling back into the cave. Hoped that the fight was over, dropped his hands, but the monk regained his feet, attacked again. Jack stepped in, grabbed the man in the armpit. Absorbed a hard punch, slammed the monk into the cave wall. The guy rose slowly, advanced again.

"Dude!" he exclaimed, "I wanna give up—before I hurt you."

"You're not ready for the third instruction," the monk yelled. "And you will receive what you asked for." He kicked Jack in the left thigh. Jack lost control of his leg, fell to his knees. The monk spun, kicked him in the jaw, knocked him unconscious.

He woke minutes later: alone on the ledge. Peered in the cave but there was no sign of his assailant. Rubbed his jaw, felt like the experience had been a painful dream. Abashed at the monk's easy victory, thankful to be alive, he looked for Milady. She was lying on a rock, unaware of the fight.

The waters of the pool looked green and brown except where the roaring waterfall landed: there the water was white, foamy. The sky was cloudless, had a rich blue color; a flock of doves swooped, disappeared in the forest. He caught a movement on the trail. Upon closer inspection, saw a Kafir boy approaching.

Milady looked up, waved, made a perfect dive into the water. He glanced back at the cave, thought about diving into the deep pool. Flexed his fingers. Milady was still underwater; he could see her dark body swimming to the edge of the pool. Incredible figure, long hair trailing. He thought of their lovemaking, readied himself to dive into the pool.

Jumped far out, straightened his body, covered his nose with one hand, plummeted feet first to the water. It came fast—looked like he might not clear a rock outcropping—then he hit the water with a crisp, hard cut.

He and Milady were dressed by the time the boy reached the pool. The boy called, waved at the two. Milady waved back while Jack gulped down the last sandwich.

"What's up?" he asked through a mouthful of food. The breathless boy, unable to understand, looked at Milady. She spoke rapidly in Pathan, the boy answered. Milady turned to him. "Robert wants us to come immediately. Something about catching a ride today. To Pakistan. We must go at once." The three hurried back to the vil.

Milady and Jack walked to the command center where she sent a villager for Robert Arses. Moments later, Arses arrived, pulling the patch over his eye. "Good news," he shouted. "U.S. Air Force pilots headed for Karachi. They'll pick us up."

"A helicopter?"

"That's right, lad. A Blackhawk. Party time tonight. What?"

"When're they arriving?" He felt a surge of excitement at the idea of escaping Afghanistan. Suddenly remembered telling the monk in the forest temple that he wanted a helicopter. Felt a shiver of fear at the coincidence.

"They're on final." Robert headed for his hooch. "Grab whatever cargo you want to bring." Milady dashed away. He poured a cold cup of tea, sat down to relax—the thought of getting to Islamabad was tremendously exciting. Odyssey would be over. Everything was happening so quickly, he felt dizzy, disoriented. Minutes later, Milady returned with a travel bag and Jack's Taliban bag. She wore a tiger-stripe fatigue outfit with pants tucked into her boots, a clean white puggaree on her head.

He heard the distant sounds of a helicopter approach the fort. Drained his tea. The two walked outside, crossed to the gate.

Foraging chickens scattered in a panic when the large helicopter with one tail prop, one four-propeller rotor, settled onto the helipad. The words: US Air Force above the cabin hatch. When the engine died, three men in blue coveralls emerged; the pilot, co-pilot, dressed in flight suits, climbed out. All hurried around the side of the aircraft, urinated.

Robert Arses passed through the gate, hailed the men when they came back around the helicopter. Arses and Jack introduced themselves to the pilot, a major called Jimmy Jinks, who grinned and shook hands.
"Congratulations on your escape, Lieutenant. We're excited to help you." A black guy, about thirty years old, with short hair, round pleasant face, a big smile.

"Thank you, sir. I can't tell you how much I appreciate your assistance. How'd you hear about me?"

"The whole net's been buzzing about an American officer who escaped the Taliban." Jimmy smiled, waved at the aircraft. "This's a new bird.
Sikorsky S-70A the Pakistani Air Force purchased. We're taking it to Karachi from Incirlik in Turkey." "How come?"

"Some general wants to approve the purchase of a squadron's worth. We came through Turkmenistan to get around Iran, you're right off our flight path. And when we overheard the Brit's call—Mister Arses here—we diverted to pick you up."

The co-pilot walked up, introduced himself. His name was Ben Holland, a captain. He smiled, showed teeth covered by braces, dashed a lock of hair off his forehead after he shook hands. He looked younger than Jimmy, was very skinny, with red hair, freckles, ears that stuck out, looking like seashells. Holland walked forward to check something on the undercarriage.

Another man, also black, about thirty, yelled, threw a bottle to the pilot. He introduced himself as Natrone Smith. Tall, lanky, with long hair for an airman, a white spot on his cheek.

The pilot joined the co-pilot, who was inspecting a wheel. The last man, handsome, about twenty-five, with brown curly hair and a trim body, introduced himself as Phillip Crangal.

Robert, Milady, Jack—all climbed aboard the aircraft. Crangal and Smith smiled, checked out Milady. She smiled shyly, probably excited by the attention, put her hand on Jack's arm. Benches inside were situated along the bulkheads. The red-headed co-pilot joined the pilot in the front of the helicopter. In seconds, they were airborne.

The co-pilot, a lieutenant like Jack, offered a shiny flask. He drank, tasted scotch whiskey. Handed the flask back, realized that all the men were drunk. Glanced at the pilots but could only see the backs of their heads.
"You guys thought about partying in a bar 'stead of 10,000 feet over it?
What's your range?"

"Goddam far enough, if this headwind lets up," Smith responded with a laugh. He glanced at Jack. "You a pilot?"

"Not licensed," he responded, "but I've flown our chopper at home in Montana. Chasin' lost cattle."

"Well, not to worry, Jimmy'll get us there."

"So you're going to Karachi?"

"Yep, party tonight. After we drop you off in Islamashit." Smith drank from his flask, offered it to Milady. She smiled, shook her head.

The helicopter took off, followed a canyon created by the river, climbed to 2,000 feet above ground. He glanced at Milady, smiled. She flashed a tremendous grin, squeezed his elbow. Fifteen minutes later, he felt the helicopter bank into a turn to the west. He looked out the hatch, saw that the helicopter was diverting around a huge dust storm.

Later, woke with a jolt, realized that the engines were sputtering to a stop. He glanced out the hatch—they were still thousands of feet in the air.

The helicopter tilted, went into a slow, descending spin.

Chapter 38

On his second visit to Baluchistan, Yassar Ahmoud watched in amazement as Rama Razi finished a huge lunch—a platter of Indian chicken moglai. The colossal man's ability to eat was beyond belief. Curry that had spiced the dish permeated Rama's Bedouin tent.

Rama snapped a finger, a beautiful Arab girl emerged, with long black hair, a transparent veil revealing a beautiful face and wonderful breasts. She took the empty platter away. Rama snapped his fingers twice, another girl brought an iced coffee tray. In the back part of the air-conditioned tent, Arabian music came from unseen musicians.

Rama smiled. "I have a lovely girl for you—perhaps this one—if you care for a diversion after our meeting. What have you got for me, Ahmoud?" Yassar Ahmoud ignored the girl and announced, "I still have the bomb secured in a cave in the Hindu Kush. I have a ship ready to pick it up in Karachi. The ship is owned by a cousin of mine."

"Karachi!" Rama exclaimed. "Much too open. Bring it to Chah Behar, here in Baluchistan. I can bribe the Iranians to look the other way. It'll be much safer."

Yassar Ahmoud barely contained a smile of joy. The dreams were coming to fruition. He would soon be The Man.

Chapter 39

The airmen yelled jibes, curses, taunts at each other and the pilots: the helicopter's engines ran out of fuel, coughed to a stop. Jack watched the pilot throw the aircraft into an auto-rotate mode, prayed the guy knew how to affect the engine-out landing procedure.

Aircraft plunged towards the earth at a rate of descent of thousands of feet per minute. Milady buried her head in his shoulder. Robert sprawled on the floor, a shocked expression on his face. Yells increased in volume. Helicopter continued to plummet towards the earth, in a slow spin, a steep dive. When the spinning ground rushed to meet them, the pilot flared, completed the auto-rotate maneuver, stopped the bird in mid-air. It landed with a deafening, but survivable jolt.

Aircraft bounced back in the air, passengers flew across the cabin. Rebounded one more time with another crash, settled to a stop. An electrical fire broke out in the cockpit; passengers dashed outside when smoke and flames bloomed. Co-pilot grabbed a fire extinguisher, put the fire out.

"Every landing you survive is a great landing," Jimmy Jinks announced when he shakily staggered out of the BlackHawk, surveyed his passengers. They all sat or sprawled on a brown dirt road surrounded by towering cliffs. Jinks appeared dazed by the hard landing, started to ramble. "We're in the infamous Khyber Pass of the Safed Koh Mountains—crossed by Alexander the Great in sometime BC—an' by our Brit pals in the early 1840's. That's when Elphinstone's army of seventeen thousand was wiped out to the last man, who was named good Doctor Brydon."

"Shut up, Jinks. Someone's coming," Smith announced.

Jimmy peered east towards Pakistan, exclaimed, "Afghans, don't you know. We definitely need some aviation fuel for our

flying carriage, which Ben called for before our anticipated but regretted landing." He added with a fake British accent, "Ben Holland, I feel a bit peckish and very thirsty.
Share that flask, you blighter."

Jack studied the approaching men, who were running towards the helicopter. "Take cover, guys—might not be friendly."

Ignoring him, Jimmy continued. "And I do believe you're right. Local chaps coming to assist us. How jolly." The group looked where Jimmy pointed. Shots rang out. Bullets whined off rocks, ricocheted off the metal frame of the aircraft. Group scattered in all directions, looked for cover. Jack took a breath, ran into the smoky helicopter, searched for a weapon. More firing ricocheted off rocks, and the BlackHawk. Pistol shots when the pilots, Arses, and Milady responded.

Smell of burnt plastic filled the cabin. He saw a stubby, rifle-sized military green box, ripped it open, trying not to breathe. Inside, a Army dismissed OICW! Elated, he broke open an adjoining ammunition crate, grabbed bandoliers of 5.56mm ammo, two six round clips of 20mm grenade shells, jumped out. Scrambled behind a boulder, breathing hard to clear his lungs of the smoke. Arses was crouched there, firing his revolver. Heard
Arses mumble,

"When you're wounded on Afghan plains,
And the women come to cut out your remains.
Jest roll to your rifle an' blow out your brains,
And go to your Gawd like a soldier."

Arses glanced at Jack, nervously giggled. "Rudyard Kipling had it right, lad. We're in a bit of a pickle."

"Maybe we'd better consider givin' up," Jimmy Jinks yelled from under the helicopter. Shots banged. Jack hurriedly loaded the OICW's six round grenade clip and the rifle magazine. Hit the selector toggle used to switch from rifle fire to grenade mode, turned on the sighting system. Looked into the small screen on the back of a digital video camera, mounted like a telescope. Aimed the OICW at Taliban wannabes moving up the road towards the chopper. Numbers appeared on the screen—acquired range of three hundred meters to the group. Adjusted the rifle until the red dot on the screen was on the soldiers, fired.

The grenade launched, seconds later, the bomblet's minicomputer exploded the 20mm shell amongst the Taliban. They disappeared in the cloud of dust created. A man limped out of the dust cloud, Jack shifted to the rifle mode: put the laser dot on the charging man. When it acquired him, he fired a two round burst. The man dropped like a sack of spilled potatoes. Spotted men on a ridge. Toggled back to grenade launcher, fired. Bodies flew, slid down the cliffs until they landed with crashing thumps on the road. Changed back to rifle mode, aimed at two men approaching from the east; when the heat-sensing camera spelled out the distance to the closer man at two hundred meters, tumbled him, put the dot on the farther enemy. Shot him—the guy kept coming. Fear rose—what was it going to take to stop this guy? Fired again and again—the guy showed nothing until his knees slowly buckled and he looked down, then fell face first on the road, his rifle firing into the ground.

Arses, who had stopped firing, was watching in amazement. "By God, we've got Buck Rogers on our side."

"I was thinking more like Matrix Neo," he yelled back. Ran to a boulder, ducked down next to Milady. "With this, I can take on the whole goddam Taliban." Mopped the sweat from his brow, fired again. Returning fire slammed off the boulder. Rose, dropped a charging soldier at a range of one hundred meters, after the dot appeared on the man's chest.

Outgunned, the attacking Talib forces fell back, ran to boulders, hid. He switched back to grenade mode. It was a video game, now. Spotted the boulders where four men had dove. Aimed at the rocks and when the dot settled, triggered a round. Screams of terror rang out, enemy reeled into sight. He aimed at another hidden group, fired with the same result.

The rest of the attackers threw down their weapons, realized there was no hiding from the weapon, ran in terror.

"I'm super glad we invited you to the party," Jimmy said. "I knew we were hauling special weapons to the Pakistani Army, but I never imagined in my wildest dreams…"

Ben pointed west. "Here's the fuel truck. I called Camp Rhino Control a few moments before we crashed." A U.S. Air Force fuel truck approached, skidded to a stop. Two armed airmen and another Air Force enlisted man climbed out, surveyed the group.

The one guy laughed. "You fellows almost made it to Peshawar, over there in Pakistan. You want a fill or a tow back to Jalalabad?" Laughed again. Pulled a hose out of a port on the tank of his fuel truck, walked around to the BlackHawk's fuel tank, refueled the helicopter, then turned the truck and departed with waves and cheers from the airmen.

Against his better judgment, Jack helped Milady back on the chopper. He asked Jinks, "Dude, are you good to go?"

Jinks laughed. "No sweat, Marine. We'll get you to Islamadreadful by early aft. I can fly this bird in my sleep."

Jack thought fast. "How about checking me out in this BlackHawk? I'd love to try it." Jimmy Jinks, swayed, peered at him with one dark eye closed. "Why not, pal. You deserve a treat. Take the left seat."

He took off, struggled with the heavy aircraft, but quickly got the feel of the cyclic control stick, adjusted to the extra weight. In moments, after a couple of dips, dives, he stabilized. The whooping group settled back, relaxed. Milady came forward, leaned against him. "Are all Americans crazy like you and these men?"

"Crazy? I'm the sanest guy I know in a world gone mad. Did you see those crazy fuel guys drive up like they're in the middle of Kansas City?"

Milady exclaimed, "These pilots have drunken parties at ten thousand feet

—you hang out with tigers and shoot space guns."

"Well, you're not exactly rowing with all your oars in the water, Milady," he responded with a smile. He checked the altitude. Milady slugged him in the arm in mock protest. "My life is wonderful. I strike the Talibs. I live in the free mountains of Kafirstan. I travel to Islamabad with a handsome mysterious warrior." She hugged him. "Who leads a more wonderful life than I? What woman wouldn't trade with me?"

"If you don't return to your seat, you'll lead a short life, lady," Ben
Holland declared. "He needs to fly this bird."

As the flight continued, he thought of the women he had known—he could not think of one of them who would have traded for Milady's life. Mara was the only one that possibly could endure Milady's existence. She had grown up in a society engaged in a life and death struggle. She carried an air of danger. He thought of Ashley Dupont. A city girl. She'd crumble at the first sight of trouble—call her mom, go shopping. He shifted his thoughts to their destination when Jimmy Jinks grabbed his arm, pointed out a brown sand storm to their front. It looked like it rose to over 50,000 feet in the sky.

"Not going to Islamacrap today," Jimmy announced. "It's socked in.
Have to come with us to Karachi, catch a ride back tomorrow."

Pursed his lips in frustration, turned over control to Ben Holland, gave up his seat to a more sober Jimmy Jinks, who entered a heading for a refuel in the Pakistani city of Quetta.

An hour later, Jimmy called Quetta Control. A voice over the loud speaker instructed him to begin a descent on a one hundred seventy degree heading. Jack looked down, saw they were flying over a fertile valley surrounded by bare brown mountains. He potted a caravan of camel-riding nomads headed towards an area of shabby housing that was Southwest Asia's version of the suburbs, laughed at the Asian commuter traffic jam. Five minutes later, Jimmy landed in Quetta. A ground crew approached, tied the BlackHawk down.

After congratulations, thanks, goodbyes, the pilots walked towards the terminal, entered a restaurant. Jack thought about kissing the ground, fought the impulse. Man, how bad is it when you think Pak-a-toon is heaven. As the three walked through the terminal, a crimson-robed monk approached him, looked directly in his face. He turned away from the man, glanced at his friends. The three entered a cab. Arses asked, "What that all about?"

"Beats me. Scary guy. Maybe he's lookin' for an offering." Who cared? Good ol' Pak-a-toon. Now all he had to worry about were crazed mullahs, nutty Colonel Farley, overzealous General Harmbruster, and oversexed Miss Elle.

Chapter 40

"Milady, Jack, and Robert made a brief stop in Quetta's busy open market: Arses identified it as the largest bazaar in southwestern Pakistan, and purchased for Jack, two changes of clothes, a cheap sports watch, toiletries, shoes, and a travel bag, after arguing and shouting with a tiny, wizened, hunch-backed shopkeeper over the prices. The three crawled back in their waiting cab, the driver took them to the Serena Hotel.

"Best hotel in Quetta, fronts on Lytton Road," Arses said of their lodging. "Overlooks the waters of the Hori Nullah River." The lobby was clean, potted palms fluttered from the draft of overhead fans connected by an elaborate pulley system.

The three took a two-bedroom suite, cleaned up, changed clothes, walked down the stairs to the lobby for dinner. Milady wore a bright blue sarong, a white silk top that revealed a bare midriff. She looked spectacular in the Islamic atmosphere.

"I need an international line," Jack told the desk clerk. The darkskinned, bearded man stared at him with intense black eyes, did not respond until Milady spoke in harsh, cutting Pashtu, whereupon he smiled, pointed at a desk. She walked to it, picked up the telephone; Jack sat down while she spoke into the receiver. Arses waved from across the room, disappeared.

Five long minutes later, Milady handed over the telephone. He gave the telephone number for his aunt in Menlo Park to an English-speaking operator. Numerous clicks followed, until he was delighted to hear the housekeeper, elderly Mrs. Hansen, answer the phone. "Mrs. Hans—it's me."

He heard a scream, "Jackie, is that you? Are you okay, honey? We heard you were lost in some God-forsaken place." He grinned, happy to hear her voice. "I'm fine. How're you?"

"Oh, I'm exhausted—I just walked from Drager's with an armload of groceries—but it beats driving thirty miles to Red Lodge for fixin's."

"Dad around?"

"Oh, Jackie, he went to Redwood City. He'll be so disappointed that he missed you. He'll be back later. Can he call you? Are you sure you're alright?"

"I'm great. Have him call the Hotel Serena in Quetta, Pakistan. Write it down. Tell him. I'm fine" He spelled the city name, then said, "Goodbye." He hung up. It was like a hang up on reality. Tears filled his eyes when he thought about the lost ranch, his dad, relatives in Montana and Menlo Park. He glanced around, dashed the tears away, joined Milady. The host approached, escorted the couple to the restaurant where he sat them at a window table over-looking the Hori Nullah's brown waters. Arses arrived with a frosty bottle of beer in one hand and a bottle of red wine from the bar. The three sat in white wicker chairs under a slowly revolving fan, watched different types of boats and scows sail by, making up the busy river traffic.

Jack sipped his wine—it tasted cheap, but it was great just to have it, to share it in a safe place. "Is there a consulate here in Quetta? Where I can report in?" Noticed an ominous-looking, crimson-robed monk standing on the riverbank, staring through the window.

Arses smiled. "Afraid you're still in the sticks, old chap." "Can you guys come to Islamabad?" Jack asked.

Arses grinned. "Not popular in 'Abad. Besides, I just learned we have to see someone in Karachi." Milady and Robert Arses glanced at the monk. She said, "He wants something. I'll go ask him." Stood, walked out of the restaurant. Spoke, returned to the restaurant.

"What's he want? Looking for a handout?" Arses asked.

"He wants Jack to go to his superior. Tonight."

"Why? White men that rare around here?" Milady threw her long black hair back, sipped her wine. "He mentioned the third instruction. Said you'd know what he meant."

Feeling a flush of fear, Jack gulped his wine. The old monk in the temple. He said there would be one more instruction. I thought that was a dream—like the first time in the mountains above Shangri-la. And the statue cave guy said I wasn't ready for the third instruction. Noticed
Milady's full lips on the rim of the glass; leaned forward, kissed her.

"Might be fun," Arses said. "I see a chap—I'll be back."

A moment later, he heard a woman's voice scream, "Jack Flashhardt!" Felt a hand on his shoulder, looked up, saw red- headed Melinda O'Reilly, the newsbabe. "You're saved! And why wasn't I invited to this party?" He jumped up, bear-hugged Melinda, delighted to see her.

"You escaped!" Melinda squealed. "I must have the story."

He turned, took Milady's hand. "Milady, meet my friend and comrade in arms, Melinda O'Reilly." The two women shook. "She and I played patty cakes with bandits on the KKH Highway. On my first assignment for the
UN. She drives a mean getaway truck."

Melinda looked back at Jack. "Speaking of the KKH trip— you were all talking about the missing biobomb. I have a British news source that will pay hugely for the bomb. One million pounds. Interest you?"

Jack frowned. "Even if I was, I'm U.S. military." Suddenly, the Irish newswoman forgot about him. "The Milady? Oh, my God! You're the Kafir
Princess?"

Milady blushed, nodded her head, pleased at the recognition. Melinda focused her eyes—she had been drinking. "I must interview you. Can we meet here in the morning?"

Jack regarded the beautiful redhead, glanced sideways at Milady, who said, "I don't know what will happen tomorrow." Melinda turned to him. "Please, Jack, I need to talk to Milady. She's become famous from Istanbul to Hong Kong. But the West hasn't heard her incredible tale. Her struggles against radical Islamists." Melinda held out her glass, he poured wine.

"I can't speak for Milady. She's her own woman."

Melinda looked at Milady. "Can I meet you tomorrow?"

Milady said, "Yes." The drunk reporter, grinned, drank the entire glass, walked to a group of pilots at the next table.

Milady tossed her long hair in irritation. "She's so old those overinflated tits pull the wrinkles from her face."

He laughed, "Don't be jealous, she's a special gal. But I wouldn't trust her. She's only out for her story. She won't care what happens to you." He thought of Melinda's easy taking of him to ensure a ride to Hunza.

Milady tossed her head. "So, I shouldn't talk to the old bag."

"Help you become more famous. But do you want the Mujs knowing more about you?" He drained his glass, sat back. After a lamb chop and curry potato dinner that had smelled wonderful and had tasted great, he felt exhausted from the day's trials.

Noticing his mood, Milady said quietly, "Jack, I want you."

He smiled. "I love it when you talk nice."

The two left, un-noticed by Arses who was still at the bar.

In the suite, Milady walked to the bed occupying one corner of their bedroom. She pushed aside the canopy, undid her sarong and when she turned to him, her magnificent, muscular black body stunned him.

She un-buttoned his shirt, un-did his pants, knelt to take his boots off. She pressed her powerful frame against him, pushed him onto the bed.

A knock at the door. He ignored it until he remembered the call to his father. Cursing under his breath, he covered himself with a towel, answered the door. A bellhop announced a telephone connection in the lobby. After Jack explained to Milady, he hurriedly dressed, went with the bellhop. The lobby was quiet, Arses was gone. He held the old-fashioned telephone to his ear. "Dad?"

"Jack, thank God, you're okay! Mrs. Hansen gave me the news. When I lost your cell phone call, I felt so helpless. I got on the horn to the Marines and demanded they get off their asses and start looking for you."

"Thanks, Dad. I'm okay—and I met some great people after I talked to you. They helped me get to Quetta in Pakistan. I'm flying to Islamabad tomorrow." He felt dizzy from the joy of hearing his father's voice; pressed his free hand against the desk for support.

"That's wonderful, Jack. How bad were you hurt?"

"I was wounded, but it wasn't serious. Just a blow to the head. A slight concussion—knocked me out. Happened when I was captured—when we rescued Omar." Who the hell hit me? he wondered for the hundredth time.

"I'm so glad you could free Omar. He told me the whole story in a letter. I'm proud of you, son." The two spoke for long minutes, said goodbye. When he crossed the lobby, he saw the monk standing by the elevator door. Jack stopped. The cleric said, "Come, Kshatriya."

He thought of Milady waiting upstairs. "Forget it, pal—I'm not a warrior anymore, I'm in the UN." Tried to move past the monk, but the man blocked his way, pointed at the front door. He looked, saw a black Mercedes Benz sedan parked at the curb. On impulse, he decided to go outside, tell the monks to get screwed, quit bothering him. Followed the young man, saw two more monks standing by the sedan. One of them opened the door, stepped aside. When he leaned over to talk to the back seat's inhabitant, the three monks violently shoved him into the car, slammed the door. Driver gunned the engine, the car raced away, with Jack sprawled in the empty back seat, his knees on the floor.

The car sped through near deserted streets. A rainsquall had moistened the paving, it gleamed from the infrequent streetlights and neon signs announcing roadside businesses. Streets turned into dark stretches of empty gloom. He tried to open the locked doors but could not, the windows wouldn't go down.

"What's up? Where're you taking me?" *They're going to kill me. Some enlightenment.* "Hey, guys," he said to the driver and the passenger, "Lemme go—I promise I'll make bigger donations next time they pass the plate in church." The passenger in the front seat looked at him, didn't get it, didn't respond. Hoping to calm himself, he added, "An' I promise not to fall sleep during the sermons." No answer.

After ten long minutes, the big sedan stopped next to a large body of dark waters. Monk from the front seat held the car door open for him. Humidity was high near the water, temperature felt to be about 70 degrees. The monk pointed at a powerboat tied to a rickety dock—the sleek inboard vessel was twenty feet long, looked like a 1930's style, wooden speedboat. A man, also dressed in a crimson robe, was at the helm.

Looked around, saw no help, made a decision to play along with his captors rather than run, walked out on the pier; boat driver, who stared straight ahead, did not look up when he stepped on the vessel. The cleric untied a mooring line, the craft pulled into what he figured had to be the Hori Nullah.

Crossed the black water, watched another boat, showing a dim red light on its bow, follow at a distance of about two hundred meters. "We got a convoy," Jackk muttered. A half hour later, after a rapid transit across moonlit waters, craft coasted to a stop at a dock on an island in the river. Following boat curved northward, disappeared. Lights of the city were scarce on the banks.

A white-domed shrine, its peak visible in the moonlight, on the hundred-meter-long island. Walked toward it, smelled a heavy odor from fragrant and exotic frangipani flowers. A large hollow drumbeat came from an unknown location, reverberated across the island. It sounded like the word "Doom," repeated over and over. The sound penetrated his body, resonated.

The white marble temple gleamed in the bright moonlight, grounds around it immaculately groomed. Climbed fifteen wide steps to a first level, slowly ascended another fifteen steps, where a group of monks prayed at an altar; they turned like a giant crimson pinwheel, all pointed to a third set of stairs.

Climbed the last nine steps, walked across a veranda until he confronted an old priest sitting on an elevated seat in the center of the sanctuary. Shaft of moonlight lanced through a skylight above him, spotlighted the cleric.

Smiling man wore a full-length white robe, had shoulder-length, white hair, his face shadowed in the dark. He said, "Kshatriya, welcome to Quetta. Thank you for visiting our order." Another British accent.

"Why'd your men force me to come here?"

The monk held his hands outstretched, said with a harsh, demanding voice, "Dangerous demons hover over Southwest Asia. You must fulfill your dharma—your warrior's task for Dragon God Baal."

"What d'you mean? You guys keep, like, pumpin' that dharma and kashit-ree-a crap. What's that have to do with me?"

"You are a kshatriya—a member of the warrior caste. A significant player on the field of souls. Born in the Year of the Dragon. You're a Lung Tik Chuan Ren—descendent of Dragon."

"I'm a gringo."

The monk regarded him with hidden eyes, voice still strong. "The Dragon, or Lung, is one of the most powerful and lucky signs of the Chinese Zodiac. Dragons are divine mythical creatures that bring ultimate prosperity and good fortune."

"Asking someone what their sign is went out of fashion a while back," he said. "Astrology's a bit dated."

The monk continued to ignore him. "You traveled to Shangri-la. You visited our ancient temple in the heights above that valley. No one has visited the valley in over twenty years. Ever since the Soviets destroyed the only access. For some reason, Dragon God Baal called you to him. He's so old that few know anything of Him, our worship of Him, its rituals, its purposes—except our tiny order of followers and the few faithful inhabitants of the valleys surrounding. I don't know why you are special, but you must visit Dragon God Baal again."

"I didn't travel to Shangri-la," he protested. "Blown there by wind while searching for the lost biobomb in the Hindu Kush."

"What does the bomb contain?"

"Nasty bugs: Spanish Flu, smallpox, and anthrax." The monk leaned forward. "Perhaps the mystery is solved." "How so?" Jack asked.

"In the Fourth Century, Constantine, the Roman Emperor canonized the Bible. Some books were left out. For example, the Book of Thomas of the New Testament, re-discovered in Egypt about fifty years ago, was left out. It contained sayings of Jesus Christ. The Book of Mary was also left out. It revealed the return of the Dragon Avatar, sent to Earth by the Almighty. It was mentioned later, in The Revelation."

"Why was a book left out?"

"Written by a woman. And there was a plague in the Fourth Century. A plague of anthrax in Europe. The Avatar was blamed. Now, anthrax has returned to the Dragon. There must be a connection. That is why Dragon God Baal called you. It was no accident. The oracles reveal he is ready to act. Even my old friend, Edgar Cayce, predicted soulic activity at this time."

"The Mu and Atlantis guy?"

The monk smiled; his teeth flashed white. "Yes. Ed noted that Polaris

—the North Star—would shine directly into the main entrance to the Great Pyramid a few years after the turn of the new century. In 1932, he predicted a great number of Atlantean souls would then migrate to Earth and possess humanity.”

“I’m a Christian. I don’t believe in gods in caves or pyramid soultraveling. My god stays safe and sound behind an altar where I can keep an eye on him. Doesn’t run around in snow-blown caves, pant hot salsa breath. In fact, we’ve got him nailed to a cross so he won’t wander. I’ve got no reason to visit your god. I don’t believe a god would look like a dragon, anyway.”

You’re right,” the monk said. “He’s not a god, he’s an avatar. But the folk insist on naming the unnameable.” The monk leaned forward, his face appeared out of the shadows: a very old white man! He waved a hand in dismissal of Jack’s words. “Dragon God Baal was called Thuban until Polaris became the Pole Star when the Earth’s North Pole shifted its focus in the heavens. The name Thuban derives from an Arabic phrase meaning
—-.”

“Look,” Jack interrupted, “let’s skip the history lesson in the dark on an unknown island where I’ve been kidnapped. Let’s bottomline this right now.”

“—-also vanquished by Hercules in his 11th labor, to acquire the golden apples. He has been called Dragon God Baal since Alexander stole him, but he’s actually only an avatar from the Universal Almighty. He has been on Earth so long, his followers think the statute is the god. So we continue with that construct.”

“Where’s the real god?”

“Can anything be bigger than God? Can God be in a place?”

Jack looked around. “If he isn’t size challenged.”

“God is everywhere, he is everything. Does an atom in the rock you sit on know what it is or what dimension it exists in?”

“So, like, I guess he doesn’t have much time for us.”

"The quantum physics of man begins to touch the tiniest bit
of God.
But God touches everything, knows everything."

"All marginally interesting if you're in divinity school. But
what're you doing here, anyway? You're a white guy."

"Perhaps you've heard of me. I'm Hugh Conway."

"The hero of the novel?"

"Hilton wrote it as a novel, but it was a true story of the Hindu
Kush— beyond the River of Time—beyond the Himalayas."

"That'd make you over a hundred years old!"

"Yes, well, you've been to Shangri-la Vortex. You discovered
the secret of the Tarn Waters."

"Yeah, right," Jack said. "How come they don't work on you?
You look your age." The old man swung a gnarled fist through the
air. "I and many others have been cut off from the Tarn Waters since
the blasted
Russians—-"

"Blew up the tunnel," Jack interrupted. "You claim the water
really works. And others outside the valley know about it?" "Select
few worldwide," Conway said. "Now the pressure to re-gain access
is building to an incredible level."

"So the stuff works? And who are the select few?"

Conway gestured as though he were chasing a bug. "A secret
society.
Not for you to be concerned about."

The choir humming and the drum beating stopped. Jack
looked around, saw no movement. Wondered why. "Sounds like a
crock to me!"

"There is a more important issue. Our avatar now guards a
most dangerous egg. The American bomb that many search for in
the Hindu Kush has been accidentally—or not—hidden in his lair."
Jack leaned forward. "So you know about the bomb?"

"Yes," Conway replied. "And we want you to remove it. We don't want the avatar irritated or distracted. He has more important occupations. He will return the emerald shield to certain members of our… you must hurry. The Muslims seek this bomb. Those who want the bomb threaten our order. And we'll be at risk until it returns to American hands." The old man looked around. "Although it is a shame you irresponsible Americans are allowed to even possess such a terrible wesaapon."

"I've got a feeling you're at risk right now. A boat followed us to the island." Jack looked around—all was quiet. "Your drums have stopped. What's that mean?" Conway turned his head to the side. A young man approached, handed him a wooden box wrapped in a black silk cloth. He shut his eyes for a moment, prayed, held it out to Jack, "To that end, we have had this prepared for you—it will help you in the near future."

Jack took the box from the priest. Opened it: an empty, short sword scabbard resting on a black silk cloth.

"This scabbard was made from the hide of a sacred white komodo dragon. The straps are from the mighty jungle cobra. The diamonds come from an ancient mine in the depths of the sacred mountain, Annapurna. The warrior's device for this scabbard has much power. The silver and gold trim is from a Tibetan gomba's mine on the flanks of Chomolungma."

"Chomolungma? That's Mt Everest."

Conway smiled. "Yes, that's what we Westerners call it. When you gaze upon its heights, you will know it is Chomolungma, Mother Goddess. Note the word lung in the mountain's name. The Dragon God came from the sacred mountain. He will soon return. When he does, he will require your services."

"This is great," Jack said. "What'm I supposed to do with it? Hit somebody over the head? Where's the sword for it?"

"There'll be many troubles and successes for you in the days ahead. But you must fight the battles. Be slain and attain heaven or be victorious and enjoy the earth. But if you are true to your salt, if you give fidelity to your leaders, you'll fulfill the covenant with your superiors."

"Too much salt creates high blood pressure."

Conway stood and shouted, "Stop the derision! Listen: you must go to Dragon God. Awaken him. Remove his emerald armor, keep it safe until it is given to the chosen." He sat again. "Dragon God possesses the blade for this scabbard. You must acquire the sword. It is very old and has much power. You will need it. It memorializes Dragon God's escape from the
Emperor of the East. It will save you in the end."

Conway pointed at the silk cloth. "And the silk cloth is your map. Search out the anthrax eggs before men discover and hatch them. The map will lead you."

"I don't believe in your maps… your god."

"You must believe in your dharma," Conway responded. "Time grows short. It's a question of our survival. The continued existence of our avatar.
The fulfillment of his destiny on Earth."

Hearing a a distant thud, Jack looked into the darkness. Heard a sigh, saw the young monk collapse to the side. A sharp rattle of an automatic weapon shattered the silence. Jack threw himself to the ground, crawled to the fallen man. A black stain crept across the moonlit white marble from the monk's body. "This guy found his destiny a little early."

"You must leave at once," Conway said in a frightened whisper.
"Hurry. Go to Dragon God Baal. Secure the sword—it is your weapon.
Beware the big ones—they lurk in the dark corners beneath Dragon God Baal."

Jack looked around, thrust the scabbard and cloth inside his shirt, bolted into the darkness. Thought, *What's this beware bullshit?* He ran across the grass grounds. Heard shouts, gunfire behind him. Bullets whined, twigs popped in shrubs at his side. Ran until he reached the river's edge. With no hesitation, he dove, swam under icy water until his lungs ached.

Eased his head out of the water, saw he was about twenty meters downstream of the island, the current carrying him. Cold water made it hard to breath. He forced a gulp of air, plunged under the water, swam. The next time he surfaced, he began a distance-consuming crawl towards the shore. Worried about the cold water—hypothermia. Heard an engine roar to life, the craft with the red light on its bow crossed back and forth.

A tubby houseboat drew near, he saw a slender young woman lean over the bow, watch the water. Decided to take a chance, called out. The girl straightened, looked until she spotted him. She turned, went to the wheelhouse. Seconds later, the engines stopped, the boat drifted towards him. A man edged to the bow, threw him a rope. Once on the boat's wood deck, he asked, "Speak English?"

"Of course," the man responded. He was about sixty, wore a turban, a long, dark shift. The girl was taller, much younger, very pretty, even in the darkness. "Who're you?" the man asked. "What happened to your craft?"

"I'm an American. I was held up by robbers," he improvised. "I jumped in the river to escape. Thanks for stopping. I need to get to Quetta —the Serena Hotel." He rubbed water out of his hair. Tried to stop shivering.

"Satan's hotel," the old man said. "I am Mufti Zubair."

"Can you and your daughter——-"

"My wife," Zubair corrected with a snarl. "Koolreer, regain your veil. There's a stranger present." He scowled and heavy wrinkles carved his face into lines. "And get him a blanket."

"Can you and your wife give me a lift to Quetta?" "We go right by it," the girl ventured.

"Silence. Am I the captain of this vessel, woman?" The old man turned back to the wheelhouse. "Get him food. He looks like he has missed many meals." The girl, who had covered her face to the eyes, returned with a rough woolen shroud, led him to a tiny galley, lit a propane stove. She portioned a piece of dried fish, a scoop of rice into an old brass skillet. "Do the women in America really wear high heels?" she asked in a low voice. "And paint their toenails?" she whispered the last question. She dropped her veil, her face was strikingly beautiful, with large black eyes, dark skin, a perfect nose, lush lips.

"Women in America have the same freedom to live and screw up as men," he responded. Wondered why such a beautiful girl was with an old man. The smell from the warming food filled the galley.

"My idol, Mara Bhutto, lives free. She's a professor."

"Mara's a pal of mine. Sorta."

The girl's eyes brightened when she looked at him. Just then, Mufti Zubair peered through a port window. The aged man noted the happy look on his wife's face. His face disappeared when a shouted voice hailed the boat. Mufti responded in Urdu. Koolreer gasped. "My husband has just told seekers that an American is on the boat."

"I gotta go," he exclaimed. Looked at the fragrant food with regret. Turned, Koolreer caught his hand wouldn't let go. "Take care," she said. He tore free, tiptoed to the starboard side of the boat, away from the hailing voice, steeled himself for the shock of the cold water, slipped over the side.

An hour later, back in the hotel room, he woke Milady—she sat up, a worried expression on her face. He un-wrapped the silk fabric, put the box aside. The front of the black silk cloth was embossed with a silverencrusted picture of a man lounging on his back. Two horns grew out of his head. A long vine grew out of his navel, culminated in a large, white lotus flower, in the middle of which another man sat. Above the second man, a dragon brandished a long knife, rode in a chariot pulled by a pair of demonheaded horses across a plain.

"There is Vishnu, God of Gods," Milady said after she inspected the cloth. "The lotus growing out of his navel is the Universe as we know it. The Buddha sits in the lotus flower and dreams our world into existence. Buddha also gives us a dragon that will save our world from evil." She looked up at him. "But what is strange… the horns. Vishnu doesn't have horns." She paused, then said, "Where've you been? Your clothes are damp. Where did you get this? It's a rare temple rubbing."

"Those weirdoes in red robes that hung around yesterday grabbed me and hauled me across the river to an old monk. An Englishman named Conway. He gave it to me. He knew of me." Jack turned the temple rubbing over, saw the reverse side of the religious scene was a map of the Hindu Kush Mountains. The valley of Shangri-la was clearly marked and a tendril of smoke trailed out of a cave on the side of a mountain above the valley. At the top of the column of smoke sat the Dragon God, breathing flames.

Milady shivered. "What is it? It looks evil."

He caressed the silk rubbing, was astonished when the map faded away. The fragile, etched rubbing disintegrated, left a residue of silver dust in his hand.

"What happened?" Milady asked. "What was it?"

"A map. But it's gone! There was trouble. I got it wet in the river." He dropped the empty silk cloth, turned, looked at Milady. She fell back on the bed, put her arms out to him. He took his clothes off, climbed into the bed. Their love-making was slow, intimate, pulsing, intense. They joined together twice more during the night— each time was a dream of heaven.

The next morning, after a room service breakfast of over-cooked, rubbery eggs, bitter yogurt, cold toast, he went to the lobby, couldn't reach Islamabad, called the U.S. Consulate in Karachi. The operator connected him to the OIC, an Air Force major, and he related his experiences since his escape from the prison camp in

Afghanistan. The major suggested that he write a full report for MAACPAK on the way to Islamabad. After making a reservation for a flight, he called the office in Islamabad again, got through, left a message for Gil that he had escaped Afghanistan, was arriving in Islamabad at noon.

On the way to the airport, Arses and Jack summed up plans for a rescue mission to Shangri-la to save Dickey. They agreed that Jack's route over the peaks was too difficult for ordinary men, so a helicopter appeared to be the best solution. They decided to try and find one that could fly over the high cliffs.

At the gate, Milady cried while she hugged him. "It was wonderful last night and this morning, Milady," he whispered in her ear. "Thanks for everything."

"My crazy American warrior. Come back to Kafirstan. Come back, my love. Help me fight the Taliban."

"I'll try, Milady. Be careful." He gave her another hug, shook hands again with Robert, who said, "Ta ta, Jack, my lad."

"Thanks for the ticket," he responded. "I'll get the UN to reimburse you."

"Don't forget," Robert added with a smile, "as soon as you're squared away, we go for Dickey. That'll be thanks enough"

Nodding in agreement, Jack walked across the tarmac to the waiting Thai Airways jet. A smiling Asian flight attendant stood at the top of the stair, escorted him to a window seat in the crowded aircraft. When the jet began to taxi away, he saw Milady run out. He grinned, waved until the jet pulled away from the mountain girl. *This UN gig. It keeps me moving. And how can I make a close connection with a bizarre, wonderful woman like Milady when I'm leaving town faster than a roofing salesman with a cash advance?*

Chapter 41

On descent to Islamabad Airport, Jack finished writing a stark situation report about his capture and escape. He mentally debated putting in the story about the map but the whole thing seemed too crazy to put on paper. Glanced at his watch: almost noon. Wrote a letter to Amy Anderson's family, notifying them of her death. Can't lie, he thought. But I don't want to say she was raped and committed suicide. He carefully crafted the letter and put it in his pack for later delivery to the American Embassy.

After the landing, the senior flight attendant smiled, handed him Milady's worn .45 and battered holster when he reached the outer hatch. He crossed over the heat-blasted tarmac, walked through the airconditioned terminal, was shocked to see his UN superior, red-faced Gil Acton and his tiny girl, Fazila; his black pal, Arabic-looking but very blackskinned Omar Johnson; grinning Chopstick Mick Nakamura, gorgeous Mara Bhutto, Bruno the lean Russian, his brother, Billy Howling Dog, and evil-looking Bulldog Mahoney, the huge former drill instructor. They were waiting next to a Mercedes limousine in front of the terminal.

About twenty American military men that he didn't recognize stood on the sidewalk, held a huge, garrison-sized, bright American flag. The group cheered, clapped when he emerged. The sight of his friends, the men holding the red, white, and blue flag, pummeled his senses and emotions. He simultaneously hugged Billy, Omar, pounded a grinning Bruno, and laughing Gil on the shoulders. Returned Mahoney's salute, shook hands with the grinning Marine, who laughed, stuck a cigar back in his mouth. Mick gave him a bear hug, his eyes disappeared as he smiled. Bulldog gestured at the Americans. "These guys are from MAACPAK, Lieutenant. We followed the situation reports since your escape. Everybody off duty

in the Ops Center wanted to greet the American who escaped the Taliban.
You're a hero in Islamabad."

Mick raised his arm. The crowd of military men shouted "Hip, hip, hooray," three times, then broke into song:

> *"When Jack comes marching home again, hurrah, hurrah.*
> *The men will cheer and the boys will shout,*
> *The ladies, they will all put out.*
> *And we'll all get laid,*
> *When Jack comes marching home, hurrah!"*

He walked into the crowd of young men standing in the late morning sun: all grinned, slapped him on the back.

Golden-skinned Mara sported a short haircut, held a bouquet of flowers, pressed her wonderful breasts against his chest, gave him a kiss on the lips. The crowd cheered louder. A few catcalls, whistles rang out. Abashed, he looked around, grinned, noticed Fazila frown, wondered why she was unhappy.

As his friends surrounded him with greetings and laughter, Jack felt pain in his head. Tears formed, crossed his cheeks. He shouted with an emotion-thickened voice, "Thank you all for coming. I'm overwhelmed. I look forward to meeting you all."

Omar hugged him again, exclaimed loudly, "Sweet!"

The crowd cheered. Gil yelled, "We're all going to the Marriott, mates.
Everybody's welcome. Drinks on the UN."

With ringing cheers in the background, the friends all climbed into the limo; Gil opened a bottle of Dom Perignon champagne, passed it around. The bearded, turbaned chauffer looked back with a gap-toothed smile, pulled away from the curb. The group laughed, talked, passed the champagne around again. By the time the second bottle had been opened and consumed, the limo stopped in front of the Marriott. They jumped out and the smiling host, dressed in a faded tuxedo, quickly seated them at a linen-covered table in the bar. Billy on Jack's right. Gil and Fazila directly across the table. Bulldog and Mick on each end. Mara and Bruno on his left. He recognized her perfume, couldn't figure where he had encountered the faint odor.

The host waved at a waiter, directed him to take the flowers.

Bulldog stood, offered a toast: "Here's to you, L. T. And to three generals: General Peace, Plenty and General Pussy."

With Bruno conducting, the group broke into a song:

"Jack worships Ares more,
Oh, for he so loves a war.
Oh, so to add to his lore,
So we'll find him some gore.
Oh, so hear it for the Corps,
Aye aye, Sir, Blood, rape and whores,
For Jack worships Ares more."

"How in the world did you do it, bro? How'd you escape from the Taliban?" Omar asked over the table-pounding chants, reinforced by the rest of the welcoming crowd as they entered and sat at the next table. The waiter returned with the blooms in a white ceramic vase, placed it in the middle of the table. The centerpiece of the arrangement was a black orchid; white roses surrounded it.

"I got shot in the head and was blinded at Papa's front door," he answered. Thought, *One of the people here hit me.* He looked at each face —no reactions. "A few days into my fun Taliban vacation, my sight came back. I hid the change from the guards. They thought I was helpless, so I was able to just walk out one night. Then it was a foot race." He glanced at Mara. She wore a long silk skirt, light blue in color, a white, long-sleeved blouse. The smell of her perfume was wonderful.

"How'd you survive in the mountains, mate?" Gil asked.

He laughed. "Piece of cake, old buddy. Friendly wildlife and natives.

Combatants were lousy shots, mosquitoes sucked." He beckoned a waiter. "I want a huge roast beef sandwich with everything on it. Tomatoes, onions, mayo, horseradish, ketchup, lettuce—everything. I've had raw fish, Afgone rice an' veggies 'til I wanna puke."

Mara put her hand on his upper leg, squeezed it. "Jack, it must've been horrible. Are you sure no one tried to prevent your escape?" She traced her fingers over the scars on his bare arms.

"Well, I did encounter minor resistance, but nothing serious. I got these scratches from my personal jail trainer, Hakim. Ugly little gay guy. All in all, I think they were glad to get rid of me." He glanced at Mara, saw tears in her eyes. He tried to remember whether he had seen her cry before. The sight looked familiar.

She noticed his stare, squeezed his leg again. Slowly slid her hand to his inner thigh, began to rub it under the table.

Distracted by Mara's hand, he smiled. Felt his face grow hot, tried to understand Mara's actions.

Bruno asked, "You lay waste like Montana Cossack you are?"

Jack reached across Mara, patted Bruno on the shoulder. Looked at the others, grinned. "In fact, while you guys have been winning the war of terrorism at your desks in Islamabad, I'm happy to say, Bruno, that I whacked a bunch of anti-Russian Afgones. And an old T-55 tank left by your Soviet pals, when they hauled ass north with their tails tucked firmly between their legs."

"So you continue to slaughter young, innocent Talib fighters of Afghanistan," Bruno smiled broadly. "Oh, Jack, you regressionist Capitalist swine. I don't know what we're going to do with you— except to pour you a drink."

Bulldog Mahoney exclaimed, "Congrats again, Lieutenant."

"Thanks, Gunny. I gotta say, since I last saw you, I've no love lost for those Taliban pricks. I'd like to whack all the bastards. I say, let's get it on."

"Great speech, Jack," Bruno said. "Makes me want to join up the U.S. Marines and Green Berets, or fart or something." He belched, which inspired a round of laughter.

"Throw a goddam party an' don't invite me an' I'll have you all in the brig." A gravely voice rang out. Jack turned to see General Harmbruster approach the table. The Marine general wore cammie BDUs, his aide trailed, wearing a khaki uniform. The young officers all scrambled to their feet, saluted. Four chairs and Omar fell over when all leaped to their feet.

"Belay that, men. At ease," the general shouted. Returned their salutes with a casual gesture. Leaned over, helped Omar. "Goddam Army poges can never hold their booze."

"How's it going, General?" Jack asked.

"Where the hell you been, boy? I was lookin' for you."

"He was captured by Taliban forces and taken north, General. But he escaped!" Omar exclaimed. "That's after he rescued me from Taliban Mujs in Hunza."

"I've been following your adventure. Goddam amazing! Tell me all about it." Harmbruster sat in an chair across from him.

"General," Omar added, "I tried to get the Marines to help when Jack was captured but they weren't interested. The Marine Corps is pissed at
Jack."

"No shit, Sherlock. I'm the only Marine in his corner." The general looked at him. "Say, how'd you pull that escape off, Lieutenant? Tell me all." Fazila poured him a Singapore Sling from a huge ceramic pitcher..

"Tell you what, General." Jack pulled several sheets of folded paper from his pocket, handed them to Harmbruster. "Here's my report. There's also some notes I stole from my Taliban captors. Some are in English— some in Arabic or Urdu. We need to get the papers translated. You can read my report at your leisure."

"Efficient use of time," the general responded, gripped the papers in a hand marked by burn scars. "Symbolizes the command presence you showed during your ordeal. You deserve a promotion. No more silver bar. Railroad tracks for you. You're now a captain, my boy." He glanced at his aide who stood behind the general. "Captain, make it so." He handed the papers to the captain, raised his glass. "To a Marine." He tossed down the Singapore Sling, held his glass out.

Fazila poured another round of drinks. Jack sipped his drink—it was cool, refreshing. Thought of the filthy water in the prison camp, shook his head. Mara, noticed his distracted air, squeezed his thigh. He saw tears in her eyes, wondered at her emotions. "So how do you feel about the gaddam Moo-slims now, Jack?" General Harmbruster asked. "You look like you lost a few pounds during your ordeal. You're skinny as a Lincoln rail."

"General, I'm ready to kick some Taliban and al Queerda ass before they can whack us." He glanced at Mara.

"Atta boy," the general shouted. "About time you came around. Kill 'em for Christ. I can't wait to read your report. See me at 1000 hours tomorrow. Don't rise, men." The general left.

"Heady circles for a junior officer," Bruno observed. "I've never talked to a general in the Russian forces."

"He's a piece of work," Jack observed. "He knew my dad." His sandwich arrived, he took a big bite. It was delicious. He chewed, looked at his friends. "Heaven can come in small packages," he observed. "And how can anyone without a roast beef sandwich on the menu claim to be civilized?"

Gil ordered another pitcher of Singapore Slings but Jack switched to bottled water. The group got progressively inebriated. The afternoon wound down until only Mara and Jack were sober. Mara looked at the group. "Let's go somewhere and get some dinner, Jack. I'm hungry."

"Yeah, why not? But you're buyin'. I don't have any dollars or rupees.

Hey, guys, Mara and I are goin' for a quiet dinner. We'll catch you all later.

Thanks for everything."

Mara picked up the flowers and the couple left the party, worked their way across the bar. On the street, they caught a taxi to a small restaurant in central Islamabad. In the cab, he wondered, why Mara was acting so strangely.

Chapter 42

Happy to see an American-style dinner menu in the little Islamabad restaurant, Jack ordered a top sirloin steak. The meal was average but he enjoyed the sensation of eating a non-curry smelling dinner in a small eatery on a quiet street. He shut his eyes, imagined he was in a restaurant in Palo Alto. Mara ordered a cobb salad but ate little. Occasionally she stroked the flowers she had brought from the party.

"What's troubling you, Mara?"

She looked across the restaurant table at the American. Her head was swimming, trying to keep the fractured factions of her emotional life straight. "Jack," she said, "will you go home now? You're becoming highly visible. Continual exposure to danger is a most deadly disease in Pakistan.
In fact, it's terminal."

He cut a last piece of steak, chewed while he thought about her statement. Steak was tough—not like the beef raised at the ranch. Thought of the hills of the Flying Eagle Ranch back in Montana. Dad, Ashley. Green grass, a cold beer—wading through huge snowdrifts in winter. He sighed.

Mara added, "I'm saying, you're at great risk. You'll die if you stay in Pakistan." She pronounced the work like an American would, a strange trait for a native. He had heard another local use the pronunciation, but he could not recall who it had been.

"You don't seem political. How d'you know?"

She reached across the table, grasped his hand. Had a stricken expression on her face. "Believe me, Jack. There's an assassin looking for you right now. An implacable, unrelenting murderer has been ordered to kill you."

"Every American's a target. Nothing new about that."

Mara clenched her fist. "Will you take me home?"

"Sure." He beckoned to the waiter, requested a taxi. After Mara paid the bill, the couple walked to the entry. A battered black Toyota taxicab screeched to a stop in front of the restaurant, Mara gave the Chinese driver an address in the Market Zone. A cool wind blew smoke, dust through the air.

"So, I finally get to see your late dad's palace."

"No, I'm staying at a friend's apartment for a few days."

"Oh, too bad. I always wanted to be a guest in a palace. Maybe some other time?"

Ten silent minutes later, the cab parked in front of a grocery with apartments above. Narrow street, no Caucasians, scene looked creepy.

Jack said, "I guess, I'll just drop you off, Mara. I'm tired and I have to report in early. Do you mind?"

Mara opened her eyes, sighed, either in regret or tiredness. "It's been a long day, Jack. Maybe tomorrow night would be better." She climbed out of the cab, turned and said, "On second thought, Jack, come up. You can sleep on my sofa. I'm sure it's more comfortable than some of the places you've slept lately. That way you won't have to go all the way to Gil's."

He could not voice his uneasiness nor could he think of an excuse.
"Okay, thanks."

At that moment, back at the Marriott Hotel, Gil held tiny Fazila's hand while she vomited into a toilet bowl. She got off her knees, fought dizziness for a moment, pressed her hands against a tiled wall, washed her face in the sink. Gil smiled with a sympathetic air, the two returned to the group in the bar. He held a chair out for her. "You look ghastly pale. Feel better?"

She stared at the Australian. "Yes, but I must tell you something. In private. Let's go over to the window." The two walked to a security rail.

"What's up? Want to go home?"

"It's Mara. I think she plans to kill Jack."

An astonished look crossed his face. "Come on! Why?"

"Because, Gil. She's a Chinese assassin. But some other force controls her now. And they say they'll imprison or kill her sister if she not kill Jack."

Gil studied her face, tried to determine whether she was telling the truth. "But who would want him dead?" After he spoke, he wondered, *If Mara's a Chinese Communist, what is Fazila?*

She shuddered with nausea. "I no know. Probably al Qaida. What does it matter? She is the Black Orchid. Don't you see? She took the flower with her. The black orchid."

Suddenly believing her, he said, "We have to warn him. Where'd they go?"

Fazila shook her head."She show me a flat in Market Zone. Or maybe her villa."

"She wouldn't kill him in the Bhutto home." He grabbed her elbow, led her to the group, examined the others. Billy was slumped over the table, snoring; Bruno was pawing a waitress; Omar, the Negro officer, was gone; Bulldog Mahoney, chewing on a cigar, looked semi-coherent. Gil walked to Bulldog, leaned over and whispered, "Jack's in danger, mate. Come with me?"

When the big Marine realized Gil was serious, he stood and said,

"Let's go." He shook Billy and poked Bruno. With a stumbling Fazila in Gil's grasp, Bulldog pulling Billy along, the men rushed down the stairs, outside. An empty Humvee was parked in front of the hotel. Bulldog jumped in the vehicle, the others followed.

"What'n hell's goin' on?" Billy shouted.

"Jack's in trouble. Lock an' load time." Bulldog yelled.

"How far is it?" Gil asked.

"Not sure," Fazila admitted. "I've only been there once."

"Fazila told me Mara's an assassin. Gonna kill Jack."

"You're shittin' me," Bulldog shouted. "I'll kill the bitch."

In Mara's flat, Jack noticed the apartment was devoid of personal memorabilia, was stuffy—like it had seen little use. Could have been an impersonal hotel suite. Corner of the room, a cockroach confidently postured ownership indignation at the intruders. Above, a ceiling fan slowly revolved, cast flickering shadows on the drab plaster walls.

Mara came out of the bathroom. "I'll make tea. Lie back and relax."

She pointed at a hook by the door. "Hang your gun there."

Glanced at the hook: it was screwed into the cracked plaster wall. Took off his belt and holstered gun, but dropped it and his bag on the floor next to the sofa, listened to the sounds Mara made in the kitchen.

She re-appeared with a tray, two fragile china cups engraved with gold filigree. Placed the platter on a low, glass-covered bamboo table in front of the sofa, smiled, sipped tea. He took the other cup, noted that it looked too fancy for the lowlife apartment, wondered why Mara was staying there. He drank the hot black tea, looked into her green eyes—she looked blank, like she was on drugs. Tea was refreshing but he was too exhausted to enjoy it.

Put down the cup, stretched out on the couch, struggled to keep his eyes open, slept.

Mara studied the young American. Her friend. Attractive even in sleep. She wished they had been lovers. Wondered what he would have been like. Swallowed hard, drew a dagger out of a pocket in her pants. Pulled it out of its sheath, stood over him. She thought of his imprisonment in Afghanistan. Wondered how he had managed to escape his prison cell. He lay on his back. She aimed the blade at his chest. His lips were parted, she thought of kissing him. She looked at his sleeping face. Her muscles would not move, her heart beat rapidly. She put the knife behind her, stroked him on the cheek. He turned over. With his face now hidden Mara felt empowered, raised the knife. After a brief hesitation she sobbed once, stabbed.

<h1 style="text-align:center">Chapter 43</h1>

Bulldog Mahoney pounded the steering wheel when the evening traffic jammed up on Shalimar 7 Street, almost shattering it with his huge fist. He angled to the right, drove on the sidewalk, scattered pedestrians. A policeman waved his hands but Bulldog continued, his horn blew until he was past a two-car accident.

Gil shouted, "Do you see anything that jogs your memory?" Fazila looked at both sides of the street. "No," she wailed.

In the apartment, Jack felt impending doom: tried to wake but couldn't. Felt trapped in a nightmare. With a shout, opened his eyes. Saw a violent movement. Threw himself to the side. Slashing pain into his shoulder blade! An awful slice hit a rib, glanced off. Thought he was shot, grabbed his pistol, stared at Mara. Finger tightened on the trigger of his .45. No one in the room.

On her knees, eyes wide with shock and fear, Mara gasped.

"What the fuck?" Extended the gun. "Where is he?"

"Jack. You must leave. My team'll be here in seconds."

"Your team?"

"They'll kill you. I'm… sorry, run." Mara began to cry. She begged, "Please don't kill me." He spotted the bloody knife in her hand. Blood on her hand. Aimed the pistol at her, grabbed his bag and belt, edged around her. Ignored the fierce pain, blood draining down his side like a gusher from an open faucet, ran to the door, opened it a crack. Peered into the empty hallway, heard feet drum up the stairway. Ran the opposite direction, clambered up a narrow flight of stairs.

On the next floor, tiptoed to the room above Mara's apartment. Opened the door: an old woman looked up, pulled a shawl over her face, cowered in fear. Ignored her, gasped for air while he crossed to a broken patch of plaster wall, lowered his ear to listen, heard a door slam.

Man shouted, Mara answered. Frustrated, he stood up, looked around, saw no escape from the room except the door he had entered. Crossed, threw the door open, moved to the head of the staircase. An Asian holding a pistol, Jack shot him in the chest. Guy smashed against a wall, stretched for Jack with grasping hands, curling fingers. Slumped to the floor.

Gunshots in the narrow stair were deafening. Shot twice more at new targets, smashed through a tangle of three men sprawled on the steps. Slashed at one attacker's head as he vaulted over the team. Three long leaps, he was into the hall outside Mara's door. Ran past it, down the staircase, out the street door.

Passersby, startled by the gunfire, shrank back as he bolted onto the boulevard. Looked around, two armed men across the street ran in his direction. He fired, missed, ran through screaming crowds abandoning the sidewalk. Seconds later, tripped over a yelping dog, crashed into a small kiosk displaying green melons and yellow apples.

Jumped up, darted into a small cross street, panted for breath. Shots rang out. Old woman grunted, grabbed her abdomen, fell to her knees. Thirty steps down the alley he glanced back, saw men pursue. Fired a shot, the men ducked for cover. Individuals and groups huddled along the alley walls, sitting, lying on the ground. Vaulted over several. They looked up, he saw horrible, wounded, scarred faces.

Lepers! Glanced over his shoulder—pursuers did not follow him into the fetid-smelling leper colony. With a sick, weak feeling, buckled his holster on and crept through the colony. Silent eyes stared out of frightened faces, followed his intrusion—alley stretched on forever. Tried to inspect his back, blood was draining down his clothes, messy but didn't look lifethreatening.

No windows, just doors. Saw his chance—a pile of scrap lumber along a wall. Ignored the pain in his back, threw his bag up, leaped, reached the eave of the adjoining building. Pulled himself up to the flat tarpapercovered roof, sprinted across it. Jumped a ten-foot gap, saw a rooftop window: it was jammed. Kicked the window, knocked out jagged edges, crawled through. Inside, he leaned against a wall, tried to catch his breath. Pain in his back flared. Reached back, ran his thumb along the wound—it hurt but didn't feel deep—sliced shirt was sopped with blood. Ran down a stairway, emerged on a street. Started to feel faint. Concentrated on shutting down the pain. Heard a honking vehicle, elated when he saw Gil, Bulldog, Bruno, Billy and Fazila in a Humvee that weaved, knocked aside slowmoving vehicles with ratcheting crashes of sound.

Yelled at his friends. Seconds later, Bruno and Gil jumped out, grabbed him. Billy knelt on the street, fired at a pursuer, who ducked behind a clothes cart.

"He's bleeding bad!" Gil exclaimed.

"Great to see you guys," he panted. "Got any tequila, maybe some spare blood?"

"Lay him on his stomach and find the wound," Bulldog retorted. "Put pressure on it. Hurry."

"It's not that bad. Mara stabbed me with a knife. Get us outta here. Not shitting you—bad guys all over. How'd you get here?"

"Fazila told me what's goin' down, mate," Gil answered. They guided him into the back seat. Gil grabbed the blood-drenched, frayed shirt, ripped it open. The slash across his back was very bloody. Billy jumped on the bumper, Bulldog crashed through the traffic, knocked a bicycle cart aside when he skidded into the middle of the street. Raced past a policeman's outstretched hand. Police car hit its siren, gave chase.

Humvee and police car careened through the streets. When the police caught up, the driver motioned Bulldog Mahoney to the side of the street. Billy gave the policemen the finger, then pulled his huge pistol, blasted out the pursuer's windshield. A second police car approached. They tore around a camel cart. Terrified dromedary reared up, twisted into the path of the onrushing police cars.

Everybody whooped in triumph when a police car crashed into the cart, spun the braying camel around.

A traffic jam forced Bulldog onto the sidewalk again. He pulled onto it with his horn blaring.

They turned a corner, down an alley, continued on to MAACPAK Clinic; two U.S. Army orderlies standing in front saw the Humvee skid to a stop. They grabbed a stretcher, ran to the side of the vehicle, loaded Jack's sprawled body onto a stretcher, raced into the hospital.

Chapter 44

At 2100 hours, Jack emerged from the emergency room: he had received sixty stitches in his back, codeine for pain, a tetanus shot, an antibiotic shot for infection, an IV saline solution was hanging from a makeshift IV tower.

Relieved that his wound was superficial, he climbed into a wheelchair. A smiling woman nurse wearing a white veil, a long gray dress, pushed the clanking wheelchair through a noisy, disorganized hallway. Antiseptic and soap odors filled the air. Jack grinned at his friends and his brother in the waiting room; they all looked shocked at the pallor in his face when they greeted him. Noting their expressions, he tried to smile. "Thanks, guys. I want to thank you for pulling me out of that nightmare."

Gil exclaimed, "I can't believe you're up. What happened?"

"I fell asleep on Mara's sofa, an' she stabbed me with a knife. Luckily, all I got was a surface wound. She flipped out, warned me to escape.
Unbelievable."

"I'll kill the raghead bitch," Bulldog growled.

"No," he said as Gil pushed his wheelchair outside. "I want to talk to her. Find out who's responsible. She warned me at dinner. Told me people want me dead. I need to find out who."

"Why would anybody wanna single you out?" Billy asked.

Jack looked up, down the empty street. "Maybe, I'm too smart. Maybe it's my bad breath. I need rest. Gil, can you take me to your place?" "Stay in the BOQ, Lieutenant," Bulldog interjected.

"More secure," Bruno agreed.

"Yeah, you're right." He glanced at his Australian friend.

Gil nodded, "I feel so guilty, mate."

Jack slowly climbed into the front passenger seat of the Humvee, carefully leaned back, winced from pain. "Don't sweat it. I was suspicious of her from the start." He shook his head. "I don't know why. She acted real strange tonight. Like she was on the rag or something."

"What a ghastly nightmare!" Gil exclaimed. "Just imagine. Mara's the
Black Orchid. She's killed Americans, Pakistani politicians and officers." Fifteen minutes later, they pulled up at the tiny Bachelor Officer's Quarters at MAACPAK: it was a dreary two-story block building that reminded Jack of the smaller Afghan prison without the bullet holes. Flanked by his friends, he walked in, showed his ID. The Army corporal behind the reception desk—a fat youth with a Southern drawl—assigned a room. "I'll have your gear sent over, mate," Gil said.

"Thanks. I'm scheduled for General Harmbruster at 1000 hours." He stroked the hospital gown. "That reminds me, I'll need a uniform for my meeting. I wish I'd had a haircut."

"I'll scare up a barber, bring him to the BOQ—they're cheap around here," Gil said. He turned to Bulldog. "You'd better come early and pick up
Jack's gear and a uniform. I'll make sure it's pressed."

"We'll just pick you up, Lieutenant," Bulldog said. "After I get your gear from Gil. Mess hall at 0830?"

"That'll work," he half-saluted, headed for his assigned room. It was spare but spotless—a bed, a table, fiberglass chairs. He took two codeine tablets from a packet the doctor had given him, fell into bed. His mind overloaded with thought, he stared at the ceiling for long minutes, fell asleep.

Opened his eyes the next morning with a slight codeine hangover, was momentarily frightened when he looked up at a PFC standing over him. Young black man carrying clothing. "Thanks. I'm awake now. Which way is the head?"

"To your left, sir," the PFC responded. "Just down the hall. The duty sergeant sent you this shaving gear, soap and a towel, sir. Also, clean skivvies and socks. And the Marine sergeant gave me these BDUs, sir. He and a lance/corporal are in the mess hall, waiting for you." The young enlisted man turned, left the room.

When he sat up, a stab of pain from his wound flared. He concentrated on the monk's teaching, was amazed when the pain faded away. Twenty minutes later, dressed in the BDUs, a pair of boots, he joined Bulldog and Billy in the mess hall. A woman appeared with steak and eggs, potatoes, toast. "Wow!" he looked at the food. "All I can say is, wow."

"Welcome back to the real world," Bulldog said with a grin.

Billy added, "Real as it can get in this shithole of a country."

Bulldog reached into his pocket, pulled out two captain's bars, placed them next to Jack's plate. "I also got a haircutter standing by. He'll do you after chow."

"Hey, that's great, Gunny. But I'd better not wear railroad tracks 'til I make sure the general remembers my promotion."

An hour later, he presented himself to General Harmbruster's clean-cut aide, whose name he had forgotten. The short black captain smiled, led him into the general's office. It was spare in décor, with a cluttered desk, two chairs for guests, a picture of the President, American and Marine Corps flags. General Harmbruster rose, greeted him with an immense smile.
Glanced at his buzzcut hair, clean-shaven but emaciated face. "Lieutenant.
You look sharp—considering your ordeal."

"Good morning, General. Thank you. But I was injured last night and I feel weak. May I sit down?"

"What d'you mean, Lieutenant?"

"Well, sir, last night, a few hours after I saw you at the hotel bar, I was attacked by a local assassin, the Black Orchid. She stabbed me in the back. I managed to escape."

"It's healthier to leave them laughing, Flashhardt." The general laughed. When Jack did not join him, he said, "My God, son. You live a hectic life. Let me see your wound."

"Not much to see, General." He unbuttoned his blouse, drooped it down his back. A bandage covered one shoulder.

"Goddam, that's a major bandage!"

"Yes, sir. And all I really wanted was to go to law school, drink beer, chase blondes and be a tree-hugging, pseudo intellectual peacemonger." He looked at a chair and asked, "May I sit down, General?"

With a look of concern, the general said, "Of course, son."

Jack gingerly settled into a chair. The general looked at sheets of paper on his desk. "On a quasi-training mission, you landed in a remote valley by accident and fought your way out after you discovered a plot to attack an American city." The general looked up. "Just what we wanted and expected from you." *Wanted from me? I thought I escaped Colonel Farley's clutches when I refused orders.*

"Then you freed your Army friend, got wounded and captured, escaped from a prison camp. Again, perfect.*" Perfect? Then was I sapped on purpose?* "Your escape in the Corridor sounds like a barroom tale for the most hard-bitten warriors. A running battle, a tank attack, a chopper crash and a fire fight in the Khyber Pass—it must have been a blast!" Harmbruster's face broke into a wide grin. *You call being imprisoned by maniacal Taliban, chased by fanatic terrorists fun? But… galloping across that cornflower meadow, chasing Arses, ducking an invisible, howling 100mm tank shell, a struggle at the tank—it was tremendous.*

General Harmbruster looked at him. "I got an email from an Air Force type—a Major Jimmy Jinks. He said you saved his bacon in the Khyber Pass. Well done. Admit that you've had a grand time. Teddy Roosevelt or Winston Churchill would have loved it. I think it was Churchill who said there's nothing more invigorating than being shot at and missed." The general pounded his desk, grinned.

"Today, you're getting a Purple Heart for your wound in Hunza, and a Silver Star for rescuing your friend. And I'm recommending you for a Navy Cross for your escape. That Intel about the Chinese—al Qaida meeting is prime."

Jack flushed, felt a charge of pride go through his body.

The general picked up his phone, called his aide into the office. "Get that photographer in here." A corporal bearing a camera entered, the general came around his desk. "A record never hurts, son. Lord, knows, I'm tired of this undercover nonsense." *Undercover? I'm UN, General.*

The general's aide, bearing a box, walked in, stood at ease.

General Harmbruster pinned a Purple Heart and a Silver Star on his blouse, the photographer took several pictures. He felt a flush of amazement and pride go through his body when the general shook his hand. "Thank you, General. I'd like to make a couple of award recommendations for two enlisted men. I had help from great Marines and soldiers, or I wouldn't be here."

"That'll be fine, Captain. Nothing more than you and your men deserve. You know, Doug MacArthur got seven Silver Stars as a company grade officer in World War I. It's our nation's third highest medal." The general grinned, gestured at the chair in front of his desk. "I may not be Smedley Butler, the Corp's most famous Marine, but I've been around— almost since Caesar crossed the Rubicon back in 49 BC. Of course, if you're still determined to go to school, I can arrange a transfer to a reserve unit stateside, and you can go back to law school. Become a JAG attorney."

Jack reflected on the fulfillment of his hopes and dreams. Yes! he thought. I'm outta this insanity, back to the real world. Law school, airconditioning, Dad—maybe even Ashley. Screw fanatical Muslims, crazy monks, weird Dragon Gods. Upon reflection, he realized he had to mention the bomb. "That sounds great, General, but I've something else I must discuss with you. Something too wild to put in my report. In Quetta, I met with a leader of a religious order at his island temple. He gave me a present. A sword scabbard. And

he told me the sword for it is in a temple in the mountains. And, that the bomb the U.S. is searching for is near the temple.
He gave me instructions on how to find it."

The general leaped to his feet. "That's wonderful!" Lowered his voice and added, "I knew bringing you aboard would pay off. We'll form an MEU action force and take it back."

"Not that easy, General. The map self-destructed during my escape from the island. I've no proof or directions to the bomb."

Stopping in midstride, the general gave him an angry stare. "Can you make a copy? And what do you mean—escaped?"

"The map wasn't exact, General. I think it'll take a survey on the ground. There's a temple and a cave in the Hindu Kush, west of Hunza Valley, near the Chinese border." Stopped, remembered he had never mentioned his first visit to the temple. "I think we have to find it. I think al Qaida plan on setting it off in Frisco." Startled, the general stared at him.
"Can you get a copy of the map from the religious order?"

"They might not be much help. They were attacked by unknown agents while I was visiting them. I barely escaped. We'll have to check it out and try to get the head man here. Conway. Get him to re-draw the map."

"Tell me where the island is," the general ordered. "I'll send a team right now."

Chapter 45

In his BOQ room, after enjoying two toasted BLT sandwiches, a glass of cold whole milk for lunch, Jack fell asleep. The luxury of drifting to sleep without worrying about some maniac trying to kill him, or imprison him, or starve him, or beat him, or seduce him, was an indescribable feeling of security. He awoke at 1600 hours, winced at the stiffness from his wound, called Gil from the telephone in the lobby.

"Hey, mate," Gil said. "How're you feeling? Up to a meeting with Miss Elle? She wants an update on your adventures."

"Sure, why not? I've been asleep. Can you send a vehicle?"

"Righto, mate."

An hour later, Gil escorted him into Miss Elle's office. Jack looked around. Arranged flowers on her big desk, bright blue curtains framed large mullioned windows. An Abba CD was playing in the background. She stood in front of her desk.

"Mister Flashhardt," she said, "I'm so happy to see you alive and well." She wore a gray linen suit that showed off her tall, slender body, and the blonde hair piled on her head.

"Thank you, ma'am, it's good to be back."

"You've lost weight. We must fatten you up or you'll give the United Nations a bad name." Miss Elle sat down, glanced at his crotch. He settled very carefully into a leather couch. Miss Elle frowned. "Gil told me you were attacked and slightly wounded by a Chinese assassination cell. I can't understand why a United Nations officer would be singled out, but it may be retaliation for the unauthorized rescue operation. The one you conducted on the Chinese border."

After he related a toned-down, abbreviated tale of his escape, Elle expressed wonderment and sympathy, then dismissed him. As he left the office, he glanced back: Miss Elle was staring at his rear end. She looked up, colored.

Bulldog and Billy were waiting in his office. They took him to the BOQ; he concentrated on absorbing and flushing away pain, fell asleep in his room. He woke at midnight, stared at the ceiling and tried to recall law school, but failed. It was resting in a dreamy, fuzzy, misty non-reality. He could not see himself walking with a briefcase or an armful of books—he could only see a weapon in his hands.

The next morning, being in a secure environment was again an incredibly wonderful feeling: he relaxed, happy that he had no pressure or time constraints. The room was stark—the windows had no curtains—but its immaculate condition made it seem American: home, reality. He went to the bathroom, took a careful shower, shaved, dressed, walked to the mess hall for breakfast, returned to his room for more rack time.

In the afternoon, a knock on the door surprised him: it was Billy, wearing a khaki uniform, a UN blue hat. He said, "I hope you're ready to get out of this armpit of a country." Billy ran his fingers through his hair. It had grown, looked like it would soon be long enough to braid.

"You read my mind," he smiled. "I'd settle for the peaceful shores of South Central Watts, a spelling bee in Detroit, even a biker bar in east Orange County. He glanced at his brother. Yo ever make it to Cook's Corner when you were stationed at Camp Pendleton?"

Billy smiled, nodded his head up and down . "How's the back?"

"Dude, it hurts, but it's not serious."

"Gil had a talk with Fazila," Billy said. "He's like totally pissed at her. She knew about Mara from way back. So he threw her out." Billy shook his head and added, "The question is… what the hell're we doin' in this snake pit?"

Jack made a wolflike grin. "Killing snakes. Let's go to the office."

At the UN building, Gil greeted them. "Hi, mates. Jack—as usual— you've saved my bacon."

"Wha's up, Gil?" he asked as he sat down.

"Miss Elle's going to a government function tonight and I was slated to escort her. Now you can do it." Gil crumbled a paper, threw it in the wastebasket under his desk.

"Come on, Gil. Why isn't she going with her husband?"

Gil raised a restraining hand. "Mate, this'll be good for you. It's a reception and dinner held by President Zardari. You'll get a chance to meet the Head Cheese. Or in this case, the Head Muttonhead, I guess." Gil clapped his hands together. "Anyway, I've got a date tonight—and Elle's husband doesn't attend functions."

Jack smiled, "Your magnanimous offer's irresistible. I'd like to meet the president. But what's the dress?"

Gil glanced at his uniform. "You could wear dress blues or even a civilian suit."

"How's Fazila?"

"I dumped the bitch—I'm sorry, mate. I was the cause of it all. If I hadn't introduced you to Mara..."

Jack rose from his chair. "Fazila saved me in the end. Heart was in the right place."

Looking into his eyes, Gil said, "You're more forgiving than me, but I don't give a shit. The bitch should've told me that her friend was going to try and gut you like a perch." He stood, shooed the two out. "Take the day off. I'll tell Miss Elle about the change."

"She won't care?"

"Naw," Gil responded. "Just so she has an escort that can stand and chew gum at the same time. In fact," Gil grinned, "she suggested it. Said it was a chance for you to meet the president."

"So who's the new babe?" Jack arched his sore back.

"We'll see. Mick set me up," Gil said. "Let's all get together at noon tomorrow."

"Glad your love life isn't disrupted. I don't have evening dress—better get my blues cleaned." He and Billy left Gil's office. An hour later, he had the NCO at the Bachelor Officer's Quarters send for a cleaner to press the uniform, shirt, and tie he pulled out of his footlocker. While the dress uniform, his father's when he served as a young officer in the Corps, was being readied, he showered, shaved, tried to read a Louis L'Amour novel about an American pilot crashed and on the run in Siberia. He could tell the author, like most writers, was clueless about the reality of survival in the wilderness: the fear, the hunger, the cold, the filth—but it helped him go to sleep.

The duty sergeant sent the cleaning man up with his blues at 1730. The trousers, blue, with one-and-one-half inch scarlet stripes up the seams, had been fitted at OCS but were loose on his reduced frame. The leather shoes sparkled like mirrored black glass. The jacket, made of black broadcloth, fit well around the shoulders, the brass buttons with globe and anchor insignia gleamed. He noted the stiff collar: there was a label—Horstman of Philadelphia—and an English-made, white detachable liner.

At six PM, a PFC knocked on his door, told him a car was waiting. He donned his white cap with a brim as black and shiny as his mirrored shoes, walked down, climbed into the back seat of the Embassy Mercedes. Whiteblonde Miss Elle, dressed in a pale-blue, sleeveless, low-cut dress, was sitting in the far corner of the Mercedes. She was spectacularly beautiful. He caught a faint odor of perfume—smelled like fresh lilacs.

"Hello, Miss Elle." He inhaled, savored her scent.

"Jack, call me Elle when we're alone," the Norwegian said. She glanced at her watch. "Excited about meeting the president?"

"Of course." He studied her beautiful bod— *Not as much as a chance at meeting you skin to skin, but—* "How long'll the event last, Elle?"

Leveled her intense blue eyes on him. "I'm not sure how many will go through the reception line. The dinner will last at least an hour, then the president will give a speech in Urdu and one in English. How's your wound? Inhibit your movements?"

"I'm much better. Just a surface wound." Her hands, grabbing his back. Milady had got his mojo working, even with this... unfortunately married babe.

"That's good," Elle said with a throaty tone. "Are you enjoying your service with the United Nations?"

"It's certainly been interesting so far." Get the feeling Elle is on the make. *Like to service you, babe. Wish you were single.*

"Having young officers from various countries around the world serve with the UN gives us an opportunity to pass the institution's values on to the countries to which they return." Elle looked at him, glanced at his crotch. "It's important that the UN maintain a strong relationship with the
United States. Any UN official that doesn't build a strong rapport with the
U.S. is doomed as a career diplomat."

"You sound like a UN brochure," he observed. *How about trying to establish close relations with me? Ait—remember, she's married.*

She smiled, stroked his arm with soft fingers. "You're right. Let's forget diplomacy for tonight and enjoy ourselves." *Enjoy. Is that a promise? Stop it, stupid—she's married.*

Fifteen minutes later, they entered the fabulously decorated palace with its polished marble floors, clumps of exotic flowering plants growing in ancient brown ceramic pots. Elle explained that the pots were recovered from an excavation of an old fortress in Lahore. They moved through the reception line and when Elle reached President Zardari—a plain-faced, short man, he greeted her and presented his wife. She was a black-haired woman with a friendly peasant's face. Elle introduced Jack, mentioned that he had been imprisoned, had escaped from the Taliban.

"So you're the new American hero." President Zardari smiled, shook his hand. "Congratulations. How did you manage?"

"It's a long story, Mister President."

His wife grasped the president's forearm and said, "Husband, don't you think recognition is in order for this young American?"

"Excellent idea, my dear," President Zardari exclaimed. "I'll have an aide contact you at the UN offices, Mister Flaser. We'll have a ceremony and you will be awarded… the Pakistani Hilal-I-Juraat." "Thank you, sir." *What the hell is that?*

Zardari added, "We're very happy to recognize bravery, initiative, and resourcefulness in one of our allies' finest warriors."

Elle took his arm, they passed into a room where diplomats, politicians, military officers stood in groups, drank champagne. "Fetch me a glass of champagne, Finest Warrior," Elle ordered over her shoulder. She joined two Pakistani men in Western suits.

Feeling like an overdressed servant, he worked his way through the crowded room, asked a bartender for two glasses of champagne. The man poured from a bottle of Dom Perignon. Impressed with the president's taste, he downed both glasses. The man smiled, refilled the flutes.

A guy with a familiar face approached him: David Holland, an FBI agent he had met in Montana during the ranch pre-trial. "Step over here with me," Holland said in a low voice. He turned, walked to a clump of large-leafed plants in a corner. Had a very muscular upper body, was dressed in a black linen suit. Light brown hair neatly combed, brown eyes wideset. Jack followed the agent he had met in Billings when the FBI had investigated the Crow Indian claims against the ranch.

"What up, Sir? You chasing camel rustlers for Pakistan?" Holland grinned. Had a great smile with friendly eyes that encouraged trust. Jack didn't.

"I transferred to the CIA, kid. I was in BAM for awhile, but even more action here. Looks like you're doin' okay. Especially after your ranch disaster."

"Hey, I'm a dress waiter for the UN." He checked out Holland. The man looked tired. "What's BAM mean?"

"By Any Means. But that's in the past, kid. I heard about your adventure in Afghanistan. I'm proud to know you, Jack. You're one tough guy." Here came a set-up. Guy wanted something.

Holland grasped his elbow. "General Harmbruster told me to contact you. Predictive analysis indicates someone is going to haul the bomb to the US. But I guess higher-ups decided they didn't want the Marines overtly involved in the recovery of the biobomb. Too hot. Nobody wants credit or blame. But the general's not backin' down. So for now, I'm your contact man with Harmbruster. He said to tell you he sent a team to Quetta. All the monks on the island…"

"What about them?"

"All the team found were dead bodies. But no white man." "You're shittin' me!" Law school—he could see it fading away.

Holland shook his head. "Nope. So it's up to you, the general said. And if you find the bomb, you're gonna be the target of enemies that'll want to relieve you of it."

"Yeah, like that makes sense. But what'm I supposed to do? Auction it to the highest bidder?"

Holland frowned, grabbed his arm. "Cut the crap! That bomb's one deadly chunk of ordnance! And it's too hot to even recover. We're talkin' deep denial from everybody concerned. They're runnin' for cover on this one like scared cockroaches. I'm gonna send a QUALCOMM satellite phone to your BOQ tomorrow. It's small and it'll work anywhere. Has a built-in GPS and a tacked-on blasting cap. Just turn it on and it's programmed to call me. If you don't leave a message, I'll call back in six hours, send a signal— it'll ignite. So all you have to do is pack it in a couple kilos of C-4 and it'll blow up the bomb. Also, exactly after the six hours, I'll have a B-52 strike ready with BLU-82s—that's 15,000-pound Daisy Cutters. So leave a message sayin' "This is it." and the GPS in the cell phone will show me where it is when you call. Oh, and the cell has a builtin camera, so take a picture of the bomb and send that. I wanna make sure you've got the right ordinance. We'll bomb that location… say thirty minutes after the cell phone blows up. With a CEP of ten feet—that's circular error probability for you ground pounders—we'll close up your caves forever. You can say, "Sayonara, Long Island Iced Tea Bomb, no mas, no mas."

"What about the al Qaida? What if they get there first? Can I use the cell phone to order out pizza? Wouldn't want them to think I'm inhospitable."

Holland appraised him. "I can see you're the same smartass you were as a civilian. I'd a thought the Corps woulda beat it out of you. Anyway, the LIIT bomb can't fall into enemy hands. You heard its capabilities."

"They give smart bombs IQ tests? Can it dance? Tell jokes?"

"You could put toilet paper on its nose and wipe a Taliban's ass if he bent over. And more importantly, the sonic wave it emits penetrates the earth two hundred feet, clears a path. Deep underground bunkers are the hottest thing going for the baddies to protect their munitions and barracks. We even found airplanes buried way deep with elevators and shit like that in Iraq. 'Course the raghead sandpounders were so stupid, they let sand contaminate all their buried planes. But our B-52 strikes couldn't touch them until this bomb was developed."

Jack held up his hand, "Yeah, I know all that crap."

"We got a lotta people on this. The flu bug in it is vectored by birds and humans—it'll put tens of millions of people on their deathbed within days. There's no defense for it. There's no vaccine. It's incurable and it hits the victim in minutes. They start feelin' real sick, right away."

"Why in hell did you people let it loose on the world?"

"Well, it's only supposed to go off inside contained areas like bunkers and caves. It follows ventilation and kills everybody."

Jack shook his head, looked around the ballroom. "I don't know why I ask. There's something about government that takes ordinary, sane people, turns them into imbeciles."

"Cut the political chatter, kid. You ain't votin' on this. Just hope you find the bomb before the villains do, an' make sure they don't get it. Your country'll be grateful," Holland ordered.

"I don't want to end up in the brig."

Holland smiled. It was not pretty. "If you do, I'll visit."

"Thanks a whole hell of a lot. And when do I get funds and written orders?"

Holland glanced around. "It's too hot. Nobody wants to touch it," he admitted.

"Yeah, well, I don't wanna work on it either. The general tried to suck me in before. But now he's promised to send me to JAG, back home. I'm outta here. Get someone else."

Holland looked around. "You're the man. You know how hard it is to find climbers qualified to work on this?"

Jack exclaimed, "I don't care! I'm outta here."

On the way back to Elle with the champagne, General Harmbruster hailed him. "A two-fisted drinker, ehh, Lieutenant? Let's shed a tear for
Lord Nelson."

Jack paused, careful to balance the drinks. "What's that, General?"

"When the British hero, Lord Nelson, died during the Battle of Trafalgar, the British preserved him for burial by sticking him in a barrel of brandy. They shipped him to England in the barrel. On the way, sailors would ask permission to shed a tear for the admiral. Then they'd go below decks, drink from Nelson's barrel and piss in it to maintain its level of fluid.
Hence the toast: Let's shed a tear for Lord
Nelson." "General, in a word—yuck,"
Jack responded.

Harmbruster grinned. "That's swabbies for you—they'll drink anything. Any progress on our problem? Did Agent Holland tell you about the massacre? Are you exploring a lead here?"

"No, sir. I'm just here as Miss Elle's escort. But Holland told me about the dead monks."

Ignoring the reference to the monks, the general exclaimed, "Good show. She's a real looker. I met her at an Embassy function just before you started workin' there."

Jack stared at the general. "You did? Excuse me, General." He walked towards Elle until he felt a hand grasp his arm. Short Mick Nakamura and tall, lean, big-handed Omar dressed in Service "A" uniforms. He grinned, greeted them, "Hey, Mom, Mick, what's up? What're you doing?"

Omar smiled. "We're both serving as temp dog robbers."

Mick pointed with a nod of his head at two Army generals. "I come halfway around the world to be a goddam gofer. Pisses me off, but what're you gonna do?"

"I spose you wanna go shear Syria or slam Iran," he smiled. "But we had fun in Hunza."

"Only good action I've seen lately—our rescue of this green beanie," Mick affirmed.

"And I'm still paying for my famished Hunza chowin' down on fricasseed eyeballs!" Omar exclaimed.

"Hey, at least you can laugh about it," Jack commented. "I gotta get back to Miss Elle." He spotted her and moved to join her. Just as he reached her, a host announced dinner, and after courses of grilled salmon, slabs of smoked pheasant, rice, various vegetables, the president gave short speeches in Urdu, English. Towards the end of the speech, Jack popped three pain pills to calm his wound.

After the dinner, Elle told the driver to return to her residence, a villa on the east side of Islamabad. It was a well-maintained English Colonial structure, with a tile roof, stuccoed walls. They passed through a courtyard and a servant opened a side door to the parlor. Elle said, "You look tired, Jack. I won't keep you long. Would you like a drink?"

"I'll just have water if you have it. I just took some meds." Sat down on a comfortable sofa, took off his jacket, looked around for danger, immediately fell asleep. When a noise woke him hours later, he was covered with a light blanket, his shoes and cap were on the floor next to the sofa. He saw Elle standing in the doorway, dressed in a full-length, multilayered nightgown. "Come to a more comfortable bed," she said.

Felt dopey from the medication, got up, took Elle's outstretched hand, shuffled behind her. She led him to a bedroom with a four-poster bed; he yawned, sat down. Elle unbuttoned his shirt. He shucked his pants, socks and shorts, climbed under the covers, fell asleep.

When he awoke at sunrise, Elle was lying next to him under the covers, caressing his chest. Her odor was clean, alluring, her touch was soft, stimulating, unending. He stared at the pink silk canopy that hung from the four posts at each corner of the bed and draped down the sides. The walls, ceiling beyond were a light creamy, unmarked color. *Must be her bedroom. She took me to bed and I fell asleep. Remember, she's married. Where's her husband?*

Elle continued to caress him, her hand slowly circled across his breast. He shut his eyes, reflected about waking under an insect-infested pile of leaves in the mountains of Afghanistan. Her hand dropped lower. Remembered waking on a coarse, smelly pile of Afghan rugs in a rude mudbrick hut. Elle's hand circled lower, rubbed his right hip, moved across to his left hip. Thought of lying on the dank, dirt floor in Yassar Ahmoud's prison camp, sick from drinking foul water. Ran her fingers through his pubic hair, rubbed his balls.

He turned, embraced the beautiful woman. Her body was muscular, lean, hard. She smiled when she looked into his eyes, moved closer. He kissed her, pulled the nightgown over her head, stroked her naked breasts, moved his hand down until it rested between her legs. Elle sighed with pleasure, arched her lean body towards his grasp.

He rolled on top, entered her. She rose to meet his thrusts with a passion that he had never experienced before. Her hands gripped his arms and back with a strength that belied her appearance. Elle clawed his upper back. He climaxed, was immediately grateful she had not ripped his wound open. Thought, *My first married woman. Guilt? Where the hell is the husband?*

Elle misinterpreted his nervous smile as one of satisfaction, said with a soft voice, "Young men are too quick with their own gratification. You must think of a woman's needs." Kissed him passionately, climbed on top, whispered, "Now, let's start over and make love my way."

Chapter 46

A small café near the Islamabad UN offices: the lunch customers appeared to be Pakistanis who worked for foreign embassies and businesses; the majority wore Western clothes. Jack was trying to enjoy a croissant and cheese. The CIA's QUALCOMM satellite phone was on the table next to his coffee. He regarded the phone, sent by Holland to the BOQ. Wondered if it could spontaneously explode. He glanced around, saw a white man standing in the doorway of the crowded, noisy cafe. The man, wearing casual civilian clothes, approached.

"Howard Hucks, CIA," the man said when he sat down. "Flashhardt, our station's been trying to track you down."

Jack sipped bitter coffee in a tiny cup. "Really? Didn't know I was so popular. Well, I've been on a paid vacation up north. Now, I'm outta here.
Back to the States."

Hucks, a solid-looking man of about thirty-five years, with black curly hair, a handsome face, about two inches under six feet tall, appraised him. "Congrats on your escape." Hucks checked out the cell phone, Jack slid it into his pocket. Hucks continued, "You have enemies in Pakistan. What's the deal?"

"Cool. I dunno, maybe my winning personality?"

"Yeah, we got a thick file on you. Hard to figure—a young guy like you." Hucks waved at a waiter, pointed at his coffee. His fingernails were chewed down. "Hate this local shit, but that's probably all they have. Where's a Starbucks when you need one?"

"Dude, why d'you have a file on me?"

"I'll ask the questions, kid," Hucks growled. He pointed at the waiter, made a hurrying motion when the man noticed him. "They hate to be pointed at," Hucks said with a sly smile. "I do it often as possible." He looked back. "Last night, you met President Zardari. He's gonna give you a medal."

"You followin' me around?" He looked around—"Where's Agent Holland?"

"No, we got it from a telephone tap." Hucks picked up coffee the impossibly thin, black-skinned waiter placed in front of him. "You know there's a hit on you—unofficially? And I don't mean the Black Orchid, who can't carve her way out of a paper shithouse." Hucks looked at him. "How's your back?"

"Cool it on my back—thanks for your concern," Jack responded sarcastically.

"Would've solved a lot of wasted effort if she had carved you up a little better." Hucks poked a finger. Suddenly enraged, Jack growled,
"Look, asshole, I don't need to take crap from you."

Hucks glanced around the crowded café. Faces turned. "Not bad, kid. I like you, and we got a deal for you."

"What's the deal? Aces and eights?"

Hucks chuckled, said in a low voice, "Yeah, right—dead man's hand. When Zardy gives you the medal, waste him."

"You crazy? Why would I do that?"

The CIA agent looked around with just his eyes. "For some reason you're on Colonel Farley's hate list." Pulled out a cigarette pack of
Pakistani Gold Leafs, extracted a cigarette, lit it with a Bic lighter. Jack saw English, Urdu warnings on the pack: "Smoking is injurious to health—
Ministry of Health." *Whole damned country is dangerous to my health.*

Hucks continued, "Like I said, there's lotta sympathy around the station for you. You're a doer. Some of us locals figgered, here's your chance to prove your loyalty to the U.S."

"But why President Zardari? You running out of Taliban targets? You killed all the al Qaida while I was gone? Wasn't Osama enough?"

Ther agent ignored his jibes. "The local honchos have decided he needs to go. This isn't D.C. level, or even COS—Chief of Station. Eventually, Washington will figger it out but nobody wants to wait for them to pull their heads out of their asses. So it's only a matter of time that we get a gunner next to Zardari. Then it's lights out— the party's over."

"But why would the U.S. want to do him in?"

Hucks glanced around, leaned forward. "Because Zardy's a deadly combination of weakness and corruption. It's not like he's an elected democrat—the last election was rigged. And, he and Mushy let their buddy, Khan, sell nuclear technology to North Korea. Sold it to Iran, too." Hucks held up his cup.

Jack took a bite of his croissant. Suddenly it tasted dry, pasty. He washed it down with bad-tasting, worse-smelling chicory coffee. Quit whining—it beats the shit outta licking raindrops off the bars of a cage. "What if your local honchos change their minds between now and a successful… assassination? Do I get a replay? And who's Mushy? Do I have to waste him as well?"

"Not gonna happen, G.I. He runs around, pretends to chase al Qaida, turns over low-level operatives. No, Zardari's cashed all his chips." Hucks poked at a slice of bread. "Mushy? He's retired— Musharraf was the prez." Billy Howling Dog walked up to the table. "Hey," he called. He was dressed in woodland BDUs, a UN baseball hat. He sat down, glanced at the CIA agent.

"Take a hike, kid," Hucks said. "We're busy."

"Billy's with me."

"Should I throw this asshole outta here?" Billy asked.

"Shut your yap, kid," Hucks ordered.

Billy threw a left jab from his heels. Hucks jerked up a forearm, blocked Billy's fist—the force of the blow still knocked him backwards. The waiter started yelling in a high-pitched voice.

Rising, Hucks grinned at Billy, said to the waiter, "It's okay, my pal's just showin' me he loves me."

"You must leave." The waiter turned, headed back to the kitchen, muttering to himself.

Hucks looked at Jack. "So what do you think? Take care of the problem, you're off my desk."

"Why not? But how do I get out of there alive? I've got a better chance of dodging you than knocking off the president."

"Don't worry, kid," Hucks lit a fresh cigarette, inhaled deeply, glanced at Billy. "We can get people in the palace—we just can't get any armaments close to Zardari. His interest in you is heaven-sent. He takes military guests to a shooting range in the Palace. That'll get you the weapon and opportunity. And we'll supply guides to get you out of there. Just make sure there're no witnesses an' it's back to the States for you. Headaches over, no mas, no mas."

You must think I'm really stupid, he thought. "Well, if you can get me out, you got a deal." Holland and Hucks partners?

Hucks rose. "Just play it out and I'll have resources ready when you pull your caper."

Do people really talk like this? This guy is right out of the comics.
"You got a deal. Want me to make it a package and throw in their Parliament? I know a bomb I can fire up their asses."

"Zardari will do just fine, smartass," Hucks growled. He ground out his cigarette on Jack's plate, looked at Billy. "Nice jab." He rose and left the café.

"Who 'uz that creep?"

"CIA. Figures I work for them, I guess. He's nuts. But why should he be any different than the rest of the head cases in this dump?" Jack threw a few rupees down and asked, "You eat yet?"

"Yeah, I grabbed chow. What'd the guy want?"

"Just wants me to off the president, is all. He's got bad breath, I guess. Seems like giving him breath mints'd be easier."

"No gov'mnt around here 'ud be better than what they got."

He glanced at Billy. "Yeah, right! We gotta figure how to get out of this mess with my skin intact."

"There you go with that "we" shit again, Flashy. How about you just don't go to the medal ceremony?"

"Dude, you're bubbling over with great ideas. Gonna send my remains back in a wood casket or a body bag?"

"Plant you under a banana tree," Billy responded cheerfully. "That way, I'll think of you every time I slip on a peel. So that CIA guy was serious? I didn't think the U.S. would just off some country leader."

"The CIA killed the Diem brothers back in the 1960's."

"Diems? They related to De Eminem?" Jack laughed, took out the cell phone, regarded it.

"What're you gonna do?"

"Obviously I'm not gonna shoot the president. I'll figure something out. The ceremony's tonight. I got a message at the BOQ to be at the Presidential Palace at 1800 hours."

"Want company?"

"No, I want you out of it in case something goes wrong. That way you can help me later."

"Okay," Billy said. "I got a class to take. Gun safety."

Jack laughed. "Probly your version of gun safety is to shoot everybody in sight and claim accidental discharge. May as well teach a bull how to make china cups."

Smiling, Billy said, "Fun-ny! Let me know how it goes hangin' with the politicos. I'll check in with Gil."

An hour later, Jack met Gil at the UN office, didn't reveal his CIA assignment. The Aussie congratulated him for the medal, suggested they meet at the Marriott Hotel bar at 2100 hours.

Back at the BOQ, he took a long nap, cleaned up, donned the Dress Blues uniform, attached his new medals and captain's bars. After he dressed, he caught a cab to the palace.

An ISI major, slender and tall, with a British-style mustache, very dark skin, dressed in a dark green Pak uniform, was waiting for him at the entrance. "I'm Sadiker Dang," he said.

"I'm dang sad too," Jack responded. The man didn't get it, or ignored the lame joke, so he swallowed an additional attempt at humor. They turned, entered the palace, marched down a long marble hallway. He flashed on the dark cell in the Taliban prison, shook the image out of his head. Sadiker stopped outside a door flanked by two stiff guards. "No weapons in the president's presence. Must search you."

"I'm clean," he said. Sadiker searched him anyway, giving special attention to his inner thighs, his groin. Repulsed by Dang's caresses, Jack noticed a tic in the man's dark face, smelled a hint of perfume, wondered if the guy was gay. They entered a reception hall, a male receptionist escorted the two through to a large office decorated with ficus-type trees in the corners. President Zardari sat behind a teak desk overlaid with vivid pink marble. Walls were covered with black charcoal drawings of Indus River scenes, a Pakistani flag hung on the wall behind the desk.

A general stood to the side of the desk, an Army photographer stood by the door. Sadiker stopped, saluted, so he followed suit, even though his Marine training normally forbade indoor salutes.

"Welcome, Captain Flash," the president said. "Meet my able assistant, General Shaikn." The short general smiled when he shook hands with Jack. President Zardari added, "The general will do the honors of presenting you with the Pakistani Hilal-I-Juraat which is awarded for acts of courage and valor."

Prompted by Dang, Jack stepped forward to receive the medal. Sadiker Dang, read a proclamation:

"For conspicuous bravery. While a prisoner of the Taliban in the Northern Areas, U.S. Marine First Lieutenant Jackson Flashhardt, serving with the United Nations, escaped from his Taliban captors, and thereafter formed and led a Kafir guerrilla team that succeeded in eliminating a Taliban tank and three personnel that were pursuing in an attempt to re-capture him. Personally leading the forces, Lieutenant Flashhardt showed initiative, superb planning and execution in the defeat of the invading enemy. For these actions, Lieutenant Flashhardt is awarded the Hilal-I-Juraat."

Signed,

Lieutenant General Shaikn Baikn

For,

President Ali Zardari,

Islamic Republic of Pakistan

The general saluted him, pinned the medal on his chest. It was round with a crescent moon, a star in the center, hung from a red and green ribbon. Jack saluted, accepted the president's hand, shook it. The photographer took a picture, blinded him with the flash. Jack felt pride, even if the medal was silly-looking, and even though the action had actually taken place in Afghanistan, not the Northern Areas.

"Come," the president ordered. "I want to shoot." The four men went through a side door, entered a small shooting gallery. Jack said in a low voice, "Mister President, there's something I must tell you in private." "After we shoot," the president ordered. He picked up a .45 semi auto from a table, fired three rounds at a target ten meters downrange. Handed the pistol back to the general, who fired three rounds.

Jack was the last to shoot. Heart rate raced while he regarded the smiling president. Three men, three bullets. Raised the gun, turned to a new target, felt it, fired the three rounds. When the targets were returned, Zardari's shots were grouped near the bull's-eye. Baikn's were in an outer ring. Jack's had shredded the bull on his target. The president smiled at his success over the general, frowned when he saw Jack's target. "You're righthanded. But I noticed your right eye was closed when you shot." "Actually," Jack said, "I had both eyes closed when I shot."

"Amazing trick!" The president autographed the target, handed it to him. "I don't live in the Palace," he said. "Come to my private day quarters, Captain, and we'll share a drink." The president dismissed the others, led Jack to his personal quarters in the palace. A guard opened the door, the two passed into a starkly furnished room with a bar at one side. A uniformed soldier, ugly, hard-looking, stood behind the bar.

"I'll order, he doesn't understand English," the president said. He spoke rapidly in Urdu, the soldier poured two glasses of Johnny Walker Black Label.

Jack said, "Mister President, an attempt is being made on your life." The president stared, his drink raised halfway to his lips. He picked up a telephone, spoke in Urdu. A moment later, a man dressed in a suit entered the room.

"This is Javed Hussain Shah, my Security Chief." Zardari said. "Javed is head of our country's security forces, including ISI. He knows of no new plots against my life other than the normal desire to kill me, held by tens of thousands of Taliban and other Muslims, Buddhists, and even Bhutto's daughter. Tell him what you've told me." Jack regarded the newcomer: man was short, slender, dressed very neatly in a black Nehru-style suit. About thirty-five, condescending look.

"All I know is a man approached me in a restaurant and suggested I kill the president. He knew of the medal ceremony. Said I should kill President Zardari. He said I'd be killed if I didn't follow his orders." He hoped his omission of the fact that the man was an American would go unnoticed.

"Well," Zardari appeared to relax. "That just sounds like an attempt based on opportunity. Nothing to worry about. Javed Shah will arrange to have you fully de-briefed later. You may leave now, Captain. Good luck." Zardari walked him to the door. Sadiker was waiting, led him to a tan Toyota SUV parked near the entrance to the palace.

He asked Sadiker to take him to the BOQ. The soldier driver negotiated the crowded streets with one hand on the wheel, the other on the horn, tooted at every perceived hindrance. At the BOQ, Jack asked if he could be dropped at the Marriott Bar. Sadiker agreed. He ran upstairs, put the new medal in his footlocker, changed into civilian clothes and hiking shoes, returned to the waiting Toyota. Sadiker was talking on a cell, nervously smiled at him while he listened. He gave a short instruction to the driver, the man drove away. When the vehicle was out of sight of the BOQ, it pulled over and Sadiker asked, "Would you please get out of the vehicle?"

Mystified, he climbed out of the rear seat. Driver got out, pulled a gunmetal gray, long-barreled revolver, pointed it.

"I must ask you to put your hands together," Sadiker commanded in an apologetic tone of voice. Handcuffed him with plastic ties.

"What's going on?"

"You're under arrest for participating in a conspiracy to assassinate the president," Sadiker responded.

"What? Are you crazy?"

Sadiker said, "Get back in the vehicle."

Saw no option, climbed into the front seat. The driver put away his weapon. Sadiker climbed into the back. Three hours later, after silent, strained travel out of the city, during which the driver and Dang conducted frequent conversations in Urdu, the vehicle passed through farmlands, small shabby adobe hamlets on a paved road, later a dirt road.

The Toyota halted at the checkpoint entrance of a large village. A guard stepped out of a hut, lifted the pole gate by hand, waved the vehicle through the checkpoint. While they traveled through the village he stared at people who walked or idly sat on the ground.

Sadiker said, "This is a leper colony." They stopped at the gate to a fenced enclosure. It was a heavy metal-linked fence about three meters high, had concertina barbed wire rolls above the links. An electrified wire was strung at the very top. A guard swung open the metal gates; the Toyota entered.

"This's your new home," Sadiker said in a pleasant voice. They stopped in a square open area of packed dirt surrounded by plywood-sided huts with metal corrugated roofs. "You'll stay here until a military tribunal interviews you and decides your fate."

Dismayed at the dismal surroundings, Jack asked, "Do I get an attorney?"

Sadiker grasped his arm, guided him out of the vehicle. "There's no telephone here and I don't know when your tribunal will meet. I've served five years and there has never been one held." The driver drew his pistol, Sadiker cut away the plastic ties.

"This's crazy!" he exclaimed. "You can't just leave me here. At least call my superiors."

"You'll be notified when the tribunal's ready."

"But why a leper colony?"

"Nobody will look for you in the middle of a lepertorium." Sadiker over his shoulder with a broad smile as the driver drove away.

Watching them disappear, he felt helpless, swallowed a lost feeling. A loitering guard swung the gate shut, a swirl of dust flew up in the twilight. He turned, looked around. Saw several darkened buildings in a row, trudged to a hut with an open door—it was empty—he slumped to the plywood floor. He was tired. *Maybe I'll be able to make sense of this tomorrow. And Billy's alerted.*

Hopefully, I can be tracked down. But a leper colony! That Pakistani fuck is right. No one's going to look here. Why did I ever open my fat mouth? How stupid can one guy get?

Chapter 47

Despite his surroundings, Jack slept soundly, woke up hungry. Rolled off his bare cot, looked outside; the wind was blowing hard, the early morning sky was gray with a low ceiling that partially hid distant mountains. Perfect. Couldn't be any more depressing if Dean Koontz had scripted the scene.

He had no idea where to go, so he sat in the open doorway while he waited for activity. Wind continued to howl, kicked up dust devils. Scraps of trash plastered against the border fence. Finally, he stepped out of the hut, walked around, looked for an administration building. Found nothing, but when he passed the construction site for a new structure, a tall, sturdy, dark-skinned man exited a hut, surveyed the scene. Head and thin face shaved. Wore a well-worn green Pak uniform showing ripped-away insignia. Guy looked like an Oriental villain in an old movie.

Jack hurried across. "Am I supposed to report? Can I eat?"

The man looked at the new prisoner with a frigid, appraising glance, said in English, "Eat at the fence. You have money? You buy food." He pointed at the tall fence where an old woman was waving at them. Jack patted his pocket, his wallet was there. Opened it, counted money—there was about a hundred dollars in American cash, fifty dollars in rupees. Bitterly wished he had Holland's cell phone—he'd left it at the BOQ. He avoided puddles, walked to the fence. When he drew near, the veiled woman, clad in a black burqa, displayed a mutton stew. Food smelled wonderful—realized he had not eaten since lunch the day before. At least this beat the hell out of the Taliban prison.

Her left hand, missing all its fingers, was wrapped in a ragged bandage. Visible parts looked like raw flesh. Scratch the idea that it's better than the Talib dump. The woman put down a basket she had carried across her shoulder, took out a bowl and spoon. She held them up. "One hundred rupees." She pointed at the food. "Twenty rupees."

"You got it, lady," he said with a smile. Above, electricity coursed through the top wire: snapped, hummed.

As she filled the bowl with a stew, the wonderful odor welled up to his nose. He inhaled deeply, pulled three dollars out of his wallet. Noticed the woman had twinkling eyes above her veil. She scratched her head: her right ear was eaten away. She handed the dish through a small hole in the chain link fence with the hand that had scratched—met his eyes. He regarded the bowl dubiously for a second, looked up, noticed her stare, accepted it and handed over the money. Maybe this was part of their torture treatment. The old woman limped away. He looked at the bowl of noodles covered with mutton and vegetables, sat down, spooned the food into his mouth. Tasted salty but was filling.

Finished, he put the bowl down next to the hole, followed the fence around the perimeter. Discovered that a rapidly flowing river ran along the camp, about ten feet outside the fence. In the distance, a bridge crossed the wide expanse of brown roiling water. Across the river, farmlands.

When he neared his starting point on the perimeter, he mentally summed up his observations, realized that there were ten huts in the camp. The man that had given him directions stood with two other men, next to a pile of lumber and a partly-completed building. He smiled, approached the group. The hard-looking bald man grinned, showed a large hand free of leprous sores, shook hands. "Welcome to Camp Hope. I'm Hammar. Former brigadier, Pakistan Army." Had a hawk face with a big, beaked nose, piercing black eyes, deep wrinkles.

"Hello," Jack introduced himself.

"Here is Akram and Akbar," Hammar smiled again. Waved his hand.

"You walked the perimeter. What do you think?"

"Basic. Real basic. But that's okay, I'm not staying long. I suppose the electricity on the top of the fence is available for running television, computers, and microwaves."

"Probably fatal if grasped," Hammar observed. "Guards respond at once if the fence is disturbed. Also, they have sensors in the earth. They respond to tunnel-making activities. If you have money, you'll be all right.
The lepers feed us, as you discovered." Hammar looked at the fence. "They're the only outsiders you'll see in Camp Hope."

"What's going on here?" he pointed at the construction.

"More barracks. And we must build an admin building. Our resort's growing as Bastard Zardari's difficulties multiply."

"You know him?"

Hammar smiled—it was not a pretty sight. "I was one of his generals. I commanded the Seventh Infantry Division before I was relieved for too much independent action against the local tribal authorities." Hammar smiled forlornly. "I'm a rare breed—a Catholic in Pakistan. I hate the mullahs. Anyway, don't stand on formality here. Just call me Hammar."

Jack was tempted to ask what had happened to the general. Instead, he strolled over, checked out the piled materials. Spotted some long beams as well as framing lumber, sheets of corrugated metal roofing.

"And don't think about building a bridge over the fence. The guards ignore us but they patrol the fence once every hour."

Jack wheeled around. "Do you have tools?"

"Yes, of course." He appraised Jack. "I know you think of escape, but I've been here long and have studied without success. There's no escape from Camp Hope."

Looking back at the fence, Jack smiled. A hundred feet from the closest huts, another ten feet to the water. Felt a thrill track through his body. "Who's building the new huts? Can I help?"

Hammar gestured at the other men, who watched the American. "We earn a pittance which helps pay for our food and other needs. We also work in the fields under guard. You can help but we cannot stretch the money."

"Good!" He rubbed his hands together. He felt a need to begin an escape plan. "When do we start?"

Chapter 48

When Ashley Dupont stepped off the Indian Air airliner at Islamabad Airport, the heat hit her like a fist in the face. The sky over Islamabad was blue, but tinged with the heaviest smog she had seen since a trip to Mexico City a year earlier: the air smelled putrid. She glanced at her watch—it was two PM. The flight from San Francisco had taken twenty-three hours with a stop in Tokyo.

Excited about her long-awaited employment as an assistant associate producer for CNN, she had stopped in Islamabad on the way to her assignment in Kuwait. She hoped to renew the relationship she had abruptly ended with Jack Flashhardt during a fit of depression after her miscarriage. She wore a tight, white cotton sweater and a blue skirt that showed everything about her fabulous lean figure.

As Ashley descended the boarding ramp placed against the side of the plane, she looked for Jack. She had written a letter to him at the UN offices because his father, Bill, had been very encouraging. The letter informed Jack that she was going to stop off in Pakistan on her way to Kuwait. She expected him to be waiting, despite their horrible troubles in Palo Alto. She was eager to start over and was investing two weeks to do it.

A Marine, an American Indian, approached and greeted her, "Hey, Ashley." There was no question in his voice. But, she figured, that was to be expected: few looked like her in the States, let alone this remote part of the world. And when she was with Jack, people stopped to stare at the couple, expecting them to be movie stars.

She answered, "Who're you? A friend of Jack? Where is he?"

The man smiled, "I'm Billy Howling Dog, Jack's brother. I work for Jack. He's missing. His boss got the letter about your arrival and sent me to pick you up."

"Missing! How long? Where is—what's he doing?" She searched his expressionless Indian face: square jaw, Indian nose, piercing grey eyes—he was striking. Though he was obviously just out of his teens, he looked as mean as a raptor she had once seen up close at the San Diego Wild Animal Park.

"Half-brother," Billy added. He smiled, his face mellowed for a second, returned to its hostile state.

"He's talked about you." Ashley looked around at the absolute chaos of the busy airport. The noise, the stench, the activity was overwhelming. People walked about, airplanes taxied, helicopters landed, took off. "Can we please get out of here?" she suggested. "It's too loud to think. My head's spinning."

"I've got a vehicle," Billy said. "Where you stayin'?"

"The Imperial." The two walked through the crowds. After Ashley went through Customs, Billy loaded her bags in the embassy Toyota Landcruiser he had left in front of the terminal.

Ashley climbed in the Toyota, asked, "What happened?"

"I dunno. Jack went to the Presidential Palace to receive a medal from the president and that's the last I know—-"

"The president? Of Pakistan? I can't believe this!"

Ignoring a wildly-gesturing traffic cop, Billy pulled into heavy traffic.
"I called the palace but they say he was taken to the BOQ—the Bachelor's Officer Quarters—and they don't know anything else. I talked to the corporal who was on duty. He confirmed Jack got to the BOQ, left wearing civilian clothes."

"And he's just missing?" She had thought of him all the way around the world, hoped he would accept her back into his life.

A half hour later, Billy swerved through heavy traffic, pulled to the curb. "This's your hotel." Ashley looked at the four-story structure. It looked like it needed to be washed. She saw patches of crumbling stucco.

Waving at the uniformed doorman, she pointed at her bags in the back seat.

"Let's get out of this heat."

The two Americans walked into the lobby, sat in over-stuffed armchairs. Ashley noticed expensive-looking Afghan rugs scattered haphazardly on the marble floor.

"What're we going to do? What else do you know?" Ashley was tired, sweaty, thirsty, needed a bath. Overhead fans were belt-driven instead of manned by a pukka wallah as she had imagined. Otherwise, it looked like an Indiana Jones movie set.

Billy said, "Let me order you a cold drink." He rose, grabbed a man in a white and black outfit, told him to bring two beers. When he returned to the chairs, Ashley sat back with her long legs spread wide, her arms draped over the sides of the chair.

He sat next to her. "The last time I talked to Jack, he was with this CIA guy who wanted him to kill—to assassinate President Zardari."

"You're not serious!" Ashley accepted a glass of beer with ice cubes from a waiter, drank. It was cool but tasted flat.

"Yeah, I am. Jack said he was just gonna shine the CIA guy on—and he did, 'cause nothing happened at the palace."

Omar Johnson and two soldiers dressed in camouflage uniforms with rolled-up sleeves joined them. Omar bent over, kissed Ashley on the cheek, gently patted her with a huge hand. She jumped up, hugged him, then short Mick Nakamura. It was comforting to see familiar faces from Palo Alto.

Mick introduced Bulldog Mahoney, who was very tall, very hard-looking. The three pulled chairs, sat down.

She said to Omar, "I'm so glad to see you." She put down the flat beer.

"What in the world is going on with Jack?"

He responded, "You're a wonderful breath of home—sweet!"

She glanced at Mahoney and Mick. "Thank you for being here for Jack. This is a shock to me. I expected him to meet me at the airport and now he's——"

"Missing," Mahoney concluded her words. His eyes flashed. "And when we find out who's responsible…" he bit back words.

Ashley was surprised to see that all the men, like Billy, wore poorly concealed holstered handguns on their hips or shoulders. They looked hard, mean—except for very black Omar who had the air, manner of an accountant, despite his uniform. She couldn't imagine him shooting at anyone.

She asked, "Who kidnapped him? Have you reported it?"

"I doubt the Taliban would screw around with a kidnapping," Omar offered. "They kidnapped him once, he burned them bad." He glanced up at a waiter, ordered beers.

"Mara Bhutto has good connections with the Pak government," Mick said. "She's our best source to find him."

Ashley looked perplexed. "Who's that? I'd like to talk to her— maybe she'll help find out where he's being held."

"Gil, Jack's boss, is looking for her," Omar said. "His ex-girlfriend and

Mara are friends. He promised to bring Mara here."

"If we find that he's being held somewhere, what do we do? Call the

Embasy?"

No one suggested a solution. They each thought about taking on a government twelve thousand miles from home.

"We call in the Marines?" Omar asked.

"They've posted Jack as AWOL," Mick responded.

Omar snarled, shook a huge fist. "Why's he have so many enemies in the Marines?"

"Because he doesn't follow the grain," Mick said. "He doesn't bleed Marine Corps green, so he pisses off most senior officers. And they can't intimidate him—that really pisses them off. And when he got himself transferred to the United Nations, they washed their hands of him. But there's more to it."

"What do you mean?" Omar asked.

"I went to my commanding officer," Mick explained to Ashley. "And we went to General Harmbruster for help, but the General told us to keep our noses out of the whole affair. He said Jack was right where he needs to be."

"That's crazy!" Omar objected. "So they're saying he's on a… secret mission, one he hasn't told us about? Maybe even he doesn't know about?"

"What about the UN?" Ashley asked. "Can they find him?"

"They're a bunch of incompetent fools," Omar retorted. "Gil is a good guy but he's an office poge. He's the best of the lot."

"I feel so gritty. I need to check in and take a shower," Ashley said to the group. "Could you wait for me?"

"Yeah, no problem," Billy flashed a big smile, checked out her figure. "Dress conservatively," he cautioned.

A half hour later, Ashley re-joined the four, gratefully sipped a glass of water. She wore a pink Polo T-shirt, baggy jeans.

A woman, exotically beautiful, accompanied by a lean, smiling blond man with a snub nose, walked up to the group. The masculine-appearing, golden-skinned woman was dressed in a blue European dress suit similar to several Ashley had noticed in the most expensive shops in Paris the previous summer. She was tall in three-inch black heels; she wore a single strand of pearls around her neck over swelling breasts. Everyone grew silent, Ashley felt the group tense up. The woman stared at her, sat down in an empty chair, maintained a rigidly straight posture. She had broad shoulders, a mannish, short haircut of shiny black hair. Ashley guessed she was a lesbian.

The white man smiled. "You're Ashley. And I'm Gil. I work with Jack." He looked at the others, "G'day, mates. Here she is— don't be too hard on her. She's only a sheila, after all."

"Do you know where he is, Mara?" Omar asked.

Ignoring him, Mara, asked Ashley, "Who're you?"

"Ashley Dupont. I'm a friend of Jack. From California." She wanted to say girlfriend, but wasn't sure what Jack's relationship had been with this beautiful woman.

Mara looked down. "I had nothing to do with his disappearance. I'm very sorry for what I did to him. He gave me open friendship and I betrayed him. But——"

"Bitch!" Both Bulldog and Mick uttered the expletive.

Mara glared at Mahoney, looked down. She continued, "I was blackmailed. The ISI kidnapped my sister, Fatima. They held her in Afghanistan. They told me to kill him. Or I would never see her again." She looked around at the group. "Don't you see… that's what I do. I thought it would be easy. I thought I had no choice. But… I couldn't in the end." She looked at the others. "My little sister——" she broke down, emitted an anguished wail. "My precious sister… her body was found, abandoned on a dike. Fatima is dead! Raped, stoned to death. Beheaded."

Ashley listened to Mara's words with mouth open, in a state of shock.

After a moment, Mara looked up at the group. "I'm a Communist. I hate Pakistan. I hate this evil land for hanging my father. I hate it and I swear they'll pay. I'll do anything to help Jack. You must believe me." Bulldog Mahoney snarled, "Great act. But I don't believe you for a fuckin' second!"

"Why not give her a chance? Let her find Jack," Ashley responded.

She was drawn to the girl, repelled by her, hated her all at the same time. But she couldn't doubt Mara's anguish over her missing sister.

Omar said, "It's hopeless to think any of us can find him." The Eurasian beauty looked at the others through her tears. "If Bastard Zardari had him arrested, I can find that out. Maybe I can also find out where he's being imprisoned. But you'll have to free him. I cannot do that."

Ashley searched the Pakistani woman's green eyes, startling in her golden-skinned face. She caught a tiny flicker in the woman's gaze. Did it reveal sincerity? Or lies?

Putting down a saw, Jack glanced around the Pakistani prison encampment, at the highly electrified fence that surrounded it, up at the sun. He wiped fresh-smelling sawdust off his brow.

General Hammar smiled, his black eyes opaque. "Too hot?"

"It's even cookin' in the morning."

The other prisoners kept working, Hammar occasionally shouted incomprehensible instructions. The general's personality made him a natural foreman, and the new prison bunkhouse, now framed and sheeted with plywood, was almost finished. Jack confirmed for the tenth time that three big rafters were still lying in a pile of lumber. An escape plan had formulated in his mind the first time he saw the heavy rafters. "Know anything about ancient siege weapons?"

"Of course" Hammar said. "I studied at Victory College at Sandhurst —the British equivalent of West Point. How do you think I made it to this elevated state of grace as a carpenter?" He grinned. "There was the ballista —the first catapult, invented by Alexander the Great's father, Phillip. In the 4th Century B.C. And the Romans—or most likely Archimedes—invented the improved trebuchet. It was a long wooden arm resting on a pivot, and it acted as a lever."

"Trebuchet wouldn't work without a big counterweight. How about a common catapult? How far do you think a catapult made of one of those beams could throw a skinny Marine?" He pointed at the three twenty-footlong rafters lying in a pile.

Hammar stared at the beams. "I should imagine a good distance, if it was carefully built. And the man was light."

"Yeah, I used to weigh about 180 pounds but I endured a successful diet when the Taliban entertained me in a Muj prison."

"A simple catapult. Not counterweighted—just flexed." Hammar looked at the fence bordering the bank of the silty-brown Kurang River. "I'll bet I could sail over the fence and into the water." He looked back at Hammar. "You're pretty skinny, yourself, General. You and I could make like Daedulus and Icarus." Hammar laughed, pounded his thin thigh with delight. Dust puffed off his clothes. "My boy, you're a genius. Hopefully, we'll not fly too close to the sun." They returned to work; when the others quit in the early evening, the two went to Hammar's hut, began to sketch plans by the light of a guttering candle. The next day, they built the framework for the base of the catapult out of doubled-up framing studs.

Chapter 50

The mirror of the Regency Hotel room on Islamabad Club Road, threw a manly image of Mara back as she adjusted her flamboyant silk tie, splashed on a musky aftershave, moved her man's snap-brim hat to an attitude angle. She had discovered, after she questioned several government bureaucrats, that Major Sadiker Dang was President Zardari's personal hatchet man. She had also learned that he was a homosexual. The masculine look that she saw in the mirror reassured her. It felt safe, comfortable, more right than Mara wanted to admit to herself. Her informant had told her that Major Dang was in The Simpering Satyr most nights from six to nine PM, so at eight PM, she flagged down a cab at the hotel, rode to the underground nightclub on Rama 5 Street. The hookah bar was more crowded than any other popular establishment in Islamabad. A smoky, opiate-smelling pall hung over the entire place, the dog urine smell of marijuana was in concentrated spots, a pulsating U2 tune played over raucous conversations. Two young men danced wildly on the room-length bar, shaking their bodies at each other.

Swaggering in, Mara stopped at the marble-topped bar, ordered a Perrier water. The bartender had lipstick on his lips, rouge on his cheeks, fake eyelashes. She sipped the water, surveyed the club, finally spotted Sadiker Dang sitting at a table with a peroxide blonde woman in a revealing Western dress. Sadiker wore a khaki uniform with a presidential braid on his shoulder. Mara watched out of the corner of her eye, became convinced that the blonde was a cross-dressing male. She walked across the bar, leaned over, stared in Sadiker's eyes for seconds, continued to the toilets. Ignoring the urinals, she entered a stall, walked out seconds later, casually zipped her pants before she re-entered the barroom.

"Bonjour, M'sieur," she greeted Sadiker in a throaty voice when he joined her at the bar. Despite her haughty manner, her heart was beating rapidly.

"Are you Pakistani?" He asked.

"I'm from Hong Kong," Mara responded.

"Do you work in 'Abad?" He had a twitch in his cheek.

"No, I'm on my way to Ankara. I'm a manufacturer's rep for a Hong Kong company, LAI." She pronounced the initials like the word lay. "We make sex toys for the American and European markets. My name is Monsieur Bang Cock." Mara shut up, dropped her eyes slowly, stared at Sadiker's crotch.

"Lay. Interesting name. I'm Sadiker Dang. Your tan is wonderful. How would you feel about a joyride in a booth?"

"Ohh," Mara moaned. "You're forward, but I prefer privacy."

Sadiker frowned, then smiled. "I must be home soon. Perhaps tomorrow?"

"I'm at the Regency. Room 1265. Come at two?" At two PM the next day, two soldiers knocked on Mara's door, wordlessly searched the suite. Mara watched, afraid they might find a clue to her real nature. Suddenly she remembered the bra and dirty panties she had thrown in a corner behind the toilet. The men searched the closet, drawers, the bathroom, but neither saw the telltale undergarments behind the toilet. The two silent men then left, ignored the shy female maid sweeping the hallway, the old maintenance man removing a duct cover on the wall. Five minutes later, Sadiker Dang knocked on Mara's door. When Mara opened the door, her two disguised operatives stepped behind him, grabbed his upper arms, shoved him into the suite. He stumbled forward, Mara savagely punched him in the stomach with the butt of a cane. Sadiker sprawled, Mara kicked him in the head, knocked him out. She heaved a sigh of relief at their success.

Fifteen minutes later, Dang regained consciousness. His arms were handcuffed to the bedposts with plastic strip cuffs. He felt a searing pain in his lower abdominal area, just above his penis; he looked down, was horrified to see the handle of a stiletto protruding from his body. A red stain was pulsing, bubbling, growing on his khaki pants. He watched in terrified fascination. He tried to pull his legs up but they were tied to bedposts. Sweat trickled into his eyes, burning them. He smelled feces—his own.

Golden-skinned Mara moved into sight, leaned over him. He noticed and was astonished by her large breasts.

"Why?" Sadiker sputtered. He bit his lip to keep from screaming.

"You'll tell me what I want to know, Mon Cheri. Or you'll lie here until you rot," Mara whispered.

"Any—-" he could not speak through the pain.

"Where is Jack Flashhardt?"

Terrified, Sadiker bit his lip, moaned. Mara twisted the knife handle.

Sadiker writhed from the agonizing pain. "I'll tell you! The American's at

Bharakan Leper Colony. Bharakan, Kurang River."

Mara pulled the stiletto out. Her two operatives held Dang's head in a tight grip while Mara put the knife to his throat. "If you lie, you'll end slowly."

"Truth," Dang, filled with despair, groaned horribly. "The American's at Bharakan. Secret prison camp. Speak… truth."

Avoiding his jugular vein, Mara carefully slashed his trachea and voice box with a vertical cut of her razor-sharp stiletto. She wiped the blade on his uniform shirt. The operatives released his head. Dang tried to shout but only a groaning, sputtering, whistling sound emerged. His attackers left the room.

Chapter 51

Squatting on the bare ground next to the three-meter high fence that divided the prison from the leper colony, Jack glanced at his watch: time for the food lady—he hadn't asked her name. The river flowed just beyond the fence, a distinct smell of dead fish coming from the slow-moving water. He worried about the strength of the beam for the catapult escape attempt. He and Hammar had wanted to shoot sand bags towards the river the night before, but had been afraid the action might alert guards. He spotted the old food lady, dressed in her usual black burqa, walk across the clear area between the village and the camp. He noticed she wasn't limping. The veiled food-seller stopped on the other side of the fence. "You've gained weight. Prison must be good for you."

Shocked to hear Mara Bhutto's voice, he staggered off his haunches, landed in the dirt, looked up at the assassin.

"Yes, it's me," she said. "I'm here to help. Major Dang told me how to find you."

"Danged Dang? He put me in here. Why'd he tell you?"

"He felt a need to share, believe me." She held out a large bowl of stew. "Eat. Someone may be watching." Her eyes were dilated, her skin flushed. "It's not poisoned. Want me to try it?"

"That might not be a bad idea, given our relationship." Looked into her green eyes. "Never mind. Shit'll probly kill me on its own." He looked at the food, put the bowl aside, anyway.

"Your friends asked me to find you. To help them find you."

"Who?"

"All of them. And an American woman. A skinny blonde woman from California," she added with a biting tone.

"Ashley? She's in Islamabad?" He thought for a moment, looked up at her. "So? Why'd you bother? You want me dead. But what made you think that you could kill me, Mara? You're a professor, not a hardened—"

"I was blackmailed. And I could've killed you. I set it up to look like a failed attempt." She wiped her damp face. She was sweating, even in the early morning air. "It's true. I'm… I'm the Black Orchid." She covered her face with her hands. "I was trained in China. I'm a Communist, like my father. I hate Pakistan and everyone in it. They killed my daddy!"

He sat back on his haunches, wondered if she was acting. "A black orchid's a myth—I looked it up. You're just a common killer. But, I see your point, Mara, and it'll kill your soul. It'll destroy you. Get out of here.
Do you have any money? Let me help you."

She began crying. "You're in prison and you tell me to escape? People are the same everywhere."

"People are not the same everywhere, Mara. People in America are good. We're about good, truth, happiness—not like snarling, hate-filled, suspicion-ridden, fanatical Muslims. We help each other. Wait—go stay at my ranch in Red Lodge. We have plenty of room at the Flying Eagle Ranch, even though we lost all the acreage. Dad would welcome—I wouldn't tell him you tried to turn me into a shish kabob—might make him a vegetarian."

She looked at him. "How can you possibly forgive me?"

"To get you out of here. You need help."

Mara looked around, wished he would eat the poisoned stew. "I must leave or I'll be suspected. Your friends want to assist your escape. Do you have a plan?"

Despite his offer, Jack harbored suspicions. She looked sincere. Why would she go to this trouble? He decided to take a chance. "I'm going to escape tomorrow night. There's a bridge about a half click below the camp. Tell them to wait there at midnight." He pointed at his dirty shirt and pants. "And I need BDUs and boots. Tell them to be ready in case I'm chased by guards. I'll be in the river. Swimming."

Mara tried to still her excitement; he had not eaten the poisoned food, but now she had another chance to execute him.

Chapter 52

At 2300 hours, the three-man guard squad made their hourly patrol of the prison camp. Hammar and Jack watched the shuffling patrol return to their encampment outside the fence, hurriedly took the catapult out from a pile of lumber.

They fitted the base plate together, set it down in the agreed upon position. Two of the prisoners scooped out temporarily re-filled trenches for the forward and rear crossbars of the base plate. When the base plate was fitted together, they dropped it into the meter-deep trenches. More of the prisoners arrived, crowded around to help: they filled the dirt back on top of the crossbars, tamped it by jumping on it.

By the light of the moon, Hammar and three prisoners carried the weighty catapult arm over, fitted it into the heavily reinforced slot in the base plate. The arm had a bar that made it a cross, and jutted into the air at about a thirty-degree angle. Together, Jack and Hammar struggled to pull the arm down. Three prisoners joined them, the five men pulled with their combined weights until it curved to the ground, with a heart-stopping creak. They fitted a rope brace over the end of the arm. The two ends of the hemp disappeared into the ground, tied to buried crossbars.

Jack shivered in the cold, nervously sang in a low voice, over and over: "Fly me to the moon, let me play among the stars."

"Don't worry. It worked for Archimedes and the Romans when they conquered Sicily." Hammar's teeth gleamed white in the moonlight. "Just think of Daedulus and fly to freedom, young Jack. I'll be right behind you."

Gingerly, he crawled onto the catapult arm. Made sure he was in the center of the crossbar, spread his arms on it. Heart pumped blood in his throat. Wanted to crawl off, but steeled himself. "Do it," he whispered. The arm released with a sharp sprang, he exclaimed, "Ohh, my God!"

Soared up, away from the catapult, over the fence, into the heavens, over the river. Rushing air cold on his face. Below, the glittering reflections of the moon on the stream. Feared he'd sail over the waters, crash on the shore beyond. Moon flashed through his vision: he tumbled, again saw water below. Gritted his teeth, put one hand over his nose, the other over his crotch. Landed in the silvery path of water with a jolting crash.

Water through his fingers, up his nose, pained his sinuses, but the feeling of success overrode any hurt. Broached the water laughing, swallowed water. "Yes!" Envisioned Shania Twain singing an old Dean Martin song:

"When the moon hits your eyes, like a big pizza pie, That'sa freedom..."

Coughing and sputtering, he stroked downstream, relief flushing through his body. Water was ice-cold: ecstatic, he ignored it. Heard the "sprang" of the catapult. Glanced up, saw a body fly, tumble into the water just upstream.

The general surfaced, caught up to him, flashed a grin of triumph. No sign of guards on the bank next to the camp; they swam towards the bridge.

He spotted figures standing in the middle of the structure. Friends or foes? Swept closer, one of the men threw a rope over the side. Adjusted his direction, took a chance, grabbed the rope. Hammar also grabbed the free end, the two were pulled towards shore. He looked up at the bridge, saw a big man—maybe Bulldog—step back from the rail, move sideways until he was behind another individual. The big man punched that figure, hoisted him over the rail of the bridge, threw him into the river.

Jack felt the bottom, staggered towards the reed-lined bank. Heard splashes under the bridge, glanced, could see nothing in the darkness. Pulled Hammar, moved into the reeds. Waded through the shallow water— tremendous relief—saw Billy walk around, look into the dark waters under the bridge. He joined his brother, hugged him.

Crawled up to dry ground, collapsed in the grass. Raised his head, looked back at the black waters: no sound. Walked back to the bank, listened, all was quiet.

"Jack!" Ashley ran up, embraced him. Astonished, he squeezed and kissed her with relief and joy. He shivered, even in her warm embrace.

"Let's get outta here!" Mick shouted. All scrambled up to the road, crowded into a Land Rover with side benches. Several rifles on the floor.
Bulldog Mahoney drove.

"What happened?" Jack asked. "Who fell in the water?" He feared Mahoney had killed again.

"The Bhutto bitch," Mahoney said. "Leaned over too far. Gone. Just as well, no chance now for her to do you in." Jack was horrified but decided to change the subject. "Guys, this's General Hammar. He came out with me."

"Congratulations, General," Mick said. The others murmured a greeting, sounded intimidated by Hammar's rank. Jack was elated: free and with his friends. He hoped that the guards had not noticed the escape, called to block the roads.

Chapter 53

After five tense hours over a poorly paved, narrow asphalt road in the rented British SUV, the group stopped at a restaurant on the shores of a large lake, fifty miles north of Islamabad. The establishment looked like a Mexican beach hut, with a palm frond roof and sides. It had no windows. Scarred tables and chairs were scattered around the brick-floored patio.

It was just after sunrise, the skies were a cloudless blue. Jack felt wonderful—he was free, surrounded by armed friends. Friends that could hold off an army. It was great.

General Hammar pounded on the door of a mudbrick house behind the restaurant, woke up the owner. The group ordered food, and after the tousled man made and poured fragrant coffee for the group, he prepared breakfast. He stroked his long black beard and shouted to his wife to bring condiments. He turned on a diesel generator and then an old record player for his guests. It played what Jack, a Blues enthusiast, was surprised to recognize as an Elmore James medley of Muddy Waters, Son House, and Dust My Broom. Jack looked around the humble restaurant and tried to imagine an old blues piano player at a battered piano.

While they listened and waited, then ate refried rice and scrambled eggs, Jack regarded his friends, seated or sprawled on flimsy chairs. They looked deadly but tired. He thanked them all again for the successful rescue effort. He explained why he had been imprisoned, then outlined the mission he had decided to take to find the deadly smart bomb lost from the B-52 bomber.

"Before I was relieved from duty and imprisoned," General Hammar interrupted, his shiny black eyes darting from face to face like a black laser light show, "I heard of this bomb. The Chinese and Pakistanis have been sneaking SOG units into Afghanistan, looking for it. Question: if al Qaida has it, what if the bomb's transported to America and detonated in a major city?"

"Never happen!" Bulldog exclaimed.

"Really?" Jack asked. "I'm not aware that the Navy or Coast Guard board common freighters. Say a small boat carries the biobomb warhead, invisible to a radar screen, to a freighter coming from Singapore carrying a load of toys. No reason to suspect the ship and no one inspects until it docks —"

Mick interrupted, "Shut up! So it sails into San Francisco Bay and is detonated just as it crashes into the Golden Gate Bridge." Jack continued, "If the ship was loaded with flammable materials like oil or liquefied natural gas, the smoke cloud, carrying the germs, could drift over San Francisco and cause massive panic, death, injury."

"But it would kill everyone on the ship," Ashley protested.

He looked across the bar. "Ashley, first thing you have to realize is that we're dealing with maniacs who're willing to sacrifice generations to win their cause. Not hundreds or thousands of soldiers: generations of soldiers. And not even soldiers. We all know that. They're cowards: bunches of old guys expend innocent women and kids against soft targets to further their hateful cause. Rather than fight soldier to soldier." He looked at the others. "It's not like they're giving up a lot. Most of 'em live like their ancestors have for thousand of years—in mud huts. If we hadn't given them guns, they'd still be throwing rocks and spears. They sit around and pump each other up all day long with their religious hate bullshit."

"What makes you think San Francisco?" Omar asked. He had retracted his conversion to Islam, but he still acted defensive whenever Jack referred to Islamic fanaticism.

Jack glanced at Mick and Omar. "Our government has a lot of people working on the missing bomb. But when I escaped, I stole a laptop from the Muj prison. I was able to retrieve an email from someone in San Francisco who wrote about a mock attack. You,

Mick, Ashley, and I, have friends, relatives in the Bay Area." Jack continued, "Earlier, I found an email that asked when the Giant's baseball season starts at AT&T Park. Then, in Quetta, I was given a map to the bomb's location by this weird religious group at their island temple on the Hori Nullah River."

Jack looked around the tiny restaurant. A beautiful dog—a long-legged Afghan hound, sidled in, sat and watched the group. "Somebody attacked them and I had to run," Jack continued. "The map was destroyed in the river, but when I reported what I had learned to General Harmbruster, he promised funds and secret authority to pull in anybody I want. I was supposed to get it in writing, but that hasn't worked through the system yet." He looked around. "But I want all of you to help me."

Bulldog objected, "Just one thing, sir. I don't figure you for bleedin' Marine Corps green all of a sudden." His face took on its hardest aspects.

"Well," Jack said, "as a matter of fact, there is another reason to find the bomb. I may as well tell you guys—I don't want to hide anything." "What's that?" Billy asked.

"Remember Melinda O'Reilly?"

"Who could forget!" Billy exclaimed. "What a piece!"

Ashley stared at Billy, tracked around to regard Jack with accusing eyes. Trying to avoid her eyes, Jack continued, "I ran into her in Quetta.
She has a newspaper that'll pay one million pounds for the bomb."

"Wow!" Omar called out.

"We're duty-bound to destroy it or secure it for the Air Force," Mick protested.

"I agree," Jack said. "I'm just sayin'—"

Bulldog pulled a huge cigar out of a breast pocket and stuck it in his mouth. "So what do you want to do, Lieutenant?" He asked.

"That's a shitpot of money," Omar added.

Jack looked around at his friends. "When we signed up, it wasn't to get kickbacks from people who don't have our country's best interests at heart. I'm slow, Gunny, but I started to realize that some real crazies want to kill friends and relatives in my part of the world. I'm here to stop them and anybody else who's tryin' to hurt the U.S. I'd rather be doin' this now than have my kids doin' it later. And the only people I can count on are you guys." He looked around, wondered whether he could count on all the others. Wondered who had sapped him in Papa Pier's manor. Wondered if one of the group would succumb to the temptation of millions of dollars.

Chopstick Mick said, "I'm signing up. It'll be goo-od!" He almost bounced at the thought of the impending action.

"What a shock," Jack commented with a dry air. The others laughed. He looked around and added, "I'm convinced it's in Shangri-la, the valley I told you guys about. Robert Arses and I are going there to rescue his older brother. At the same time, I'm gonna look for the cavern where it's supposed to be hidden. Once I find it and secure it, we call in the cavalry or destroy it. But this whole thing is gonna be—like, gnarly, dudes." Everybody in the room, except the general, smiled at his jibe, nodded, raised a cup or gave a thumbs-up. "Awesome!" he concluded. "Gunny, you find us a base of operations here in the Islamabad area. Mick, you go see General Harmbruster about access to funds and munitions. And see if he can get my AWOL status lifted." He held his hand up. "Wait, maybe being an outlaw is a good cover. Let's leave that the way it is."

General Hammar cleared his voice, "There's one problem. You're
Americans. Stay in Islamabad, you'll be reported in
days." Jack said, "You're right, of course.
What d'you suggest?"

"As an operational commander, I was responsible for the territory from Afghanistan to the Line of Control with India. But we never patrolled north or west of the mountain, Rakaposhi."

"Yeah, and I was based in Hunza for a time," Omar pointed out. "The general's right on, Jack. Hunza would be a perfect base. The Paks never go there—it's disputed territory with the Afghans. And it has an old English military airstrip. And it's right next to the Afghan Corridor and China."

General Hammar added, "The U.S. Army sent a few old U.S. Army DHC-4 Dehavilland transport aircraft to Lahore for training purposes. I'll bet they haven't been used—all the aircraft just sit on the tarmac. The Caribou's a twin-engine, cargo craft. With its short field capabilities, it'd be perfect for your force." He added, "It wouldn't be too hard to liberate one for your cause."

Jack said, "I'm starting to get the feeling that you'd be a very valuable addition to our mission. Will you join us?"

Hammar shook his head. "No, I'm too well known in Pakistan to stay around as long as Bastard Zardari's in power. I have a nest egg in a
Singapore bank. I want to retire to a tongkang—a sailboat—in the Malay Straits. I'm tired of living in dust, dirt, sparse weeds, and impossible mountains."

"Think about it, General. It's obvious that we could really use you." He looked around, "Most of us are green rookies compared to your experience and leadership skills. But I can probably fly the Caribou if I'm checked out on it. Maybe you and I could go to—The whore? No, La whore? But beyond that, you've operated in circles that we have no clue about. Please think about it." He drained a cup of coffee and concluded, "That's all for now. I'm going for a swim to get the stink of prison off me. Let's plan on meeting again and get outta here around noon. I think we'll need sack time before we head out."

"One thing, Jack," Omar said. "Mick, tell him what the general told you."

Mick looked reluctant to speak, finally related, "When I went to General Harmbruster for help to find you, the General told me to keep out of the whole affair. He said you were right where you needed to be."

Jack thought for a moment, said, "I've been thinking that Harmbruster isn't as innocent as he seems. He might be the grand puppet master. I screwed up when I told the prez about the planned assassination. I probly did what I was expected to do. But why'd they want me in prison? And how'd they know I'd break out?" He shook his head. "Too much, I need a swim." He glanced at the general. "Think it's safe?"

The general shrugged, smiled, said nothing. Jack caught Ashley's eye. She slid off the barstool, joined him at the beach side of the restaurant. Eager to be alone, they walked across the sand to the waves coming off the lake.

"Jack, I'm sorry about the email. The—"

"The miscarriage? It wasn't your fault, Ashley."

She grasped his hand. "I was so depressed. You gone. Me sick. I overreacted. Now I came here to spend time with you—"

"I'm sorry I couldn't be there for you." He took her hand, held it.

"Let's talk about this later."

"Mara," Ashley said. "I know she tried to kill you. Were you friends before that?"

"We were friendly acquaintances, but that's all, Ashley." He changed the subject, "I wish we were on a beach in Thailand or Newport Beach— even Stinson, remember the beach north of Golden Gate Bridge? When we —you know, did it on the sand?" He stooped, picked up a rock, threw it in the waves. "But I've started to like nonstop adventure. It can become addicting. I'll bet it's kinda like being in the Old West."

"But it's wrong to steal an airplane from the Air Force."

He thought for a moment while they walked. "Strange. But when you think about it, we're using it to help the US. And we need it. You know, they say in the Army—"Be all you can be"—so here's my chance to become an airplane hijacker. I hear it's an exploding field. Anyway, the general's taking it, not me." Smiling, he picked up a stone, threw it in the water. "I don't know, Ashley. Like everything else around here—carryin' guns, being shot at by strangers, shooting people with no consequences or questions asked. It's all weird—Silent leges inter arma—during war, the laws are silent."

She looked into his eyes. "I must admit, there's a terrific story in all this. And I'm way out here to investigate and produce stories, so…"

He smiled, hugged her with one arm. "I get your drift, babe. You gotta exclusive."

Ashley glanced back at the restaurant. It was about a half mile away, the others were whooping, running into the water in front of the small eatery. "Thanks for suggesting the swim. I feel so dirty. I hate dirt."

Jack glanced at his friends, thought, Better get used to it, babe.

The two took off their clothes; Ashley was shocked to see how thin Jack was. She stared in amazement at the large red scar on his back, traced it with her fingers. Felt the ridges from the beating he had taken during his imprisonment.

Feeling self-conscious about his emaciated body and the scars, he raced into the water, dove into the mild, wind-driven waves. She followed. Sunlight flashed off the sandy bottom, bits of weed floated in the waves, dark green fish, hand-sized, flitted across the lake floor, dark spots against the sand.

It was warm. The brilliant blue sky, the water reflected in their eyes; the two turned, returned to neckdeep water. He embraced her hard body—it felt wonderful. He got an immediate erection. He fondled her breasts, kissed her passionately. Ashley grasped his erection. He shut his eyes, relaxed, enjoyed the moment. The sun was warm on his face. Ashley rubbed against him, climbed, put him inside her.

"Oh, babe," he murmured when he felt the exquisite sensations. The sparkling blue water turned her hazel eyes to a dark blue-green hue. She laughed aloud. He thrust deep inside her, spun her around.

Chapter 54

Charlie Davis looked about twenty years old—tall, blond, thin—too young to be a freelance pilot in Southwest Asia. He was washing the windshield on the general's old, low-wing V-tailed Bonanza, outside a deserted hanger at an airstrip south of Islamabad. A sign had identified it as Kilgar Khan Airport. The general was seated inside the aircraft. Charlie was helping them steal the Caribou.

"How long have you worked with Hammar?" Jack asked.

"I was with him for six months—ever since I went AWOL from the Corps," Davis said. "Then he got caught, thrown in the prison camp at Bharakan. I've been hanging at the Duc Doo Inn in Islamabad over on
Rama 7 Street. It's underground—meaning it serves illegal booze."

"Well, thanks for helping us. If you need a hand getting out of your AWOL rap, let me know—and good luck," Jack said. *Yeah, right*, he thought. *Like I can help him. I'm only an expert 'cause I'm also AWOL.* He shook hands with the general, watched as the young American climbed in the airplane, taxied to the end of the runway, flew away. Thought about lunch with Ashley at the Empress Hotel, the next day's trip to the far north.

The next afternoon, after a long, all day drive to Hunza in a M1123 Humvee truck, Jack, Bulldog, Omar, Mick, admired the twin-engine Caribou the general had liberated from the Pakistani Air Force. It had two massive engines, was high-winged, painted desert tan. The five men unloaded the bladder of aviation fuel they had scrounged from Major Lialot Soongoon at the military base in Gilgit, then drove to the old fort.

When they pulled to a stop, Jack reflected that the fortress still looked like it should be a prop in a French Foreign Legion film, with a young Michael Caine wearing a white puggaree and a red jacket, leaning over the battlements and observing enemy hordes charging across Hunza Valley.

Tiny Sergeant Major, the little Afghan warrior, and three of his big tribesmen soldiers dressed in tiger-stripe utilities, stood in the entry gates. All had huge grins on their faces. He introduced General Hammar to Sergeant Major—the old Hunza snapped to attention, saluted. The group passed into the fort, through the tiny parade ground, entered a dining hall where they sat at a long wooden table. A popping fire in a black metal potbellied stove in the corner warmed the room.

Jack said, "Thanks to the general, we have air transport. My first hijacked aircraft. I joined the Marines and learned a trade." The others laughed.

Two Hunza soldiers entered the room, put a platter of wonderfulsmelling fresh chapatti bread, a dish of yak butter, some kind of algae-like paste in a bowl, a pot of tea on the table. Jack chewed on a hunk of soft bread, ignored the vile-looking algae stuff, and observed, "It's obvious that we need an on-going source of cash. But our government doesn't dare fund anything to do with the biobomb. Especially when we're operating in
Pakistan. Any ideas?"

Hammar stood, walked about the room for a moment. "Alexandre Pier —or Papa—as you know him, has money. A lot of his income comes from poppy growth. It's illegal. Perhaps, he should be subject to a local taxation authority." Omar smiled a thin-lipped grin. "It's true, he's pretty rich. But I thought Papa made his money on coffee and wine."

Jack objected, "I'm not comfortable living on drug money."

"The gov'mnt idjits want us ta work for dem—they shoulda give us some dough to hop-a-rate," Billy said in a gangster accent. The group laughed, looked at each other, waited for another idea.

Jack finally said, "You know, it's not too far to Robert Arses's fort. Just about fifty miles into Afgoneistan. I have to meet with him about getting his brother out of Shangri-la. Why don't I go talk to him? Maybe the SAS'd fund an anti-Taliban op."

"How do we get there?" Billy asked. "He got an airstrip?"

"No. Bulldog, do you have a line on a helicopter?"

"Yes, sir, but we're not totally set up on it."

"Well, if we don't have it yet, we'll have to overland it." He glanced at

Omar. "We'll need a guide and a vehicle."

"I'm sure Sergeant Major has a guy that's good to go," Omar said. He went to look for the Hunza leader.

"Jack, I'll sit down with the general," Mick said, "and generate a list of materials. Let's aim for a mobile force with some punch. Maybe a Javelin rocket, a 60mm mortar, a few RPGs. A SAW. Let's set up an all-around kick-ass team."

The general added, "I'll take Mick with me—we'll go munitionshunting in Chitral, get lined up, be back in three or four days." Jack regarded the general. The man had a controlling personality. He wondered whether he would take over the group. The Americans all stared at the general. With his shaved head, lean face and bird of prey nose, he looked very hard.

Sergeant Major and Omar returned to the hall. "Got a problem, Jack," Omar said. "Turns out that the pass northwest of here is controlled by a tribal force. They're bivouacked on the pass. You won't be able to get past them."

"Well, we can't just walk through," he said. "My Punkiban passport is expired. How about if we take a truck through with a load of stuff. We'll hide in the back."

"Pretty risky," Omar said.

"Well, we'll go through at sunrise," Billy said. "Shouldn't be too many up and about. And if we get busted, we shoot 'em and haul ass."

"So violent," Mick said in a mock-breathy voice. "Ohh, I wanna come." He bared his teeth, his canines looked ready to rip out a throat. Jack laughed, then ordered, "No, we need you to work with the general. I promise we'll satisfy your bloodthirsty soul later."

The next morning, Jack and Billy rode on benches in the back of an old canvas-covered GMC truck, headed towards the Afghan border. They had strewn the bed with empty and half-full bags of rice, battered wooden boxes. Two stave barrels that smelled rancid were labeled in Urdu and English: PORK LARD. The foul odor reminded Jack, by contrast, of Ashley's wonderful presence during the night.

An hour after dawn, they reached the guard post. The Pak driver slammed the truck to a stop. Jack and Billy were lying under a pile of musty-smelling straw. Guard approached, held his breath because of the unholy, unclean pork lard, lectured the driver, who slipped him a handful of rupees. Accepting the bribe, he angrily shouted for the truck to go on; the truck shifted into gear, lurched into Afghanistan.

"Made the first hurdle," Jack sat up, pulled straw out from his collar. "Excited about seein' your tank-killing babe?" Billy asked.

"Not really," Jack responded.

"How come?"

Jack laughed. "I'm too polite—Milady'll kiss me with her wonderful lips, put her fabulous breast in my hand, her hand down my pants and——"

"You'll be too polite to stop her."

"And then Ashley'll yell at me for bein' too polite." They laughed, dug MREs out of their packs.

The old GMC broke down after navigating forty miles of tortuous roads. The brothers left the driver to pound on the gearbox with a hammer, continued on foot into the mountains for the last ten miles. Just before sunset, they saw Milady's fort. Robert Arses, warned by guards, came out of the gate strapping on his eye patch and shouting a hello. Jack laughed, the two men embraced. He introduced Billy to Arses and the three walked to the comm hut.

"Go get Milady," Arses directed a boy sitting on the floor. The boy jumped up, ran out the door. "Haw, haw," Arses laughed. "I'm glad you're off your bum and back in the Great Game, Jack."

"Yeah, Robert, here I am again. Can't seem to kick the dust of
Southwest Asia. And I've dragged my brother, Billy Howling Dog, into it."

"An American Indian in the Hindu Kush? That has to be a first." Arses smiled at Billy, checked out his short braids. "Out for bloody al-Qaida scalps, are you?"

"Well, long as I'm here," Billy said with a self-conscious grin. He looked like he didn't know what to make of the bombastic Brit.

Milady burst into the hut, hugged Jack, almost knocked him down. Kissed him on the lips. Abashed at her forward behavior, she stepped back, smiled at the others. Billy stared at the spectacular black girl in amazement. She wore form-fitting camouflage pants and a woolen sweater that showed off a perfect body, had covered her chest with crossed bandoliers of brass ammo, long hair ran down her back.

"You're too late for High Tea, but just in time for a bit of din din,"
Arses said. "Milady's already dressed for the High Table."

"Let's go to my kitchen and eat," Milady linked her hands through the two American's arms, flashed a brilliant smile, led them into the wind. Over a meal of fried trout, boiled yams, slices of apple—served by two smiling village women—Jack told Robert and Milady about what had happened to him since he had left them in Quetta, then related his funding problem.

Arses admitted, "I tried to get into Shangri-la—couldn't wait to rescue Dickey. But the winds were so violent, the helicopter pilot refused to continue. Said we'd be killed."

Jack speculated, "There's something about the configuration of the peaks around the valley."

"Exactly. Creates a bloody vicious whirlpool of air," Arses continued.
"We'll have to come up with another plan."

The four discussed the reasons for the American visit. Jack outlined their mission, detailed their needs. Arses and Milady listened without comment until he had explained his situation.

"Killing a bunch of Taliban is bloody wonderful." Arses said when Jack stopped talking. "But what about rescuing my brother?" He looked at the Americans. "Tell us the rest."

"The missing biobomb," Jack decided to reveal all. "We're supposed to find it. I'm convinced it's hidden in Shangri-la. In a cavern. Don't know exactly where. We'll kill two birds——-"

"With one stone," Arses interjected.

"Who do you think hid the bomb?" Milady asked.

"Far as we know," Jack observed, "somebody found it and sold it to Chinese terrorists. Then al Qaida got it back, somehow. They have a tribal force in Barog Pass."

Startled, Arses asked, "What the hell're they up to?" "Maybe they're getting ready to move the bomb," Billy said.

Arses stroked his chin. "By Jove, I think the Redskin has a point.
Damned clever. No wonder you fellers wiped out Custer."

The four discussed possible plans until they all yawned. After goodnights, Milady led them to a mud brick hut. Billy sank down on a pile of rugs. Milady grasped Jack's hand and led him from the hut. "I'm so happy to see you," she murmured. They hurried through the increasing wind. At her one-room house, they stopped inside the doorway, she hugged him again. Her son was sleeping in a corner of the room. An oil lamp illuminated the room with a pearly glow.

"It's so wonderful. I'll help you any way I can. You know that." She pulled him onto the floor, embraced him. Her long hair cascaded over him, smelled fresh. She pushed him onto his back on the sleeping mat until she realized he wasn't responding. "Jack, what's wrong?"

He took a deep breath and said, "My American girlfriend and I have ended our separation. We're back together. I love her."

Horrified, Milady cried out—sobbed. Tears flowed down her black cheek, hit his face. She buried her face in his neck, held him tightly. She pulled blankets over their bodies, silently cried. Exhaustion overcame him, he fell asleep.

Chapter 55

"Awake, Jack realized he was alone in Milady's cold Kafirstan house. He rubbed his face, thought of Milady's spectacular body, went to Billy's hut. The Indian sat crosslegged in the entrance, cleaning his pistol with a toothbrush and a small bottle of oil. He grinned, "You look too rested. I'd a figgered the babe woulda destroyed you—tonsil-hockeyed you to death."

"It's not that way 'tween us now that Ashley's in Pakistan."

"What a waste." Billy assembled his pistol, reloaded it. "You shoulda called for help."

"If you're done whinin' about my love life versus your pathetic sex life, let's hustle some chow." The two walked to the comm hut.

Arses smiled when they entered. He spoke to three children and the kids sprinted away. "They'll fetch you brekky. Have a spot of tea." He poured two mugs of strong-smelling black tea.

Jack looked around the Brit's well-kept headquarters. "So, Robert, how've things been going? Any serious trouble?"

"The Americans have pounded the Taliban to bits again. They're basically all in Pakistan now, or hiding in the mountains." Arses grinned,
"Pretty quiet around here. Boring, actually."

"Too bad, Robert. But we need assistance. I've been given a mission that no one wants to support. Can you help? Cash to buy supplies? We need about sixty thousand dollars for material. I know it's an outrageous amount, but there it is."

"Money's not a problem," Arses responded. He went to a footlocker sitting next to the wall, opened the creaking hatch. It was full of U.S.
currency of various denominations.

"Where'd that come from?"

"Contributions from the local farmers. And my girls send money home from Karachi." Arses closed the chest. He smiled at the two astounded

Americans. "We collect taxes from the poppy growers. Biggest crop in Afghanistan, you know."

"And prostitution?"

"I send the local girls to Karachi for a year. When they come back, I arrange a marriage and give them a dowry," Arses replied with a defensive air.

"So we'll be supplied by druggies and hookers," Billy concluded with a smile. "My kind of operation. I love it."

"Yes, well, we do our best," Arses said. "And whether a bullet is bought with cash from a sailor or comes from a poppy field, the Taliban and odd Chink troublemaker dies all the same. I call it Free Enterprise. They're snakes in the grass and we kick their ass." He lifted the lid, pulled out a handful of bills. "We'll be able to help you. And when you whack al-Qaida and Taliban, you'll make our lives easier. And knowing how bloody good you are at that, young Jack, I figger it's a good investment."

Jack sighed. "I guess we shouldn't look a gift whore in the mouth,

Billy. It's just hard to be a criminal 'out feeling like one."

Laughing, Arses counted out eighty thousand dollars in worn, one hundred dollar bills. "I need a receipt. For SAS. Must show them a paper trail, what?" Jack signed a receipt for the money, showing a payment from SAS funds, put the cash in his pack.

Sensing the American's discomfort, Arses smiled. "It's a terrible world, young Jack. Bad guys all over the place. I think it's rough justice to use their own money against them. After all, these aren't the playing fields of Tom Brown's Rugby School."

"Our problems're solved," Billy said. "All we gotta do is kill the

Taliban, find the bomb and live happily ever
after." "Don't forget my brother,
Dickey," Arses added.

"He's at the top of the list, Robert," Jack smiled.

At that moment, Milady entered. Behind her, a teenage girl and Milady's son, Kim, carried several kettles of food. Kim grinned at Jack and said, "Seat y'self." Jack laughed and hugged the boy, sat him on his lap.
Felt comfortable with the kid, especially after he had told Milady about Ashley. Milady watched the children spread a breakfast of fragrant scrambled eggs, fruit, fresh tea on a wood plank table. The three men pulled up chairs and ate. With swollen eyes that did not look friendly, Milady left.

The Englishman noted her coldness, said nothing. He pointed at a map of Southwest Asia hanging on the wall. "It's about fifty or sixty miles to Shangri-la," Arses jabbed at a spot on the map with his fork. "Once you take care of the Taliban, we'll get Dickey out."

"You're right. We're gonna have to get rid of the border camp first," Jack said as he studied the map. "They're sittin' too near the only possible way into the valley."

Arses looked at him, responded, "Might be a tall order to eradicate them. The Americans are busy in Southern Afghanistan."

"We don't have a choice other than humping over the summits—and I don't see that happening." Jack smiled. "But I have a plan. When we passed through their camp, I noticed they've made a couple of key errors in setting up their fortifications." He outlined an attack.

When he concluded his scheme, Arses bellowed with laughter. "You're goddam on the money."

"Call us the White Tiger force. And you
are..." "Hellbent," Arses replied with a grin.

"Perfect. And speaking of White Tiger, have you seen my tiger?" He looked at Milady, who had silently re-entered the room. She answered, "No, not a sign."

Arses looked at a picture of a tiger on the wall, then said, "When do you want to stage the attack, young Jack?"

"Hopefully within a week. We need time to ammo up and practice the attack. I'll call you on the satellite phone my CIA boss gave me, if you give me a number."

"Good show." Arses made a note of his telephone number. "I imagine you'll get back to Pakistan, ASAP."

Milady said, "You'll have to sneak past the border guards."

Jack laughed, "Shank's mare, Billy."

"Fifty miles?" Billy scoffed. "Fahgidaboutit! I can do that before breakfast."

"Tough guy. When can we start? And I could use a good rope."

Arses drained his tea cup. "Take a look at what I've got as far as a rope goes. Unfortunately, there's a moon tonight but it'll set around 0300. If you reach the pass an hour later, you'll be good to go. The Taliban and al Qaida usually are opiumed out by an hour after dinner."

At noon, they said goodbye to Robert Arses. Jack hugged Kim, avoided Milady, who still looked crestfallen, swollen-eyed. Jack carried a hundred-fifty-foot rope over his shoulder. The two hiked through the mountainous countryside until sunset, held up on the trail to eat a meal Milady had given them: cold chicken in a wonderful spicy sauce, with chapatti bread. "How's your feet?" Jack asked.

"Trashed, how 'bout you?"

"Same. We could use some transportation." By the time they were ready to move, the moon had risen over the eastern peaks, had illuminated the western cliffs with a pearly light. Billy stopped. Jack looked over his brother's shoulder, saw a pale tiger crouched in the middle of the road.

"Goddam big pussycat!" Billy whispered excitedly. "I'll blast it." He raised his M-4.

"Wait. I can't tell in the dark, but it might be my tiger pal."

"You mean the one that stole your deer? Some pal!"

"Yeah, that one. Dude saved my life—led me to Robert." He stepped around Billy, approached the cat.

"Watch out. He looks hungry." Billy covered the tiger with his rifle. The big cat yawned—it's eyes and fangs flashed in the moonlight, it growled again. He stopped an arm's length from the tiger. "It's gotta be him," he concluded. "Or I'd be toast. How you doin', big guy?" The tiger stood on his hind feet, enveloped Jack in his front paws. He nipped at Jack's head as the two toppled to the ground.

"How'd you find me, pal? And why haven't you been using mouth wash?"

Billy suggested, "Dogs can smell for miles—why not a tiger?"

"Must be so," he agreed. "But we gotta keep going." The two resumed their rapid march, the tiger trotted alongside. At a pace of five miles per hour, they crossed over the high pass at 0400 hours, drenched in sweat despite the frigid, high altitude air.

The moon had set, and they were in complete darkness when they slipped through the Taliban camp: no guards. At false dawn, they saw the village of Hunza and ten minutes later, entered the fort. The tiger stopped at the entrance, bounded into the brush nearby, disappeared. The two walked into the fort, found no one present. The fort was cold, deserted.

Chapter 56

Jack and Billy loafed all day, caught up on lost sleep that night. They departed to recon the Taliban force just after the sun rose over white-capped mountains that shimmered n the clear air. After a half hour on the trail, the white tiger joined them, trotted ahead through pungent sagebrush.

Billy asked, "Got a name for that critter?"

"Yep, it's Tigger. He's a Caspian Tiger. Panthera tigris virgata."

Billy waved an arm, asked, "You know Latin for everything?"

"Naw, but this tiger is special. Supposed to be, like, extinct. I called a guy at the zoo in Karachi. He was all excited. Wanted me to capture Tigger.
Said he was worth a hundred grand."

"Okay, how do we capture it? We could sell it to magicians in the States."

"I dunno. You go first."

Billy glanced at the big animal. "Tigger, huh? Winnie would apoohve," he laughed.

"Ha, ha, very funny. Save your breath."

On a rocky Hindu Kush ridge over-looking the Taliban camp, they found several old parapets made from loose rocks. They settled into a dusty trench, watched the camouflaged bare dirt camp, a click away. Men moved about in random walks.

Billy ground one rock into another. "Looks like old wars around here. Guess people never change—makes you wonder," Billy observed. "Hey, you know, Mara didn't fall into the river."

"Yeah, I know."

"Bulldog threw her over. Cuz the bitch tried to fillet you."

"But what the hell am I going to do?" Jack shook his head, rubbed his face. "Guy can't go wasting folks he doesn't like."

"So you gonna court-martial him?"

Jack sighed. "For what? Killing the most famous and successful enemy assassin in Pakistan? Maybe saving my life? He should get a medal. But it was a summary. He's not a judge."

"I gotta be careful when I kill a Taliban? Make sure it's the right time to whack 'em? You wanna publish some guidelines that I can tape to my rifle sight? Who do I ask for permission?"

Looked at his childhood buddy, "It's already been done. The ancient Greeks started it: wars should be officially declared, no fighting at certain times like during the Olympic games, don't punish or injure prisoners, exchange of prisoners—stuff like that. And now we have the Geneva
Conventions. Rules of war."

 Billy snorted. "Rules of war. Gimme a break. Everywhere I look, crazies trying to kill me. I'm gonna shoot first and ask questions later. Like my drill instructor said, Kill 'em all, let God sort it out." He laughed. "And
Chief Talking Dog'll kill me if I let anything happen to you."

"That's old school," Jack said. "Problem is you can't kill faster than they can breed. The U.S. learned that in Vietnam. So really, I think minimum casualties is the correct response. The fewer you need to kill to control a situation, the fewer downstream enemies you create who'll be focused on killing your ass." He turned his attention to the Taliban force in the pass. He pulled out the cell, called Robert Arses.

"Hell-bent, here," Arses answered. "How's it going, Tigger?"

"Okay," he said. "Our raghead buddies are still hanging around, so I think it's time to bring out Welcome Wagon."

"Roger that," Arses said. "Set it up and I'll get back at you."

After disconnecting, he said, "Billy, let's haul ass,". "We're gonna commence to kick Taliban ass."

Billy howled, "Hoorah!"

As the two headed down the trail in the fading light, he saw Tigger bound down a hillside to their path. He was relieved to hear the distinctive sound of the Caribou aircraft approaching the valley.

Chapter 57

After an hour's hike through a heavy rain that turned the lower trail into slick clay, Jack and Billy reached the fort at 1900 hours. They were saluted, waved in by two sleepy Hunza guards.

Bulldog, Omar, General Hammar, Mick greeted them when they entered the dining hall. Jack was taken aback to see Ashley sitting next to the general; she wore a tailored cammie utility outfit, looked fabulous with her blonde hair tucked under a wide-brimmed bush hat.

"Jack, I have a week before I report for work," Ashley said. She kissed him, he inhaled her fresh scent, hugged her. "When the general told me about what you're doing, I talked him into letting me come. This'll be a great story to start work with."

Shaken by her presence, he said, "Ashley, this place is too dangerous.
Especially if things don't go the way we planned."

Ashley said, "Oh, Jack, spare me the ritualistic guy whining. I've seen all the war movies so I know all about war. I'm here. Deal with it. And by the way, your Pakistani girlfriend is alive."

"Mara? I heard—"

"It's true," Omar said. "She survived Bulldog's dunking."

I'm amazed, Jack thought. *Mara, alive.* He looked at Bulldog—guy's face was expressionless. Tried not to glance at the big .454 Casull on the Marine's hip.

Ashley added, "I don't want to think you're up here playing footsies with the Kafir Princess. I read about her in Time."

Jack drank from a water bottle, regarded Ashley. "You should take over G-2 Intelligence, Ashley—you'd be a whiz." He rubbed his face. "So, you'll be, like, an embedded reporter. I guess I won't mind embedding—" Ashley slugged him on the arm.

Jack ducked away, laughing, then looked at the others. "Glad you guys are back. General Hammar, please start."

Hammar placed a new AN 94 folding-stock rifle on the table. It looked like a modernized AK 47. "Lieutenant Nakamura and I prepared a material and munitions list including fifty rifles like this: 5.45 millimeter assault rifle. Replaces the AK 101 for Russian Army. Up to 1800 rounds per minute. Gas-operated, delayed recoil action."

"That makes the Belgian P-90 sound like a popgun. Is this the rifle that fires two rounds at a time?" Jack asked.

The general raised the rifle to his shoulder. "Yes, it'll punch two bullets right through the same hole, thereby neutralizing body armor. We flew to Chitral and I met with an old friend—a man who served under me in campaigns past. I gave him the list and after he met with his sources, he told me he can get us everything we need. Including MRE meals. And he asked for a ten percent commission for a grand total of forty seven thousand dollars. You understand, these materials are stolen from the Pakistani Army."

Jack said, "It pisses me off that we have to operate like this." "Why won't the Marines support you?" Ashley asked.

Jack shook his head, "I think everybody's afraid of getting tarred by a colossal accident. They all think there's a risk of wiping out thousands of civilians. So we're hangin' out there, twisting in the wind. But for the same reasons, we can't walk away from a potential catastrophe."

"I can have forty-five Hunza ready," Omar said. "Give me a couple days with the new weapons. That'll give you time to create a battle plan. But I need some payroll for the Hunza." Jack threw his pack on the table, counted out fifty thousand dollars.

"Here's the money, General. There's extra for avgas and expenses. Take it back to your supplier and get the gear, ASAP.

Arses is ready to go with his troops. After checking out the terrain, I've got a pretty good idea what I want to do."

"And that is?" Mick asked.

He looked around the table, met eyes with each of his friends. "We're gonna take out the Taliban border force. I think the bomb'll be easy to find. It's obviously hidden in a cave near the pass. But there are hundreds of caves. We can't check 'em out until the bad guys are removed from the equation."

"Looked like at least 200 men in that camp," Billy said.

"That's an affirm" Jack agreed. "My old Marine tactics instructor would call it a target-rich environment." He looked back at the general. "One thing I'm gonna need is a sniper rifle. A good one with match quality, full metal jacket ammo. Better, an OCIW."

"I don't think I can get an OICW," the general responded. "I've never even seen one."

"I can't either, but I know I can get a SIG SG 550-1 Sniper," Bulldog interjected. "I'll need to go to Islamabad."

"No," Jack said. "No, then I'd want an M-14 with a scope or better yet, a M40A3 with the 10 power Unertl sniper scope."

"That's the 7.62 custom rifle they special make at Quantico," Bulldog said, "That'd be even harder to track down. But you can't beat a plain old
M-14 with a scope for accuracy. I'd say that's our best chance."

"Good, Gunny," he smiled. "Where would we be without you?" He held up a hand. "Yeah, I know—a bordello in Bangkok or a brig in
Bombay."

Ashley asked, "Is it really a biological bomb, Jack?"

"That's top secret, Ashley. Please don't say anything about it. We'll get in big trouble."

Omar regarded him. "You're kinda diggin' this aren't you?"

"Yeah, I'm kinda diggin' it." Jack counted out five thousand dollars, put the cash in Omar's huge hand. Omar stuffed the roll in his cargo pocket, buttoned the flap. "Sweet! That'll work, bro," he responded. "The Hunza wanna help but they need to feed their families."

Jack looked at his friends. "We're close. We'll succeed."

Mick said, "I hate to burst your bubble, Jack. You an' Billy're listed as deserters." He smiled one of his eye-disappearing grins.

Chapter 58

"Omar, Billy, and Jack, climbed in the dark to the vantage point above Barog Pass in the Hindu Kush Mountains. Long-legged Omar had trouble in the higher altitude but struggled and managed to keep up; they reached the ridge just as dawn brightened clear skies over the Himalayas.

The three took turns watching the border camp, worked on a tactical layout of the encampment, napped on the windswept ridge for the rest of the day. At sunset, they ate, rolled out sleeping bags, slept on the cold, wind-swept ledge, under a sky filled with an infinite number of stars.

The next morning, Jack poured an envelope of Gatorade into a canteen of water. "Wake up, guys. Loosen up and listen to the attack order. As Baron De Jomini once suggested, we're gonna catch them in their tents."

Billy and Omar sprawled down on the cold rocks, huddled in their sleeping bags.

"Who's that?" Billy asked.

"Worked for some Russian Czar, wrote a book on the art of war," Omar said.

"War is art? Guy was nuts!" Billy exclaimed.

"Right," Jack agreed. "Omar, what I want is for the Hunza to set up an ambush on the east side of the pass, just below where the Taliban are sitting. Arses and his force will attack from the west, forcing the Taliban to retreat right into the kill zone of your Hunza ambush."

"What makes you sure they're gonna retreat?" Omar asked.

He regarded his pal, "For one thing, their defenses are set up facing

Pakistan. So Arses will be hitting their backside. They didn't learn from
Britain's mistakes in Singapore in
    1939." "What?" Billy asked.

"Hey, you're right! It's the classic mistake," Omar responded. "All the British cannons and all their defenses of Singapore were set up aimed at the sea. When the Japanese attacked at the beginning of World War II, they came from the land side on bicycles, and overran the British from behind." "These guys made the same boo boo," Jack added. "All their primary defenses face Pakistan to the east. Arses will come from the west and be in their back pocket before they know what hit 'em. My guess is that when Arses smashes them, they'll panic and retreat down the pass." He pointed at a ridge on the east side of the pass.

"Too bad we're not meched up," Billy observed.

"Tanks'd be nice," Jack agreed. "But it ain't gonna happen. And at the beginning of the attack, I'm gonna take out their leaders with the sniper rifle. From that shelf overlooking their camp." He added, "They'll never even hear my shots. So to sum up, Arses will initiate the attack. At the same time, Bulldog will begin a mortar attack with his mortar team from a defiladed location where I'm sending them. We'll use a Javelin—if we can get one—to knock out that pack howitzer cannon in the middle of their camp. I'll take out their leaders, and when they retreat, they'll run into your ambush, Omar. You'll smear them. It'll be a reverse spectacular."

Tigger, who had been absent for a day, appeared; the tiger ignored the others, walked up to Jack, wrestled, rolled on the ground. They grappled, he scratched the big cat behind his ears, rubbed his upper neck. The big cat growled with happiness.

"Jesus Christ!" Billy exclaimed. "I hope he's been fed. And speaking of cats, what're you gonna do with Ashley?"

"She's layin' out her claim," Omar observed. "I'm down with that.
She's the best—don't blow it."

"My life is crazy, Omar," Jack protested. "How do I know she won't go sideways on me? And she's got a huge temper."

"Never know 'less you commit," Omar concluded.

The three pals headed down the mountain in single file. The tiger moved ahead, helped the men relax, confident that the cat would sense and disrupt any ambush in their path. As they reached Hunza Valley, they watched the Caribou come in for a deadstick, completely silent landing. They turned, intercepted the airplane when it rolled to a stop.

The general climbed out, followed by Mick and Bulldog. "Just in time to tote some Taliban ticklers," Mick called.

Bulldog handed Jack an M-14 rifle with a ten-power scope, a cloth bandolier of ammo packs, who cleared the heavy weapon, slung it and the bandolier over his shoulder. The general opened the cargo hatch, began unloading wooden crates. Every box rattled when it hit the ground. Mick and Bulldog unloaded the last four. The group of seven each took a container of weapons, covered with Cyrillic lettering, headed for the fort. Four Hunza tribesmen stayed behind to guard the cargo.

When they reached the fort, Sergeant Major sent twenty men back to the airplane to finish the unloading job. The entire leadership group listened to the plan over a dinner of moist pheasant, sweet-smelling yams, and brown rice, prepared by Ashley. She announced she had grown restless sitting around, and cooking food the Hunza delivered had helped pass the time.

"What if they don't retreat across the pass?" Bulldog asked. He speared a second pheasant breast.

Jack looked at the others. "The Hunza will lay down covering fire so
Arses can dis-engage. Then we'll bug out, too. We'll rendezvous at the
Caribou and fly out while the Hunza scatter."

"But, sar," Sergeant Major bent down, picked up the mortar tube at his feet. Brandishing the 60mm mortar tube, he said, "With this, sars, we will devas-ta-tate the e-vil Tal-ib."

"That's great, Sergeant Major," Omar said. "Can you assemble your troops? Hand out the new weapons?"

Bulldog watched the little man leave. He smiled, stuck a big unlit cigar in his mouth and said, "Sixty mike mike, M-2 mortar. Effective range 1,000 meters. I can shoot it in my sleep."

"Bulldog," Jack sordered, "you put a Hunza team together and set up the mortar a click south of the base on a hill I spotted."

"I'll need about ten men to hump ammo," Bulldog added.

"Take all the men you need, Gunny," he said. "Okay, this's why we're here. Arses and Milady have agreed to hit the Taliban day after tomorrow. Just before sunrise." He looked at Bulldog. "I'll show you on the map where I want you to set up the mortar. The Taliban have a 75 mike mike pack howitzer so you'll want to get in defiladed positions—the reverse slope of a hill—to protect yourself until we take it out with the Javelin." He asked Hammar, "General, what d'you think about air support from the Pakistani?"

Hammar grimaced. "Pakistanis won't fly into Hindu Kush."

Jack asked, "How about mounting the machinegun in the Caribou? We could sandbag it on the deck."

Ashley poured wine she had purchased from Papa. "Who's Milady?" she asked with a hard edge to her voice.

"The Kafir Princess," Jack said. "The one you read about." He grabbed Omar, walked outside, stood in front of the Hunza and Sergeant Major.

He yelled at the gathered tribesmen, "I want to tell the Hunza that we're gonna kick Taliban ass."

The fifty-odd Hunza roared approval, shook their new Russian rifles in the air. He raised his fist, shook it. The Hunza roared again. They were ready for the battle. He hoped they would stay that way.

Chapter 59

Yassar Ahmoud, commanding the ragged force of Taliban and tribesmen he had assembled to move the bomb, yawned in the predawn light, thought about calling for hot tea. He was depressed at the thought of another day sitting on the Pakistani border, isolated, without support. He wished for the hundredth time that he could take the hidden bomb, transport it south—but he had to wait for bad weather to provide more than just cloud cover from satellite surveillance. He needed heavy snow or a howling sandstorm to mask movement from the American surveillance satellites and unmanned spy aircraft. He wished he had the courage to remove the warhead from the bomb but he knew it would be too dangerous to fool with the volatile package. Ahmoud was leaning over to pull on his boots when gunfire pounded on the west perimeter! The whoosh and explosion of rockets and satchel charges destroyed the quiet of the early morning camp. Ahmoud dove under his cot just as shrapnel slashed through his tent walls. He rolled onto his back, pulled his boots on, crawled out of the tent.

Outside, he saw attackers run forward from the west, throw explosives at the camp. The charges exploded in the lines, screams sounded. Loud concussions buffeted him, paralyzed him.

Another mortar bloop, secons later a machine gun took a direct hit. He forced himself to act: ran to the east perimeter. Grabbed a machine gunner, directed the soldier to move the crew-served weapon to the west side, where the attack was the heaviest. He yelled at the howitzer crew to look for the mortar tube. Following the gunners to the western side, he saw more attackers run towards the lines. The force did not look large enough to overcome the camp. He relaxed slightly, until dust kicked up a half meter to his right. He ducked down behind the perimeter rampart, looked for the shooter, saw movement on a high ridge.

Billy Howling Dog rubbed sweat off his brow, wiped the smear of cammo paint on his BDUs, aimed the fifty-pound Raytheon launcher at the cannon in the Taliban camp. "We screwed up—I can't get a fire and forget lock—there's no heat source. Wish I had a TOW missile."

"Too heavy to lug up here," Jack retorted. "Do your best."

Billy fired the Lockheed Martin missile—it missed by twenty feet. He snatched up binoculars, mumbled curses, then watched Jack fire another sniper rifle round. "Just a hair left and up four feet and the guy's toast."

Jack squinted through the ten-power scope mounted on the rifle, adjusted. He wiped his sweaty palm on his pants leg. The target turned, looked eastward—so close in the telescope, he felt like he was peering at a nearby television image: it was Yassar Ahmoud! A flush of shock swept through his body. He exclaimed, "Holy shit. I thought I killed him in the prison camp." He pressed the grooved trigger when the crosshairs centered on Ahmoud, but couldn't shoot.

Billy urged his brother, "You gotta. The whole attack depends on it.

Arses won't be able to whack 'em if the leaders hold their troops."

Fifty caliber rounds clanged off rocks behind Billy after Ahmoud directed the M-2 machinegun crew to fire at the ridge.

The two dove for cover, unsure about what the powerful weapon could penetrate. Jack reviewed his Recon weapons training while he tried to dig into the rocky surface: 500 rounds per minute, cyclic rate of fire; muzzle velocity of 3,000 feet per second; max range 6,700 meters, effective range 1,800 meters. He tried to shove himself into a tiny depression as the massive gun pounded their position. Suddenly the firing stopped.

He took a deep breath. Raised the rifle, spotted the machine gunner.

The guy was trying to clear a jam in his receiver. Jack squeezed until the 7.62mm round fired. The buttplate of the M-14 slammed into his shoulder, the odor of gunsmoke drifted past.

Billy peered into his binoculars. "I saw the bullet's vapor trail go past him. Put in a little left windage."

Jack adjusted the scope, fired. A second later, the gunner threw up his hands, spun around when the 180-grain bullet slammed into him. Jack acquired Ahmoud in his sights, relaxed, fired. Ahmoud sprawled. "Got him.
Look for the next in command."

Billy was amazed at his brother's apparent coolness. "Haven't lost your touch. You 'uz the best marksman around Red Lodge."

"Somebody'll take over. A junior officer type or a senior NCO. Keep looking." Tried to quell the adrenalin sweeping through his body while waiting for Billy to spot the next target. Took long breaths. Hands still shook, gripped the weapon harder.

"There," Billy said. "The guy in the raghead turban and long skirt standing by the howitzer crew. Looks like an officer—the dumb bastard."

"I got him." He adjusted for the slight breeze, took a deep breath. Slowly squeezed the trigger. Rifle bucked again: a miss.

"Wind musta picked up a little. Or maybe a gust," Billy said. "Try again with the same dope."

Jack squeezed off a round, the officer spun to the ground from the impact of the bullet. Jack forced a yawn, hoped to release the tension in his jaw. Shrugged his shoulders, lifted the rifle. "How's Arses doing?"

"He's pouring it on. But dumbshit Bulldog's in the open on the front side of the ridge. Slugging it out with the Taliban howitzer." Billy peered through his glasses.

Jack panned the rifle scope around the camp. Attackers were advancing toward the camp's eastern perimeter. Mortar explosions continued to dance around the compound, knocking down running men.

"There's one more guy trying to organize the defenses."

"Got him," Jack said. "But he won't stand still."

"Lead 'em."

He fired three times. Thought of a running elk on a Montana ridge. Imagined the hit: dropped the guy with his next shot. Two men stooped, lifted the man. The officer hit them with one arm. "It's like watching a panoramic scene in a cowboy and Indian movie," Jack said.

"Yeah, except for once, the good guys—like me—are winning." Billy responded. "Fuck! Our mortar section just took a direct hit."

Jack glanced toward the mortar ridge, saw nothing. Looked back, watched the Taliban retreat, then form a makeshift defensive position at the eastern end of the pass. Suddenly, Omar's force opened fire into the Taliban's exposed backs with a powerful hail of bullets from two hundred meters away. Trapped between the Kafirs and the Hunza, the frantic Taliban broke and ran. Excited, Omar's force, led by long-legged Omar and short Mick, rose and charged their panicked foes. The Hunza overran the Taliban force.

"I feel like a mad orchestra conductor," Jack said. He saw the Caribou fly about a click south of the pass. He pointed it out to Billy. The Caribou banked, descended. Orange tracer fire lanced towards the battle; individuals and groups of men escaping towards the slopes slumped into stillness. About one hundred survivors scrambled up a scree field, disappeared into a cave, leaving scores of fallen comrades behind.

Lines from an ancient Greek play popped into his head:

"Many   heroes,
Persia's   bloom,
Myriads perished.
Cruel! Cruel! Asia kneels."

"Let's head down to the camp," he ordered. "We kicked their asses. Now, I gotta feelin' we'll find answers on the bomb." The two reached the pass an hour later. He broke into a run through the combined Hunza and Arses' forces, slapped backs, hugged individual soldiers. Elated by their overwhelming victory, the Hunza roared approval when he moved through the ranks.

Mick and Omar were watching their force scavenge the battlefield. The four pals congratulated each other on the victorious battle, laughed while they excitedly recounted events. Robert Arses and Milady knelt next to Captain Yassar Ahmoud. Arses had put a tourniquet on the leader's arm, just under the shoulder. Milady's face was painted in vivid colors: blue, green, white stripes.

"Better than the eyeball massacre." Omar yelled in triumph. "Man, we laid waste. There's a hundred and two enemy KIAs, so far. Sweet!"

"You really worked them over," Jack exclaimed. "Except you weren't supposed to chase them."

"The Hunza. I couldn't hold them, so Mick an' I joined in," Omar explained. "And we didn't get one scratch. The Hunza think you've got mystical powers."

Mick pounded Jack on the back, grinned—his eyes disappeared. "Man, you turned into Warrior Numero Uno, buddy. For a guy who didn't believe in war—you're amazing. I gotta thank you for lettin' me serve with you, pal. I'll follow you anywhere."

"Thanks, Mick. Up Army!" he hugged his friend.

Robert Arses added, "My boy, it was a magnificent battle."

Jack smiled, walked to Ahmoud. Lying on his back, Ahmoud looked at the sniper rifle slung on Jack's back, touched his mustache, said, "You. You shot me."

"That would be right," Jack grinned. "Just a little payback." Glanced at
Arses. "How's he doin'?"

Arses griunted. "The bullet didn't mushroom—musta been a full metal jacket. Might be a while before he offers a lady his arm. Other than that, he's okay. Missed the artery. But he needs morphine or he'll go into shock pretty fast." He opened a first aid package, pulled out a needle pack, jabbed the needle into Ahmoud's leg.

"Where's the bomb?" Jack asked. "We know it's here." Mouth agape, Ahmoud stared up at the American. His green eyes looked familiar. Tears coursed across his dust-covered face.

Jack turned to Billy, "He's no good to us. Kill him."

Billy grinned, pulled his K bar. "Can I scalp him?"

"Why not?"

Billy tapped Ahmoud's wound several times with the knife blade. Ahmoud screamed, passed out from the pain.

Jack grimaced, then said, "Gotta make this dude talk. But don't torture him."

"Maybe not," Arses said. He pulled a notebook from the man's pocket, thumbed through the pages. "There's a map. And some writing… Christ!" he exclaimed. "It's in Arabic."

Jack recalled Omar had studied Arabic at Monterey Language School. He saw his friend. "Omar," he called.

Ahmoud stirred, opened his eyes. "I'm alive," he murmured. He looked at the three gathered around him. Jack took the notebook. "Maybe this's all we need."

Ahmoud smiled with a ghastly grimace. "Won't do you any good. It's in Arabic. In a code. Go back to America," Ahmoud added with a bitter tone. "Leave Asia alone." More tears filled his eyes.

Jack glanced at the others. "I feel like we're in a riverboat melodrama. Guy can't take a joke. Maybe the morphine'll loosen his tongue. Mellow him out." Realized he was talking like a jabbering magpie. Must be in shock, myself. Noticing his nervous state, Milady stood, hugged him. Omar approached. Jack handed him the notebook. Omar shifted from one long leg to the other, looked through the entries. "Mostly personal notes. Complaints about lack of money, good weather." He looked at the man on the ground. "Here's a map. Here's the road, the pass and… must be that mountain." Omar pointed at the south ridge over the pass. "Says below it:

"See the Dragon,

"Oh, great," Mick exclaimed. "We got a poet on our hands." He prodded the prisoner with his foot. "What's it mean?" "Monk's mumblings," Ahmoud whispered.

The Americans and Milady stared at the wounded Arab. He gaped back. His shifting, darting green eyes looked like he was wondering whether he was going to live out the day.

Chapter 60

The Americans and Hunza, excepting the mortar section, returned to the old English fort by 0900. Jack constantly worried about Bulldog's team.

Omar sent for Sergeant Major's assistant. When the man arrived at the hall, Omar told him in pidgin Hunza to set lookout posts and to send someone to find out what happened to the mortar unit, then grabbed an open wine bottle, drank; the red wine trickled over his dark skin, stained his dust-covered jacket. He offered it to Jack, who took a mouthful. When Billy stalked into the dining hall, Jack offered him the bottle.

"Here's to kickin' ass," Billy said with a happy voice.

Ashley, showing wet hair from a bath, entered the room, hugged each of them.

"You did it, Jack," Mick said. "It was great!"

Billy added, "Glad you didn't work for Custer. Indians might've gone home empty-handed." He lifted the bottle, drank. "And if'n you'd been on our side…"

Jack took the bottle, put it on a table. "Let's not get big heads. Small unit tactics ain't big-time strategy. But, thanks, guys." The door to the hall crashed into the sidewall, Arses and Milady entered the warm hall. Arses clapped Jack on the back, picked up another uncorked bottle from the sideboard, smashed off the top of the bottle, poured wine into his mouth. Milady, splattered with blood from Ahmoud's wound, walked up to Ashley. Jack held his breath while the Kafir girl crossed the hall. He wasn't sure whether Milady would strike Ashley or hug her. The two were the same height, but Milady was much more muscular, looked dangerous in her wild war paint, blood splashes.

Ashley timidly smiled at the approaching girl, held out her hand. "I've heard about you. It's an honor to meet you." Milady looked Ashley up and down, smiled thinly, shook hands. Watching the women, Jack and the other men in the hall relaxed, but the two women looked guarded, stiff.

The general and a group of Hunza entered, hauling a makeshift stretcher made of a coat and pants threaded over two poles. They were carrying Bulldog, who was shirtless. His upper body was covered in blood.

Bulldog whispered with a hoarse voice, "Sing me a song, guys… the

Garryowen."

Jack glanced at the others, began singing—Mick joined in on the verse to the ancient British military song:

"We're Garryowen in glo-ry.
Instead of water, we'll
drink brown ale, And stiff
our bar bill without fail.
No man for debt
shall go to jail,
We're Garryowen
in glo-ry."

The others joined halfway through the verse:

"We'll beat the bailiffs and shout for beer,
We'll make the mayor and sheriff fear,
Our hearts are stout, we'll get much fame.
Where'er we go, they'll fear our name,
We're Garryowen in glo-ry."

Gasping, Bulldog rolled out of the blood-soaked stretcher, grimaced in pain, tried to sit up. "A swig of that bottle?"

Arses crossed the room, handed the broken-necked bottle to Bulldog; he poured red wine into his mouth, fell back on the floor. Some of the bitter-smelling wine splashed onto the scarred, wooden planks. Bulldog sputtered, handed the bottle back to the Englishman, tried to put his cigar in his mouth, it fell to the floor.

All gathered around the wounded man. Arses pulled fresh bandages out of a first aid kit on his belt. Omar left to fetch a plasma package.

"What happened, Bulldog?" Jack asked. "We saw you set up in front of the hill. You were supposed to stay in defilade, not dance around like a drunk drill sergeant in a ballet." He looked closer and realized Bulldog was in severe risk of dying.

"Sounds good back at the base, Captain," Bulldog gasped. "But none of my gooks could aim the tube. So I had to spot and aim." He gasped again after Arses wiped blood from a shrapnel wound in his side, applied a compress. "Couldn't do that behind the hill."

"Luckily, we knocked out the seventy five with a RPG," Arses said.

"Just sorry the Javelin didn't work," Billy said.

Omar returned with medical gear, handed a clear plastic bottle to Milady. She ripped off a wrapper, jabbed Bulldog's arm with a needle until she hit a vein, undid a clamp, held the bottle up and squeezed the fluid into Bulldog's vein. Omar poured alcohol on a cloth, cleaned blood off Bulldog's face.

"You don't look more than half ugly now that we got the blood off you," Jack observed. "How d'you feel?"

"It hurts. Feel bad. Don't wanna die. Lost a lot of blood—feel faint. Gimme another slug of that wine," Bulldog requested.

Ashley, her face white, her eyes wide, exchanged a glance with Jack. He nodded. She put her hand under Bulldog's head. Arses gave wine to Bulldog from the broken bottle.

"Thank you, sir," Bulldog gasped

"We need to get Bulldog medevaced," Jack said. "How many Kafirs and Hunza are injured or dead?"

Arses said, "We lost three troopers and had seven injured in the assault. I've already sent the bodies and injured back to Afghanistan. Our unit is sweeping the area for Talib survivors."

"General, it'd be great if you could fly Bulldog back to get medical treatment." He glanced at Bulldog. The big Marine turned pale, fell unconscious. Jack hurried to his side, felt the man's pulse in his neck. It was weak, rapid—it skipped. Bulldog opened his eyes. Jack leaned to his ear, "Bulldog, did you sap me at Papa's house?" The big Marine closed his eyes, sighed. Jack asked again, "Was it you?"

Bulldog whispered, Jack didn't catch it. Bulldog formed the word "No." his eyes shut. Jack checked his pulse. It fluttered again, stopped. Shocked, he said, "Bulldog's dead." He thought about CPR but with blood all over, the prospect was nil. His words silenced the celebration as the others contemplated their friend's passing. Regarding Bulldog's face, Jack recalled the mean looks, snarls and yelled commands the big man had given him at OCS, thought of the KKH ambush-rape, the bridge incident. Bulldog had helped save him after Mara's knife attack. So many memories.

"General," he said, "I can't thank you enough for your help. Can you take him to Islamabad? He needs to be sent home to his folks in Kentucky.

Not left to rot here."Hammar, a solemn expression on his face, silently nodded.

Mick stared at his friend's body. "I can't believe it. He was way larger than life. And could he make up songs? Crawl around 'Abad whorehouses and hookah dens? It's hard to fathom." He looked at the others with a pained expression. "Only the bad guys are supposed to die."

Chapter 61

Before dawn Jack hugged Ashley, inhaled her wonderful female scent, climbed out from under a wool blanket and dressed in the cold air. The long-haired blonde looked fabulous in the faint predawn light. She smiled, snuggled under the blanket. He joined Billy in the frigid dining hall. They grabbed several MRE rations from a case against a wall, headed for Barog Pass. Jack carried a 150-foot hemp rope draped over his shoulder. Both took a stubby M-4 rifle. Minutes out of the fort, snow-white Tigger joined them, knocked Jack down with a greeting tumble, followed in trace after a short tussle. When they reached the pass, they found it had snowed during the night—concealing all the shed blood, tears, death. Hid the horrible aspects of the battle. The scene was covered with mounds of whipped cream. He thought of Bulldog Mahoney. Wished he could bring the big Marine back.

They continued through the empty camp, began the climb up the loose scree slope that surrounded the base of the cliffs. An hour later, they stood at the bottom of an almost vertical cliff, perforated by many caves.

"They must've closed up the cave to hide their escape route. Don't see any Via Ferrata, so I'll just start right out," he spread out his rope.

"What's a Via Ferrari?" Billy asked.

"Ferrata—not Ferrari: a safe way. Julius Caesar formed the Sixth
Legion of soldiers in… oh, about 2,000 years ago. Legion was known as the Via Ferrata because they were safe and dependable. Caesar counted on 'em to clear the way. Now, it's a climbing term."

"More'n I wanted to know," Billy muttered, looked up the cliff, noticed Tigger sniff at the base of a shadowed line in the cliff.

"I know you're itching to make like a mountain goat, but me an' the tiger ain't romantic like you."

"Yeah, you'd take an elevator up Mount Everest."

"Goddam right. But only if I was stupid enough to want to climb the mountain. It's a Paleface sport."

"You'd feel different if you'd been dragged up and down mountains by

Dad when you were a kid. Let's explore and see what we've got." The two men and the tiger headed north along a trail below the ridge. There were countless openings in the limestone cliffs.

Finally, Jack decided to climb to the heights, look for the temple he had stumbled on in the fog, weeks before. He pulled out a screw gate with the label, Fader, on the side of it. Spread out the rope again, handed a Petzl ascender to Billy.

"I suppose I gotta make like a goddam sheep," Billy growled.

"Yep." He attached the rope to his waist harness, climbed.

"Now, you're happy," Billy accused his ascending brother. "You 'uz worried we might be able to stroll up the mountain."

"Well, I can see that there used to be a road there, but an earthquake must've wiped it out." He pointed at an ancient rockslide covered with brush and trees. "Means few have been on top of this ridge in a long time.

The monk's map showed a road to the temple."

One hundred feet up, he disappeared from sight, a minute later the rope quit moving. "Okay," he called. "Clamp on that ascender and get your half-red ass up here." He leaned over, watched as Billy slung his rifle over his shoulder, attached the hand-held, steel ascender to the rope, slid it up as far as he could reach. When it locked, he pulled himself up to a new foothold. He repeated using the ascender to ease the climb up the rope. Long minutes later, Billy grasped a hand, was pulled over the edge.

"You're getting' pretty good," Jack commented.

"Yeah—against my will! You're draggin' me all over impossible places."

Resting, the two watched below as the tiger wandered away, disappeared. They continued leapfrogging up the snow-free cliffs. Winds began to whistle. They entered a snowfield, postholed through it for an hour.

As the sun began to set over the wildly rugged Hindu Kush, they moved over the highest ridge, buffeted by frigid winds. Ten minutes later, they spotted a series of ruins: old buildings made of quarried limestone, half of which were tumbled down, spread across a flat area. The biggest temple, which Jack recognized, was also the highest. It hovered over the valley of Shangri-la, about five miles north of the pass to Afghanistan. Snowdrifts piled halfway up the walls of the shrine.

The Americans entered the temple, their panting breath hanging in the cold interior air. The ten-foot-wide vestibule's walls that Jack had thought to be bare when he first visited the temple, were covered with complicated ceramic works of art. Three complex themes were evident: one depicted monsters fighting humans, another showed humans and monsters fighting gods, and the last series showed gods and humans defeating monsters.

Ignoring the art on the walls, Billy walked to the throne, now empty, where the frozen monk had rested. Jack studied the wall, looking for an opening or a handle to a door. The wall revealed nothing. "I'm sure there's a secret room." Poking the wall with his rifle produced no results.

Billy sat on the throne to rest; suddenly a grinding noise startled the brothers. Part of the wall slid back, revealing a low entry to another room.
Billy jumped up, entered the second section. He called back, "Goddam! There's a bigass worm made out of gold and jewels! We're rich! Check out the gold."

Jack entered, stared at the dragon that dominated the temple. It was a long statue—about ten feet—had two horns coming from the head, of carved ivory. The dragon had a huge snarl on its face.

"Dracoserpens Lung orientalis—Oriental dragon," he said in a hushed tone. The statue appeared to be solid gold protruding from a block of black obsidian on the back wall. But when he moved his head, the statue morphed to create a blue-greenish hue.

"We're rich!" Billy shouted.

"Think so? It's awesome, but try an' lift a couple tons of gold. Anyway, it's bad news: Auri sacra fames—the cursed hunger for gold.
Especially in a church." "Forget the Latin poetry bullshit—where's an American flying crane when you need one?" Billy stroked the statue. "It's cold!"

The dragon's chest was covered with dark green scales shaped like teardrops. When they drew closer, they realized that the scales were huge, dark green emeralds, about the size of silver dollars, flat in the center, faceted around the edges.

One of the dragon's feet held a marble box full of emerald scales. The other claw held a knife. Its handle was gold and ivory, with three beautiful inlaid, purple-faceted stones. The blade was over two feet long and highly polished. On one side was an engraving, an exact replica of the dragon, carrying a bag. On the other side was an etching of a young Chinese woman, wearing an elaborate, floor-length gown. It was ripped, shredded, had holes in it. The girl wore a griefstricken look on her beautiful face.

He dropped his pack, looked for the monk's scabbard. When he found it, he thrust the weapon in; it fit perfectly. He felt a weird sensation course through his body.

"Dude, it's a sword," he said. "It's almost as long as my Marine Mameluke sword. This is the one the old guy told me about. But where's the pizza? Pizza knife's no good without a pizza to cut up."

"Forget chow, check out the view," Billy said. He walked to the western side wall—an approximately four foot by four foot aperture had also opened, revealing Shangri-la far below. "So that's where you live forever? Why don't we try some?"

"That's the story. At least you're supposed to live a long, long time. Probly longer'n I'd care to hang around."

"You might feel different if'n you 'uz old."

"Maybe so." Jack looked down, realized that far below he could see the lights of the village, Asgard, thousands of feet directly under the Dragon God. Thought of rosy-skinned Penel, wondered what she was doing, which light was hers. He turned back to the interior of the temple: it was constructed of white polished limestone. The dragon, four feet high, ten feet long, had reptilian eyes of vivid, pinkish-red diamonds. Its teeth were huge rubies that caught the last rays of the sun. Tendrils of steam trickled out of its nostrils and mouth, smelling of rotten eggs. "Scary, man," Billy muttered.

"Serious halitosis." "Yeah, weird." Jack looked around. "Where's the bomb?"

"Don't see it. You said the dragon was sitting on it. If that bomb isn't in the temple, it must be inside this mountain. It'd take weeks to explore all the caves we've seen. Makes me hungry." Billy pulled packs of food out of a web gear pouch.

"Yeah, a complicated mountain. Old limestone structure, full of leached-out caves and caverns, penetrated by a volcanic vent. Could use a thousand men to search it."

"Maybe you could get these local guys to explore all those caves," Billy proposed.

"Yeah, but that'll take forever, catch the attention of everybody who wants it. How do we fight them off?" He heaved a sigh of frustration. "But the bomb has to be somewhere below us. Conway—that old guy on the island said the bomb was cached under the dragon."

Clouds rolled in; visibility dropped to just a few feet. Winds howled over the ridges. The two sat down in front of the dragon, gnawed on MRE meals of half-frozen beef stroganoff. After eating, the two wrapped up in their sleeping bags, drifted into restless, high altitude sleep.

Jack woke hours later, noticed that the wind had stopped. Became aware of a sound like a rumbling roar of surf. Visibility on the dragon's ridge was still bad. He got up, walked toward the sound coming from beyond the temple. Outside, a patch of night sky where the stars glittered through the cloud cover. Remembered the poem's order: first, you see the dragon, then you hear the dragon. Ploughed through snowdrifts, toward the overhead rift in the clouds. Sound grew louder until he stood over the source of the noise.

A vent in a crevasse emitted a strong smell of sulphur in a blast of hot air that whistled out of the vent. He stood next to the rushing air, thought, *Then you smell the dragon. See, hear, smell.* What did it mean? He returned to the camp, Billy was coughing, gasping in his sleep. Jack went to the dragon room, aimed a small flashlight, studied the magnificent gold statue. Sat down, fell asleep: dreams—a voice. "You must awaken Dragon God." Answered, *Doesn't look like he's too aware. Sits there like a lump on a rock, like a statue.*

The voice: "Are you familiar with a totem?"

Sure thing. Big stick, lotsa carvings of ugly animals.

"Dragon God is a totem. He was placed in this dimension for purposes that are not completely understood. But he is here to awaken, to lead, to help Mankind."

Actually, it's humanity nowadays. Includes other folks. Like, women and kids, you know?

"Don't trivialize this discussion with attempts at humor."

So why doesn't he lead and help? We gotta lotta problems. Me, for instance, I—

"He must be awakened. You will do so. Soon."

Jack woke. It was sunrise. He looked around, saw no one. He joined Billy, shook him. They devoured cold MRE ham omelets with frozen raspberry sauce for breakfast, he told Billy of the strange vent, didn't mention the strange dream. After eating, the two discussed the crack Jack had found, retraced steps to the crevasse. Stood over it, felt air soundlessly flowing into the hole.

"You standing on your head last night?"

He looked at his brother. "No, I'm telling you, it was blowing out. I think it must be a natural chimney. I smelled sulfur last night. I think there must be hot springs that heat the air in a cavern during the day—the hot air rushes out at night. When the night air cools, the cold air up here sinks through the vent and flows into the cave. I'll bet hot air used to come rushing out of the dragon statue's mouth and nostrils."

"That's why they talk about dragon's breath," Billy guessed.

He nodded in agreement. "But maybe an earthquake caused this fracture and the air comes out here instead of the dragon's mouth like it's supposed to."

"Must be a big-ass cavern inside the mountain."

Jack zipped his parka tighter. "I think we'll drop in an' investigate it."

Billy looked into the crevasse, shook his head. "I ain't no cave spelunker," he said, "but I know lots of people've suffocated in caves that have low oxygen levels. This one has sulphur fumes already. We could croak in there."

"Yeah, well, it's not very healthy out here either. There's too many crazy critters that want to waste us." He donned his climbing headlamp, looped his rope around a boulder near the vent, buckled the rope to his waist harness with a carabineer, lowered himself into the mountain, hoped there was sufficient air. Wriggling down the crack into the rocky interior, he encountered a narrow stairway hacked in the side of the vent. It spiraled down into the darkness. Swallowed his fear of darkness and forced himself to move. "Follow me," he called to Billy. No answer. He knew Billy wouldn't bail, despite his fears. After minutes of waiting, Billy crawled down, Jack recovered the rope.

They crept down the stairs, reached a point where the vent opened into a huge cavern. Stairs had been swept away by a rockslide along the wall of the grotto. A ghostly light from the overhead vent, a faint radiance in the distance on the natural cathedral's west side. He secured one end of the rope to a screw he put in a crack, lowered himself to the end of the line. He was still twenty feet above the floor. He swung until his momentum allowed him to land on a small ledge on the side of the cavern. Felt for protuberances and cracks, realized that below was a body of water. He secured his slung rifle, put one hand on his lamp, dropped into the water. It proved to be more than warm: it was a giant hot spring with a temperature of at least 90 degrees. Wondered if there was such a thing as cave sharks, big-fanged cave eels. Slowly waded towards the wall of the cavern. At the base of the stairs was a wide footpath. Heard a huge splash behind him, waited for Billy.

"Goddam warm in this dragon's hot tub," Billy said. His head lamp flickered then came back.

"Your first bath in a month, right? You smell so bad, friends might shoot you outta pity."

"Dirt's healthy," Billy growled. "Germs can't get through it. Get dirty enough, bullets might bounce off."

"Dream on, dude."

When the two reached dry ground, they followed the trail around the lake. Stalactites and stalagmites stood like stern jailers and bound, silent prisoners being subjected to dripping water torture. They walked across a flat expanse with a number of darkened side canyons until they found a series of steps cut into the floor of the huge cave.

The two followed the stairs down into the darkness until Billy grumbled about oxygen levels. They ignored headaches, shortness of breath, pressed on: long minutes later, the lamp illuminated the GBU-200 bomb. They high-fived, excited and happy.

The device: military green, long, slim, ugly, on the bare rock floor. Jack walked around it, worried about radiation from the depleted uranium shielding. Wanted to touch it but afraid. Could see where the bomb had been dragged into the mountain. Cave entrance was blocked off with football-sized rocks. A foul smell.

"Weird, you know?" Billy said. "People hauled that statute to this mountain an' people dragged this to the same mountain."

"Yeah, I wonder whether their motives were similar." Piles of furs and ragged parts of clothing spread against the side of the bomb. Bat excrement splashed the side of the cave wall and part of the floor. They looked at the ceiling ten feet above their heads but saw no bats.

"Hey, Billy, we did it! I feel great. We made an once-in-a-lifetime climb, a cool cavern descent, succeeded in navigating a fabulous cave, and as a reward, found the prize everybody's been looking for."

"Goddam big egg," Billy said. "And who's using it for a wall furnace? Looks like somebody's slept here. And check this out." He held up a human skull. "Some ashtray. And if you look close, you can see knaw marks."

"Killer Tomato's been hanging out in here," Jack responded. "At least it's not crystal." Despite his airy tone, he glanced around. "I hope he's had breakfast. I gotta feeling it's the guy that chased me when I left Shangri-la.
And that means—"

"What?" Billy tossed the skull, watched it bounce, heard it crack on the floor, scatter other bones like a bowling ball among pins. "Strike!" he joked.

Jack tried to think of another way to relieve the horrible atmosphere he knew Billy was also dreading. What kind of monsters would live on human flesh, scatter bones like so much trash from a McDonald's. "Remember the woman I told you about? China Bitch? She couldn't have survived after I axed her… anyway, when I climbed out of the valley, her dad followed me."

"You think this bedding here belongs to that guy?"

"Like I said, he was her father." He broke off, thought, I didn't tell you, but she tricked me, she tried… did rape me. I thought she was…" *Too hard to talk about it.* He finally ignored the human remains, looked around. "This cave system must go to Shangri-la. I figure it goes right to Dickey Arses' fort: Haartgard. Before we destroy the bomb and contaminate these caves, let's get the team and check it out."

"I don't look forward to goin' back up that chimney," Billy grumbled.
He gently pushed a thigh bone aside with his toe.

"Don't worry, I got a better way that should soothe even your lazy ass." He walked to the cave entrance, pulled rocks out of the barrier that sealed off the entrance. When Billy joined him, he heard rattling, clinking noises in Billy's pack. "What's that?"

Billy glanced over his shoulder, grinned. "While I was waiting for you upstairs, I decided the poor dragon was suffering from scales, so I helped it out."

"No!"

"Yeah. Took all the left-over emerald scales, pried the others off his chest."

"Dude, we'll go to prison for looting."

"Hey, we're getting' low on scratch," Billy said. "Haven't seen a payday in quite awhile. I figgered it was time to make a self-authorized withdrawal. Look on it as a reverse offering."

"Holy shit!" Jack exclaimed. "I'm going to jail."

"Let's see," Billy grinned. "Leavenworth Prison with three squares or cold MREs in a snowdrift. Red dust, mud and dirt of Afghanistan, or a bed with sheets in prison. Guards to protect me or maniacal Taliban tryin' ta kill me. Check out those bones back there. Hmmm, tough choices for a poor dumb half-Indian boy—how 'bout you, White Man?" Billy dropped the pack. "Anyway, you said all the monks was killed. I figger no one owns the dragon. And we found it first.”

“Who says it was lost?”

Billy reasoned, “Our dad’s suffering ’cause he lost the ranch to the
Crow Nation. My granddad never approved of the Crow lawsuit that wiped Dad out. I guess I don’t either. And our old man couldn’t pay for your law schoolin’. That’s what got you into this mess, made you join the Reserve for tuition. I figger this way we come up smellin’ like wild roses in Greasy Grass. How d’ya think he’ll feel when you buy back the ranch with this scratch?” Billy took a breath and concluded, “Show me a JAG prosecutor that’s gonna climb over twenty thousand feet up to gather evidence.”

“All right, all right, Mister Lawyer. You talk too much. And remember, the ranch is part yours, whether you like it or not. Let’s get out of here.” He moved rocks blocking the entrance.

“First,” Billy answered, “I’m gonna hide the pack somewhere farther back in the cave.” He walked into the darkness and returned in five minutes.
With a big grin, he clapped Jack on the back and exclaimed, “We’re rich, Red Ryder.” He used the nickname Jack had gone by when they played childhood games.

Jack shook his head. “Stolen jewels in a cave are a long way from cash in Citizens State Bank in Billings, Montana, Little Beaver.” Then he remembered the old monk’s entreaty, “Listen: you must go to Dragon God.
Remove his emerald armor; keep it safe until it can be returned to the Emperor’s heirs.”

Chapter 62

The brothers emerged from the creeped-out cave just after dark, reached the fort an hour later. Jack led the way into the dining hall; they went from triumph to disaster in seconds.

Arses looked up, exclaimed, "Beastly Yassar Ahmoud kidnapped your gel, Ashley, and escaped sometime in the night."

"How'd that happen?" Jack and Billy shouted together.

Omar interjected, "Well, Ashley decided to interview him. I figured it was no sweat 'cause he was so weak from his wound. We shoulda posted a guard, but it didn't occur to me that he'd try and get away. Bummer, bro.
Major bummer."

Jack slumped down on a chair, draped his body over the long plank table. Every possible thing that Ahmoud could do to Ashley flashed through his mind. Immediately thought of Amy Anderson, the suicide from Iowa. Looked in the somber, sympathetic faces of his pals. Milady, at the other end of the table—stone-faced—said nothing. He wondered whether she had helped. "Please, God," he prayed aloud. "Protect her until I can find her." He looked around the table. "Did you check the road to Gilgit? There's not many places he could have taken her."

Omar observed, "They were nowhere to be found in the valley. He might have slipped past you into Afghanistan. He coulda passed you in the dark. He's probably gone to re-assemble his survivors so he can move the bomb."

"We found it!" Billy exclaimed. "In a cave."

The others pressed for details and Jack related the story of the climb, the descent, the discovery.

Robert Arses rapped his knuckles on the table. "Wait a second, you blokes. I'm happy you found the dragon's egg, but the primary reason I funded this operation was to rescue my brother. I don't give a Newcastle coal miner's shit about the bomb. And my brother's as important to me as your gel is to you. We need to get to bloody Shangri-la to rescue Dickey. And by the way, how much is left from my eighty thousand dollars?"

Jack thought furiously but could not think of an argument that would persuade Arses. He felt prickly sweat break out on his brow. "But Dickey's safe. Ashley isn't safe at all."

"We don't know that, young Jack." "But it makes sense," he pleaded.

"We must go for my brother," Robert ordered. "That was the deal. If Ahmoud isn't in this valley, and he hasn't left by road, he probably slipped into the cave system you spoke of. Mayhap, all the answers—including your gel—are in Shangri-la."

Jack stared at the Englishman. "I think Ashley and the bomb take precedence, and I hope you're right. I made you a promise and I'll stick to it. I have twenty five thousand dollars for you."

"We can't climb like you goats," Omar protested.

"Billy and I found a way. I'm pretty sure the cave where the bomb is, leads to Shangri-la. We should take about twenty men." He looked at Milady. She remained stone-faced.

Chapter 63

Ominous thunder echoed all night in the Himalayas, on the eastern end of Hunza Valley. Early in the morning, Jack dressed, went to Milady's room and knocked, identified himself. She opened the door, wearing only a wool sweater. It covered her to her upper thighs. A coal fire in the fireplace warmed the room.

Trying to ignore her long legs, he sat in the only chair while she sprawled on the bed. Long black hair spread across her broad shoulders. She looked tremendously appealing as her sweater crept up her body.

He took a deep breath. "We haven't had a chance to catch up, Milady. I can't thank you enough for your help."

Milady stretched her exquisite legs, smiled. "You bring us your wisdom and great fortune. It's good to join forces with you. I only wish and hope——-"

"You guys are warriors." He spoke quickly, hoped to cut off a personal tone. "I have to leave and we need someone to stay here and protect the approach to the bomb. Can you do that?"

Milady sighed, "I know you think only of rescuing your American woman." She reached out, took his hand, pulled him to her side. "Am I so lacking, Jack? I've watched this woman you chase. She's for herself. While I'll give you my all. Is it not enough?"

"Did you… did you——-"

"Help the al Qaida? No." She put her arms around him, kissed him. He inhaled deeply—her scent was enticing, overpowering. For a moment, he could not resist, kissed her back. She leaned back, drawing him prone on the bed with strong arms.

Images of making love to Milady flooded his mind, he put his arms around her. Her body heat scorched through his clothes.

Milady pulled at his blouse, shoved her naked leg against his groin, rubbed. His physical reaction to the contact was immediate, uncontrollable. Her shirt slid higher and out of the corner of his eye, he caught a vision of her bare lower body: lovely. More memories overwhelmed his mind. A word welled up without pre-thought. He exclaimed, "No!"

Pulled away, backed up. Heart pounded, gasped for breath, tried to calm his body. "I'm sorry, Milady. But I can't do this."

Her dark skin flushed, Milady stared at him. Her crestfallen expression said it all. She gulped for breath. "I'll stay here with my Kafirs. Go with good fortune, Jack Flashhardt."

An hour later, Jack, Billy, Robert Arses, Chopstick Mick, Omar, joined ten volunteer Hunza troops and ten Kafirs that Robert Arses had chosen. Each man carried his weapon, six MRE meals, ammunition, a handful of pitch pine torches Sergeant Major had provided. The small force crossed the green valley, climbed the barren slope into loose-rock scree fields, moved above the snowline.

Tigger loped down the slope, skidded to a stop next to Jack, walked, rubbed his shoulder against his friend. Troops murmured in several languages, those nearest drifted away. At 0830, the force was at the cave entrance. Jack told Sergeant Major of the danger of the strange giant men who inhabited the cave system: the old man spoke in Urdu to his men. Several asked questions, mumbled the word, Yeti, looked nervous.

Omar ordered the Hunza and Kafirs to take the lead in a column of twos. He instructed that the point soldier drop off at each side tunnel and stand guard until the column had passed.

The lead man lit a torch, started into the five-foot-high opening, but immediately yelled, brought a fingernail file, put it in Omar's huge hand.

"Sweet! It must be Ashley's," Omar said. "Tribal men or women in Pakistan or Afghanistan wouldn't bother to clean their nails." He showed it to Jack. "She's left a sign that she passed."

Arses joined them, added, "We'll find an' save her, lad."

Jack stared at the close-up, vertical mountainside; hope surged. Took out Holland's cell phone, auto-dialed. Got a recording. "This is the Daisycutter impact zone," he said. "I'll send an image of the bomb tomorrow." Tigger stayed at his side.

A moment later, the cell vibrated. Jack answered: it was Holland. "Got your message. That's great! You know anything about a stolen Caribou?"

Jack felt a tremor of fear. "What about it?"

"A Caribou was stolen from a Pakistani base in Lahore. A witness described General Hammar. He used General Harmbruster as an originating requisition order. Colonel Farley thinks it was you and Hammar. He's up in arms."

A ngered, Jack responded, "Look! You want this bomb taken care of, or what? Keep Farley off my back."

"I'm just saying——-"

"Take care of Farley and I'll hold up my end."

"When are you goin' to take out the bomb?"

Jack looked at the men entering the cave. "I need to move some personnel, set up demo. Probly tomorrow to be safe." "Don't delay," Holland cautioned.

"Don't worry—we crushed the tribals guarding it. And I've got Kafirs and Hunza troops guarding the entrance to the cave system. This thing won't see the light of day." He punched the end button to cut off further conversation.

When they saw the long American bomb, illuminated by the wavering light of their torches, the men paused, then moved into the cave, edging past as far from the device as possible. The men sniffed the foul air, noticed the human remains and hurried through the area. When Jack reached it, he took a picture with the cell phone, framing it so the human bones scattered across the caves' floor wouldn't show, moved back outside, sent the image to Holland's number. Thought, If an inanimate object can look alive, this does. Looks deadly beyond death. Ugly, beautiful, sleek: evil embodied in a green steel sculpture, not wrested from raw materials by skilled artists, but built by more common hands.

Ten minutes beyond the bomb, the cave opened into the immense cavern. The force encountered the vast underground lake with its sulfurous fog hovering like a formless ghost. In various spots, stalactites and stalagmites were still doing the jailer and bound prisoner water torture gig. A faint light from above spread across the cavern.

Jack shouted, moved forward. He instructed the point man to take the branch of the trail that traced around the southern flank of the black waters. The troop passed bubbling hot spots that grew louder as they approached, faded as they passed. After an hour's march along the shore of the hot water lake, the trail, wide enough for three men to walk abreast, headed upward along a cliff that abruptly fell away to the black waters below. Five minutes later the column halted, Sergeant Major shouted that a soldier left to guard a side tunnel was missing. Jack felt a massive tendril of fear race through his body but he maintained a stoic expression. He and Billy exchanged uneasy glances. Tigger rubbed against his leg while men cautiously searched. Tension built, the troop finally gave up after a long hour, nervously moved on.

A half click farther, they approached an arching bridge over a silent current of water that flowed out of the fogbank. The lead man held up at the sight of a man standing just short of the bridge. The Americans and Arses moved forward, stared at the figure, barely visible in the semi-darkness of the huge cavern. "Send scouts ahead," Mick suggested.

Two Kafirs moved forward. They neared the man, one screamed in shock, both backed up. "It's the missing Hunza," one shouted. "He's shishkabobed on a pole stuck in the ground."

Weapons cocked, the force advanced: the head-less man had been spitted, with the pole shoved through his crotch, out his gory neck. Sergeant Major and a Hunza levered the body down, stretched it out at the beginning of the steeply climbing stone bridge. A Kafir supplied a ground sheet, covered the body.

The force moved up the long, arched stone bridge. After slow minutes, a rampart appeared at the highest point of the span, hundreds of feet above the water. When they drew closer, they realized it was a flat-roofed structure, also built of stone.

The frightened natives held back, so Jack, accompanied by Tigger, moved forward. Entered a doorway into the one-room edifice. A foul moldy odor assaulted his nose, even the tiger sneezed. Human bones, skulls, scraps of clothes were scattered around the twenty-foot-square room. He stepped carefully, avoiding the remains. Seeing nothing alive or informative, he gratefully retreated. Jack stepped out of the structure, Tigger suddenly crouched. He glanced up, a giant bat-like shadow soared from the roof. A huge man, over seven feet tall, landed next to Jack, missed with a swipe of an enormous arm, grabbed a nearby Kafir, jumped off the bridge in one bound. The Kafir screamed for long seconds as he tumbled into the abyss. Finally, a huge splash below cut off his cries. Rising, Jack and the other men looked around. Silence stretched throughout the cavern. Several peered into the darkness.

"Holy shit!" Billy exclaimed. "I thought trolls lived under bridges, not on them. Who the hell was that?"

"Whoever, he was fearless," Omar observed. "I wouldn't want to meet him in a dark——-"

"Where the bloody 'ell you think you are?" Arses demanded. "This could as well be the bloody River Styx—gateway to Hades."

Omar looked down, added in a frightened voice, "Right."

Billy observed in a shaky voice, "He attacked you, Jack. Like he knew you."

"Let's go, 'fore we waste our torches," Mick demanded.

Trying to look in every direction at once, the force continued and moved off the bridge. Two hours later, the pathway forked to the north and south. They continued along the south fork for another hour, until it ended at a collapsed tunnel.

"There's gotta be a way past this," Jack said. "China Bitch and her pals must've had an entry to Haartgard." After a fruitless search, he and the others sat down for a short break. He looked around and up. Saw a faintly gleaming crack of light above him. Rose, jabbed with an unlit pitch pine torch: a heavy hatchway barely lifted. "Look," he said.

Mick threw his torch down, ordered, "Lift me." Omar bent over. Mick climbed on his back, pushed the hatch away, looked. "There's a hallway. It's a building." Ten minutes later, the entire force assembled in a deserted hall of Haartgard.

"Where is everybody?" Arses asked. "Why's this huge place empty?"

Chapter 64

With Tigger at his side, Jack cautiously advanced down the hall. He noted the sulphurous smell of the cave was finally gone—the air was cold and sterile. Passed through a portal into a large room: a reception hall and eating area with a high ceiling. Heard shouts, shots,clamor outside. A Kafir cautiously pushed twelve-foot-high double doors open, they stepped into the fifty-foot-wide courtyard, faced a scene of chaos.

Dozens of men stood, shoulder to shoulder on the upper walkways of the thirty-foot outer wall, firing rifles beyond the battlements. The temperature change from the castle to outside made all hurriedly button their coats. Gobs of flaming materials flew out of the sunset-tinted sky, soared over the ramparts, splattered against the walls surrounding the flagstone courtyard. Men and women rushed about on various tasks. Jack thought of his sneaking retreat from the fort long ago.

Arses, Mick, Omar, and Sergeant Major, joined Jack and observed the incredible scene. Shouts, screams, the roar of an unseen enemy host rang through the air. Arses grabbed a cowering child. "What's going on? Where's Dickey Arses?" he yelled. The boy peered at the men, stared at the white tiger in astonishment. "Mujs attack!" he answered as he pointed at the walls over the main entrance. At that moment, a small group of men fired an ancient brass cannon on wood wheels. Jack recognized Dickey Arses' distinctive top hat. "There's Dickey," he yelled. "In the top hat."

"My brother? Is that him?" Arses ran across the courtyard to one of the two stairways that coursed up to the ramparts, on each side of the closed wooden gates. The team watched Robert climb the steps, run to the 17th Century cannon. He accosted Dickey, the two spoke for a moment, stared, hugged. A flaming missile, trailing gobs of burning particles, dashed against the rampart next to the two brothers. They dove for safety as a billowing cloud of smoke and fire enveloped them. Tigger jumped, ran back into the fortress. Engulfed by confused motion, the bastion was a mass of men and women. They busied themselves at several aspects of the defense. Some carried wounded, several fought fires, others carried various crates.

"Let's go see if the brothers survived their reunion," Jack yelled over the sounds of the battle. Turned to Sergeant Major. "Will the Hunza fight alongside the people of Shangri-la?"

Sergeant Major grinned. "The Hunza are Shangri-lan kin. We will follow pukka sahibs into any battle to save True Hunza."

The Americans, the Hunza, the Kafirs, sprinted across the courtyard, up the steps to the ramparts. After the men positioned, the crackle of gunfire increased.

Jack approached the English brothers. They were lying on the rampart walkway, nose to nose, holding hands and talking. Bullets whistled, ricocheted overhead. Their clothes were singed, smoldering, their faces blackened by the fiery explosion that had detonated near them, but the two grinned, shouted at each other.

"Hey, Dickey," Jack called, "I know you missed me, but this fireworks reception is over the top."

The brothers looked up. Robert had a wide grin on his face. He jumped to his feet, hugged Jack. "All I can say is, thank you." Dickey Arses, replaced his top hat, stood, patted him on the back. "I thought you were dead and eaten by foul China Bitch," he said. "We found the blood trail leading from your room. After you disappeared. You're alive, wonder boy
—and you've brought my brother in our hour of need!"

Jack introduced Omar, Mick, Billy, to Dickey Arses; introductions were interrupted when another fireball sailed over their heads, impacted on the roof of the main hall. The group peered over the rampart, Dickey Arses pointed at the scattered groups of attackers, firing from behind rocks and hastily piled barriers of dirt. Said, "Bloody towelheads attacked yesterday at dawn. First time they've acted so boldly. But their numbers and weapons have increased." He glanced at the setting sun. "Luckily, they abate their attacks at nightfall. Damned druggies retreat to their hovels, suck their hashish for courage."

"How many able defenders do you have?" Robert Arses asked.

"What're your ammunition reserves?"

"As of noon, we had two hundred men and boys capable of standing the defense. With scarce twenty bullets per man."

"How about the enemy?" Omar shouted over gunfire.

"Hard to say, they have more attackers than possible. Somehow got an influx of fighters," Dickey answered. "And an infusion of courage. Luckily, only tried to overwhelm the fort once. Had a bloody pack howitzer. I managed to knock it out with our old East India Company culverin." He took out a rag, lifted his hat, wiped the powder smudges off his brow.

Jack shifted on his feet and mumbled, "I'm afraid we're responsible. Got in a fight with a Taliban force and the survivors retreated into the caves east of here. Must've found—"

"Another secret entrance to Shangri-la?" Dickey asked. "Seems every goddam person knows the way out except me!"

Arses hugged Dickey. "You're saved now, brother."

Mick dropped down after closely observing the attack. "They're using a catapult to fling those firebombs over the walls."

Jack felt arms surround his upper body, squeeze. He turned his head, recognized Penel Kong, his beautiful Shangri-lan lover. He turned, hugged and kissed her.

"Thou left Shangri-la without me! But thou hast returned." She flashed a radiant smile.

"Introduce us to your friends," Billy demanded. He and Wantonal, Penel's sister, were sizing each other up.

A bullet whined off the parapet. Dickey shouted, "Don't let the battle interfere with you chasing my bloody gels!"

Penel scowled. "As mine sister hath said a thousand times, we're not thy bloody gels, Dickey."

While they bickered, Jack glanced up at the towering cliffs the fort huddled against. "You ever suffer avalanches here?"

Dickey looked up. "No," he answered. "That's why the fort was built into these cliffs, many centuries ago. There are snowfields on the upper slopes, but that ridge of stone above the fort prevents avalanches." A sharp line of crags separated the snowfields from the cliffs that the fort was built against.

"Do you have any C-4?" Jack asked.

"No, but we have ample supplies of nitro," Dickey said. "Why d'you ask?"

"Better. Suppose an avalanche swept your enemies away."

Robert looked up and enthused, "I see where you're going, young Jack. If the fort's inhabitants pulled back into the mountain, an avalanche would destroy the onrushing enemy. Bloody brilliant, if it could be done." "Where d'you get gunpowder?" Mick asked.

"Potassium from bat guano in caves," Dickey said. "Charcoal from pine cones, sulfur from deposits near the hot springs. We make and add nitric and sulfuric acids to produce nitroglycerin."

"If you could hold off the Mujs long enough for me and Billy to get up to the heights, then let them overwhelm the ramparts, I could set off explosives and turn the attackers into frozen pillars of wisdom in a giant avalanche."

"Asgard and the front half of Haartgard'll be destroyed!" Penel protested.

"At least you'll have survivors for the task of rebuilding," Robert Arses said. "If the Muslims attack in force tomorrow, they'll take your fort easily. You've no choice. It's that or run." A string of bullets hit, whined off the parapet.

"Down to the courtyard," Dickey ordered, "where we can plan in relative peace." His words were punctuated by the ominous whistle of a firebomb that crashed onto the roof of the fort. A bucket brigade sprinted to the new crisis. Checking the horizon, Jack watched the sun disappear over the western heights. The air temperature dropped quickly. When the group reached the bottom of the front walls of the fort, they sat on the flagstones. Penel hugged him. Wantonal sat next to Billy, the two conversed in low tones.

"Will they quit?" Omar asked. "And start up at sunrise?"

"That was the drill yesterday," Dickey responded. He peevishly glanced at Wantonal, then added, "As I said before, the bloody towelheads suck up the drugs after din din. But I fear tomorrow morning. I think they'll launch a major attack and we'll be finished 'less we come up with a plan."

"There's another option, brother," Robert pointed out. "Your Shangrilans can come out the way we came in from Pakistan. There's a huge cavern and tunnel with a hidden entrance to your fort."

"We'll not be driven from Shangri-la!" Penel protested.

"I thought you wanted to see the outside world."

"We'll not be driven out by filthy Mujs," Wantonal added. "This is our home—sacred Shangri-la."

Omar asked, "Who's your leader?"

"Our father, king of our people, was killed in the first moments of the attack," Penel said. She stared at Omar, the first African-American she had ever seen, rubbed her forehead. Added, "In the fight to close the gates. Father fought bravely. Muslims dragged away many fallen after their battle for the gates."

Jack took Penel's hand, squeezed it and said, "I'm sorry."

"Yes," she responded. "Now, I must decide…"He pulled his knife, drew a line on the dusty flagstones. "We'll counterattack the Muslims just before dawn. Omar and Mick, you send out four teams of Hunza to take out their listening posts. Then you sneak through the lines with a raiding party and attack from their rear. You cut your way back to the fort. Hopefully, the action'll slow their attack tomorrow morning."

"That'll totally fuck up their dope," Omar agreed, flashed a thin-lipped smile. Mick grinned at the mention of action. "I like it. We'll start with bayonets until we're discovered. Then we shoot our way out of there." He smiled again at the thought. "It'll be goo-od."

"Exactly," Jack said. "Mick, I'll leave that in your bloodthirsty hands.
I'm gonna go on a schedule as though the Muslims will attack at dawn.
Omar, we'll need flares, fuses, a detonator."

"Sergeant Major should have what we need," Omar replied. "He always carries the engineering and demo supplies. I'll check."

"Great!" Jack turned to Dickey. "Billy and I'll hump a load of explosives up to the heights. When we're ready, I'll shoot a flare out over the valley. Dickey, you retreat into the mountain caves. When the Mujs mass at the walls, send up a flare. I'll set off the avalanche, bring the snows down on 'em."

Penel asked, "Can I help carry the explosives?"

"No," he said. "Billy and I'll make the climb. We're used to the altitude. Anybody else might get sick and slow us down." Eyes flashing with anger, Penel stared at him.

Billy looked at the forbidding cliffs rising from the rear of the fort. "Jesus Christ, Jack! How're we gonna climb that?"

"We'll go up the way we came from the Dragon's temple." "And if you don't set off an avalanche?" Dickey asked. "They win," he admitted. "But what're your options? You've enough ammo for a ten minute pitched battle. So if the avalanche doesn't work, you retreat to Pakistan."

"A brilliant plan, young Jack," Robert Arses said.

"What about the Monster Man of the Mountain?" Penel asked. "China Bitch has been absent since thou left Shangri-la, but the cannibal bastards continue to attack. What'll the monsters do if we invade their lair?"

"Keep your guard up. They're human, just like us. Moreover, those of you that are leaving Shangri-la, should haul ass immediately, 'cause I don't know what the explosions will do to the tunnels. They're already messed up by past earthquakes."

"As soon as we retreat into the castle, we'll head for Pakistan," Robert said. He hugged his brother with one arm, adjusted his eye patch with the other hand. "Let's hope we all meet on the other side of cave waters—and let us hope they are not the River Styx, the waters before Hell."

Chapter 65

Taking his hand, Penel led Jack upstairs to her day apartment in the fortress. It was clean, with bright colors and ornate, carved furniture. An elaborate green wool bedspread covered a down comforter on a double bed. A fireplace was constructed of hand-shaped brown bricks, faced with sparkling quartz. A mostly red Afghan rug covered the floor in front of the fireplace. A large mullioned window with an elevation above the outside walls, showed a wonderful view of the western mountains across the valley. Far below, terraced fields crept up the valley floor to the base of the dark mountains.

Penel crossed the room, put her arms around Jack, kissed him ardently, drew back. "I sense coldness thou did not show before. Then, thou were passionate beyond belief." He stared at the beautiful blonde. She looked like she could be Ashley's sister but her stilted English was jarring and reminded him of her difference. But the two women's similarities were confusing. "Things… things are different now," he stammered. "My
American girlfriend and I have reconciled."

"Really," Penel said coolly. She crossed to a small table against the wall, poured two glasses of water from a blue ceramic pitcher. She handed one to him, drank from the other. "Remember the words I spoke on the day we met? I said, Drink and be restored. These waters have healing powers. For now and forever."

"Yeah, but—-"

"Drink. This water is from the same tarn hot springs. Hast thou been ill since that last draught of Shangrilan waters?"

He regarded the water, then Penel. "Hell, yeah! I ate a wild mushroom and almost died. Drove me crazy for awhile. Forgot who I was." He gulped the sulphurous, mineraly-tasting water.

Penel frowned. "Small and black? With a white stem?"

"It almost did me in. Dickey's brother said it's deadly."

"That mushroom kills all who ingest it. Thou're alive because of the tarn waters taken on thy first visit. One side effect only: the essence of the water in thy body marshals thy life force. It is common during recovery to temporarily lose memory and sanity. Now finish the water." He realized he was thirsty, drank despite the foul taste.

Penel smiled. "Thou're now a Shangrilan."

"What's that mean? I'm from Montana. I wouldn't even know which king candidate to vote for in peaceful Shangri-la."

She smiled again. "What I mean is that our people have discovered that consumption of those spring waters once, prevents illness. Ingestion twice, and thou will live long."

"Yeah, right," he tried not to scoff at her beliefs. "I guess that means Social Security will throw me out when I tell 'em I'm retirement age but look thirty. Thanks a lot."

Penel approached him, put her arms around his waist. She smiled and said, "Joke as thou will, matters will not change. Thy American woman will grow old, sicken and die before thou reach middle age. Thou are mine, now. I will wait. Flashhardt, thou will be drawn back to Shangri-la. You were brought to the Tarn of Long Life for a reason. That is already proven."

He briefly kissed Penel on the mouth. He hugged her and said, "That's great, Penel. Thanks." *Yeah, right. Every one of these mountain kooks think they'll live a long time. They've got nothing else. But if I had to, Penel would be a great babe to spend a couple hundred years with.* Penel returned his kiss with passion hard to resist. Finally, he thought of Ashley in Ahmoud's grasp, broke away.

Chapter 66

Packing the pint jars of nitro that Dickey Arses had fetched from the Haartgard armory, Jack and Billy worked slowly. The containers were old pint-sized Ball jars, each full of a yellowish liquid.

Billy asked, "Doesn't this shit explode real easy?"

"I wouldn't juggle these bottles if I were you," Jack responded. He looked at the bottles, wondered how American-made Ball glassware had made it to Shangri-la. When he finished packing his bottles, he drew the Dragon God knife and pried the three purple, quarter-sized stones out of the handle.

"Why're you doin' that?" Billy asked.

"I gotta feelin' these stones aren't just colored rocks. I want to keep them separate, in case I lose the knife." Jack held up a purple faceted stone —it was a flawless gem. At 1800 hours, the two said goodbyes, left the fort, headed into the mountain.

It had taken the entire team seven and a half hours to travel the caverns to Shangri-la. Though slowed by packs filled with twenty pounds of nitroglycerin, the brothers made their way in four hours, through the tunnels, across the bridge with its bone and debris-filled hut. The dead man they had left was missing. They continued around the black, underground bubbling lake Robert had dubbed the Styx—the waters that separated the world from Hades.

When they reached the bottom of the collapsed stairs, Jack put a new battery in his headlamp, regarded the wall above him. He uncoiled his rope after setting the pack down. "When I get above the collapsed part, send up the packs. Make sure—"

"Yeah," Billy laughed. "Drop 'em and we're toast. Or maybe scrambled eggs. But what the hell—my legs feel like oatmeal." Jack looked around nervously. "Make sure that big guy—" "No shit," Billy agreed, broke into a low-voiced ditty:

> *"He ain't gonna munch on me.*
> *He might munch on the other guy's balls,*
> *But he ain't gonna munch on me."*

"Oh, you're in rare form, oatmeal legs," Jack laughed, happy to break the tension. Turned to the cliff: after a short climb, reached the stairs. Pulled up the packs, Billy attached an ascender, worked his way up the fixed in place rope. When his brother joined him, Jack said, "Let's go. We gotta climb five thousand feet. It'll take all night. Unless you've another hymn to sing…"

"Can't you get the janitor to turn on the escalator?" Billy grumbled while he cautiously lifted his pack. "I'm beat to shit."

"You don't want this joint's creepy custodian." He looked up the winding stairs. "I hope Ashley doesn't end up… on the bottom of an icy avalanche."

"I doubt… they'd take her to a battle. No reason to do it."

"Hope you're right. Save breath. Gotta be in place by dawn."

The sky was brightening to a bluish-white over the Himalaya range to the east as they climbed out of the cleft in the rocks near the pitched-roof temple. The brothers hurried, began their descent of the western slopes. Realizing they were late, they ignored their trashed muscles, hiked and slid a quarter mile down the thirty-degree snow slope until they reached the two-hundred-meter stretch of rocky ridge. It was light enough to see the dark-green fields far below. Jack feared Ashley was on the valley floor, prayed she wasn't near the fort's walls.

Shivering in the glacial air, Billy said, "Looks warm down there. I wonder how Mick and Omar did?" They listened, but could not hear the sounds of battle. All was quiet in the dawn light except for the moaning wind. Jack carefully unloaded the jars of nitroglycerin, packed in strips of wool. He placed a Ball jar next to the rocks, attached a blasting cap with a strip of duct tape, cautiously packed snow over the bottle so the blast would not go airborne.

"That stuff was solid when we started," Billy exclaimed. "What happened? Is it gonna work?"

"If I remember my explosives class, the stuff liquefies at 37 degrees. It's fine. Produces ten thousand times its volume in explosive gases. Take this whole ridge out. Put a bottle every ten meters. I'll set up the fuses.
We'll save one bottle for the bomb."

Faint gunfire and explosions echoed through the ridges. "It's started!
We gotta hurry! Go, go!"

After they placed the nitro jars, set the fuses, they started up the slope, struggling in the high altitude snow. It took a half hour to reach the temple. Jack worried about Ashley all the way, wondered again whether she was with the Muj attackers. Wondered if he was about to kill her.

Panting for air, Billy collapsed on his back. Jack carefully shed his pack, pulled off his gloves, dug out a flare. Sent it arcing into the heavens. A thin trail of green smoke stood out vividly against the blue sky. He flopped down, pulled out his detonator, which was the size of a car door opener. "I hope. We're not… too late. They didn't… have ammo."They started up the ancient, dust-covered steps in the dim light of Jack's headlamp.

Billy commented, "Seems like your social agenda is getting' a tad crowded. Heard about leaving a babe in every port. But you're carryin' it to an extreme. Course with Ashley bein' missing an' all… they're reduced by one."

"You're about as sensitive… as a horny bronco on a shy mare," he panted. "And it's not my fault that Milady, and Penel, and Melinda, and
Ashley… all have the hots for me."

Billy was also having trouble with the low oxygen air. "Melinda? You nailed her? Save some for the rest of us. And anyway, your charms. Didn't work. On Mara, the Black Orchid."

"Hey, can't win 'em all—she didn't know a good thing when she stabbed it," he wheezed. "Anyway. I'm worried. Ashley might…" "Hunza. And Kafirs. Pretty ammoed up," Billy gasped.

Twenty minutes later, Jack saw an orange flare shoot into the sky above the valley. "Here goes." Thought of Ashley, prayed. Keyed the electronic detonator. Below, they saw bursts of flame, smoke along the ridge. Heard cracks above and below their position. Snow settled, separated. "Let's get outta here!" They ran.

"Temple should be safe," Billy shouted.

"No, head for that cornice." They ran fifty meters higher to a massive rock cap, reached safe haven just before the snow from above roared past in a huge, cascading wall that engulfed, swept the ancient temple—smashed to pieces—down the slopes. It disappeared in a giant column of snow flurries. Snow filled the air, even after the roaring sounds of the avalanche subsided.

"Adios to the gold statue," Billy exclaimed. "I'm glad we got outta there, Flashy."

"Yeah, right. Almost adios to us." He suddenly thought of his dream in the temple. The voice had said, "He must be awakened. You will do so." Billy poked him in the arm. "Hey, guess what? This means the emeralds're ours with no trail."

"Explain to the IRS how you worked for the loot."

"Finders keepers. We'll sell them in Bangkok or Hong Kong or somewhere and pay the taxes. You're the brain. You'll figure it out. I'm rich! Billy clapped his gloved hands, danced in a circle on the rock outcropping:

"I'm rich, I'm rich,
I'm a sonofabitch and rich."

“I wonder whether we’ll live to spend it. But more importantly, we just killed hundreds of men.” He thought of the first monk’s words: “You will make the earth a lake of blood. Remember, a righteous battle leads to heaven for the fallen—they will be washed of their sins by their spilled blood.”

Flat on his back, gasping from his song and dance, Billy said, “They put their asses in a sling, not us.” Jack watched the snow dust rise, pushed by swirling winds. The flurries looked like souls ascending to heaven. Wondered how responsible he was: continued to watch snow flurries, caught, turned golden by the rising sun. Mists soared higher. Wondered how many more souls would float away before he completed his mission.

Chapter 67

"Exhausted, Jack and Billy sprawled on a snowbank for ten minutes. They wolfed down parts of MREs, then ran down the stairs, slowly dropped down the dimly-lit cave walls. Tigger sat at the bottom of the stairs, next to the black lake. Sulfurous steam from the hot waters still hovered over the lake, hid the ceiling. Jack noted that it was already 0900. "Hey, buddy," he said. "Great to see you."

The tiger growled, banged his head into Jack's midsection hard enough to stagger him.

"One of these times, he's gonna take a bite out of you." "Naw," he rubbed the tiger's soft ears, hugged him. "Tigger loves me."

Jack, Billy, and the tiger moved around the lake, approached the trail junction at the head of the waters. Tigger stopped, stared at the trail ahead. Billy spotted a pale object in the dim light cast by his maglite. "Hold up," he ordered.

"What is it? It looks like——-" "A head," Billy interrupted.

Cautiously, the trio advanced until they stood next to a Hunza's head impaled on a four-foot-high stake at the edge of the lake. The head stared, with dull sunken eyes open, towards the center of the dark waters. Its mouth hung open, tongue was black. At the base of the pole was a pile of human bones, scraps of bloody clothes. Jack exclaimed, "Must be the guy we lost on the bridge!"

Tigger delicately licked the stake where blood had drained from the severed neck.

"We might've lost him, but he lost his head," Billy cracked. He looked around. "Who put him here? Why's he staring at the lake?" Jack looked closer. A woman's belt dangled over the head. It was Ashley's belt! He sighted in the direction the dimmed eyes gaped, saw a faint area of radiance across the lake. "Mo Poo! Chin Bit's dad. He's left a message. He has Ashley."

Billy inspected the muddy shoreline. "Must be short on road signs around here. Look down there." A linear indentation, huge prints led into the water. "He took the bomb. He has Ashley and the bomb. Why's he being so sharesy with info?" Billy's voice dropped to a whisper. "Look's like he wants you to come to the party."

"Well, it may not be Cotillion, but I say, let's get it on." He shouted across the waters, "We're gonna dance, asshole."

Chapter 68

Standing at the edge of the cavern lake, Jack and Billy stared at the illuminated area in the fog. Jack felt the utter exhaustion from being up all night. He checked his watch—it was just after 0900. "I'm beat," he said. "This late night gettin' bombed, goin' ridge-hoppin's gotta stop. I hope the avalanche saved Haartgard. But I'm going after Ashley. I've a feeling she's at that lit-up area out there in the lake." He glanced at Billy. "You'll probly miss the guys coming from Shangri-la. I want you to go to Hunza Valley and get some backup. Bring them. I'll need help."

"Bullshit, Flashy! I'm not leaving you alone in here. This dump is creeped-out to the max!"

"Give me a couple spare clips for my M-9," he ordered. "I wish we hadn't left our rifles at Haartgard." Dumped everything out of his pack except the last bottle of nitroglycerin, a water bottle, three M-9 magazines, two MREs—waded into the hot water. "Don't worry, I'm just gonna do a recon. I wish we had a UAV to check out what's over there. Anyway, I'll need more help than you can give me by yourself. Get the troops, come an' we'll figure out what to do." He left Tigger and his brother, started across the lake. The tiger put a paw in, jerked it out.

He looked back and said, "I know how you feel, Tigger. I wanna do the same." Despite his fears, wading in the heated mineral water was comforting after fighting through snowbanks on the top of the mountain. Wondered how unstable the nitro was if it changed from a liquid back to a solid in the hot water. Occasional smelly, bubbling hot spots made him nervous, he moved faster to get around the super-heated areas.

As he crossed into the low-lying fog, the sight of an island formed before him. Glanced back at the empty darkness behind him, continued in water up to his neck on the underground causeway. The island was a small volcanic cone with steep cliffs around the sides that dove into the waveless still waters. Diffused light illuminated it from the cavern's roof high above —probably from a volcanic vent to the outside. He prayed that he wouldn't have to circle around the perimeter—he drew closer—spotted a large hollow lava tube. He slowly moved with his pistol drawn, towards the tube opening in the vertical cliff. The lava tunnel, which had been formed when a lava flow cooled on the outside, enabling hot lava to flow through and out of the inside of the tube, was about six feet in diameter, and stretched into the darkness of the cone's interior. Walked into the tube, maglite shining on the ground ahead, felt like a bug crawling into a garden hose. Reached the end of the tube, discovered it was blocked by a huge boulder. I ain't Sisyphus, he thought. I can't budge a boulder. Retracing steps, he emerged from the long cylinder, bleakly assessed the cliffs. Saw no other option, holstered his pistol, gulped down a bag of fruit from a MRE in his pack, assaulted the cliff just north of the tube. The lava cliffs were uncomplicated, easy to climb except for a sheared part of the cliff that had created an overhang to surmount: his only difficulty was exhaustion. He hung by his hands, thought about just letting go, dropping down to where he could rest, even sleep. Remembered the nitro in his pack, thought of Ashley, imprisoned, abused or dead. Fall and you're dead, you dumb ass. Summoned desperation energy, heaved past the projecting rock. Ten minutes later, he peered over the top of the volcano cone, into the circular caldera. Reminded him of Mount Kilimanjaro on a smaller scale and without the snow: round—like the equatorial African summit—continuous rim, steep interior walls. Flat surface below, barely visible in the dim light from the overhead vent, littered with jagged, volcanic rock piles. Numerous hotspots emitted steamy vapors.

A pathway had been improved from the lava tube, for a distance of about three football fields, to a large one-story wood timber structure in the middle of the caldera. The scene could have been a vista from Hell. Arses said it—maybe the water is the River Styx—this looks like Hades.

Half dozen other small stone-built buildings scattered around the caldera.

Saw no one about, pulled the rope from his pack, secured it to a locking carabineer, attached it to a screw he wedged deep in a crack on a large boulder. Worked his way down the steep interior wall until he reached the caldera. Left the rope in place.

Discovered that it was much hotter on the bottom. Hunkered down behind a lava flow, ate a chicken and mashed potatoes MRE. Almost choked on a chunk of bread when a small man emerged from a nearby cave, moved towards him.

"Hail, sir. Tell me who thou art? Art thou English? Russian? I speak no Russian. Name thy country. From whence hast thou traveled hither to China?" The old man appeared to be Chinese. Dressed in ill-shaped clothes that were patched together from blankets and rags. Just over four feet high. A body like Batman's Penguin.

"I'm—who the hell are you?" Glanced around, saw no one else nearby. Resumed eating, but the food now had no taste.

"Luckless stranger! Flee across the black waters of this hellish lay. Fly from this cheerless abode before thou art consumed by the jaws of the giant cannibals."

Chapter 69

"What are you? A Shakespearean foghorn on wheels? Who're these cannibals? They related to Chin Bit? They had breakfast?" Jack looked around the dim volcanic caldera, glanced at his watch: 1100 hours. *Wonder if I'll ever see the blue skies of Hunza Valley or Shangri-la again? This really sucks.* "Is he the guy been dogging me? Is Ashley—is there a blonde woman here? An American?" Please, say yes.

The old man's slanted, eyelash-less eyes widened. "Thou art the man

Mo Poo seeks to draw hither. Thou art the focus of his hate. Thou hast slain Mo Poo's daughter. Thank thy stars he traveled to Shangri-la for tarn waters of long life."

"Chin Bit attacked me," he looked around, fought a feeling of guilt.

"People of Shangri-la say she was a cannibal."

"Peoples of Shangri-la, I often heard Chin Bit proclaim, supply the daintiest meal." The old man nervously looked around the caldera, back at him. Wrinkles on his face deepened.

"Why did she—why do they eat people?"

"No one hast ever arrived here without being butchered." *Non-answer*, he thought. "How come you speak English?"

"Taught by Shangrilan prisoners. I am named Cyvual, by Mo Poo." He pronounced it as Sigh-view-all.

"What about Ashley? The blonde woman. Is she here? Is she okay?" Swallowed his fear. Stared into the old man's eyes.

"She lives."

"Has… has she been harmed?" Dreaded the response.

Cyvual vigorously shook his head. "No, imprisoned only. I know what is implied by thy question. Thou should know, he is a eunuch. They all are.
De-manned when the Chinese masters decided to end the experiments."

Unconsciously, Jack touched his crotch. "Castrated? To end what program?"

"To build an army of identical giants. It was one of Chairman Mao's
Giant Leap programs. They see best in the dark. The woman is only here to attract thee. She is the bait of this trap. She will serve when all is done."

"You said they—how many are there? All identical? That's impossible!"

Cyvual held two fingers a quarter-inch apart. "A few dozen still exist here and in Tibet. They were one hundred, all identical in appearance if not manner. They escaped the Nazi scientists and military masters of the Second Department that created them. Praise the day the monsters finally depart this sad vale."

"Nazis? They were WW2. That's ages ago!" Jack exclaimed.

"Hired from their lairs in some southern land by Mao's Collective Shield—now called the Second Department. Hired to breed the identical giants."

"Sounds like cloning. That's never been done except in animals."

Cyvual spread his arms, threw them above his head. "The Nazi scientists brought magic from their war experiments."

"Why're they cannibals?"

The old man gestured at the barren caldera, said, "What would you grow in here?"

Jack finished his food, crumpled his trash into a ball, stuffed it in his pack. Pulled his M-9, cleaned it with an oily cloth he removed from a cargo pocket. Extracted the bullets from the magazine, dried every shell; after reloading each round, his confidence grew. While he worked, he looked up at the watching old man. "What about you? Why doesn't he eat you?"

"I serve the horrible masters. At their sufferance. Each night I praise
God for surviving another day in this hellish locale. Herotmere, is what the
Monster Man calls the fortress."

Jack regarded the old man. "Just leave."

The old man grimaced. "Sir, I do not wish to die. I am confident that mine old carcass would not be sweetly chewable, but death is death."

"Tell me where the woman is."

The old man pointed at the timber structure in the middle of the caldera. "She's kept in the Hall of Herotmere."

"Not a bad pad. Who built it?"

"Volunteers from Shangri-la."

"Volunteers. Yeah, I'll bet. Habitat for Humanity of the Hindu Kush.
So how'd she get here?"

The old man looked over his shoulder. "The Pakistani soldier brought her. He left soon after. I don't know why he was allowed to leave."

Stood, put on his pack. "Take me to the fortress."

"Thou'll be captured when he returns. I'll be punished," the old man shuffled his feet. Tapped his pistol barrel against the old man's chest. "Guess you thought I was making a request. Take me to the woman or I'll blow your brains back to Pakistan."

With slumped shoulders, the old man picked his way through the rock debris towards the center and bottom of the caldera. They occasionally passed disgusting heaps of human bones, skulls, ragged remains of clothes. Ten minutes later, they reached the front of the twenty-foot-high timber stronghold. Logs were standing on end rather than on top of each other. Constructed of volcanic obsidian, twenty-seven polished black glass steps led up to the portal. The old man stopped at the bottom of the steps and said, "I must not enter. She, who thou seek, is inside. Steps will lead thee below to her confinement. I cannot help thee more."

Looking back at the blocked entrance to the caldera, Jack climbed the steps, thought, *Fear and trembling. This really sucks.*

He gripped the pistol tighter, forced himself to advance. Inside, he searched the building. The first room: a large meeting hall. The next two, each about ten by ten feet: deserted. The fourth room—someone had collected and carefully stacked human skulls to the ceiling. The hundreds of empty eye sockets stared, all aligned in the same direction, at Jack in the doorway. He offered a prayer for their souls, blocked out thoughts of the horror and suffering they had probably endured.

Fifth room was an armory of discarded weapons: rifles, submachine guns, swords, knives. On top was one of General Hammar's folding stock Russian AN 94s. Spotted the American biobomb resting in the far corner. Drew closer—it was intact, except for a dent in one of the controlling fins in the tail, another in one of the forward wings. Stared at the bomb: it still looked ugly-beautiful. *Wonder if little germs are still crawling around inside? Get Ashley, destroy it.*

He retreated to the hall, lit by fat guttering candles on the walls.

Looked around, walked to a heavy plank door, suspended by rusty, mismatched iron hinges at the end of the hall. Lifted the crossbar, forced the door open. Set of steps led into darkness. Overheated, terrible-smelling air flowed out, hit him. Smelled like an ancient foul sewer. Thought of scary movies he had watched as a kid. He'd always shouted, "Don't go down there!" Easy to say.

"Ashley!" he yelled. "It's me. Ashley, you there?"

Heard no answer, threw the wood crossbar down the steps Listened to the clatter. *Great. She's down in the Herotmere Hilton getting a massage and facial, I'm up here, scared shitless.* Started down the steps, wondered, hoped. Paused at the bottom step, shed his pack, pulled out his headlamp.

Batteries ruined by the water, lamp would not operate. Put it in his pack.

"Ashley," he yelled. "It's me, Jack."

Stepped into the semi-darkness, inspected a cell to the right. Empty. Second cell, empty—ammonia odors made it hard to breath. Piles of excrement in the middle of the floor. He looked up—the room was a septic tank of sorts. Disgusted, he backed out. Light from the stairs was diminishing. Quickly moved along the walkway to the third cell, where he called out softly, "Ashley? Come on. The Oasis Bar and Grill. Menlo Park, California. U.S. of A. It's really me, Ashley. Come out." Caught a movement, was engulfed by her hurtling body.

"Jack! Oh, Jack." Ashley clung to him. "I thought it was another trick. That horrible little man——-"

"Okay, Ashley. I'm here. I found you."

"I prayed that you would come. When they let Yassar Ahmoud leave, I begged her to give you a message." Led Ashley to the stairs. Pulled his canteen out of its pouch, put it to her lips. A long drink, she dropped her head, wailed, "Ohh, Jack, it's been so horrible!"

Stroked her greasy, matted hair. Hugged her. Buried his face in her grime-smeared neck. She smelled rank, unwashed, felt gritty. He suppressed overwhelming guilt. "Let's get out of here."

Creaks at the top of the steps startled them. He saw Cyvual: the little man struggled, slammed the door shut. Complete darkness. Ashley tried to suppress a wail, did not succeed. They sat, holding each other. For a second, he felt passion, but forced the emotion down. "I'm sorry I got you into this nightmare."

"No, I should never have told the woman to ask you for help." Ashley's voice was flat, without hope.

Gotta buck up. I'm the one responsible for this stupidity. Be strong. "Ashley, we're goin' to get out of Herotmere. I've got my M-9. Billy's bringing the guys. But what woman?"

Ashley clutched his hand. "Yassar Ahmoud. He's a she."

"No way. What makes you think so?"

"Trust me, Jack. She's disguised as a man."

Baffled, he disregarded her accusation. They talked for an hour. Despite their situation, conversation made the time pass. They planned a vacation on the Seychelles Islands, off the coast of Africa. Planned a photo safari in Tanzania, balloon ride over the Serengeti Plain. Camping trip in Yellowstone Park. They held each other, inwardly hoped it would all come true. He wished the baby had survived. Knew at that moment that he wanted this incredible woman to share his life. Knew he would do whatever it took. Overcome any obstacle to keep her by his side.

Ashley broke the spell when she asked why the giant Chinaman hated him. He related his self-defense killing of the Chinaman's daughter, Chin Bit, in Shangri-la. Left out that Chin Bit had seduced him, tried to strangle him. Told her about his imprisonment by Yassar Ahmoud, who was after the biobomb.

He saw a light, looked up. The huge Chinaman, Mo Poo, was standing in the doorway. Half-blinded by the light, Jack stumbled up the steps, pulled out his M-9. From above, Mo Poo peered into his face, as though he was trying to determine Jack's nature. Dressed in wild attire of tattered patches of blankets, castoff clothes, ragged furs, the distinctive peaked cap, the ugly, huge-headed man snarled with his distinctive basso voice.

"Let us go," Jack demanded.

"Never," the Chinaman answered. "You killed my dot-ter."

Jack fired three rounds. Dust puffed in the center of the Chinaman's chest. He staggered back, Jack kicked his ankle, the big man tripped, fell. Jack leaned over him, was grabbed, pulled to the Chinaman's chest. Stared into the man's horrible mouth. Thinking the man was dying, he yelled, "I got two words of advice for you, pal. Next life, brush your teeth!" Snarling, the giant lifted him in the air like a toy teddy bear, hurled him. Chinaman stood, shoved the door shut. Jack collided with Ashley. Pistol flew away, misfired. A feeling of helplessness overpowered the pain from crashing down the steps. Dazed, he said into the darkness, "Well, that went well, don't you think?" Ashley sobbed, cradled his head to her chest, then asked, "Jack, are you okay?" In a quieter voice she whispered, "Jack, you shot him. I saw him stagger. How could he survive?"

"I'm fine. He's probly wearing body armor. Damned underpowered Berreta. Wish I'd aimed at his ugly head." He sat up, blacked out.

Chapter 70

When Jack awoke, his head was in Ashley's lap in the pit of Herotmere. He could smell her foul odor, saw nothing; for a moment, he thought blindness had returned. Realized they were in complete darkness. "Hey," he whispered. Ashley stroked his forehead. "Are you alright? Thank God! I was so frightened. I can't stand being alone again. You've been unconscious for hours. Jack, I hit someone. Two big men came down the steps. I fired your pistol. I hit one in the foot. They locked the door again."

"That's great, Ashley. Give me the pistol." *This is the girl I thought couldn't hack the violence of Asia? She's goddam Annie Oakley!*

"It's empty." She handed the gun over.

Felt around until he found his pack. Found a full magazine: reloaded the M-9. Stood, adjusted to the pains shooting through a hip, his ribs. "This rescuing damsels in distress isn't everything it's cracked up to be —'specially since I'm the one gettin' cracked up." Crept up the steps, pushed against the door. Flimsy, makeshift iron bar barely secured the door. Thought of the Dragon God's knife in his pack. Went down, got the knife out, strapped it to his belt, carefully put the pack on. At the top, he slid the knife blade through the opening, lifted the bar above its sleeve. It fell to the floor with a clatter. The old monk in Quetta was right. Knife is saving me. Whispered, "Ashley."

She joined him, they ran into the hallway, ducked into the ammunition room. He picked up the AN 94. It was loaded. Worked the action, extended the stock. Glanced at the slender GBU-200 biobomb. The bomb's rear access panel was dismantled! Imagined piles of white dust on the floor.Ashley noticed his startled expression. "What?"

Jack didn't want to breath, didn't want to move. He slowly backed into the hallway, pushed Ashley ahead of him. "Nothing," he said. "Let's see if Mo Poo can eat a whole magazine of lead. When was the last time you ate?" "I can't remember. You have food? Why didn't you say so?"

He shrugged out of his pack, keeping his eyes on the door. "There's chow in my bag. Careful of the nitro bottle." Useless, now. Who the hell got to the bomb? Had the nerve to open it?

"Nitro! Nitroglycerin?" Ashley cautiously groped in the bag until she found a package. Pulled it out, ripped it open. Ate the food—Cajun rice with sausage and a carrot cake. Devoured it like a hungry dog would— gulping it down without chewing. Pulled out a water bottle, drank.

Watching her, he thought of their first date, a fancy restaurant on University Avenue in Palo Alto, California—just down the street from Stanford University. A cheerleader and popular girl at the school, she had been so confident, so precise in her eating style. Now she was—

"Ohh, so good. Haven't eaten in forever. I love you." An explosion rocked the building; shockwave threw them.

"Wow!" he said. "You make the Earth move for me, too." Ashley, her mouth, her lush lips smeared with food, looked up, grinned. Her eyes danced in the dim light from fat candles. They waited for long minutes after the explosion, crept to the front of the main hall. He saw men emerging from the lava tube that led to the volcanic core. Glanced at his watch—1600 hours.

"Who're they?" Ashley asked. "Your friends?"

"No, ragheads. Come for the bomb." He knelt down behind a corner of the portal. "Explosion we felt, that was the ragheads blowing open the blocked entrance."

"What're you going to do? Jack, you can't fight. There's too many." Ashley's voice neared hysteria. He fired three times before the approaching aggressors ducked for cover. After scant minutes of silence, interrupted by wails of a wounded man, a voice called out. "Is that you, American?" Voice echoed off the steep walls of the caldera. He recognized Yassar Ahmoud's voice, remained silent.

Ahmoud walked along the path to their position like a man treading on eggshells. Jack stood, hidden behind the portal, watched the Pakistani approach the fortress. Amazed that the al Qaida dared approach. Fought an urge to shoot. The al Qaida stopped about one hundred feet from the small fortress and said, "If you give up now, we'll let you go. All we want is the bomb. You can live. Go free."

"Jack," Ashley said. "We're saved."

"Shut up," he whispered. Thought of inhaled anthrax, eating his lungs.

Yelled, "No chance, Ahmoud. Let's dance or get outta here before the

Chinamen serve us all up as take-out chop suey."

"Think of the woman, Flashhardt. You're condemning her as well. For a stupid, solitary bomb."

"You're making one fat-ass assumption. That you and your raggedy ass, sand-pounding dopeheads can take me. Why don't you all get out of here? I'll let you." *What an irony,* he thought. *Now I'm defending a useless weapon. But they wouldn't let us live, anyway.*

"American, I have Mara Bhutto. I'll kill her."

"You're lying."

"I'll show you. You cannot let both women die for the bomb." Ahmoud walked back to his troops. After he disappeared, there was silence.

The voice of Mara Bhutto called, "Jack, save me."

Thought of when he had met Mara. Beautiful, self-assured woman. Dinner at Gil's. Feeding him hummus with beautiful fingers. Had thought about sex with her. She sounded terrified.

"Is that her?" Ashley asked.

"I dunno."

"Jack, I fed you in the prison camp at Bharakan. You invited me to stay at your ranch. In Montana. You said your father would welcome me." Mara's voice took on a pleading tone. "You made love to me on the shores of Rawal Lake. Jack, I'm pregnant with your child. I want to go to your ranch. Save me. They'll kill me."

Ashley punched Jack in the arm, glared at him.

"She's lying, Ashley. But it's her."

Ashley gripped his forearm. "Jack, you said… what're you going to do?"

The lying bitch tried to kill me. Also saved me. But something weird here. What can I do, anyway? Nothing.

"Eh, Flashhardt?" Ahmoud's voice came out of the darkness. "Give us the bomb, or her death will be cruel." *It's worthless, you stupid prick. Somebody beat you.* He hugged Ashley. "Doesn't matter, they'll kill us if they can. This isn't the movies where you throw down your gun and give up. There's nothing I can do for her. I—"

Mara's scream interrupted them. Cried out his name. Pleaded for rescue. Screamed again. Jack and Ashley held each other. He felt Ashley shudder against his body. Squeezed her.

Finally, there was silence. I've killed her. Attackers laid down covering fire, while others circled around to the side, jumped from rock to rock.

He tried to hit the flanking men, had to duck away when bullets ricocheted off the walls. They ran into the assembly room. Tipped over a long, heavy table, crouched behind it.

"They'll probly throw grenades, Ashley. Cover your ears."

Minutes later, they heard running steps, a shout: grenade bounced through the entrance, exploded. Gunshots shattered the air. He sighted, fired. Ducked down. Automatic fire pounded into the table, sending splinters of wood flying over their heads.

"Let's back up." They crawled along the hallway, ducked into the first room. Bullets continued to spray, stopped. Suddenly, distant gunfire! Peered around the doorway, saw an attacker standing, strangely exposed in the entrance, staring across the caldera. Sighted, shot the man in the back with a double tap. Man screamed, fell, kicking one leg over and over. Other men scrambled out of the fortress.

"It must be Billy and the team. Ashley, we're saved!"

Chapter 71

Ashley looked around the stronghold of Herotmere, "I'm under a huge mountain. In a creepy volcano filled with ghoulish cannibal freaks, crazy
Taliban. I stink, it's hot, and I need a bath. Why don't I feel saved?"

Jack laughed. "Ashley, you're the best. But I'll do the jokes." *I wish I could tell you, Ashley. Don't sweat the big freaks—we've gotta worry about microscopic creeps.*

She squeezed his hand. "Just get me out of here." Gunfire increased. He led her into the hallway. "Stay away from the door, keep watch." Put his pack down, opened it, removed the bottle of nitro. Tried not to breathe as he tiptoed into the gunroom, approached the bomb. Placed the bottle under the slim green weapon. Ashley called from the hall, "Will that little bottle destroy that big bomb?"

He glanced up. "Stay back! This's nitroglycerin, remember? It'll destroy the bomb. Turn this pile of germs into a case of mild sniffles." *Yeah, right! Ex-germs.* Took the cell phone, pressed start. Was amazed when he got a signal.

1800 hours: "That'll do it," Jack said. "Holland'll call back in six hours. We've got six hours to get out of the cavern." He put the phone next to the nitro bottle. Didn't mention the B-52 strike that would drop fifteen thousand pound Daisy Cutter bombs on the cavern entrance. Gunfire was intense in the caldera until it became completely dark. He tiptoed out of the room, gathered rags, splintered chairs, other trash lying in the main hall, piled the debris in the building entrance. "Help me."

"What're you doing?"

"Need a signal to the guys, by making this body a Taliban crispy critter. So they can tell where we are." Pulled a Bic lighter out of his pack, lit the pile of trash. Pushed the body to the fire, next to the growing flame. Smell of burning hair, smoldering clothes, barbecuing flesh.

"Burning a body!" Ashley looked horrified.

"Hey, trust me. I'll bet the guy doesn't care. Probly right now, he's busy gradin' his seventy two virgins." Took Ashley's hand, led her away from the fortress. "We'll hide in the lava field while we wait." Long minutes, an hour later, he heard Billy call, "Red Ryder?"

He estimated where Billy's voice was calling from, said, "Okay, Little

Beaver. The fire's in Billings. I'm in Yellowstone."

Ashley whispered, "What'd you mean?"

"We're from Montana. I just told him where we are. I didn't want to be too graphic, case the ragheads are waiting." Ten minutes, Billy called, "Red Ryder?" Thirty feet away.

"Here."

A minute later, Billy joined them. Behind him were several people. Group huddled together with heads almost touching. He recognized Mick's stocky body and square head in the faint light from the fire, Omar's black skin, Arabic features. "Thanks for coming, guys." Billy handed Jack night vision goggles. "They're VS-7s, Flashy. We got you on the night vision with light from the fire and on thermals from your body heat."

While adjusting the mounting straps, he smelled wet animal fur and said, "Tigger?" Big cat rubbed against him.

"Yeah, Tigger tagged along. I wasn't gonna say no."

"We knocked down a couple of ragheads," Mick said. His voice carried a swaggering tone that heartened Jack.

"How many are there?" Omar asked.

"Counted maybe thirty at first," Jack said. "Now there's about twenty five. But why didn't you bring troops?"

Billy handed Ashley a second set of goggles, helped her put them on her head, said, "Brits an' their troops hauled ass as soon as they got out of the caves. Were already gone. An' the general took Bulldog's body to
Islamabad."

"Hunza took off for their homes after the battle," Omar added. "Luckily, Bruno showed up."

Hearing Bruno's name, Jack realized he was the fourth man. "What brought you to the party, Bruno? Saloons quiet down in 'Abad? Ladies of the night on strike?"

"I heard of the troubles, Jack. You mustn't have all the fun, so I talked my way onto a Pak helicopter to Gilgit. Caught a ride up the highway. I got to Hunza just as your friends returned from the hidden caves."

Jack tried to see Bruno's face but the goggles hid it. Why was Bruno there? Was he really that much of a pal? "Guys, tell me about the avalanche."

"It worked!" Omar responded. "Sweet! We pulled back and the avalanche took everything out. Huge noise—felt like an earthquake. When it settled down, all we could see was a wall of packed snow. The Shangri-la folks were starting to dig out when we left."

"You took out hundreds of ragheads," Mick enthused. "You're a kick ass battlefield commander."

Ashley cried, "I can see!" Billy had turned on her goggles. "But everything's green!"

1915 hours: Jack glanced at his watch. "We've got five hours to fight our way out of the caves, 'cause I set a timer and nitro on the bomb to blow at midnight. Anybody still here will be toast." "Five hours!" Omar exclaimed. "It'll take an hour to get out of here. That leaves just four hours to get through the Taliban."

"Well, I hate farewell parties," Jack said. "We'll just have to throw a short one."

"Where's the bomb, Jack?" Bruno asked. "Maybe we'll have to reset its destroyer."

"In the fortress, but don't sweat it, Bruno, old buddy. We'll get out of here. I got a plan. We have five shooters plus Ashley. We'll advance in pairs and charge through their positions, keep on going. Ashley has my Beretta. Omar, you stay with her."

"Let me take the rear," Bruno said. "I've good night vision." "Makes sense," Omar said.

"Okay," Jack agreed. "We'll go up the trail to the lava tube in single file: Billy, Mick, Omar, me. When Billy makes contact, Mick and Omar break right and I'll head left. Bruno, you and Ashley lag twenty feet behind and stay on the trail. If we can't bust through, let's regroup here. Everybody locked and loaded? Tigger, you can't fight bullets. Stay here until the shootin' dies down."

"Don't tell me the cat can understand you," Omar said.

Jack put his hands on the tiger's face. "Stay," he ordered. The tiger growled from deep in its throat.

"Goddam!" Mick exclaimed. "Makes hair stand on my neck."

The team headed up the trail in single file, until, after ten slow minutes, Billy stopped. Jack looked, spotted ghostly infrared images to the front. Billy backed up, the others followed, huddled. Billy whispered, "Flashy, there's two on each side of the trail."

"Good," he responded. "They can't see us, take 'em out." Team moved ahead again, Billy moving slower and slower. Suddenly, he stepped on a tripwire: illumination flare blasted! Blinded by the light, they dragged their goggles off, charged. Jack ran to the left side, shot one man—guy fell away. Closed with another: they tried to knock each other over, failed. Taliban snarled in fear or rage—breath hot on his cheek. Smashed against each other; rifle knocked away, he tumbled down. Taliban shouted triumphantly, stood up. Jack drew his knife, slashed the man's midsection. Guy wailed, tried to contain his entrails. Machine gun opened fire, hands flew up, guy fell. The mess cascaded: odors of garlic, blood, feces, were sickening. Gagging, Jack brushed the gore aside, untangled an arm from a slimy rope of gut, scrambled away, trying not to vomit. Caught up to the others, all fell back. Flare died away: complete darkness, goggles back on.

Chapter 72

2000 hours: Minutes after the Taliban flare burned out in the air over Herotmere caldera, the team reached the fortress. The sizzling fire still faintly illuminated the top of the steps. The stench of the burning Taliban body was intense. Jack called for a headcount, discovered Bruno was missing.

"Anybody see him go down?" Omar asked. "Ashley?"

"No," she responded. "I just ran and ran."

"Okay, bro, what d'we do now?" Billy gasped.

"We can't fight machineguns," Mick said.

"I saw a pile of M-67 frag grenades in the munitions room. We can't outshoot heavy weapons, but maybe we can blow the two machineguns. I'll go get the grenades. You all move away, case I screw up and remodel the fortress." He walked into the dark stronghold, headed for the gunroom. Thought about anthrax dust. Dreaded going into the room. Passed through the assembly hall, barely illuminated by the fire, heard Bruno say, "Jack." Shocked, he stared at the muzzle of Bruno's AN 94, the man's ghostly form. "I thought you were dead. What's the deal?"

"I can't let you destroy the bomb, Jack. My superiors want it. We know its capabilities. This weapon could go right into a hardened underground bunker."

"So, all along, you've set me up. I can't believe it. You're my buddy. You saved my life back on the KKH."

"My friend, I serve FSB, Mother Russia."

"Well, jerk off, you're wasting your energy. Someone beat us to the bomb. And a B-52 strike of Daisy Cutters is going to turn this whole mountain into rubble thirty minutes after midnight."

"I don't believe you, Jack. Turn around and walk away. You'll live. I let you live. You're my friend. When my allies get here, I'll tell them you escaped."

"Okay, Bruno, just take it easy on that trigger finger." "Very slowly, Jack," Bruno cautioned. "I know your capabilities."

"Right, Bruno. Don't blast me." Caught a flash of white in the hall darkness beyond Bruno.

"Don't try anything, Jack." Movement behind Bruno. "Hey, you ever watch any old Tarzan movies?"

Startled by the odd question, Bruno said, "Of course, but now's not the time—"

"Tarzan was real tough, you know? Animal pals always hung with him. Lions, elephants, apes, shit like that." He pointed at Tigger, who approached from the darkness, crouched at Bruno's rear. "Like my buddy who's right there. If you shoot, Tigger'll have you for supper. His claws could wrap around a silver dollar—you don't have silver dollars in Russia.
Trust me—they're big."

"Shut up about your nonsense, Jack. Get out of here before I have to shoot you," Bruno commanded.

"His teeth are about the size of your forefinger. Think about him biting down on you. Tigers go for the throat so he'll probably grab your head with a paw, pull it back, bite into your neck, rip your throat out." Bruno slightly dropped his weapon's barrel. He tried not to look behind.

"I'm not sure how long you'll live. I'd shoot you to end your misery, but I'm afraid I'll hit him. He's so big. You ever notice his head is three times bigger than ours?"

"I don't believe you. You're the great cowboy bluffer. The poker player. You're lying—just like you're lying about the bomb." Bruno's voice sounded tense as a stretched guitar string.

"He doesn't believe me, Tigger. Tell him I'm not lying." Tigger growled when he heard his name. Bruno jumped, could not stop from glancing back. Jack leaped left. Flew through the air, fired his rifle.

Bruno's receiver handle, struck by a bullet, broke away—slashed his jaw, knocked him backwards. Jack rolled. Hit the rock floor, came up, steady on widened feet, weapon aimed at Bruno. "Sorry about that, Bruno. Don't know why I missed you." Shut his eyes for a second while adrenaline flushed through his body, felt blood surge through his throat. Took deep breathes, trying to calm his shaking hands. "You'll live," he said with a dispassionate tone. "Now, any other surprises? Tigger? You got any designs on the bomb you wanna bring up?"

The tiger had jumped back, now advanced and growled.

"No? Last chance. Okay, Bruno, let's get you back out to the guys, so I can go to work and, like, save our asses." They retraced their steps. Outside, he called, "Billy?"

2030 hours: The group gathered before the two and the tiger.

"What're you doing, Jack?" Ashley asked. She moved to his side, took his free hand, stared at his weapon. Pointed at Bruno with his rifle. "Bruno went sideways on us. But he bombed big-time when I shot him. He's wounded."

Omar stepped forward. "He tried to steal the bomb?"

Jack took a deep breath. "Yeah, and speaking of treachery, I gotta clear something up, guys."

"What's that?" Billy asked.

"Back at Papa's, someone sapped me. It was one of you." "What're you talkin' about, bro?" Omar asked.

"I got captured because I was hit and knocked out, not because I was shot in the head."

"Bullshit!" Billy exclaimed.

Jack laughed nervously, looked at the others, one at a time. "True story." "I can't get too pissed because whoever hit me probly saved my life. Course I figured out who did it."

"Me," Mick admitted. "I hated to do it but it was all a plan."

"Why, asshole?"

"To get you captured and hauled off to Afghanistan."

"What if they'd killed me, you dumbass!"

Mick lifted his hands. "Hey, I was under orders from Colonel Farley. The same thing happened to you when the Paks threw you in the prison camp."

"Mick, buddy, I can't believe—you guys think about asking?"

"You refused orders," Mick said. "You were a valuable asset, bein' a world-class climber. They figured you'd work it out. Jack, buddy, I was just following instruct—" Horrible screaming, gunfire, awesome bellows erupted in the lava field to their front. The group stopped to listen. Three flares arched above the caldera. More roars, screams shattered the air. "Sounds like the wild Chinamen have turned the Taliban into a main course," Jack observed. "I'm afraid we're gonna be Mo Poo's dessert."

Ashley and Omar applied a bandage to Bruno's wound while the others watched for movement to their front and sides. Billy moved forward, returned. "I got bad guys comin' on infrared."

Chapter 73

2100 hours: A voice called out from somewhere in the near distance of the caldera of Herotmere, "Luckless stranger, it is Cyvual. Do not shoot. I come forward with prisoners."

"Hold your fire, guys." Jack peered into the gloom. A figure, leading a half dozen men, emerged from the darkness outside the fire's illumination, twenty feet away. It was Penguin look-alike, Cyvual. Behind him was Yassar Ahmoud.

"Hold it right there," he ordered. "What's going on?"

"Jack, it's me, Mara." He peered into the gloom, but didn't see the woman. "Where are you? I thought Ahmoud killed——-"

"Jack," Ashley tugged his arm. "That's the woman I keep trying to tell you about."

Yassar Ahmoud walked past the tiny Chinaman, stopped in front of

Jack. "Here… I am Mara."

Billy shouted, "What's this bullshit? I'm gonna——-"

He grabbed Billy's arm. "Hold it."

Mara stripped her fake mustache off. "All along, I have been Mara Bhutto and Yassar Ahmoud." She stared at him, then the others.

Enraged, Jack yelled, "You're despicable, Mara. Or Ahmoud. Or whoever the hell you are." He and Ashley squeezed perspiring hands, remembered the wasted torment they had felt when each had thought they were condemning Mara to torture and death.

Cyvual piped up, "These are prisoners. I was told by Mo Poo to bring them. To join thee and the other prisoners."

"What the fuck you talkin' about, you little prick?" Billy shouted. He and Mick stepped forward, jammed their rifle barrels in the little man's midsection. He squealed, dropped to his knees.

"What makes you think we're prisoners?" Jack demanded. "Uh, don't shoot him. We need answers."

Cowering down on the ground, Cyvual cried, "I know nothing. I just follow direction, Luckless Stranger. Not kill me."

"Call me that one more time and I'll gut you myself."

"How many of the big Chinamen are out there?" Omar demanded.

The little man peered up. "All."

"Answer the goddam question," Billy demanded.

"Twenty. Two fell when they attacked the others."

Billy shot the tiny Chinaman in the midsection. He twisted into a squalling ball.

"What the hell?" Jack exclaimed.

"Didn't trust the little prick," Billy growled. "And he wasn't a prisoner. So I didn't violate any goddam convention rules." He spoke with a defensive tone. A smell of released bowels accented the stench of the other smoldering body.

"Mara," Jack asked, tearing his eyes away from the squirming little man, "how many of your men fell before you gave up?"

Mara turned, looked at her men. "I had eighteen when the monsters attacked. I have five now and three of them are wounded. It was hopeless.
They could see us without fail."

"They can see into the infrared. What did they use for weapons?"

"Clubs and long knives—deadly in the dark."

"Why did Mo Poo let you go before and then attack you now? You must be pals."

"I tried to identify myself but they did not realize it was me," Mara said. "After the mix-up, they treat me as the others."

"Tough luck," Jack said with a wry tone, but he figured Mara's claims were just another smokescreen.

"We're better than these raghead Taliban pukes," Mick said. "We can take the big guys."

2130 hours: The friends huddled after Bruno and the Taliban were pushed together, forced to sit on the ground. Mara approached the group. "We must join forces. It's the only way we can survive."

"You got no weapons," Mick said. "The hell good're you?"

Mara shrugged. "Help us, or we'll be killed."

"Why the hell should we?" Jack asked. "You stole the American bomb for God knows what purpose. You lied to us, tried to kill us, killed the missionary girl, kidnapped Ashley. For all we know, you're still with Mo
Poo."

Mara grabbed his wrist. "Forgive what I've done or don't forgive. But don't leave us at the mercy of the monsters."

"Jack," Ashley said. "She's right. We can't—-"

"They'd leave us in a heartbeat," he exclaimed. "And if we save them, they'll turn on us, first chance."

Omar said, "They imprisoned Jack. You forgotten that? And anyway, they ain't got no weapons."

Jack tried to read Mara's expression, but the gloom was too thick. "Aw, shoot. We can't leave 'em here. Will you and your baddies—er, buddies, swear to cool it until we're out of this?"

"Yes," Mara answered. She spoke rapidly in Urdu to her men. All quickly nodded agreement.

Glancing at the Russian, he asked, "Hey, Bruno, you sworn off bombastic behavior?" He looked at Bruno, glanced at Mick.

"Yes, my friend," Bruno mumbled. Mick studied his boots, did not add anything. The Americans pulled the table and a chair out of the hall, put them against the front wall. Climbing on Omar's shoulders, Billy managed to gain the roof. Tigger looked at Billy, jumped on the table, up to the roof.
Billy edged sideways, exclaimed in a fake kid voice, "Hey, he likes me!"

Jack said, "Yeah, right—he's just getting' ready to tenderize you for Mo Poo. Anyway, guys, we know the big Chinaman is crazy or he wouldn't be here. And he calls this Herotmere." "So what?" Mick asked.

He laughed. "Don't you remember your Beowulf, Mick? I had to memorize the whole damned poem in high school. "Herot was the name of the castle and the monsters lived in the mere. After Beowulf defeated Grendel, the line goes: The fated fugitive's bloody tracks led into the watermonster's mere. Herot means heart, mere means water. Heart of the water, which is where we're at."

"I thought these guys were Chinese," Mick protested.

"Dude must be a scholar."

"I hate to disturb this poet and philosopher's meeting," Billy's voice cracked. "The baddies—less'n two hunnert meters."

2200 hours: Jack looked, couldn't see any movement, but feared the threat of the giant men crowding closer. "We can't fight them hand to hand.
We're gonna ambush 'em."

Mick shrugged his massive shoulder muscles. "I'll show those string beans. Tall isn't everything." Jack grinned at Mick, even though his stomach felt like a shattered window. "Then we're gonna run. They expect us to go for the lava tube, but we're going over the rim of the caldera."

Omar objected, "You, Mick, an' Billy, only ones can climb."

"Anybody can go up a rope," he answered. "I left an escape line hanging from the rim of the volcano. Hope it's still there."
Billy jumped down. "I can see 'em on IR now. Hunnert meters away."

Jack directed, "Mick, you and Bruno over there. One magazine on my signal, run like hell for the tube. Omar and Billy, cover Mick with one magazine, then bug out. The rope's just to the left of the lava tube." "Jack, you can't face the man alone," Ashley protested.

He slapped his hands. "Okay, let's set up your fields of fire. And remember, there's no giving up 'less you want to be beef steak over noodles in a Chinese take-out."

Ashley hugged him. "I'm afraid," she whispered.

He squeezed her back and murmured, "I love you. We're gonna win and then it's you and me——-"

"On a beach. A sunny, white sand beach," Ashley said. "Please make it so, Jack."

"Piece of cake," he assured her. "Stick with me. We'll make it out together. I promise." He hoped he was right. Wondered how much anthrax they had inhaled in the weapons room. Wondered what was going on in their lungs.

Chapter 74

2250 hours: Jack was terrified. Stomach heaving. Behind him, the stinking fire was sputtering, spitting on the steps of Herotmere, starting to burn the log wall behind it. With his night vision goggles, he counted twenty giants, confidently stomping forward in single file on the improved path that plunged through the lava field. In spots beyond the marching-in-arow giants, he saw sulfurous steam ghosting out of fiery vents. Their faces were obscured, but they all looked the same height.

Felt his heart pounding, tightened his muscles. Clutched his rifle, touched the safety to make sure it was off. The tall Chinamen stopped in front of him, spread out. He had to look up—felt like he was looking at ghastly gargoyles towering above him. Each giant carried a club or a long Khyber knife.

"Gentlemen—I use the term loosely—what can I do for you?"

Mo Poo roared with an angry voice as deep as a lion's growl on the foothills of Mount Kilimanjaro, "You killed Chin Bit, two of my brothers in the pass."

"Look, I'm sorry about your daughter. But she attacked me. Tried to kill me." For the first time, he noticed Mo Poo show a human expression other than anger or hatred in his huge face: it was one of anguish and loss.

"What about my friends?" Jack pleaded. "They did nothing to you. Let them go. Just you and me. Anyway, why fight at all?"

"Your kind," the big man struggled for words. "You Fan Gway. Condemned us. A life of darkness."

"You're saying white men came down here?"

"Tibet. Little whites. Little yellows. We escaped."

"You were scientific experiments? Like Cyvual said?"

"Yes, little white rat. I eat you."

"Listen, Moose Shit, I appreciate the compliment, but let's not get personal."

"It is Mo Poo, no moo-'es she'-it."

"Hey, you call it poo, I call it… anyway, I haven't had a bath—I'd taste yucky. There's no reason to hate us. Come out into the world. I could sign you guys up for the NBA. Can't we all just get along?" He realized he was babbling.

"Shut up, Jack," Ashley yelled. She grabbed a burning table leg from the fire, ran down the steps, reached up, shoved it in Mo Poo's face.

The big man's straggly hair flamed, he pounded his head.

2310 hours: Billy and Omar opened fire. Several of the giants twisted to the ground. One giant raised his club, charged. Mick shot from the other direction. Jack grabbed Ashley, they ducked through the slow-moving, confused and frightened giants. Mo Poo swung a leg, sent them sprawling. He stood over them, snarled. His hair was still smoldering.

Tigger leaped off the roof, knocked Mo Poo down. The two rolled, the colossal man threw the four hundred pound tiger like a stuffed toy.

Jack jumped up, caught Ashley's hand. Together, they ran up the path across the caldera, with the tiger bounding ahead. The entire force ran at varying speeds, Jack maintained a lead to the lava tube. Stopped short of it. Tigger sprinted into the opening. Bellows of rage rang out of the tube—an ambush! He pointed Ashley towards the side of the caldera where his rope was hanging. The Taliban arrived, he diverted them to the rope. Bruno, Billy, Omar sprinted up the trail. He grabbed Bruno's arm. "That way.
Whole NBA's right behind you. Haul ass!"

2330 hours: A cluster of men was climbing the fifty-degree slope, pulling themselves up by the rope. Bruno, then Omar, started up the line.

Bellows of rage rang through the caldera. Jack turned back to confront the colossal men. "How's the ammo, Billy?"

"Not good. Maybe throw rocks."

Jack fired his rifle, slowed a giant down. Threw his empty rifle in the next giant's face. Beside him, Billy shot an attacker with his last round. It had no effect. Billy climbed, he followed, until—ten feet up, he felt a huge hand close on his ankle. Glanced down, Mo Poo looked up with a hideous grin. His face was ripped open from the tiger's attack. Teeth showed through the slashes on his left cheek, blood streaked down his neck. Relishing the moment, the big man did not jerk him off the rope. He slowly increased the downward pressure on Jack's leg. Desperate, terrified, Jack pulled the Dragon God knife. Slashed the giant across his upturned face, the knife slipped away.

Wailing, the fiend let go. Grabbed his wound, fell on his back. Jack scrambled up, looking over his shoulder while he heaved himself up the rope. Blinded by blood, the ogre staggered to his feet, reached for the rope. Hands skittered across the volcano wall, searched, grasped. Hooked nails scraped, clattered on the rocks.

Jack hung on to the rope with one hand, pulled the dangling end up with the other hand. Giant's paws drew near, blindly grasped. Jack yanked the rope just above his reach. Hands continued to search for scant seconds. Giant bent, grasped a watermelon-sized lava chunk. Threw it up at the sounds of the climbers scrambling up the slope. The rock hit a man. Tumbling down, the guy landed at Mo Poo's feet. The giant picked up the Taliban, bit into his neck, ripped out a chunk of his throat, silencing him in mid-screech. Jack shut his eyes, cringed at the sight, yelled, "Faster!" The giant blindly threw more rocks.

2335 hours: Just as he reached the top, a Taliban threw himself down the outer cliff: bounced, screamed, bounced again, splashed into the water. Jack yelled to the others, "Take the rope!" He threw it down the other side, urged those cowering on the rim to clamber down.

Missiles continued to fly up the ridge. He watched the half-blind giant Chinaman, trip, fall, rise, lurch through the lava field towards the tube. "Hurry," he shouted. Checked his watch: close. Maybe enough time to get out of the cave. Maybe not.

2340 hours: Jack reached a halfway point to the water, dropped, gripped his night vision goggles. Crashed through the surface, rose to the top of the hot water, looked for Ashley. When he saw her hanging on the tiger's neck, he felt a flush of relief go through his body. Ignoring struggling bodies, he swam to her. "They'll come out of the tube. Go."

"Jack, what about the Taliban? They can't swim. Look."

He didn't look. "Should've taken YMCA swimmin' classes—Young Christian classes. Not my fault they're Muslims. Go, go."

2345 hours: They moved away from the cliffs, towards the invisible shore. Screams and bawls of rage broke out to their rear; survivors swam, waded across the hot waters. No one looked back. They devoted every ounce of energy and effort to reaching the shore. Bellows, screams of dismay as men were captured, heavy splashing drew closer.

2351 hours: He caught up to Mara, just when she slumped forward. He hesitated, his mind flashing on the mock execution, the starvation, the back stab; he grabbed her by the arm. With Ashley on one arm, Mara on the other, he pulled the women toward the invisible shore.

2355 hours: They heard an eager yowl behind them. He glanced into Mo Poo's ripped-open, bloody face. The giant stretched his long arms. Reached for Ashley. Jack thrust Mara towards the giant. Heaved her between Ashley and the Chinaman.

2357 hours: The Chinaman grabbed Mara; she fought off the giant, glanced once, locked eyes with Jack. Continued to struggle, slowed the giant, who was trying to get free. He pushed

Ashley forward, then turned back. She dashed to shore, sprinted with the others toward the cave exit.

She glanced back, saw Jack smash his head into the giant's midsection. The Chinaman, Mara, and Jack, tumbled underwater.

2358 hours: Survivors and the tiger splashed to the edge of the lake, ran without looking rearward. Omar had lost his goggles, Ashley grabbed his hand. Billy, Bruno, and Mick, followed.

2359 hours: They all staggered to a halt, the tiger sprinted ahead. "Can't stop," Mick said. "Bomb will—" he was interrupted by an explosion that threw all to the cave floor. "No time. The anthrax could come on the blast cloud. Run, run."

"I gotta get the treasure. The emeralds," Billy said.

"Don't stop," Ashley yelled. "Don't do it."

"Fuck that!" Billy shouted, disappeared into a side tunnel.

0001 hours: The others turned, sprinted for the entry. A roaring sound increased in volume, the blast cloud caught the running team, threw them all to the ground.

Dread flushed through Ashley's body. She scrambled up, grabbed Omar, pulled him toward the entrance. Outside, the four stopped to catch their breath.

"We can't stop," Bruno yelled. "Jack said bombers going to destroy the entrance."

Omar suddenly realized Jack was missing.

"Run!" Ashley screamed.

The four stumbled down the snow-dusted scree field, across barren sand and rock, through a kneedeep stream. Tigger was lying in the cold water, lapping it up.

0010 hours: At a line of jagged boulders, a kilometer from the cave, Ashley, Omar, Mick, and Bruno, still dripping from the hot lake's waters, shivered in the cold mountain air. Ashley embraced Omar, buried her face in his neck. Jack was gone!

0015 hours: The sky was brilliant with stars, the moon high above, just about to disappear over the mountainous barrier to Shangri-la. Hunza valley was bright as day, beautiful in the light. Ashley looked at the magnificence around them, mentally checked her physical state. She remembered Jack's warning: "There's no defense for it. There's no vaccine. It's incurable and it hits the victim in minutes. They start feelin' real sick, right away." She felt no illness, wondered if the nitro had destroyed all the germs with its powerful blast. "Anybody sick?" She asked. No response from the exhausted team. Maybe, she thought, the nitroglycerin worked like a Deus Ex Machina—a god machine in ancient Greek plays—a device that intervened to save the day when the characters totally screwed everything up. She and the others looked back at the blackness that marked the entrance, hoped to see Jack and Billy.

0016 hours: Suddenly, two figures emerged, dashed down the moonlit snow-covered scree field. Ashley cried, her emotions surging to unbelievable heights.

0018 hours: A roaring, a whistling in the sky.

"Down! The Daisy Cutters," Mick yelled.

All dove behind boulders, but still felt a buffeting force from the huge bombs that rocked the ground. The two running men and the entire face of the Hindu Kush Mountains disappeared in huge rolling clouds of smoke and dust. Ashley cried out again, collapsed. Mick and Omar grabbed and supported her before she hit the ground. They slowly lowered her and knelt next to her, consoling her as she wept.

"Look!" Bruno shouted.

The three jumped to their feet, looked over the boulders: two men running across the stream. Jack and Billy, arm in arm, laughing and shouting, reached the line of boulders. Jack, then Billy, piled over the boulders, mobbed their waiting friends.

"Oohrah!" Billy shouted. "We got rid of the germs, I got the gems and

I live to spend the loot. An' I'm not sick."

"What're you talking about, Billy?" Ashley asked.

Jack laughed with relief and joy. "Oh, yeah, I forgot to tell you. Post proelia preemie—after the battle comes the rewards." "What d'ya mean?" Omar asked.

"Billy and I are giving you and Mick a pile each when we sell the emeralds. Without you, we would never have made it out."

Mick stepped away from the ledge. "For me? Is it legal? You stole
'em."

Jack smiled, "That's the beauty of it. The original owners are all dead.
And the temple was totally destroyed in the avalanche." "Still—" Mick protested.

"Don't you see?" he grinned again. "The temple was on disputed territory: the Durand Line, remember? Neither Afgoneistan nor Pakmanland ever accepted the 1893 border creation, so neither one can tax us or claim the treasure."

Billy danced in a circle. "We're gonna sell hunnerts of carats of perfect emeralds—Oorah!"

"So, Mister Indian," Bruno asked, nervously glancing at the tiger as it joined Jack. "Now you are true Capitalist. What'll you do with the money?"

Smiling, the Indian said, "My sister, little Willow wants to start a day care center an' pre-school back on the Rez. I'll fund it with a purified soul. Buy a little ranch, round up a couple of maidens, make babies—get drunk every night." He continued, "Course, I gotta spend a little time covering Jack 'fore I go back to Montana, or Talking Dog'll scalp me."

"But, Jack, you still have Marine Corps and United Nations obligations," Omar said.

"I figure they owe me," Jack said. He hugged the beautiful girl next to him, patted the big tiger's shoulder. "And I've got a date with a mountain.
Chomolungma—Mt. Everest. I'm gonna climb it. It'll be grand."

The End

Postscript:

Omar Johnson was transferred back to Task Force Dagger out of K-2 in Uzbekistan. In an action against the Taliban, he lost a leg at the knee, received partial disability and retired to his home in Portland, Oregon.

Mick Nakamura applied for flight school, went through rotary wing training at Fort Rucker, Alabama, and became a pilot, served at several Army duty stations in the Middle East.

Bruno Utecht returned to Russia and continued his assigned duties with FSB, Russia's intelligence service.

Ashley Dupont broke off her relationship with Jack Flashhardt during the trial, went to Kuwait and worked as an assistant associate producer for
CNN.

Milady was reportedly captured by Islamic Uighur separatists in Northwestern China, buried to the waist and stoned to death.

Robert Arses was arrested on the KKH Highway near the Chinese border, and was sentenced to one year in Kashgar federal penitentiary for violating China's borders.

Billy Howling Dog received five years in Fort Leavenworth military prison for attacking and breaking Colonel Frederic Farley's jaw on the witness stand, during his brother's trial for the theft of an Air Force airplane, treason, and desertion.

The GBU-200's germ package disappeared.

DRAGON GOD OF THE HINDU KUSH: THE RETURN

by

Wayne T. Haaland

Fort Leavenworth Prison, Kansas

The ex-Marine finished his early morning sit-ups, rolled over on the concrete floor to start his push-ups. He paused to wipe sweat off his face with a towel draped over the bunk; sound of steps approaching in the hall stopped him. One of the first things he had noticed inside was increased auditory sensation: sometimes there were measured steps in the hall, oftentimes there were shuffling aimless steps, but there were never hurried steps like those he heard now, skidding to a stop outside his door. Alarmed, he rose.

The solid steel door swung open, it was Billy Howling Dog, his childhood buddy, his teenage enemy, his grown half-brother. "Hey, Jack—I think we're getting out of here!"

Jack replied with a scornful tone, "Yeah, right! My choices are narrowed to nineteen, six, and a wake up—or Peckerwood Hill Cemetery.
But, what're you doing here, Billy? How'd you get a key to my cell?"

Billy glanced out the door, stroked his braids, looked back at his older brother. "They sent me down from the Warden's office. You got a visitor and I was s'posed to tell the day watch to bring you. But they're all out on coffee break. Only like, the video monitor guard there. He couldn't leave his station, gave me a key card, sent me over."

"A visitor! Dad?"

Billy shook his head, his braids danced on his shoulders.

Jack Flashhardt pointed at his surroundings. "Nobody else knows about this, 'cept Ashley."

"No, check this out—it's General Harmbruster's aide. He says in the
Warden's office, like, he wants to see you ASAP."

Jack looked into Billy's grey eyes. "You using?" Billy had become addicted to Oxycontin, an opiate-based drug known as Hillbilly Heroin.

"Yeah, but I'm cool."

Jack sat on his already made-up bunk, wiped sweat off his face, thought, *I'm not going down that road again. And I can't leave the cell without an armed escort. Too dangerous. Everybody in here wants a piece of me. Unless... we're ready to make the break.*

Billy walked to the door, looked into the hallway. His strong body odor infused the sterile cell's atmosphere. "I figure the general wants you for another impossible mission. And if you get out, I'll get out, too. I was freakin' wrong back in Afghanistan when I said this dump'd be better than the bush."

"I'm not lookin' for another working vacation in Afghanistan," Jack responded. "Rather get a job pickin' up' Britney Spear's costumes during her concerts."

"You're like, a riot," Billy said.

Jack took a deep breath. "No, but I'm probably about to start one. Let's go."

The brothers peered into the hallway, saw no one about, cautiously set out for the admin center. Concrete bulkheads of the high security section quietly echoed their tentative footsteps. Rounded a corner, an unseen inmate shouted an alert: "Traitor's out!" Yells repeated the alarm, echoed down the halls, through the cellblocks.

Jack felt tendrils of fear. Thought of retreating to the safety of his cell. Flush of shame, surge of anger—a swell of resolve overcame his doubts: thought of blue skies unscreened by prison bars, an American flag rippling in a fresh breeze. Clenched his fists at unseen enemies. Wanted to smash things. Looked up at the security cameras: red 'active' lights not showing. Someone had turned the cameras off. The guards know what's down. Good or bad?

A minute later, the two rounded another corner of the wide, gray cellblock hall, encountered five prisoners led by a big, multi-tattooed white prisoner with a long torso and short legs. The brothers recognized the former Army sergeant: he was in for selling stolen weapons from a National Guard armory in Madison, Wisconsin, to God's Purpose—a white supremacist force in Tillamook, Oregon. Muscles piled on muscles—his neck looked the same size as Jack's waist. Blue eyes like Jack's, but closeset. Blond hair like Jack's, but shaved—a bulldozer of a figure. A dirty look from him would send anybody scrambling to a 911 call for help. In the background, a fat, whitehaired, flatfaced guard watched. Licked his thick lips with eager anticipation.

"Hey, guys, we got a date with the warden," Jack said. "You can only get sloppy seconds." He noticed horrid tattoos all over the muscle man's exposed skin. As the man's physique flexed, the devil faces grimaced, scowled, appeared to snap their mouths.

"You ain't goin' nowhere, traitor!" the leader growled. His eyes glared with hate. "Been waitin' for you. Flashhardt. Fix you up right now. Don't need no warden."

Jack saw that he was two inches taller, at six feet, then the monstrous man, whose wide body blocked the passage. "Can't we all just get along?" he asked.

His Brule Sioux half-brother raised his fists. "Get outta the way or we'll go through you," Billy snarled. An inch taller than Jack and twenty pounds heavier at two hundred pounds, he showed no fear on his dark face. Two more white prisoners, one tall and skinny, the other average size. Both had shaved heads, wore orange prison garb. Last two were black men, who didn't normally hang with the whites—they wore white doo rags.

"Ax em if'n they wans' give up, take a beatin', bro," one of the blacks said.

"Yeah, I's gonna mess up his pretty boy face," the second black guy exclaimed. "Maybe get some white meat, close t' bone."

First one added, "Ohh, those pretty blues, eyelashes! Sweet!"

The white leader shook his head. "No, this deserter scum's goin' way beyond a beatin' or a screwin'."

"Come on, Mister Bobby," the other black whined. "He's too pretty ta waste."

Tattoo snarled, "I want these filth dead."

Jack said, "Guys, I'm no traitor. I'm an all-American sunshine boy. I sent an absentee ballot last election. I'd volunteer for jury duty… well, skip that last incredibly patriotic attribute. You guys thought about signin' up for anger management?"

No response. No more taunts. The rape thing changed the situation. He glanced at Billy. They hadn't counted on that. They couldn't fake a whipping if it ended in rape. He stared at the complex tattoos of devil faces on the leader's arms and neck. The faces snarled: the five prisoners attacked. Three piled on Billy, he went down. One man flew off the pile, another screamed.

Jack punched Tattoo in the midsection—like hitting a concrete block. "That hurt at all?" He asked.

"Nope," Tattoo grinned. He grabbed Jacl's wrist, flung him against a bulkhead like a skinny rag doll: stunned, he bounced off, back to Tattoo like a child's rubber ball on a string. The man wrapped his hands around Jack's thin middle, squeezed. Garlicky rotten-meat breath was horrendous. A second man punched him in the back of the head, once, twice. Twisted away, guy missed, hit Tattoo.

Jack swung: midsection, jaw—no effect. Sunk teeth into a fiend's image on Tattoo's collarbone: felt it crack. Desperate, stuck a thumb in the muscle man's left eye, gouged it out. Tattoo squealed, squeezed harder. Jack felt his ribs popping, smacked the dangling eye as he struggled to breathe. Tattoo howled, fell to his knees, clutched his face.

"Dude, see my point of view?" Jack taunted. Kicked Tattoo in the head as he would a resting soccer ball: head thunked, twisted away.

Second black: Jack punched him twice, guy fell. Grabbed from behind, he headbutted backwards, heard a smashing crunch, scream of pain. Arms released, he swung around, kicked the guy, then took two steps, field goalkicked the man on top of Billy. Freed, Billy jumped up, yelled a taunting war hoop, punched his attacker twice, a third time. Grabbed him by the ears, lifted him, threw his head into the bulkhead. Man grunted, collapsed.

Jack hit the last guy; he and Billy high-fived. "Piece of cake!" Jack shouted, then winced as pain shot through his ribcage.

Four more white convicts rounded the corner, waded into them. Knife slashed at Jack: he threw up his arm, knife sunk home. A biting, searing pain. Ignored it, pushed against the wielder so he couldn't free the knife. Two crashed into each other, Jack got his free hand under the other's jaw, pushed his head back. Fingers slipped into the man's mouth, got them out just as the man clamped down with his teeth. Grabbed the man's lower lip, stripped it away from his face, flesh ripped to the jawline, the bloody flap and lower lip dangled, danced. Prisoner howled, fell to the floor screaming.

Knife had penetrated his arm, protruded on the other side. He swung at a second man, the knife slashed the guy's face: an ear-shattering scream! He felt no pain, just a sucking, freeing sensation when he pulled the knife out. Saw blood splatter the floor, realized it was his, felt a sickening sensation sweep through his body. He slashed a man who was on his knees, gripping Billy's leg.

Man squalled, held on: Jack stabbed, got him in the shoulder blade; guy arched his back, the knife wrenched out of Jack's hand.

Billy rolled free, picked up the wounded convict, threw him into two advancing men. Billy charged the pileup, punching wildly. Jack slugged the last, leaning, retching man in the jaw, guy careened off the floor, collapsed. Dizzy, Jack swung around, steadied himself against the bulkhead, saw the guard lift his baton. Jack looked around, no convict standing. Forced himself to appear stunned, held still. Hit in the forehead, saw stars, consciousness faded to a dim reality. Fell to his hands and knees, landed on Tattoo, still shielding his dangling eye. Waited again. Looked at the tattooed demon visages—they scowled, snapped at him. The images were terrifying. Thought, wait a minute—he's out cold. How can he flex the tattoos? Must be hallucinating. The guard's kicks began lifting him off the floor. He struggled to his feet, leaned against the concrete bulkhead, snarled at the guard, then tried to smile: the man drew back, blew his whistle. The escape was on.